THE INHERITANCE OF
ORQUÍDEA DIVINA

THE INHERITANCE OF ORQUÍDEA DIVINA

A Novel

ZORAIDA CÓRDOVA

WHEELER PUBLISHING
A part of Gale, a Cengage Company

LIBRARY OF CONGRESS CIP DATA ON FILE.
CATALOGUING IN PUBLICATION FOR THIS BOOK
IS AVAILABLE FROM THE LIBRARY OF CONGRESS.

ISBN-13: 978-1-4328-9380-4 (hardcover alk. paper)

Published in 2022 by arrangement with Atria Books, a division of Simon & Schuster, Inc.

Printed in Mexico
Print Number: 01   Print Year: 2022

Para Ruth Alejandrina Guerrero
Gordillo

Yo quiero luz de luna
para mi noche triste,
para sentir divina
la ilusión que me trajiste,
para sentirte mía, mía tú
como ninguna,
pues desde que te fuiste
no he tenido luz de luna.
— FROM "LUZ DE LUNA"
BY ÁLVARO CARRILLO

RHIANNON ROSE SULLIVAN MONTOYA

m. Michael Sullivan

TATINELLY MONTOYA

m. Reina Delgado

Félix Antonio Montoya Trujillo

REYMUNDO MONTOYA RESTREPO

MARIMAR MONTOYA

m. Jordan Restrepo

Parcha Graciela Montoya Restrepo

(Unknown)

Pena Lucero Montoya Galarza

Pedro Bolívar Londoño IV

m2. LUIS OSVALDO GALARZA PINCAY

m1. PEDRO BOLÍVAR LONDOÑO III

ORQUÍDEA DIVINA MONTOYA

m1. Washington Gordillo

Isabela Belén Montoya Urbano

Roberta Adelina Montoya Urbano   m.   José Andrés Montoya Salazar

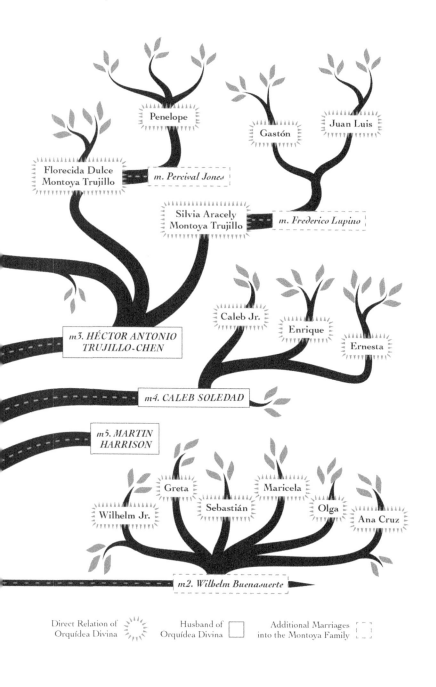

Penelope

Gastón

Juan Luis

Florecida Dulce
Montoya Trujillo

m. Percival Jones

Silvia Aracely
Montoya Trujillo

m. Frederico Lupino

Caleb Jr.

Enrique

Ernesta

*m3. HÉCTOR ANTONIO
TRUJILLO-CHEN*

m4. CALEB SOLEDAD

*m5. MARTIN
HARRISON*

Greta

Maricela

Wilhelm Jr.

Sebastián

Olga

Ana Cruz

m2. Wilhelm Buenasuerte

Direct Relation of
Orquídea Divina

Husband of
Orquídea Divina

Additional Marriages
into the Montoya Family

CONTENTS

11

■ ■ ■ ■

PART I
INVITATION TO
WITNESS A DEATH

■ ■ ■ ■

0
The Invitation

You are invited to my home on May 14, the Year of the Hummingbird. Please begin to arrive no earlier than 1:04 p.m., as I have many matters to settle before the event. The stars have shifted. The earth has turned. The time is here. I am dying. Come and collect your inheritance.

Eternally,
Orquídea Divina Montoya

1
THE WOMAN AND THE HOUSE THAT HAD NEVER BEEN

For many mornings, there had been nothing but barren land. Then one day, there was a house, a woman, her husband, and a rooster. The Montoyas arrived in the town of Four Rivers in the middle of the night without fanfare or welcome wagons or cheesy, limp green bean dishes or flaky apple pies offered in an attempt to get to know the new neighbors. Though in truth, before their arrival, the townspeople had stopped paying much attention to who came and went anymore.

Finding Four Rivers on a map was nearly impossible, as the roads were still mostly gravel, and the memory of the place lived only in the minds of those who remained on purpose. Yes, there had been railroads once, great iron veins hammered into the rocky ground connecting the dusty heart of a country with an identity that changed depending on where lines were drawn.

18

If a traveler took a wrong turn on a highway, they used the Four Rivers gas station and old diner. When any visitor asked what four rivers intersected to give the town its name, the locals would scratch their heads and say something like, "Why, all the rivers have been dried out since 1892."

Other than Garret's Pump Station and the Sunshine diner — offering bottomless coffee for $1.25 — Four Rivers could claim a population of 748 people, a farmer's market, a stationery store, the world's eighth largest meteor hole, the site of a mass dinosaur grave (which was debunked by furious paleontologists who had nothing nice to say in their journal about the prank pulled by the graduating class of '87), the only video rental store for miles, Four Rivers High School (winners of the 1977 regional football championship), and the smallest post office in the country, which was the only thing preventing them from becoming a ghost town.

Four Rivers was special for reasons the living population had all but forgotten. It was, in the most general sense, magic-adjacent. There are locations all over the world where power is so concentrated that it becomes the meeting ground for good and evil. Call them nexuses. Call them ley lines.

Call them Eden. Over the centuries, as Four Rivers lost its water sources, its magic faded, too, leaving only a weak pulse beneath its dry mountains and plains.

That pulse was enough.

In the dip of the valley where the four rivers had once intersected, Orquídea Montoya built her house in 1960.

"Built" was a bit of a stretch since the house appeared as if from the ether. No one was there when the skeletal foundation was laid or the shutters were screwed in, and not a single local could remember having seen tractors and bulldozers or construction workers. But there it was. Five bedrooms, an open living room with a fireplace, two and a half bathrooms, a kitchen with well-loved appliances, and a wraparound porch with a little swing where Orquídea could watch the land around her change. The most ordinary part of that house was the attic, which only contained the things the Montoyas no longer had use for — and Orquídea's troubles. The entire place would become the thing of nightmares and ghost stories for the people who drove to the top of the hill, on the only road in or out, and stopped, watching and waiting for a peek at the strange family living within.

Once they realized they had a new permanent neighbor, the people of Four Rivers decided to start paying attention again to who came and went.

Who exactly were these Montoyas? Where did they come from? Why don't they come to mass? And who, in God's grasshopper-green earth, painted their shutters such a dark color?

Orquídea's favorite color was the blue of twilight — just light enough that the sky no longer appeared black, but before pinks and purples bled into it. She thought that color captured the moment the world held its breath, and she'd been holding hers for a long time. That was the blue that accented the shutters and the large front door. A few months after her arrival, on her first venture into town to buy a car, she learned that all the ranch-style houses were painted in tame, watery pastels.

Nothing about Orquídea's house was accidental. She'd dreamt of a place of her very own since she'd been a little girl, and when she'd finally acquired it, the most important things were the colors and the protections. For someone like Orquídea Divina Montoya, who had attained everything through stubborn will and a bit of thievery, it was not just important to protect it, but to hold on to it. That is why every windowpane and every door had a gold laurel leaf pressed seamlessly into the surface. Not just to keep the magic in, but to keep danger out.

Orquídea had carried her house with her for so long — in her heart, in her pockets, in her suitcase, and when it couldn't fit, in her thoughts. She carried that house in the search for a place with a pulse of magic to anchor it.

In total, Orquídea and her second husband had journeyed for 4,898 miles, give or take a few. Some by carriage, some by ship, some by rail, and the last twenty solidly on foot. By the time she was done traveling, the wanderlust in her veins had dried up. Eventually she'd have children and grandchildren, and she'd see the rest of the world on the glossy postcards that covered the entire refrigerator. Like some, for her one pilgrimage was enough. She didn't need to measure her worth by collecting passport stamps and learning half a dozen languages. Those were dreams for a girl left behind, one who had seen the pitch-black of the seamless sea and who had once stood at the center of the world. She'd lived a hundred lives in different ways, but no one — not her five husbands or her descendants — really knew her. Not in the way you can know someone, down to their bones, down to the secrets that can only be augured in bloody guts.

What was there to know?

Five foot one. Brown skin. Black hair. Blackest eyes. Orquídea Montoya was untethered to the world by fate. The two most important moments of her life had been predetermined by the stars. First, her birth. And second, the day she stole her fortune.

Her birthplace was a small neighborhood in the coastal city of Guayaquil, Ecuador. People think they know about misfortune and bad luck. But there was being unlucky — like when you tripped over your shoelaces or dropped a five-dollar bill in the subway or ran into your ex when you were wearing three-day-old sweatpants — then there was the kind of bad luck that Orquídea had. Bad luck woven into the birthmarks that dotted her shoulders and chest like constellations. Bad luck that felt like the petty vengeance of a long-forgotten god. Her mother, Isabela Montoya, had blamed her sin first and the stars second. The latter was true in more ways than one.

Orquídea was born during a time when the planets converged to create the singularly worst luck a person could ask for, a cosmic debt that was not her fault, and yet fate was coming to collect like a bookie. It was May 14, three minutes to midnight, when Orquídea chose to kick herself out of the womb before getting stuck halfway, as if she knew the world was not a safe place. Every nurse and doctor on shift rushed to help the lonely, young mother. At 12:02 a.m. on May 15, the baby was finally yanked out, half dead, with her umbilical cord wrapped around her little neck. The old nurse on shift remarked how the poor girl would lead an indecisive life — a foot here and the other there. Half present and half gone. Unfinished.

When she left Ecuador for good, she learned how to leave pieces of herself behind. Pieces that her descendants would one day try to collect to put her back together.

It took twenty years and two husbands, but Orquídea Divina made it to the United States. Despite having been born on a cosmic convergence of bad luck, Orquídea had discovered a loophole. But that's to come later in her story.

This is about the woman and the house that had never been — until one day, they were undeniably there.

On their first morning in Four Rivers,

Orquídea and her husband opened all the windows and doors. The house had been enchanted to anticipate all of their needs and provided them with the basics to get them started: bags of seeds, rice, flour, and salt, and a barrel of olive oil.

They'd need to plant right away. However, the ground surrounding the property was cracked, solid rock. Some locals said the fissures in the ground were so deep, you could drop a penny straight to hell. No matter how much it rained in Four Rivers, it was like the clouds purposely neglected the valley where their house now stood. But that didn't matter. Orquídea was used to making something out of nothing. That was part of her bargain, her power.

The first thing she did was cover the floors in sea salt. She poured it between the floorboards, into the natural grooves and whorls in the wood. She crushed thyme, rosemary, rosehips, and dried lemon peels, scattering them into the mix. Then she swept it all out the front and back doors. It was magic she'd learned on her travels — a way to purify. She used the oil to restore the shine of the wood floors, and then to make the first breakfast she and her husband would have in their new home — fried eggs. She sprinkled fat crystals of salt over them, too, cooking the white edges until perfectly crisp, the yolks so bright they looked like twin suns. She could savor the promise of what was to come.

Decades later, before the end of her days, she would recall the taste of those eggs as if she'd just finished eating them.

The house at Four Rivers saw the birth of each one of Orquídea's six children and five grandchildren — as well as the death of four husbands and one daughter. It was her protection from a world she didn't know how to be a part of.

Once — and only once — did the neighbors arrive with shotguns and pitchforks trying to scare away the witch who lived in the center of the valley. After all, only magic could explain what Orquídea Divina Montoya had created.

Within their first month there, the dry bedrock had sprouted spindly grass. They grew in prepubescent patches at first, and then blanketed the earth. Orquídea had walked every inch of her property, singing and talking, sprinkling seeds, coaxing and daring them to take root. Then, the hills around them softened with wildflowers. The rain returned. It rained for days and then weeks, and when it stopped, there was a

small lake behind the house. Animals returned to the area, too. Frogs leaped across
mossy rocks and lily pads floating across
the surface. Iridescent larvae hatched thousands of fish. Even deer wandered down
from the hills to see what all the fuss was
about.

Of course, the shotguns and pitchforks
didn't work. The mob barely got halfway
down the hill before the land reacted.
Mosquitoes swarmed, ravens circled overhead, the grass grew tiny thorns that drew
blood. Discouraged, they turned around
and went instead to the sheriff. He would
run the witch out of their small town.

Sheriff David Palladino was the first Four
Rivers local to introduce himself intention-
ally to Orquídea. And though they would
go on to have an amiable relationship, which
consisted of his keeping her grounds clear
of nosy neighbors and her providing a daily
hair-restoring tonic, there was a brief moment during their first encounter when
Orquídea feared that, though she'd done
everything right, she would have to go away.

Back then, Sheriff Palladino was twenty-
three and on his first year of the job. He
still had peach fuzz on his upper lip that
wouldn't grow and a full head of hair that
made up for his too-wide nostrils, which let

you see the tunnels of his nasal passages. His bright blue eyes gave him the effect of an owl, not wise but scared, which wasn't good for the job. He'd never made a collar, because in Four Rivers there was no crime. The only murder on record would happen in 1965, when a truck driver would be found gutted on the side of the road. The killer was never caught. Even the fifty-year feud between the Roscoes and Davidsons was resolved just before he took up the seat of Sheriff. If the last Sheriff hadn't died of an aneurysm on his desk at the age of eighty-seven, Palladino might still be a deputy.

After days of pressure from the townsfolk to find out about the newcomers (Who were these people? Where were their land deeds, their papers, their passports?), Palladino drove down the single dusty road that led to the strange house in the valley. When he arrived, he could hardly believe what he was looking at.

As a kid, he'd ridden bikes with his friends, shredding their shins on the bare rocks. Now, he inhaled the dark, freshly turned earth and grass. If he closed his eyes, he'd think he was far away from Four Rivers, and in some verdant, distant grove. But when he opened them, he was inarguably in front of the house owned by Orquídea Divina Montoya. He lifted his wide-brimmed hat to scratch his wheat-blond hair, matted at the temples in worm-like curls. As he rapped his knuckles against the door, he noticed the way the laurel leaves on the wood shimmered.

Orquídea answered, lingering at the threshold. She was younger than he'd expected, perhaps twenty years old. But there was something about her nearly black eyes that spoke of knowing too much too soon.

"Hi, ma'am," he said, then stumbled on his clumsy tongue. "Miss. I'm Sheriff Palladino. There's been some coyote sightings around the area, killing off livestock, and even poor Mrs. Livingston's purebred hypoallergenic poodle. Just wanted to swing by and introduce myself and make sure y'all are all right."

"No coyotes that we've seen," Orquídea said in a crisp, regionless English. "I thought you might be here about the mob that tried to visit me a week ago."

He blushed and lowered his head in shame at being caught lying. Although the story about coyotes was mostly true. Among the complaints he'd received was that the new Mexican family were witches who used coyotes as familiars. Another call had said that the dried-up valley no one ever went to except for vagrants and vagabond youths looking to skip school was being changed and they couldn't have that. Four Rivers didn't change. Palladino couldn't understand why anyone would be opposed to change that looked like this — fresh and strong and vibrant. Life where there was nothing before. It was a goddamn miracle, but he had to do his duty by the townspeople he was sworn to protect. Which brought him to the next complaint. *Illegals,* a woman had whispered on the phone before hanging up. The family in the valley had shown up in the middle of the night, after all. Land was not supposed to be free. It had to be owned by someone — a person or the government. How had it gone for so long without being claimed?

"Would you like some coffee?" Orquídea asked with a smile that left him a little dizzy.

He'd been raised to never refuse a kind, neighborly gesture, and so he accepted. Palladino tipped his hat, then cradled it against his chest as he entered the house. "Thank you, miss."

"Orquídea Divina Montoya," she said. "But you can call me Orquídea just fine."

"I studied Spanish at the community college. That means 'orchid' right?"

"Very good, Sheriff."

She stepped aside. A young woman about half his height, yet somehow, she felt as tall as the wooden beams above. She looked at his feet, watching carefully as he stepped over the threshold. He couldn't have been sure, but it looked like she was waiting to see, not if he would enter, but if he physically could. Her shoulders relaxed, but her dark eyes remained wary.

As tall as he was, he felt himself shrink to put her at ease. Even left his gun in his glove compartment.

For the most part, David Palladino was like every other citizen of Four Rivers who'd never left. He didn't need to be anywhere else, didn't want to go. Before he found his purpose as a police officer, most days he was happy to get out of bed and get through the day. He believed in the goodness of people and that his grandmother's soup could cure just about any injury. But magic? The kind that people were accusing Orquídea of? He chalked it up to old folks with dregs of lost myths stuck under their tongues. Magic was for the nickel machines at the summer carnival.

But he couldn't deny that when he entered Orquídea's home, he felt something, though he couldn't truly name the exact sensation. Comfort? Warmth? As she led him through a hall filled with family portraits, he ignored the feeling. The wallpaper had been sun-kissed and the floors, though shining and smelling of lemon rind, were scuffed. There was an altar on a table in the foyer. Dozens of candles were melting, some faster than others, as if racing to get to the bottom of the wick. Bowls of fruit and coffee beans and salt were front and center. He knew some of the folks from the Mexican community nearby had similar reliquaries and statuettes of the Virgin Mary and half a dozen saints he couldn't name. He sat through every Sunday mass, but he'd stopped listening a long time ago. His grandmother had been Catholic. His memory of her had faded but, standing in the Montoya house, thoughts of her slammed into him. He remembered a woman nearly doubled over with age, but still strong enough to roll a pin across the table to make fresh pasta on Sundays. He hadn't thought of her in nearly fifteen years. The scent of rosemary that clung to her salt white hair, and the way she wagged her finger at him and said, "Be careful, my David, be careful of this world." Ramblings of an old woman, but she was more than that. She'd watched him while his mother was sick and his father was breaking his bones at the mill. She'd prayed for his soul and his health, and he'd loved her infinitely for so long. So why didn't he think of her anymore?

"Are you well, Sheriff?" Orquídea had asked, glancing back at him. She waited for his reaction, but he wasn't sure what it was he should say.

He realized that he was still standing in front of the altar, and his cheeks were wet. His pulse was a frantic thing at his throat and wrists. He pressed his lips together and did his best impression of politeness.

"I'm peachy." He wasn't sure if he was, but he shook the emotion out of himself.

"Make yourself at home. I'll be right back." Orquídea went into the kitchen and he heard the water running. He sat in the large dining room, the barest part of the house. No wallpaper or decorations. No drapes or flowers. There were stacks of papers out on a banquet table fit for a dozen people.

Now, he wasn't trying to pry. He believed in the rights of the people of his township, his small corner in the heart of the country. But the papers were right there inside an open wooden box. The kind his mother had once used to store old photographs and let-

33

ters from her father during the war. From his cursory glance, he recognized a land deed and bank records with her name on it. Orquídea Divina Montoya. Part of him was bewildered that it was all here in plain sight. Had she been putting everything away? Had she known he would come? How could she? It didn't make a lick of sense. But there was the proof in front of him. Documents that could not easily be forged. He was relieved. He could tell the very concerned citizens of Four Rivers that there was nothing out of the ordinary about the house and its inhabitants except — well, other than that they had appeared out of nowhere. Had they? The valley had been abandoned for so long. Maybe no one in Four Rivers had been paying attention, like the time a highway sprung up where there hadn't been one before. Surely there was no harm done here.

"How do you take your coffee?" Orquídea asked as she walked into the dining room clutching a wooden tray offering two cups of coffee, milk in a small glass jar, and a bowl of brown sugar.

He drummed his long, thin fingers on the table. "Plenty of milk and plenty of sugar."

They smiled at each other. Something like understanding passed between them. Neither of them wanted any trouble, he was sure of it. So, they talked about the weather. About Orquídea's distant family, who had passed the house down to her. He didn't remember any Montoyas from Ecuador around these parts. He wasn't sure where Ecuador *was,* if he was being truly honest with himself. But then again, it was possible that he didn't know everyone. Perhaps the world was bigger than he thought. It had to be. It certainly felt that way while he sat there drinking her strong coffee. Coffee so rich that it made him stop and sigh. It was not possible but somehow, he could taste the earth where it had been cultivated. When he smacked his tongue against the roof of his mouth, he tasted the minerals in the water that helped the plant grow. He could feel the shade of the banana and orange trees that gave the beans their aroma. It shouldn't have been possible, but he was only learning the beginning of it all.

"How did you do all of this?" he asked, setting the cup down. There was a chip on the side of the roses painted against the white porcelain.

"Do what?"

"Make coffee taste like this."

She blinked long lashes and sighed. Afternoon light gilded her soft brown skin. "I'm biased, but the best coffee in the world is

35

from my country."

"I say you'll be sorely disappointed if you stop by the diner. Don't tell Claudia that. But the pie is to die for. Have you had pie? Is your husband home?" He knew he was rambling, so he drank his sweet coffee to quiet himself.

"He's out back, gardening." She sat at the head of the table, resting her chin on her wrist. "I know why you're really here. I know what they say about me."

"Don't listen to them. You don't look like a witch to me."

"What if I told you I was?" Orquídea asked, stirring a clump of sugar into her cup. Her smile was sincere, sweet.

Embarrassed, he looked down at the dregs of his pale coffee, when a birdsong called his attention. There were blue jays at the windowsill. He hadn't seen one of those around these parts — maybe ever. Wondrous. Who was he to judge that? To judge her. He'd sworn to protect the people of Four Rivers, and that included Orquídea.

"Then I'd say you make a bewitching cup o' joe."

They shared a laugh, and finished their coffee in a comfortable silence, listening to the creaking sounds of the house and the return of birds. It wouldn't be the last time that the surrounding neighbors tried to question Orquídea's right to take up space on that land, but that coffee and those papers would buy her a few years at least. She had traveled too far and done too many things to get where she was. The house was hers. Born from her power, her sacrifice.

Fifty-five years after Sheriff Palladino came to call, she'd sit at the same table, with the same porcelain cup, stirring the same silver spoon to cut the bitter out of her black coffee. But this time her stationery would be out, crisp egg-shell paper and ink she made herself. She'd send out letters to every single one of her living relatives that ended with: "I am dying. Come and collect your inheritance." But that is yet to come.

As Orquídea walked the young man to the door, she asked, "Is everything in order, Sheriff Palladino?"

"Far as I can see," the Sheriff said, returning his hat to his head.

She watched his car amble up the road and didn't go back inside until he was gone. A strong breeze enveloped her, hard enough to make the laurel leaves on her doors and windows flutter. Someone out there was searching for her. She felt it only for a moment, but she doubled the protection charms on the house, the candles on her altar, the salt in the grain.

There would come a time when her past caught up to her and Orquídea's debt to the universe would be collected. But first, she had a long life to live.

2
INTRODUCTIONS TO THE PROGENY OF ORQUÍDEA DIVINA

The invitation arrived at the exact moment Marimar Montoya burned her tongue on her midnight cup of coffee. She felt a strange surge ripple through the apartment, as if a phantom had made the lights flicker, the TV turn on, and her computer screen freeze. She grimaced and set down the porcelain cup. It was part of an ancient set from her grandmother's cabinets, one of twenty-four. She'd shoved it in her duffle bag on the morning she left Four Rivers, just after Gabo, the skeletal rooster, started to crow.

"Not now," she muttered, slapping the translucent blue shell of her iMac G3. She'd bought it refurbished for fifty dollars from the fancy prep school on the Upper East Side after they upgraded their systems. All Marimar had needed was a way to get on the internet and a word processor where she could attempt to write a novel when she was actually supposed to be working on her college papers.

She licked the tender tip of her tongue against the roof of her mouth and fruitlessly clicked on the mouse. Then gave up and spun around in her swivel chair.

She hadn't realized how late it was and still had five pages to go in her Gothic Literature essay about Edgar Allan Poe's "The Fall of the House of Usher" and his use of fucked-up families. Rey was working late at the office again. The apartment they shared was in the heart of New York City's Spanish Harlem, and though she'd lived there for six years, she'd never gotten used to the building's faults. The lightbulbs that blew out days after being installed, the serpentine radiator, the creaky floors, the rusted pipes that ran hot in the summer and freezing in the winter. Still, it was the place Marimar and her cousin Rey had nurtured into a home.

She was reaching for her phone to message him when she noticed the slim square envelope beside it. There was no stamp, only her name and address:

Marimar Montoya
160 East 107th Street, Apt. 3C
New York, NY 10029

She glanced around the living room for anything else out of place. The worn leather sofa with the woolen blanket depicting llamas on the Ecuadorian highlands. Rey's paintings from high school and a print of Georgia O'Keeffe's *Cow's Skull: Red, White, and Blue* she had bought in front of the Met on her first field trip. A solid mahogany coffee table her aunt had rescued from a sidewalk on Fifth Avenue and made Marimar and Rey carry for twenty blocks and three avenues. A stack of magazines, most of them stolen from the office of Hunter College's literary journal, supermarket coupons, bubblegum-flavored gum, a moldy Nalgene emblazoned with Rey's accounting firm logo, free NYC-branded condoms in the rotting fruit bowl, the open box housing a half-eaten pizza pie that she'd devoured after work.

Everything was as it had been when she started writing. Except the open window. Instantly, Marimar knew where the envelope had come from.

She got up and went to the window. Downstairs, a group of high school kids were talking shit and sharing chips and quarter waters out of thin black plastic bags. A strange bird lingered on the fire escape. It looked like a blue jay, but it was too big for the kind she occasionally spotted in Central Park. She leaned halfway out the window to grab it, but it flapped away from her grasp, the color leaching out of its feathers as its body rounded into the lazy mass of a common city pigeon. It made a gurgling sound and flew away.

"Tell her to use the phone like normal people," Marimar shouted at the bird.

The kids below looked up and, realizing who it was, tittered and whisper-hissed the words *bruja loca*.

Shutting the window and turning the latch, Marimar returned to her desk. The computer was still frozen on the spinning rainbow wheel of death, and so she picked up the envelope. No one wrote letters anymore, not the way she'd seen her grandmother do it. Orquídea would sit at the large dining table with her stationery box, a little metal spoon, and tubes of wax she made herself. Marimar had wondered who she wrote to since Orquídea didn't have any friends that Marimar knew of, and for a period of time, all their family lived in the same big house. Her grandmother had only ever responded with, "I'm writing letters to my past."

Marimar peeled off the wax seal and opened the envelope. It had been six years since she'd spoken to Orquídea. Though her grandmother sent them a Christmas card every year — for some reason those did go through the United States Postal Service and always smelled of cinnamon and cloves — Marimar had never reciprocated. Now, she held the new letter to her nose, breathing in the scents of Four Rivers. Of coffee and fresh grass and the seconds before torrential rain. There was also something extra that hadn't been there when she'd left, but she couldn't name it.

Marimar withdrew the sturdy cardstock and read the elegant cursive. She shut her eyes and felt a tugging sensation right behind her belly button. Orquídea was so many things: evasive, silent, mean, secretive, loving, and a liar. But she wasn't dramatic enough for this.

Wasn't she?

When Marimar was five and chased fireflies around the hills, her grandmother told her to be careful because they could really burn. When Marimar was six and decided she didn't want to eat chickens in solidarity with Gabo and his wives, her grandmother had told her that the dead chicken's soul would go to chicken hell if it wasn't completely consumed. Orquídea told her if she swam to the bottom of the lake, there would

43

be a passageway waiting there to take her to the other side of the world where sea monsters lived. That baking during her menstruation curdled milk, and cooking while angry embittered the food. Tiny, little untruths that Marimar now chalked up to things grandmothers said.

She took a deep breath and reread the letter. No, the invitation. *The time is here. I am dying. Come and collect your inheritance.*

Marimar picked up her phone and went to text Rey, but the screen glitched.

"Fucking hell," she muttered. The flickering lights, the computer, her phone. It was all Orquídea's doing. Certain technology just didn't pair well with things that came from her grandmother, not even Marimar herself.

This couldn't wait. She pulled her jean jacket from the back of her chair, grabbed her keys, Walkman, and headphones. When she attempted to lock the door, the key jammed for two minutes before she was able to turn it. Crossing the street, a cab took an extra sharp turn and nearly rammed into her even though she'd had the right of way. As she hurried across the crosswalk, she stepped into an ankle-deep puddle that she swore hadn't been there before.

Finally safe on the other side, she took a

moment to hit play on her Sony CD player and press the foam headphones against her ears. The heavy bass blared as she made the uphill trek along Lexington Avenue to Rey's office. It was only thirty blocks and she needed the fresh air anyway. She made this walk every day to school. It hadn't been much different than walking up the hills around her grandmother's house in Four Rivers, except she'd traded rocks and grass for glittering concrete. Both had cut the strong muscles of her calves and thighs.

El Barrio came alive after sundown like the goblin markets she'd read about in poems. Here, the streets were loud and always smelled of fried meat, dough, plantains, and the underlying rot that rose in billowing steam from New York City's sewers. She stopped at the kosher deli crammed between two buildings that looked like they might cave in overhead. Outside, four old men played cards and checkers on rickety tables and plastic chairs. Two boys not old enough to shave whistled as she stepped inside. She bought two bagels with extra cream cheese and ignored the same boys who sucked their teeth, accusing her of thinking she was all that. One of the men wearing a bright blue Mets jersey looked up and caught her eye, telling her, "Dios te bendiga, mamita."

To him and his blessing, she said, "Goodnight."

When she got to the corner of the street, a homeless man flashed his penis and tried to chase her with his stream of urine.

Marimar couldn't quite figure out why New York City refused to love her. She'd moved there for high school, after her mother's tragic and untimely death. She was thirteen and she'd loved Four Rivers once. Still did. With its green hills and clusters of dragonflies that went with her everywhere. But after her mom died, Orquídea left Marimar no choice but to leave.

Most kids would want to trade Nowhere, USA, for the Big City. Four Rivers was *technically* somewhere. It just wasn't somewhere most people wanted to be. Only Marimar wasn't sure she was a Big City kind of girl. Back then, she didn't know what kind of girl she was, except an orphan living with her tía Parcha and cousin Reymundo in a cluttered apartment facing a street that was always crowded with traffic like one of Manhattan's clogged arteries. The city's tough love provided a series of lessons that a soft place like Four Rivers could never teach her. She'd learned how to arm her face the minute she stepped out the door

46

because of boys and men who cast lines her way like she was another fish in that filthy Hudson they called a river. She learned New York evolved because it survived on blood. It was loud because it was a symphony of people shouting their dreams and hoping to be heard. Marimar had longed to add her dreams to that song but when she tried, her voice was a whisper.

New York City, six years later, would not be claimed by Marimar. It was not a place that could be claimed, though many tried. New York seemed to reject her like she was the wrong blood type. She'd been mugged twice before she learned to fight back and discovered that when someone didn't like you, they'd tell you to your face. When she'd started working at sixteen, she realized she couldn't keep a job. There was something about her that her employers didn't like after a while. Things would start off fine. She'd say the right things, go above and beyond. Then, like clockwork, after three months or so, something flipped. Suddenly, she was too pretty, too ugly, too smart, too dim, too short, too quiet, too loud, too — everything, and not enough at the same time. There was always a reason. Once, a manager at the college bookstore told her she was distracting paying customers because people came in just to look at her.

Marimar was stunning like her mother, with hair that fell in rippling dark waves and framed impossibly dark eyes. Brows that were once bushy and would be on trend years later. A nose that had been deemed "ñata" by her grandmother, though she'd never explained the meaning. Small but round at the tip and a little flat. It made her look too young. Button-like. Her skin was the brown of hazelnut shells and running up and down her arms and across her chest were beauty marks in the same pattern as her mother and grandmother.

Sometimes Marimar felt like there was this hole inside of her, amorphous like the negative impression of a tumor. When she was in Four Rivers, she didn't notice it as much. New York made her notice it for sure. Maybe it was that everyone in this city could see right through her, see the parts of her that were incomplete. Maybe it wasn't New York's fault. Maybe she wasn't unlucky, cursed like Tía Parcha liked to claim. Maybe Marimar just needed to figure out how to accept that this is who she is — a girl with missing pieces.

At least here she didn't stick out like she had in Four Rivers, where she'd gone to school with seventeen boys named John and thirty-two Mary-Somethings. Even she was, *technically,* a "Mary Something" too. People thought it was Mari-Mar. María of the sea. But her mother had meant "mar y mar." Sea and sea.

Why had her mother named her that, of all things? Why hadn't she asked when she had the chance?

When she returned to Four Rivers, she'd have to try and find out.

Marimar was nearing Rey's office building but couldn't quite let go of the pent-up breath in her chest. Part of it was the invitation to attend a funeral for a woman who was, by her understanding, still alive. Part of it was just an effect of walking these streets.

At that moment, her Walkman fritzed and when she opened the battery cover, found they were oxidized. She walked the rest of the way in silence. Turned left on Sixty-Fifth Street, panting, a cold sweat matting her baby hairs against her temples. The city glittered before her in multicolored lights and shadows, and a strange sense of longing washed over her. As hard as it was, she had fallen in love with this city, and wanted New York to love her back. To be just a little bit easy. If she went back to Four Rivers, maybe she would never get the chance.

She pressed the button to her cousin's offices, assuring herself that yes, New York would be waiting for her when she got back.

But didn't she know? New York waits for no one.

Reymundo Montoya Restrepo was supposed to be alone in the office all night but was interrupted by the familiar, haunting squeak of the mail cart's wheels. He blinked weary eyes at the red digital clock on his desk that read it was just past midnight, then looked up to see Paul the Intern making a beeline for him.

"You're still here?" Rey asked, his voice groggy from misuse.

"Mr. Leonard said that I should always be around in case someone needs my help," Paul said.

His name wasn't actually Paul — that was the name of an intern from five years prior. Paul had been an intern for about three years, the longest in the accounting firm's history, mostly because he loved being an intern but also because he was so terrified of Mr. Leonard that he'd never remind him that his six months were up. One day Paul, with his mousey brown hair and milk-white skin, was hospitalized from stress and burnout and never returned. The next day there was a new intern, hired by Leonard's secretary. That second intern had walked into Leonard's office determined to make a name for himself, to be distinct, to impress the man whose eyes were always so glued to his computer and papers that they were shrinking every year.

"Heya, Paul," Leonard had said in a Brooklyn accent so thick you needed a pizza cutter to slice it. "Take these to Jasmine, and don't forget I take six sugars and half-and-half in my coffee. I think you forgot yesterday because it tasted like I rinsed my mouth with an ashtray."

"Yes, Mr. Leonard," the young boy said, and so was born an infinite number of Paul the Intern.

Rey had once been Paul the Intern, but he'd changed that after he put in the required six months. He'd asked Jasmine the secretary to put him in as Mr. Leonard's 1 p.m. interview. Maybe no one had thought of doing that before, but Leonard looked up.

"Can I help you?"

"I'm Rey Montoya, I just finished my internship and I'm here to apply for a full-time position."

Leonard watched him with his beady eyes, moving around like a crab's. His wide mouth became even wider, showing teeth yellowed by red wine and cigarettes. "Montoya, eh? Oh, you killed my father, prepare to die."

Rey had endured an entire lifetime of that joke. The only reason he used Montoya instead of Restrepo was because it was slightly easier on the English-speaking American tongue. It was remarkable how people treated him differently depending on which last name he used.

Still, he laughed at the joke and swallowed his own pride as he picked up a pen from Leonard's desk and waved it in the air like a Spanish rapier.

"Exactly. Here is my résumé and I have the last six months to speak for my work."

"You been working with Paul? I haven't seen you."

"We split the floor, sir."

"Graduated Adelphi in two years? Impressive." He pressed a button on his phone. "Hey, Jasmine, get Mr. Montoya here set up. We're about to get fucked by the IRS and need all hands on deck. And Paul's late with my coffee."

The new Paul the Intern started later that day, and Rey was assigned a tiny desk at the far end of the office.

Now, Rey leaned back in his chair and

looked into Paul the Intern's face. "What's your name, kid?"

"Krishan Patel," he said.

"Do you really want to do this?"

"I just want a college credit." He scratched the side of his face and broke a pimple along his jaw.

"Then go home. If you come back tomorrow, figure out how to make people learn your name."

Krishan nodded, but Rey could tell he wasn't listening, not really. Instead, he picked up a stack of packages from the cart and dropped them off on the desk beside Rey's. As the kid started to leave, he jolted to a stop and turned around.

"Oh, almost forgot one."

He handed Rey an envelope that looked like it had traveled from the late nineteenth century, wax seal and all. Then, Krishan was gone.

Rey didn't have time for mail that didn't come in manila envelopes from the firm's clients, so he put it aside and got down to work, punching the numbers on his calculator like the world's least satisfying game of whack-a-mole.

Rey hated numbers, but he was good at them. He could make sense of them, at least. Always could. He wasn't sure where he got that talent from, and sometimes he wished he'd gotten Marimar's photographic memory, or the twins' musical talent, or even Tatinelly's ability to charm unsuspecting suckers into pyramid schemes. His mother had dropped out of high school to chase after a soldier whose motorcycle had gotten a flat on their road. His father, the soldier, had been an army grunt who'd been killed in combat when Rey was eight. He'd been a good man, as far as Rey remembered. When he started to forget, all he had to do was rummage through his father's old things he could never get rid of. There was a folded flag that hung at an awkward angle on their living room wall. The three crates of vinyl covering an entire history of rock, from Ray Charles to Metallica. His mother had also kept his collection of terrible Hawaiian print shirts that he liked to barbecue in when he was home. And even worse, sterling silver jewelry of flames and skulls from his teenage days as a metalhead in Queens. It was, all together, an altar to toxic masculinity, despite the fact that his father had been the first person to realize Rey was gay. He'd also been the first person to tell Rey there was nothing wrong with him, and he'd hold onto that through his adolescence and current attempt at adulthood.

54

Rey had thought that he could get through anything as long as he remembered that he'd been loved by two parents who had burned hard and bright, and quickly, like matchsticks.

Jordan Restrepo took every moment to be with his Parcha and his Reymundo when he wasn't deployed. One time, Rey and his dad were playing baseball in the park, even though Rey hated baseball. It was his dad's excuse to talk to his son. At some point, Reymundo regaled him in painful detail about what the second grade was like. All the boys were bigger. All the boys were grosser. Rey didn't know how to be like them, soft and quiet like a drop of dulce de leche as he was. The kind his mom scooped up out of half coconut shells from the bodega. There was this class play and Reymundo wanted to be in the role that sang and danced with a boy named Timothy who had hazel eyes, and Reymundo wanted to marry him. Rey didn't know what "marry" meant, but his mother liked to yell at her sister over the phone that way. "If you love that summabitch so much, marry him." "If you love misery so much, marry it." And so on. All he knew was that marriage was for love and he loved Timothy.

"Easy buddy," Jordan had said. He held

little Reymundo's round face for so long, and Rey was never sure what his old man had been thinking. But the memory was sharper than the rest from his earliest years. He could always recall the tears in his dad's eyes. Not because he was upset, but because he was worried. "You have to wait until you're my age to get married, okay?"

"Fine," Reymundo had said, in that way bored little boys had.

Sometimes, when he was unsure of himself, Reymundo thought back to that moment. To the certainty that he'd never been more himself than with his dad, hating baseball, talking about a boy he wouldn't kiss for another ten years. Sometimes, on Rey's worst days, he pictured his Army hero father — with his chunky boots, gap between his teeth, scars crisscrossing his white skin — and told himself, *If my dad could cry, then so can I.*

Rey would never marry Timothy, but they kissed in the halls of their high school at sixteen, and then one last time in Timothy's room. Before Tim's dad came home and had a fit. He asked, "What would your father say if he were alive?"

And Reymundo only smiled, because he knew in his heart what the answer would be. "He'd say that you're a homophobic fucking asshole, Mr. Green."

He never saw Timothy again after that, and no one fucked with him either. Rey knew who he was in his bones. He'd lose himself often, but he had memories, lodestones to guide him home.

Now, as he dug through stacks of taxes and poorly kept receipts, he was overcome with a worry that hadn't been there before. His skin didn't fit, his clothes were too tight. There was something so wrong, so bone-deep he couldn't scratch it hard enough to get rid of the feeling. He looked around the office, dark except for the green glass lamp on his desk. It felt like someone had pumped oxygen into the room. He thought about calling for the intern, but his eyes fell on the letter he'd tossed aside. It had begun to smoke.

Rey cursed loudly and, in an attempt to pick it up, knocked over a stack of folders. He played hot potato with the envelope as the wax seal melted off in a quick burst of flame.

He stomped on the letter, the envelope having burned off while somehow leaving the cardstock inside perfectly intact, save for the black smudges from his fingertips.

He read the words and muttered, "Fucking hell."

It was after midnight, and when the buzzer rang, he knew who it was. He gathered all his things and texted his boyfriend to say he had a family emergency and would be gone for a couple of days. He'd have to call Jasmine first thing in the morning. At least Krishan was still there, waiting to clean up his mess.

When Rey got downstairs, Marimar was leaning against the side of the building, holding a brown paper bag.

"She almost set my office on fire," he said.

Marimar shrugged and bit into her bagel. "A pigeon broke into our apartment."

"Did it also catch on fire?"

"Nope."

"Most grandmothers send five-dollar bills in Hallmark cards or tin cans full of toffee." They walked to the corner and he hailed a cab and gave the address.

"Who do you know with grandmothers like that?" she asked incredulously.

"I don't know, but they have to exist."

"Stranger things exist, I guess."

They got back to their apartment and packed. Before 2 a.m., Rey and Marimar were in his old truck, the one he'd kept from his dad and was usually parked in a little lot near the East River. A gaudy skull hung from the rearview mirror beside a wooden rosary that had belonged to his paternal grandmother.

"I say there's no way the old witch is dying," Rey said.

Marimar bit the skin around her thumbnail raw. Orquídea would slap her hand when she saw her. The engine came to life and they peeled into crosstown traffic.

"Only one way to find out."

Tatinelly tried to keep cool, balancing a bowl of ice cream on her belly. The flavors had been scooped out from four different pints — pistachio, cherry chocolate swirl, vanilla rhubarb, and passion fruit sorbet. It was the only thing she could stomach on her eighth month of pregnancy. Olympia, Oregon, was not known for its warm weather, but on that spring day, a heat wave descended out of nowhere, trapping the soon-to-be mother with the struggling air conditioner unit.

She rested her head back against the arm of the sofa and sighed. The baby hadn't kicked in a couple of days and she'd tried everything to stir her because that silence made her nervous. Her doctor, a young man who'd never carried a baby himself, told Tatinelly that everything she was feeling and not feeling was perfectly normal. But this was her and Mike's first child (first of many, she hoped) and every pinch, ache, or fever dream made her worry.

Tatinelly Sullivan, née Montoya, grew up an only child, and though she'd had many cousins, at a certain point, everyone in her family just left the house they'd grown up in and never went back. It was difficult to explain to Mike the house where she'd come from. The things her father and grandmother had believed in. Stories of real, true wishes, and women who divined the stars, of slippery mermaids, and enchanted rivers. Stories about ghosts that could enter the house if they didn't lay down enough salt. Fairies living in the hills of their family estate in Four Rivers, disguised as insects. Magic things. Impossible things.

Mike had been born and raised in Portland. He was tall, wiry in a way that gave the impression of having been stretched. He'd played baseball and basketball in high school, and every morning he rode his bike on the trails that led into the woods for thirty miles. The best part about Mike was that he didn't change. She could go through his routine blindly, like muscle memory.

It was silly, but the night of her graduation from Four Rivers High, Tatinelly had made a wish. She didn't want much. She wasn't like Marimar, who wanted the world to explain itself, or like Rey who, burned with fire and color inside, or her younger cousins who wanted fame and money. She wasn't even like her dad who had wanted to be the mayor of a town that didn't exist anymore.

Tatinelly wanted a good life, a good husband, and a baby. That was it. That was enough.

The moment that wish left her lips, the magic her grandmother had talked about felt real for the first time in her life. She saw signs everywhere. For Texas, of all places. That night, she left a letter to her family, fit her worldly possessions in the suitcase her mother had intended for world travel, and trekked up the steep road that led to the highway. The first car she'd seen was an SUV, driven by a woman heading to Texas.

From there, Annette, the driver, gave her a room for the night and a job opportunity. All she had to do, for a small fee, was sign up to sell internet services for a company called DigiNet. Tatinelly, who'd never shown interest in much of anything, was really very good at it, and after days, her downline of coworkers was becoming an extensive network of men aged eighteen to forty-five. She'd even recouped her start-up fee and enough to rent her own studio apartment. Then one day, Annette and Digi-Net vanished. No weekly meeting in Annette's kitchen, no car in her driveway, no internet connection. Tatinelly had to go all the way to the mall to get her service switched back, and there, she noticed a Help Wanted sign at a phone accessories counter. She was offered the job instantly.

A few weeks later, she met Michael Sullivan, who was visiting from Portland on a business trip. He didn't need three phone cases and a battery charger that lit up when he plugged it into his car, but he bought them anyway. He'd been taken in by her smile, sweeter than anything he'd ever tasted. Her eyes were large with a slight tilt to the edges. Her light brown hair fell in long tangled waves down her slim figure. She had the effect of a doe trying to get across the I-10 and he wanted nothing more than to protect her, guide her to the other side.

It was the most impulsive thing Mike had ever done, but he asked her on a date. They went across the parking lot to an Italian restaurant that had never-ending bowls of pasta. By the fifth hour of slurping up fettuccini Alfredo, Mike excused himself, walked across the street to the pawnshop, emptied his savings account on an emerald ring, and returned to Mezzaluna.

Tatinelly said yes, of course. Her family didn't understand why they couldn't wait a few years, but most of them had come to the small wedding in the Oregon woods where Tatinelly Montoya became the first of her cousins, aunts, and uncles to take up a new last name. Tatinelly Sullivan.

The Sullivans didn't believe in ghosts or family curses. They only used salt in food, sometimes. They never got speeding tickets and always read the Terms & Conditions. They never fought or yelled or wore colors brighter than pastels. They loved their son and they loved Tatinelly, too, even if they were young for marriage; it just meant they had more time to be together.

Her grandmother couldn't be at the wedding, but Tatinelly had known, even as a little girl, that Orquídea Divina did not leave Four Rivers. She wondered if perhaps she couldn't.

Now, pregnant and enduring unseasonable heat, Tatinelly wasn't sure why she was thinking of her grandmother, whom she hadn't seen in the two years since she'd left Four Rivers. It wasn't that her family didn't get along. But Tatinelly had always felt

63

apart, distant. It was like loving something from far away and not needing to be part of it. She kept Four Rivers in her heart and the Montoyas with it.

As Tatinelly Sullivan, she had a good house surrounded by trees and flowers. She'd been married for six months, though as far as her mother knew she was also that much pregnant. She had everything she had wished for. A selfish part of herself, one that Tatinelly didn't know was there, wanted one more thing — her grandmother. Tatinelly wanted her child to have the wondrous, strange, magical Orquídea Divina in their life. Her life. Tatinelly was almost positive, though Mike wanted to be surprised.

It was then that she felt a kick so strong, that the bowl, perfectly balanced on her belly, tipped over, and she wasn't fast enough to catch it.

The front door opened and in came the earthy, sweat-drenched scent of her husband in his black and neon bike gear and helmet.

"Honey?" He kicked off his shoes at the door and walked to her with a stack of mail in hand. "You've got a letter from your grandma. That's weird. It's not stamped."

"How about that," she said wistfully, even as pain seized her belly. Tatinelly grinned and breathed through the roundhouse kicks from within. "You're going to be strong, aren't you, my little one?"

Mike took in his perfect wife with her perfect belly in their perfect home. Then, the ice cream bowl on the floor.

"What's going on?" he asked, picking up the mess so she wouldn't have to stand.

Tatinelly guided his hand to her belly where he felt the thump of their child's foot, anxious and ready to be in the world.

"We're going to see Orquídea Divina," Tatinelly said. She knew it. Somehow, as ordinary and plain as she was, she knew in her bones what that letter said.

Mike frowned but chuckled. "We are?"

She smoothed her belly right where the kick was the strongest. She spoke to her child directly now. "You know, Orquídea Divina was a fierce little girl, too."

3
THE GIRL WHO GREW ON AIR

Isabela Montoya needed a name for her newborn daughter. Names were important, even if she couldn't stay within her family's tradition. Before her father interceded, Isabela had almost been named Matilde, after Matilde Hidalgo, an illustrious suffragette who was the first woman to graduate high school in Ecuador, the first woman to cast a vote in Latin America, first to receive a bachelor's degree, and on and on. A woman of so many firsts, the patriarch of the Montoyas thought the name too revolutionary. Instead, Isabela Belén Montoya Urbano was named after an aunt, whose mild temper and skill at the piano had won her a successful marriage.

The new mother rifled through her mental catalog of family names. Cousin Daniela was too ugly. Berta was too prim. Caridad was a gossip. There was her aunt Piedad, who was the kindest of all her provincial relatives. But naming her bastard daughter something that meant piety was too ironic for her taste.

The maternity ward was crowded with narrow cots and new families. Isabela's mother cut through the room to get to her daughter's bedside. Her hair, which had been onyx black the night before, was threaded with silver strands. The woman's face was hard as marble, her slow, careful steps like she was walking across a tight rope. Guayaquil was a crowded city, but not that big. She feared someone would recognize her, see her breaking her husband's decree that no one, not even the gardener, was allowed to visit Isabela and the child. A girl, at that.

Roberta Adelina Montoya Urbano stood beside her daughter. She took the baby's hand and pried apart newborn fingers with nails still so delicate they were almost see-through. She inspected the color, the lines on the palm of her hand like she'd determine her whole future.

"Mamá," Isabela said.

Roberta shut her eyes. She withdrew a crinkled white envelope from her purse and set it on the bedside table. A good Catholic woman, she had to be able to say to her husband that she hadn't spoken to Isabela.

But he'd never said anything about giving her money.

Isabela drew her baby closer and watched her mother walk away.

A pretty young nurse rounded her bedside. She checked on Isabela's every comfort, and asked, "What will you call her?"

In the Montoya family, it was tradition to name the first child after the father, wherever he was. But she couldn't imagine saying his first name for the rest of her life. They'd spent one night together, and then he was gone. Before his departure, he'd given her two things, only one of them a gift. An orchid, a species which only grew in Ecuador. The ship he worked on was exporting them to Europe, but he'd stolen one for her. It was a beautiful flower unlike anything she'd ever seen — white and darkest plum and soft. She still had it, but now it was beige, pressed between the pages of a book she couldn't will herself to ever finish. The second was her daughter, weightless, fragile, like the same flower, which didn't need solid ground to grow.

Orquídea.

Once the sucres in the crinkled white envelope had been stretched as far as they could go, Isabela secured a job working long hours at a doctor's office on the other side of the city, and a tiny house in an industrial stretch of land by the shore. Though she lived a stone's throw from her childhood home, the Montoyas didn't want anything to do with the unwed mother and unlucky girl. A bastard daughter was never to inherit land, titles, her father's surname, or even love, which would have been free, had that strain of the Montoya clan been in possession of it.

As she grew, Orquídea quickly understood that if she wanted something, she would have to learn all the things that no one would teach her. At five years old, she walked the quarter mile to the pier. An old fisherman, who was nothing more than leathery brown skin and bones, taught her how to fish and clean the pink guts out for dinner. She gave the scraps to the cats that slunk like lazy shadows around the corner from her house.

That long dusty road flanked by cement houses with tin roofs was called La Atarazana, named after the old colonial shipyards. The ships were long gone, but Isabela made a home on the desolate shoreline, and soon, others followed. Among them, Orquídea was known as the peculiar little brown girl with unkempt black curls. Only cats liked to follow her around.

When her mother finally enrolled her in school, she learned to read and write. She also learned how to fight the girls from good families who made fun of her name, her skin, her whole existence. How to take a beating from the teachers who left her arms and hands stinging from the ruler, and later from her mother's belt for having to be humiliated by having a daughter who fights like a puta machona.

She learned how to stitch her only uniform when the seams split and holes appeared in her socks. She learned where to pinch schoolboys who tried to shove their hands under her skirt or grab the new peach pits of her breasts. She learned how to draw blood from those pinches. She learned to bite and to frown, because it was the only way to avoid getting robbed on the way home from school. When pinching didn't work, she learned to wield her fishing knife. She'd hold it up to a boy's crotch and say, "I can gut a fish in two seconds. What do you think I can do to you?" Her heart raced and she was called nasty, rude, savage. But there was no one else to protect her.

She learned that no one was ever going to want her, for reasons she couldn't control, and that praying to chipped statues of la

70

Virgen María and el niñito Jesús didn't come with anything but silence. She learned to survive and survived by learning.

By the time she was thirteen, she was a full-blown beauty, with lustrous black curls, skin like the darkest honey, but still peculiar and still followed around by cats, though roosters had begun to join her daily parades to the river shore.

Perhaps one of the most important things that Orquídea learned during her adolescence in Guayaquil was the identity of her father. She met him once but didn't get his name.

On the day that she met her father for the first time, she was seven. Everyone mistook her silence for being dim-witted, but Orquídea was as sharp as the knives in her pocket. She saw the truth in people's lies. She saw the sin in their deeds. And she saw her own face in a stranger's. Her father, a Colombian fisherman turned sailor who'd sailed into town only once before that, was tall, with deep black skin, and the kind of smile that made women dizzy. He went back to Isabela Montoya's old house but was told by a local boy that she no longer lived there, and for a sucre would show the sailor the correct house.

He was delighted to discover that the

71

woman had struck out on her own but was not yet married. Isabela wasn't home, but Orquídea had been at the table drinking café con leche and reading a book for school.

They recognized each other without needing to speak. Sometimes blood recognizes blood. It was in the beauty marks that formed a perfect triangle over their left cheekbones, in the way they craned their heads to the side to examine the oddity before them. It was in the crooked slant of their full lips, which accentuated a dimple that would claim hearts across time zones and hemispheres.

But then he spoke. He did not say his name. He did not ask for hers. He withdrew a salt-stained coin purse from the inside of his vest, took Orquídea's small hand in his. He placed the pouch on her palm and said, "Don't come looking for me."

He returned to the docks, and that was when Orquídea learned that she was exactly like her father, untethered, belonging to nowhere and nothing and no one, like a ship lost to the seas.

4

THE PILGRIMAGE TO FOUR RIVERS

Thirteen hours into their drive, Marimar leaned over to touch the radio and Rey slapped her hand away.

"We've listened to this song a hundred times," she shouted, sucking on the dregs of her drive-through soda.

"Fifty. Don't be so dramatic."

"You have the musical taste of a frat guy named Chad."

Rey laughed, one hand on the wheel and the other resting on the open window. The I-70 was empty across the stretch through Indianapolis. Other than stopping to pick up some greasy food, they'd made excellent time.

" 'Here I Go Again' is a *classic,* " Rey argued. "When it's your turn at the wheel, you can pick the music."

"But you won't let me drive."

His light brown eyes narrowed with mischief. "Exactly."

"Fine. When we get to the house, I'm the designated DJ."

Rey sucked his teeth. He reached for his cigarette box and pulled one out from the yellow pack. "Do we really have to do this?"

"The answer is still yes," Marimar answered. She was barefoot, her heels propped up on the dashboard. Red painted toes wiggled against the cool midwestern air. "She's our grandmother."

"Orquídea Divina is finally lonely. And old. She wants attention and this is the only way to get it." He lit his cigarette with one hand and tossed the metal lighter, another relic from his long-dead father, in the messy catchall below the radio.

"How old is she?" Marimar wondered. "I want to say that she's somewhere between sixty and eighty."

"You know, one time I tried to go through her things to find what she was hiding. Why she was so secretive. She had a fucking python in her drawer."

"It escaped from a nearby zoo."

"And it just happened to be in her dresser? Okay." Rey scrunched up his face in mock-agreement. "It bit me."

"Pythons aren't poisonous. Also, I think everyone's tried to go through grandma's things and never found a snake, or anything

74

super expensive worth all the secrecy. Maybe now we're going to find out."

"The valley's worth gold. You think she'll divide it among the remaining children? Oh, I call the record player. Maybe you'll get the porcelain tea set to complete the one you stole."

Marimar rolled her eyes and stared out at the flatlands, the highway that stretched ahead of them like an infinite movie backdrop that never seemed to get any closer. Something inside her twisted at the thought of dividing her grandmother's things like a pie. It was bound to get messy.

"You're not sad?" she asked.

The song restarted and Rey exhaled his disillusionment with his cigarette smoke. "I would be if she had picked up the phone every once in a while. Most grandmothers shower their grandkids with presents and praise."

"Is that what you want? Gifts and a pat on the back?"

"I got my fucking Bachelor's in two years instead of four and got my CPA license. I think that deserved something." He flicked ash outside his window and leaned his head back. "I'm calling it. She's just being dramatic. She's probably sorry that she kicked everyone out of the house, and this is the

75

only way to get us to come back."

"*Or,* she's telling the truth and we've been making too many stops. We might get there too late. What if she's really sick?"

"Such a different tune than when she drove you away and you came to live with us. I believe your words were 'I never want to see that old witch ever again.' "

Marimar remembered sitting in her room after her mother's funeral. Cause of death was drowning. How had her mother drowned in the same lake she'd swam in her whole life? How could her mother, who'd won meets in school and swam in the Pacific Ocean, have drowned? It didn't make sense, but Sheriff Palladino had said her mother must have hit her head on the dock and lost consciousness. By the time they'd found her, it was too late.

Orquídea liked to say that their family was cursed. But she wouldn't say why. Marimar didn't always believe her until that day. It had made her furious. What was the point of all of it? All of the candles, the salt in the grain, the roosters, the fucking laurel leaves meant for protection. Every reliquary her grandmother believed ordained their family with good luck was worthless because Pena Montoya, her beautiful, erratic, aloof mother, drowned anyway. If they were cursed, it was because of Orquídea. Marimar was only thirteen and certain of it. She became a wild thing. She shattered vases, jars full of roots and herbs, bottles of amber liquor. She took a kitchen knife and began cutting out Orquídea's precious golden laurel leaves, their delicate petals etched so deep in the door and windows that she barely made a scratch.

The enchantment of the valley broke. Marimar couldn't stand it. She boarded a bus. She took with her a duffle bag of clothes, a potted plant, and her stolen porcelain cup with big roses painted on the sides. She cried the whole way to New York.

She wasn't crying now on the road leading home. "You can still love someone even after they hurt you."

"Doesn't mean we should." Rey side-eyed her, his full mouth smirking, the cigarette burning as quickly as his nerves.

"Maybe she was right about the family curse," Marimar said. She tried for joking but it came out morose.

"Latino families just think they're cursed because they won't blame God or the Virgin Mary or colonization."

At that, she snorted. "Maybe we're not like other families."

"Don't you ever feel lied to?"

Marimar eyed the radio. White Snake on a loop felt like a specific kind of torture. Her vision drifted to the perfect, periwinkle sky. "You have to be more specific."

"Like all of her stories. The fairy creatures and magic shit."

"All grandmothers tell their grandkids stories," Marimar said.

"Yeah, but I always felt like Orquídea meant them. I thought she was being literal when she talked about the monsters waiting outside the house. That if she left, something would come and get her. Get us, too."

"Maybe her monsters were real once, did you ever think about that?" Marimar turned to look at her cousin. His eyes and crooked nose were all his father, but those high cheekbones and lips were his mom's. She remembered the boy she used to chase around. He'd use aluminum foil and tin to make himself an armor. They'd go by the lake and race up the hills and protect the land. They'd wait for the monsters that never came.

"Maybe," he said, and the word lingered between them. "That's only because we don't know her. Not really."

"Did you ever ask?"

He sucked his teeth and jammed the butt of his cigarette in the ashtray. "Did I ever

78

ask our grandmother about her life? *Obviously.* All she'd say was that she was born in Guayaquil, Ecuador, and moved to Four Rivers with Papi Luis. Once, I said I needed her help for my class ancestry project, and she said it didn't matter. I failed my fucking family tree because I couldn't fill it out."

"Yeah, I'm sure your kindergarten GPA was real affected."

"It was seventh grade, bitch," he said. "Remember when your mom died, and you asked Orquídea to get in touch with your father, and she said you were better off not knowing him? Like —"

"I know you worship your dad, but that doesn't mean everyone wants to or does. We don't know what her reasons were for the things she did."

"Well, I wanted to know. Don't you think it's strange that Orquídea never leaves her property? That she has a cemetery full of her dead fucking husbands? She spent our whole childhoods saying how important it was to stay together, to be a family, but when her kids wanted to go their own way, she kicked them out. Orquídea doesn't just push people away; she scorches and salts the earth. That's not right. That's fucked and you know it."

Marimar gnawed on her cuticle again. She

remembered when she was a little girl and did the same thing, her thumb would be raw practically down to the bone. She'd watched in the open, airy kitchen as her grandmother had cut a leaf from her aloe vera plant, split open the green fleshy skin with the precision of a surgeon. She scooped out the jelly from inside and slathered it on her skin. It burned, and later on, when Marimar stuck her thumb in her mouth, she cried at the rancid taste, but she'd stopped sucking her thumb by the end of the week.

Marimar knew that Rey was right. Their grandmother wasn't perfect, but she had come from a different time. They didn't know her. But what more did Rey want?

"Do you remember lighting those votive candles and making wishes," he asked. "She said they'd come true."

"Yeah," she said. "What did you wish for?"

He took a deep breath. "A boyfriend."

She grinned wide. "Was that the summer you were caught in the barn with the Kowalski boy?"

"Best seven minutes in heaven I've ever had." He drummed his fingers to the bass of the song, the crescendo that lent itself to the open road. If he closed his eyes, he could picture his father playing air guitar at the Yankees Stadium parking lot while they pregamed with hotdogs. "You?"

"Better grades, straight teeth, to meet my dad one day." All Pena had told Marimar about her father was that he'd swept into Pena's life like a storm and vanished just as quickly. Marimar knew Orquídea had been opposed to the union because when the subject of her father came up, she'd bite down on her tongue and grumble. Marimar knew he'd left her mother a silver ring emblazoned with a starburst, which was lost in the lake when Pena drowned.

If she could go back, if the wishes whispered to the candles on their grandmother's strange altar could actually come true, she would have been more discerning with them. Maybe ask the universe for a computer that worked or a story inspiration that went past chapter three instead of wishing to meet the father she'd never seen. "At least I got braces that year."

"One time I asked her why she didn't have a trace of an accent. I barely even heard her speak Spanish. And you do remember what she said?"

"She said she mixed dirt from the backyard, red rock clay, and peppermint leaves in a bowl and then scraped her tongue with it." Marimar was laughing so hard she could barely breathe. "Then you did that to try and pass your German class."

Rey could practically feel the grit of the dirt in his mouth and the earthworm that he hadn't noticed.

"It's okay to be gullible kids, Rey," she told him, nudging her arm against his. "That's the whole point of being a kid. You believe things before the world proves you wrong."

Why did his grandmother make him so mad? Thinking of her sometimes filled him with a sense of naivete that made him uncomfortable. Like he'd spent a lifetime watching a magician and then learned how simple her tricks were. He'd thought of his grandmother as a witch, a bruja with a house that buzzed with magic. Pantries filled with never-ending supplies of coffee and rice and sugar. With land that was always green and fertile. It wasn't her fault that he'd become logical — that she must have had a steady shipment that came when he had been too busy chasing farm boys, or that her land was in a valley called Four Fucking Rivers and of course it was fertile.

Orquídea's legacy was flash and secrets and half lies. Sweet memories that curdled with truth and bitterness over time. She wasn't a bruja and she wasn't powerful. He didn't want to be anything like that. He was mad at himself for realizing too late that her stories were just stories. That she wasn't a witch with magic tucked away like a silver coin between clever fingers, snatched behind a fool's ear. She was just a lonely old woman who had survived a great deal of loss. And yet, despite everything she was and couldn't be, she was a fixture in his mind. Orquídea Divina Montoya could not die. Not now, not ever. It worried him suddenly.

"I don't feel lied to," Marimar finally said.

"Good for you," he said softly, and turned up the volume. The road ahead was open, and he hit the gas, like if he went fast enough, he'd fly.

5

THE FLOWER OF THE RIVER SHORE

The day her mother married for the first time, Orquídea helped her get ready. She'd glued river pearls to a diadem and spent all night sewing the veil. Her future stepfather promised to give Isabela Montoya the world, but Orquídea still wanted her contribution to be perfect. On the big day, mother and daughter sat in the small room with a vanity. It was the last time they'd be alone together for a while.

"You look like a queen," Orquídea said, admiring her work in the mirror.

"Come here." Isabela reached for her daughter. She was a young woman now dressed in a blush pink dress and gleaming white shoes with buckles on them. Her arms and legs were strong from swimming and walking and fishing. Her long, perfect curls wild with humidity and river water; beautiful brown skin that looked soft as velvet. Her elegant features caught all the wrong attention. Some of the locals called her La Flor de la Orilla, *the flower of the shore*. A name Isabela detested because it sounded cheap.

Orquídea didn't like it because she knew she wasn't a flower, delicate and pretty and waiting to be plucked. For what? To be smelled? To sit in a glass of water until she withered? She was more than that. She wanted to be rooted so deep into the earth that nothing, no human, no force of nature, save an act of the heavens themselves, could rip her out.

"Things are going to be different for us now," Isabela promised. "Better."

Before Orquídea could speak, the door opened and Roberta Montoya waltzed in, clutching a hat box and a smaller ring box. She greeted her granddaughter with a curt nod, then turned to Isabela.

"I wore this on my wedding day, and my mother on hers," Roberta explained, lifting the hat box lid. "God has given you a second chance, and so will I."

Isabela was stunned. Not because of the intricate lace veil spilling out of the box. But because it had been so many years since she'd heard her mother's voice that she had forgotten the cadence of it. Roberta removed the pearl diadem and Orquídea caught it before it hit the floor.

"Why are you standing there, girl?" Roberta snapped at Orquídea and shoved the smaller box against her chest. "Make yourself useful. Deliver these cufflinks to Mr. Buenasuerte."

Orquídea looked to her mother, waiting for Isabela to interject. But she only stared at her own reflection, hidden behind gauzy white lace, as if the moment her husband peeled it back she'd be a new woman.

The wedding was small, but elegant. Orquídea was forced to give up her seat for her grandmother. From the balcony of the church, she watched Isabela get her second chance at happiness. None of them — not the Buenasuerte clan, not the priest, and certainly not the Montoyas — noticed her up there, anxiously plucking out the pearls from the bed of glue on the diadem. And none of them knew that if not for Orquídea, the flower of the shore, there wouldn't be a wedding, a second chance, to begin with.

She had spent the afternoon fishing when she first caught the attention of the man who would become her stepfather. He was a land developer and civil engineer. One of those men who waltzed into small, muddy neighborhoods and provincial towns. They laid down concrete, foundations for the city, roads and boardwalks. They left their mark. They always left children behind, too. In Ecuador, a place still transforming, still changing into what it wanted to be, a civil engineer was as common as the tomcats that prowled the neighborhoods. It was a respectable and secure job, with projects being commissioned by the government.

Along the strip of houses near the river where Orquídea lived, there was nothing to develop. At least, that's what Wilhelm Buenasuerte decided upon cursory inspection. As he trekked the unnamed road all the way to the shore, he tucked his gold pendant under his shirt, rolled up his pants to the ankles to avoid the mud, and kept his hands in his pockets.

When he retrieved his handkerchief to mop sweat off his stern brow, his wallet fell, and Orquídea Montoya happened to be walking home at that moment with her basket of fish to fry for dinner. She gathered his wallet and shouted after him. Though her clothes were clean — except for the usual splatter of river water — and though she showered every day, Wilhelm took a step away from her, startled by the child that came up to his hip.

She offered his wallet back. "You dropped this."

Wilhelm Buenasuerte was born to a German mother and an Ecuadorian father. That is to say, his father was half Spaniard and half Indigenous, part of the mestizaje of the country. But he considered himself Ecuadorian to the bone. His eyes were not quite brown and not quite green. His nose was not quite crooked and not quite straight. His hair was not quite blond and not quite brown. His skin was not quite white but whiter than most. He was proud of everything that made up his whole. That was why, after being educated in Germany, he returned to his father's land — his birthplace — to make it better, to make it more.

"Thank you, child," he said. He took out a five sucre note and placed it in her hand.

By then, Orquídea had hated when men shoved money in her fist. Her father — the man who'd fathered her — had done so. The men who bought fish from her did it, too. Once, a man tried to give her ten sucres so she'd follow him home. She was only ten and she'd thrown dirt in his eyes and run all the way home and barricaded herself in. She did not think this man was that way, but who was she to say?

That was when her mother came bounding down the dusty street yelling her daughter's name. Isabela Montoya's porcelain white cheeks were flushed, and her black hair had come undone from the sensible bun she always wore it in.

When she got a good look at the classy, distinguished man in front of her, Isabela relaxed. "I hope my daughter is not bothering you, sir."

Wilhelm Buenasuerte was too stunned to speak. Something inside his chest gave a terrible squeeze. For a moment he considered whether or not he was having a heart attack. He was too young for that, but his father had died from one, hadn't he? No, it had to be something else. The woman before him was dressed for an office, with a beauty that was so delicate, he felt the incomprehensible urge to do everything he could to protect it. She wore no wedding band, but she had a child that was perhaps twelve. An early mishap of her youth. His father had always told him women were easily led astray and they needed good men to keep them in the ways of family and God. Wilhelm Buenasuerte considered himself a good man.

"No bother at all, Mrs. — ?" he held out his hand and paused to allow her an introduction.

"*Miss* Isabela Montoya," she emphasized her availability.

He gave the dirt road another once over. The wide río Guayas held a quiet promise. Suddenly, Wilhelm could see a highway that would cut through here one day. A boardwalk would stretch all the way to the cerro Santa Ana. First, these shacks and dinky fishing canoes needed to go. Perhaps he'd been in too much of a hurry to dismiss this spot of land. Wilhelm Buenasuerte found a reason to stay.

Orquídea never spent the money Wilhelm Buenasuerte had given her. But on the day of her death, she would return it.

6
THE FIRST DEATH OF ORQUÍDEA DIVINA

Marimar knew they were almost home when she licked her lips and could taste a hint of salt.

They'd spent the night in Lawrence, Kansas, at a cheap hotel in the downtown college area. They were both too wired to sleep, and spent the night drinking at a bar covered in neon lights with a country metal band caterwauling their way through pop covers. Everything closed at midnight, so she smoked Rey's cigarettes and gave money to a howling busker while Rey got his palm read by an undergrad covered in piercings and tattoos. They woke up before sunrise, showered, and got back on the road.

"What did the fortune-teller say to you?" Marimar asked.

"She said I'd save someone's life one day," Rey said.

"Cryptic."

"And that I'd take a trip and meet a hand-

91

some stranger." The last bit he said with a coquettish emphasis.

"Fancy. Maybe he has a brother and we can double date."

"Maybe he'll have an evil twin and we can live out one of my mom's favorite telenovelas."

"Don't they all have evil twins?"

"We should have brought her with us to tell the family's fortunes."

They went on and on for the rest of the drive, talking about anything and everything that wasn't their family. But when the air thickened with the pungent smell of unturned earth and wildflowers, of salty air when they were so far from the sea, they fell quiet.

At first, she thought that nothing had changed in these lands — not the unyielding sun, not the hungry wild earth, and not the tire-eating road that led all the way home. But then she breathed deeper and found a new scent — something that hadn't been there when she'd left six years before. It was the same thing she couldn't identify on the invitation — decay.

Marimar kept the windows rolled down just enough that the wind whistled past and dry leaves made their way between the cracks and onto her lap. She held a green leaf by the stem. For a moment, she thought she could close her eyes and see the makeup of its whole being, the tree it had come from, and the earth that nurtured it. She held the leaf to her nose and wished she had a book with her to press it into. Then she let it fall to her feet among the drive's collection of fast-food containers and empty coffee cups.

Rey's truck jostled from side to side, his trinkets swinging from the rearview mirror.

"You'd think she'd have the road paved by now," he muttered.

"Paving roads?" Marimar said, taking on their grandmother's stern voice. "That would make it seem like I want people to find their way here."

Rey put the dusty red jeep in park behind a neat row of cars off the side of the unnamed road that lead to Orquídea's house. "That's as far as this piece of crap is getting."

The other factions of the Montoya clan were already there. Enrique's Lamborghini was covered up with a black tarp. Cousin Tatinelly's pink Beetle was sandwiched between two silver sedans. There were other cars she didn't recognize, all parked at a hasty angle, but there were a lot of family members she hadn't seen in years. When she'd lived there, it had only been Orquí-dea, her step-grandad Martin, her mom, Tía Parcha, and Rey. She hadn't seen this many people there, maybe ever. There certainly weren't this many people when her mom died. Orquídea had told the other Montoyas to stay away for their own good. Marimar still hadn't forgiven her grand-mother for that. And yet, when Marimar inhaled the valley air so deeply that her lungs hurt, she couldn't wait to get to the bottom of the hill.

Rey pulled out his pack of cigarettes and slapped it against the palm of his hand. "Let's just get this over with."

"Nothing brings family together like the promise of riches," Marimar said, slamming her door shut. She was barefoot. When she was little, she'd liked to wiggle her toes in the ground like they were worms. But the dirt was too dry now, and she dug through the back seat until she found her beat-up penny loafers.

Rey shook his head but marched dutifully on beside her, pulling out a white invitation bleeding black scrawl, his thumb tracing his grandmother's perfect calligraphy. He won-dered if she was pulling one of the games she did when he and Marimar and Tatinelly were kids. She'd hide items around the house and give them clues, like they had to find something that had many eyes but could not see. Marimar had brought a button, Rey had brought a potato, and Tatinelly picked up a picture from the fireplace mantel. Maybe this invitation was a riddle, too. *Come and collect.* Maybe she wasn't dying . . .

They began their walk down the steep hill. Marimar used to run across the green trying to wake the fairies that lived among the twisted gardens. Orquídea liked to tell stories of the winged creatures that protected the ranch with their otherworldly magics born right from the stars. Orquídea had promised that if Marimar found her spark, if she showed potential, she'd wake the fairies. But no matter how much she tried and tried, Marimar's power would not wake, and she never saw any — there were too many bugs and dragonflies in the way.

Arm in arm with Rey, Marimar fought the urge to sprint into the tall grass fields and search for the winged beasties once again. But if the fairies had once protected the valley, they were long gone by now. The grass was yellowing the closer they got to house. The stench of unturned earth became more pronounced. For so long, the people of Four Rivers had called the Montoyas witches and other crueler things, but there was no magic here by the state of things, if there ever had been.

"Jesus, what happened?" Rey asked.

Was Orquídea simply too old to keep the land thriving and healthy on her own? The rest of Four Rivers had seemed fine on the drive in — the diner, the gas station, the video store — like it had been petrified in time. But this — this was different.

Marimar remembered one terribly hot summer. It was so arid, she felt like she was growing lizard skin. They didn't have an air conditioner because they'd never needed it before. But her mother, Pena Montoya, wasn't going to stand for the drought. She put on a record and dialed up the volume. She dragged Orquídea and Marimar outside and said, "Let's call down the rain."

Then they went outside, their voices singing to the sky, their bare feet kicking up dust. And when the sky broke open with thunder and lighting and what looked like shooting stars, Orquídea rushed them inside, and Martin mixed up a lemonade that was ice-cold and tasted bitter and sweet and perfect.

The pressure behind Marimar's belly button returned. She was overcome with the sensation that something was about to end and there was nothing she could do to stop it.

"This is depressing, and she's not even dead yet." Rey wedged another cigarette between his dry lips. This time his hands shook as he cranked the lighter's spark-wheel.

Marimar wanted to laugh, but the crowd gathered in front of the homestead gave her pause. She remembered Orquidea's stories of angry villagers who tried, and failed, to run her out of town when she and her late grandfather had arrived. But this wasn't a horde of strangers. This was her family.

"Why is everyone standing outside?" she asked.

Rey looked at his watch. The invitation said no earlier than 1:04 p.m., true solar noon. Orquídea was punctual, yet it was nearly three.

At the end of the road, nestled at the junction of surrounding hills, the ranch resembled a toy house with dozens of tiny dolls gathered around. If Marimar closed her eyes, she could picture everything within its walls. The floorboards that groaned in the middle of the night, as if the wood was still alive and trying to stretch free. Tall candles and rivers of wax melting into every crack they could find. Great open windows that

97

let in the sweet smell of grass and hay and flowers. Fat chickens and pigs Marimar and Rey tormented while their mothers, Pena and Parcha, tended to the gardens. Back then, the ranch was palatial. Their own private world among the sky and mountains, and Orquídea Divina was the queen of it all.

Marimar swatted at a dragonfly that kept buzzing around her head. Rey puffed out his cigarette smoke and it took on the shape of a hummingbird.

The final stretch of the road was steep, the wind at their backs reaching out like hands and pushing them the rest of the way. When they were little, they'd race and roll down. Now they were trying to keep their balance, feet dashing until they landed in front of the ranch, where aunts and uncles and cousins they hadn't seen in years waited.

Seeing them all like this was a unique experience. They weren't the kind of family that celebrated holidays, except for the anniversary of Orquídea's arrival to Four Rivers. It was her grandmother's version of New Year's, which she gave silly names to. The Year of the Apricot. The Year of the Chupacabra. Once, she'd let her uncle Caleb Jr. name the year, and he'd chosen the

Year of the Pterodactyl because of his dinosaur phase. Marimar removed the invitation from her back pocket and unfolded it. She traced the words *the Year of the Hummingbird.* Orquídea's favorite bird.

"What's going on?" Marimar asked.

A disgruntled sound vibrated through the crowd.

"Orquídea being Orquídea," Aunt Reina said through lips so pinched, her lipstick was feathering out like tiny veins.

Marimar counted her cousins, aunts, and uncles, but kept losing track. She leaned over to Rey and mumbled, "I guess this is what twelve years of four husbands looks like."

"Goals, question mark?" Rey said with caution.

It was an impressive gathering for a woman who had claimed to come from nothing and been wanted by no one as a child. When Marimar had asked why everyone in the family carried the last name Montoya, even though it was the maternal last name, Orquídea simply said that she wanted to leave her mark, and besides, she went through all the trouble of giving birth each time.

The offshoots of Montoyas went as follows:

Marimar and Rey represented their dead mothers, Pena and Parcha Montoya, and the family branch that sprung from their grandfather, Luis Osvaldo Galarza Pincay, who had made the journey from Ecuador to Four Rivers with Orquídea and Gabo the rooster. He'd died when their daughters were small, from something Orquídea called a patatús, and Marimar understood it roughly meant a fright. Pena Montoya was never married, and all Marimar knew of her father was that he'd left before Marimar was born. Parcha Montoya Restrepo, as an act of rebellion, gave Rey the middle name of Montoya instead.

Next was Héctor Antonio Trujillo-Chen, a Puerto Rican-Chinese professor who'd wandered down the hill in order to inquire about the aroma of coffee. He'd been guest lecturing on the subject of agriculture at the community college when he drove by. After his class, he returned to call on Orquídea, who had taken to his lovely eyes and sturdy height, and they were married the following spring. They had three children, who were all present. Félix Antonio Montoya Trujillo-Chen, his wife Reina, their daughter Tatinelly, and her husband Mike Sullivan. Florecida Dulce Montoya and her daughter Penelope. Silvia Aracely Montoya Lupino, her husband Frederico, and their twin sons, Gastón and Juan Luis.

After Héctor passed, from an infection brought on by experimenting with plant hybrids, came Caleb Soledad. Caleb, like most people, ended up in Four Rivers because he'd gotten lost. He had no phone, no quarters hidden in the glove compartment, and the tank of gas, which he'd just filled, had somehow leaked out and left him stranded two miles away from the house. He was a chemist, by way of Texas, driving around the country trying to come up with the perfect perfume. They fell in love in her garden, and when Marimar had first heard this story, she'd definitely thought that meant they'd had sex. The Soledad-Montoya siblings had the same strong brows, angular jaws, deep olive skin, and green eyes as their father. There were the twins, Enrique and Ernesta, and Caleb Jr. None of them had children yet.

Marimar looked around for Orquídea's fourth husband, Martin Harrison, a retired Jazz musician from New Orleans who had found his way to Orquídea's front porch because, somehow, he'd heard the sound of her music all the way up the road. He was not among the impatient legion of Montoyas.

It was then that Marimar realized what her aunt Reina meant by "Orquídea being Orquídea." The pressure behind her belly button intensified. Marimar pushed her way through and darted up to the house, a swarm of dragonflies now trailing around her head. With every step, her heart descended into the pit of her stomach. Her childhood home was nothing like she remembered it, and even though she was expecting some wear and tear, she was not ready for this.

Dark green ivy and vines crept between the wood panels, through shattered windows, all-consuming, as if devouring the house back into the ground. Roots broke through the porch like tentacles, strangling the door handle to shut the way in.

And if Orquídea Divina was still inside, it shut her way out.

Rey marched up the front steps and stood beside her. His fingertips brushed against one of the windows, dragging a finger along a hairline fracture that led to the stamped gold laurel. A single leaf was peeling off the glass.

"Grandma?" Marimar beat her fist against the door. When she pulled her hand back, there was a thorn lodged into the tender side of her palm. It hadn't even stung.

Rey blinked away his surprise. He pulled a handkerchief from his pocket and handed it her. "Here."

She dislodged the thorn, but only a single drop of blood fell.

Rey grabbed one of the roots that didn't seem to have any thorns and yanked. It was like trying to pry open an iron fence.

"We've *tried* that," came a voice behind them.

Tío Enrique, the second youngest of Orquídea's sons, stuffed his hands into slim fit trouser pockets. "But please, tell us what you would do that we haven't tried for hours."

"Shut up, Enrique," Rey snapped, trying to grab the root that kept the door from opening. He kicked at the vines. He picked up a large rock, but they just seemed to grow thicker, wilder.

Enrique chuckled, more amused than offended at having one of his nephews speak to him that way. Then something cruel gleamed across his features. "Praise the Saints, you finally have a backbone."

"Ignore him," Marimar muttered and cupped her hands against one of the least obstructed windowpanes. There was too much dust on the inside. She remembered Monday mornings when they poured Orquídea's homemade cleaning liquid and scrubbed the whole house from ceiling to floor. The longer she tried to look, the more the vines shook, and the house let out a loud groan.

"What should we do?" Tatinelly asked, her voice like the susurration of leaves on the breeze. "This little one's starting to get hungry."

Reymundo did a double take. The last two years had been good to Cousin Tati. She placed her hands on her pregnant belly and sat on the bottom porch steps. Her husband — a thin man with sunburned patches all over his arms and nose — hurried close to her side. He looked like a rabbit caught in a snare. They should've all been afraid. They should've all been horrified at the state of the house. But there they were, getting angry and frustrated instead.

"Didn't she hide keys inside the big apple tree when she was mad?" Rey asked. "Maybe —"

"The orchard is withered," Enrique said dismissively, and stuck out his chest like Gabo, the rooster.

The family gathered closer, staggering along the creaky porch steps. Their bright colors made them look like wildflowers sprouting between overgrown yellow grass.

"What else have you tried?" Marimar demanded.

"Knocking," Tía Florecida ticked off words on her slender fingertips. "Shouting. Breaking down the door. The house did *not* like that, but Ricky never listens. I used to sneak out through the back, but it's all sealed."

"She just needs time," Tío Félix reassured them. He had a black mustache though his thick wavy hair had gone salt white.

"You're right, Daddy," Tatinelly said in that pretty, soft way of hers. Where Marimar felt like a blowhorn, Tatinelly was a windchime. Marimar had always wondered how her cousin was able to maintain such a calm disposition. Even in the face of the strangest circumstance their family had ever faced, Tatinelly *giggled.* "Isn't it curious?"

Rey crossed his arms over his chest. " 'Curious' isn't the word I'd use."

"What would you use?" Juan Luis piped up from the crowd in his prepubescent squeak.

"I'd say this is *fucked,*" Rey said.

Marimar tried to bite down her laughter. The twins and Penelope were delighted at the swearing and repeated the words like cockatiels. The matrons not so much.

Tío Félix nodded, tugging at the tip of his

chin. "I'm beginning to get worried."

"B-beginning?" Mike Sullivan asked. He'd twisted the invitation into an unrecognizable scrap.

"What more did we expect?" Ernesta sighed. "I swore I'd never come back here."

"Who invites people over and then keeps them waiting outside?" Reina, Félix's wife asked. Her feathered lipstick kept spreading.

"You don't have to be here," Caleb Jr., the youngest of the Montoya progeny, reminded her. He had all the heat of a stove burner set to medium. Though he'd left Four Rivers to continue and expand his father's perfume empire, he loved his mother and would not stand for a negative word about her.

"Aniñado, momma's boy," Florecida muttered at her baby brother. "Why don't we call Sheriff Palladino?"

"What's *he* going to do? Tip his hat at the roots and tell the house to have a peachy day?" Enrique waved a dismissive hand.

"I don't see *you* doing anything but trying not to get your bespoke shirt dirty," Caleb Jr. said.

Ernesta shoved a finger against his heart. "Don't start."

That kicked off chatter that sounded like

a swarm of wasps. Everyone was looking to Enrique for answers that he didn't have. The truth was that none of them knew how to get into the house. They had been gone for so long, they'd forgotten how to play by Orquídea's rules.

Rey leaned against the warped wooden porch and drew out one of his cigarettes while the squabble continued outside a house being strangled by giant roots. Tío Félix and Tatinelly's husband, whose name he never seemed to remember, also bummed one.

"Isn't it weird," Rey whispered to Marimar, "to think that we're all related?"

She took his cigarette and pulled on the bitter smoke, drew it deep in her lungs until she felt the heady rush of tobacco. "Cats are related to lions."

Rey retrieved his cigarette, his hands trembling still. "Which ones are we in this scenario?"

Marimar shrugged. "I don't want to know."

"Stop it!" Silvia said, slapping her hips in a way they'd all seen Orquídea do a million times.

Tatinelly shook her head softly, staring past everyone at the yellow grass that blanketed the ground beneath their feet and rubbed her belly in a steady, hypnotic motion. "This can't be good for the baby."

"Enough!" Félix shouted. "We aren't here to fight with each other."

"For once you're right, brother. We're here to collect what is ours." Enrique shrugged out of his slate gray blazer and shoved it into Gastón's hands, who handed it to his twin, Juan Luis. The kid put it on, and it fit him like a trench coat.

"Everyone, wait here." Enrique rolled up his periwinkle blue sleeves up, cursing as he marched down the porch and around back.

Marimar nudged Rey and they followed him.

The buzzing sound of their family faded as they waded through overgrown dry grass. Further back, the orchard really had withered, but not in the way Marimar had expected. Each and every tree was split down the center, like they'd been struck by lightning.

She and Rey exchanged concerned glances, but neither trusted themselves to speak. What had done this? Why now?

The gardens and the greenhouse were brown, wilted bits of what used to be lush green. Dead and rotting and ruined. The stench of it shoved into their noses and mouths.

"There," Marimar said, pressing her arm across her nose.

Enrique stomped up to one of the small sheds which was in better condition than the main house since it wasn't covered in vines, but the roof had a visible hole on one side. When he opened the door, it came right off the hinges. Martin took up carpentry in his old age, but the place looked like it hadn't been used in years. There were stacks of wood and machetes, axes, hand saws, and rusted letter openers littered on the surfaces.

"I can't wait to sell this slice of hell into a million fucking little pieces." Enrique's rage frothed into expletives as his hand closed around what he was looking for.

"See, when I cursed like that, Orquídea would make me eat a jalapeño," Rey said from the entryway. "Seeds and all."

Enrique inhaled his resolve. A ray of sun beamed down on him from the hole in the roof. He was King Arthur, except instead of Excalibur, Enrique held up a warped machete that couldn't be used to slice a palmetto leaf let alone hack through solid wood. He slung the rusted weapon over his shoulder. His jade-green eyes were bright, and he flashed a desperate smile that was all teeth.

"What are you doing?" Marimar stepped into the doorway to bar his way out.

"I'm tired of waiting. That woman has made my life miserable since the day she realized I'd never carry any of her godforsaken superstitions."

"They're not superstitions." She could practically feel her anger licking at her skin right down to her toes. Hadn't she left Four Rivers and Orquídea's nonsense behind? Why was she defending it now?

Enrique barked a bitter laugh. "Keep telling yourself that. You're still children hanging on to her every word. Haven't you realized? There's no magic or secrets here. It's an evil. Anything that has to do with Orquídea dies. That's what got my sisters and my father. That's what got Martin."

"Martin is dead?" Marimar sucked in a sharp breath. She felt cold from the inside, like an ice sculpture was building within her. Martin with his wide, toothy smile. Martin, who had cared for them like they were his own grandkids.

"She didn't tell you either? He went peacefully in his sleep, at least," Enrique said, and for the first time there was something like compassion in his deep voice. "See? She doesn't care about anyone. If you were smart, you'd leave. After we settle up, whatever family I have, they'll never know any of this or her."

He shoved his niece and nephew out of the way.

Rey flicked his cigarette butt on the ground and whispered in Marimar's ear, "For the sake of the world I hope he's sterile."

"Come," Marimar said, and pulled her cousin along after their uncle. "He's not getting away with this."

The crowd of Montoyas parted to make way for Enrique. Enrique, who had taken all the money his father had left him in a trust and opened up a vodka distillery catering to young celebrities and the playboy millionaires he aspired to be. He wanted nothing more than to own this valley. He'd buy his family out if he had to. There was money in land development, and he could quadruple his fortune if he made the right sale. But there was nothing left for anything to prosper here, not anymore.

He wielded the machete high over his head as he marched up to the door.

"Stop!" Marimar shouted, but Enrique did not listen, and he brought the machete down on the roots that kept the door shut. The vines rippled. The roots twisted. The house let loose a deep, guttural moan. But the machete was like a fist against solid brick. Enrique couldn't stop now, so he kept hacking away at a root that petrified with every strike. Another thick root reached out and struck him across the face. He grunted and when he recovered there was the shadow of a perfect handprint on his cheek.

On the next strike, Enrique went for the gold laurel leaves on the glass windows and was pushed back with a great force. He turned to the worried faces of everyone around him and, for the first time, something like fear bolted across his eyes.

"Stop!" Marimar shouted again, and this time, even the mountains trembled with the sound of her cry.

"It'd be easier to burn it to the ground," Rey said, looking down at his lighter. The cherry of his cigarette lit up the angles of his face from where he stood in the shadows. He didn't mean what he said. He'd loved this house once. He wanted to hate it. He had hated it when he'd been far away. But now that he was here, now that he heard it crying, he wanted to make it stop.

Orquídea Divina had survived in a world that didn't want her and she survived the magic that claimed the lives of her husbands and daughters. Enrique, though he was her son, didn't understand her. Most of them didn't. Not truly. If they had, they'd be inside the house.

Come and collect. Those were the exact words Orquídea had written. They were here to answer an invitation. All of them.

"That's not how Orquídea works," Tatinelly said.

Marimar nodded. Any other day, she would have laughed at Enrique getting punched in the face by magical roots, but they had somewhere to be. Someone waiting for them. She pulled out the invitation again. *Come and collect.* She thought of the way her grandmother hid things in the hollows of trees. How she spoke to the birds that brought seeds to her windowsills and sent them on errands.

"Remember that time my mom came home drunk," Rey said, "And even though the locks hadn't been changed, her key wouldn't work? Orquídea was in the den and we had instructions to not let my mom in."

"Yeah," Marimar said. "I forgot how she finally got in."

"She said she just apologized and asked nicely, but now I can't remember if my mom had been talking about the house or Orquídea."

"Maybe we should ask nicely," Tatinelly

113

suggested.

They scoffed and laughed at her, but Marimar held on to that thought. No one wanted to be summoned, no one truly wanted to be *here.* She was sure that not one of the other Montoyas had announced themselves. They'd seen the obstacle and gave up when the answer wasn't obvious. But perhaps it was obvious.

Tatinelly got up, her belly nearly tipping her over. Rey held out a steadying hand since he was standing closest to her. She walked up the five porch steps and stood in front of the door.

"I've come to collect," she said in her windchime voice.

Instantly, the roots gave way, relinquishing their hold on the doorknob. The house released a deep sigh that shook the entire structure. Dragonflies and lightning bugs flitted in the dark open hall, their hazy glow illuminating the foyer. Floorboards peeked beneath layers of dirt, which must've come in with the roots and vines that broke through like ripped stitches.

Marimar and Rey didn't wait for the others. They were right behind Tatinelly, turning left into the living room, where Orquídea Divina liked to sit, facing the fireplace while drinking bourbon as the sun set behind the valley. Her valley.

The old bruja was right where she'd always been. Her warm brown skin was cracked like parched earth, and her hair, still ink-black despite the years, was braided into a crown around her head. Those black eyes crinkled at the corners, her mouth split into a dark smile.

Rey felt his own heart spike with relief and terror combined.

"Mamá?" Marimar gasped.

"Oh, my saints," Tatinelly said, pressing where her baby kicked hard.

"Fuck me," Rey said, reaching for a cigarette, but he was out.

"What did I tell you about staring?" Orquídea asked, her voice strong and raspy as ever.

"Do it?" Rey grinned.

Because how could they not stare? Orquídea Divina Montoya was the same as she'd always been from the waist up. It was the rest of her that needed some getting used to.

Thin green branches grew straight out of her wrists, her inner elbow, the divots between her finger tendons, like extensions of her veins. They wrapped around the high-backed upholstered chair with the laurel leaf embroidery. Flower buds the size of pearls bloomed from the branches sprouting out of her beautiful skin.

Her peacock-blue dress was pulled up to show her knees, where flesh and bone ended, and thick brown tree bark began. Most spectacular of all were her feet, now turned into roots. The same roots that tore through the floorboards and dug straight into the earth, searching and searching for a place to cling to.

7
THE GIRL AND THE RIVER MONSTER

Before she arrived in Four Rivers, before she came to steal her power, before her mother married, Orquídea was just an ordinary girl who spent most of her days by the river. Until one day, she had her first taste of the impossible. On the same day, she made a deal.

It happened during an unusually dry summer when no one could catch a single fish. Not even Pancho Sandoval who'd been fishing in the same river since he was younger than Orquídea. Pancho was slender but muscular, the kind of body built by hunger and manual labor, his skin reddish brown from days under the equatorial sun. He was worried. They all were. No fish meant nothing to sell. No food. No food and no money meant sickness.

Everyone in the city felt the strain. Jobs were scarce. Isabela's office cut her days. She took a job cleaning houses for a fraction of the usual wages. They ate white rice with a fried egg on top for every meal for weeks. Orquídea did the only thing she could. She skipped school and took that familiar road to the end of the pier.

The río Guayas was always clay brown, the rich earth giving it its color. Green weeds covered in thorns floated across the surface and always snagged her net. There was no breeze. There was no reprieve from the heat. Even the river was too warm to swim in.

"Pancho, can I borrow your canoe?" she asked, shielding her eyes from the sun with the flat of her hand.

"There's nothing there," he lamented. "Some of us are thinking of going a little ways south to scare up some luck."

"Well, so am I."

"You should be in school. I didn't go to school. Now look at me."

She did look at him. Pancho could weave hammocks faster than anyone. He could swim across the río Guayas like a fish. He could climb the mango tree with his bare feet. But no one needed hammocks, and there were no fish, and the mangoes were rock hard that summer. Some people just had a talent for things, but they were born poor or ugly or unlucky, and all they could say was "look at me" and try their hardest.

"I am looking at you," Orquídea said. "I have a feeling. I need to be here. Let me take your canoe. I'll split whatever I catch with you."

Pancho mopped the sweat on his face with the front of his shirt. He wheezed his cracked beer-bottle laughter. "I don't know if you're the devil's child or an angel's."

Orquídea shrugged. She'd already met her father and he was neither.

"Fine," he relented. "I'll go with Jaime and the boys."

Ten and stubborn, she went out. Her arms hurt from the push and pull of the oars. Her head spun from sweating all the coffee and water she'd drank that morning. Guayaquil was laid out before her, an ever-changing landscape that was always at war with itself. It had the blood of fighters in its soil. Its rivers. And turmoil gives rise to monstrous things.

The time of myths was long gone, but there were still stories that lingered. Stories she overheard from the wrinkled mouths of women who had witnessed and survived more than the turn of the century. They spoke of water spirits that liked to play tricks on humans. To keep them in their place, groveling in the dirt with sand in their eyes.

In all her time fishing, she'd seen strange things. Inexplicable things. Fish with human teeth, a blue crab the size of a tortoise, a lizard with two heads. She'd hear the wind speak to her when she stood at just the right angle. She thought she'd seen a human face poke its head out of the water before swimming across the river to the shores of Durán.

"I know you're there," she said.

She couldn't see the bottom. She could barely see the flat end of one of her oars because the river had so much sediment. She hoisted the oar up and over, laying it across her seat.

"I know you're there," she said, this time louder.

Orquídea stood up, her borrowed canoe bobbed on the surface of the river. A clump of leaves floated by, a plastic bottle tangled up at its center.

"If you tell me what you want, then I'll find a way to help you," she said.

Heat scorched her neck. She cupped a bit of water in her hand and splashed it on her skin. She sat, resting her elbows against her knees. Her mother had always told her not to sit that way, that ladies sat with their legs crossed and not open. But she wasn't a lady

120

out on the river. She was just like everyone else — someone who wanted answers and maybe a little bit of help.

The river grew increasingly still. The wind died. Even the ships and cars, whose sounds made the city feel like a constant scream, stopped.

A creature crept out of the murk and over the side of the canoe. Orquídea didn't have a word for it, other than "monster." But what was a monster, really? She remained where she was, showing neither fear nor revulsion at its crocodile face and reptilian humanoid body less than three feet tall. It had the patterned belly of a turtle. She noticed neither sex nor belly button. Its webbed hands ended in sharp yellow claws, but not as sharp as the toothy smile it flashed.

"What do you want, Bastard Daughter of the Waves?" the creature asked.

"My name is Orquídea."

"You do not bear your father's name. But he is of the sea. A sailor through and through."

"I don't claim him."

"Ah, but the water claims you. Hence — your title. Now, what do you want?"

Orquídea decided not to argue with the river monster. "I want you to bring the fish back. People are starving."

"What is that to me?" the crocodile monster said, pressing a clawed hand to its chest, as if indignant to the accusation. "I have lived in this river since before the time of men. Before iron and smoke polluted these waters. I have lived in this river since before it ran red with blood and your people set the coasts on fire. What do I care if humans starve?"

Sweat ran down the sides of her temples. Not because she was scared but because her insides were squeezing water out like her body was a wet rag.

"I know why you're angry. The world is bad and sometimes good things happen, not the other way around. But if you have been here since before strangers came to these shores, why starve us out now? Why are you angry now?"

The creature turned its face to the side. Yellow reptilian pupils stared at her, unblinking.

"I have always been angry, Bastard Daughter of the Waves. The other day, I was in the shallows near Puná, and I watched a ship unload garbage into the waters. I was buried under it for days and no one came to help me. The other fish and crabs couldn't hear me."

"How did you get out?"

It remained silent for a long time, showing the uneasy stillness of the animal it took its likeness from. "A little girl was rummaging through the waste. She cleared a path. I scared her."

"So, you hate us and starve us, but a girl helped you. That doesn't seem fair."

"How did you even know I was here? No one knows my name."

"Someone does. Someone remembers you. When I was a little girl, there were these old women who talked about the crocodile monster who waits on the shore. That once, it wrestled a fisherman and lost."

"I did not lose," the monster said, but its words were sour, angry. "He cheated. Anyway, I don't understand why you're trying to help them. I have seen you on the shore since you were old enough to walk alone and remember the way back home. Or perhaps, this river is the only home you want to claim."

Orquídea shrugged. "As long as I have a place to lay my head down and the roof doesn't leak, I'm fine. But the reason I care is because I need to eat, too."

"Then I'll make you a deal. I'll let you catch fishes for two years."

She shook her head. "What about Pan-

123

cho, who let me borrow this canoe? Tina, who welded the hole on the bottom so it wouldn't sink? Gregorio, who made him the nets? It's more than just one person."

"They are not your blood," the river monster reminded her.

"No, but they are part of this river and the river is my blood." She smiled wryly. "You said it yourself. I *am* the Bastard Daughter of the Waves. Maybe that makes you and me cousins. Family in some way."

The river monster snapped its mandible in the air, but Orquídea only laughed, unladylike and coarse and wonderful.

"What about this," she said. "Whatever I catch, I will let half of what's in my net return to you."

"Can you make that promise for everyone?"

"No, I can only make it for myself. If you want to make a deal with all the other fishermen, you're going to have to show yourself."

The river monster made a reptilian hiss at the back of its throat, then stared at Orquídea a little longer as their canoe was gently pushed by the current of the Guayas. It was so very tired of this world, of these people. All it had ever wanted was respect. And here Orquídea was, acknowledging it.

"You have a deal," the river monster said. It crept back over the side of the canoe; a ridged-back tail was the last thing to sink beneath the surface.

Orquídea paddled back to the shore and left Pancho's vessel tied up in the pier with the others. The next day, she told him of her bargain, and that they should all do the same. No one believed her, of course, but Orquídea kept her word. From then on, whatever she caught, she threw half back into the waters. When locals saw that this girl, the runt they called "Niña Mala Suerte" with her cosmic bad luck, was able to make a catch, they tried making their own bargains with the river. Some cleaned up the bottles and cans from the shore. Others offered stories and conversations. By the end of that season, the heat broke, the fish returned, and so did the rain.

The river monster was never seen by anyone other than Orquídea, though there were rumors that it had been sighted by a gringo American tourist couple who documented exotic wildlife on their vegan travel blog. All they had to show was a blurry photo.

The ancient creature felt the day of Orquídea's death, a connection carried from root to dirt to sea. And for the first time in centuries, the river monster wept. They were, after all, family in some way.

8
THE UNEARTHING OF LUCK

Orquídea gripped the arms of her chair and watched her children and grandchildren spill into the living room.

"You're all late," she said, voice rough as gravel.

"*We* were on time," Enrique said, pushing his way to the front of the crowd. The shadow of a partial handprint was still visible on his cheek. He yanked off his ruined silk tie and tossed it on the ground. "We've been just outside for hours."

"Ricky." Félix gently squeezed his brother's shoulder. "We're here now."

"Abuelita, you're, like, a tree," Juan Luis said.

His twin elbowed him, sucking his teeth. Gastón stage whispered, "Bro, you can't just say that grandma is a tree."

"But she is!"

One by one, they went to Orquídea. Hugging. Kissing her cheek, her forehead.

Squeezing her rough, wrinkled hands covered in tiny branches. All, except Enrique, who glowered at the roaring flames in the fireplace. When he turned around, the green of his eyes moved, like embers had leapt into his irises and caught fire.

"Mamá Orquídea!" Penelope shouted. She was thirteen, but still so young. Younger than Orquídea had ever been allowed to be at that age. Her thick curls were gathered into pigtails which made her look younger. But still, Penny ran to her grandmother, kneeling at her side and setting her face on her lap. Orquídea shut her eyes and took a deep breath as she gently stroked her granddaughter's shoulders. "Mom said we were coming to your funeral. But you're still here. Are you really dying?"

"Not for a few more hours."

Penelope looked up with wide brown eyes and naïve worry. "Are you stuck?"

"When I was born," Orquídea began, "it was May 14. I only came out halfway. The doctor and nurse thought I was dead. It wasn't until minutes after midnight that they were able to pull me the rest of the way out. My mother used to tell me that because of this, I would always live a life in between. My death is no different. So, yes, Penny. I suppose I am stuck. Not really

128

here, nor there."

Aunt Silvia poured herself some wine and nodded thoughtfully. She liked to translate her mother's stories into something like reason. "That was likely shoulder dystocia, and also likely because of the shape of your mother's uterus."

"May 14," Marimar said. "That's today."

"I thought you hated birthdays," Ernesta said, pinching the crooked bridge of her nose. "You never celebrated them. I never even knew what day it was. Did you?"

Her siblings shook their heads, as if none of them had ever truly realized that they didn't know when their mother was born. Marimar, like Rey, had snooped but never found a birth certificate or proof. Proof of what? That her grandmother was a real person and not some traveler from some faraway magical kingdom?

"I spared you my birthdays. Which is why I'm asking you all to celebrate my death."

"That's a bit morbid," Rey said. "And I happen to love morbid."

Orquídea peered into the embers in the fireplace. For a moment, her eyes were milky white, but then she blinked, and the dark of her irises returned. "I know you have questions. I don't have answers. I did the best I could. I knew the price y lo hice de todos modos. Ya no tengo tiempo."

The Montoyas traded worried glances. Orquídea never slipped between languages. It took Marimar and some of the others a moment to mentally translate their mother's mother tongue. She knew the price and did it anyway. She's out of time.

Marimar took a tentative step forward. In her mind, Orquídea was as imposing as a mountain and as mysterious as the sea. She imposed hard rules. She filled their minds with whimsy. She would laugh one moment and then lock herself in her room the next. It was as if there was something jagged within her, a bruise that she had passed down to all of her kids, and maybe even grandkids. But this woman transforming in front of them was showing something Marimar wasn't used to seeing — fear.

"It's okay, Ma," Caleb Jr. said, his voice was soft, but his forehead lined with worry.

Enrique grimaced. "*None* of this is okay."

There was a rustling sound, like loose pages carried off by a breeze. Ears popped. Floorboards and hinges creaked. A group of strangers appeared at the living room entrance. Five of them in total. They shared a family trait of beige skin, black hair, and haughty sneers. They all looked like they'd escaped out of an old photograph from the sixties. Three women all in dresses. Two tall men in white button-downs tucked into belted brown slacks. Even though they clutched invitations in their hands, they looked like intruders. Sparrows among hummingbirds.

Ever the diplomat, Félix waved them in. "Welcome! Give us a moment."

"Who the hell are they?" Rey muttered to Marimar.

"Secret family?" she suggested. Marimar had a vague sense of déjà vu, like she'd met them before.

One of the women sniffed at the air. Her hazel eyes settled on Orquídea with a quiet resentment. She took in the dust blanketing nearly every surface. The dirt soiling her sensible black dress shoes. She touched the golden stamp of the Virgin Mary resting against her chest.

After an uncomfortable stretch, the oldest man of the bunch approached Orquídea, who somehow managed to look like a queen rooted in her throne.

"Wilhelm," Orquídea said in greeting.

"Sister," he said. There was a delay of sound when he spoke.

"Sister?" Florecida repeated.

Marimar felt a tiny surge of vindication and grinned. "Called it."

"These are the Buenasuertes," Orquídea explained. "My brothers and sisters."

"I thought you were an only child?" Caleb Jr. asked.

Orquídea gave a solemn shake of her head. The vines sprouting from the ground coiled around her chair, sprouting green buds. Her eyes went white then black again.

"She ran away from us after mother married our father," Wilhelm said.

Even though he was standing right there, he looked like he had stepped out of a photograph, one of those old ones filtered by a shade of ochre or burnt sienna. Marimar had noticed it before, but now it was more pronounced. Like the longer they stood there, the more faded they became.

"I ran away because I would have rather taken my chances on the street than spent one more minute under the Buenasuerte roof," Orquídea said. "You saw to that."

Wilhelm sucked his teeth and smacked the air. "We were children. You were too sensitive. You've always been too soft."

The Montoyas present let loose a collective scoff.

"Believe what you want, *brother*. I am disappointed your father or Ana Cruz is not among you. I wanted to see you all one more time. I wanted you to know that I did not die or vanish like my mother believed."

"*Our* mother was sick over you," the woman with the tightly set lips said bitterly. "She died thinking you hated her."

"I suppose I did, at the time. I don't anymore."

"She told me what you did," the woman with the hazel eyes said, then gestured to the high ceiling. "How you got all of this."

Orquídea's laughter was a deep rumble. "I couldn't water a houseplant with the things you know, Greta."

Greta balled her fists at her hips. Rey and Caleb Jr. slowly made their way to either side of Orquídea's chair like sentries.

"Peace, Greta," said a third Buenasuerte, lanky, with hair so black it looked like an ink smudge. He placed a gentle hand on his sister's arm, the way Tío Félix had done to Enrique, and it was good to know that all families were the same in certain ways. There were those who felt too much, those who felt too little, and others who knew how to deal with those feelings. "If our sister is ready to put the past behind her and apologize for what she put our mother through, we are here to listen."

"You misunderstand, Sebastián," Orquídea said. "I did not invite you here to apologize. Isabela Buenasuerte was who she

133

was, and I know, in my bones, that I was nothing more to her than a burden. I will carry that knowledge with me to my last moments. You mistook her sickness over me for guilt."

"Then why call us here?" Wilhelm asked.

The ochre pallor of the Buenasuertes became shades of gray, a true black-and-white photograph. Even the air around them warped and faded at their edges, like they were on another plane of existence.

"To tell you the truth, I was hoping your father would be here."

"His health is poor," Greta said. "Ana Cruz remained behind to care for him."

"Pity. I would have liked to see Ana Cruz again," Orquídea said. "Reymundo, be a dear and bring me the cigarette box on the mantel."

Rey did as he was asked. The cigarette box was made of silver, emblazoned with a starburst and the initials BL. Marimar had tried to open it once, but the little lever at the side wouldn't budge.

Of course, when Orquídea tried, the lid popped up to reveal an ancient, waxy green bill.

"Cinco sucres," her voice regained its clarity. "That's how I met your father and that's how my mother's life changed, and that's how all of *you* came to be. That's how my life changed, too, I suppose, but I always knew that I was on a different path than my mother's. Even before I was born, we diverged. I've kept this note for decades, sealed, not even spending it when I had nothing else to my name because it carried a promise."

"What promise?" Wilhelm asked.

"That I would never be indebted to anyone ever again, especially men like your father. This was a loan, and I want to pay it back."

Orquídea held out the bill. The five Buenasuerte siblings remained still, offended, bewildered. Wilhelm looked like he was about to start foaming at the mouth, but he stomped across the living room, his feet barely making a sound as he snatched the sucre from Orquídea Divina's hand.

"You might not be indebted to anyone," he said, "but by the looks of all this, your descendants will pay the price. Whatever you did, I hope it was worth it."

The Buenasuertes left soundlessly, and they did not look back.

The Montoyas stared at Orquídea who grinned deeply with her eyes closed.

"Was that necessary?" Reina asked.

Orquídea met her daughter-in-law's eyes

and said, "What is it like to live without rage in your heart?"

Reina knew better than to answer.

"I, for one, am loving this family reunion," Rey exclaimed, going to the bar cart to select a bottle of amber liquid. He poured himself a large helping, then remembered the others in the room. Raising the glass, he said, "Salud, motherfuckers."

"All right, everyone," Félix said loudly, twisting his hands in that nervous way of his. "At this rate we'll never get dinner finished in time. Reina, Silvia, Caleb, you're with me in the kitchen. Penny, Marimar, Rey, you're on cleaning duty. Juan Luis and Gastoncito, help Ricky bring the dining table in here."

Enrique snatched Rey's drink from his hands mid-sip and took a seat in the chair opposite his mother. "I'm busy."

"I'll do it," Frederico, Silvia's husband, offered.

"See? So helpful." Enrique grimaced at the burn of his stolen drink.

"What about me?" Tatinelly said, rubbing her belly. "We can help."

"Tati, you rest for now," Félix said.

Enrique laughed. Gestured to the shoots of branches sprouting between his mother's knuckles. "Of course, you're all fine with this. None of you question anything she does."

"On the contrary," Silvia said. Her hair was pulled into a bun so tight it looked painful. "I question it all the time. I'm just okay with not having answers. I accept our mother the way she is. You're just a needy fuck."

There was a moment of uncertainty. Hurt and anger momentarily crossed Enrique's features before he hardened his resolve.

Félix's eyes softened, like he was waiting for his little brother to come to his senses, to soften and yield like they always had. Juan Luis and Gastón didn't know anything about the world, but they knew their uncle Enrique was a jerk and needed to be taught a lesson. Tatinelly squeezed her husband's hand. Rey poured a new drink. Marimar waited. Ernesta looked up at the portrait over the mantel, the one of her mother as a young girl. She had a look on her face, like someone who was daring the universe to fuck with her. Little did they know, it had.

Félix let out a resigned sigh and then spurred into action. He clapped his hands together, jolting everyone out of their momentary indecision. "Let's go, let's go, let's go. Kitchen, cleaning, dining table. Now!"

The Montoyas spread out, racing out of the living room, arming themselves with brooms and kitchen knives, like witches going to war.

Tatinelly loved this house. Unlike most of her cousins, she had been born at the Four Rivers hospital. Her mother had refused the tradition. Her exact words were, "I'm not giving birth on a ranch like a prized hog. It's 1990, for Christ's sake!" The nurses had all gathered around the little girl, the first Montoya to be delivered at their hospital. Tatinelly had come right out, like she'd been counting down the seconds, like she had *wanted* to get the show of living started. She didn't cry. She didn't fuss. The most extraordinary thing about her was how normal she was. Tati's mom had told her, years later, that the nurses had placed bets to see if she'd come out with webbed feet, claws, or a third eye. But Tatinelly was ordinary in so many ways, and she was perfectly content with that. Still, she didn't like feeling left out, so she always said she'd been born in the same room as the other Montoyas.

Her family was different, off to others, but they were hers. As she and Mike made their way upstairs and into the guestroom, Tatinelly rubbed her belly and hummed a song that had been stuck in her head since they left Oregon. She imagined that the creaking floor and wheezing hinges were singing back. The house had seen better days, but this particular bedroom was spotless. It was almost like Orquídea had known . . . The wallpaper pattern was of rose petals, so faded it had taken on a dusty mauve shade from too much sun exposure. When Juan Luis and Gastón were born, she remembered peeking through the skeleton keyhole. There was so much screaming, so many women running around. None of that had startled her, but the one thing that had was the moment the twins were pulled out from between their mother's legs, and the rose petals on the wall moved.

She told Mike as much. He set their overnight bags on the four-poster bed and made a strangling sound he'd never made before.

"Are you sure?" he asked. "You were very little."

Tatinelly went to the window and basked in the warm light. From this room, she could see the plot of graves out back. Orquídea's husbands and her aunt Pena. The grass around their family cemetery was the only part of the property that wasn't affected by the drought.

"It doesn't matter if I'm sure," she said softly. "It's what I saw."

He jumped on the bed and folded his hands behind his head. He hadn't gone on his bike ride that morning and his pent-up energy had him wiggling his toes. "I have to tell you, honeybee. I — I'm not sure this is where we should be."

Tatinelly felt a strong kick from her daughter. Restless, eager. "Why?"

"It's just not you." Mike sat up. The mattress so thick it didn't even groan as he stood. He paced in circles for a time, like a bee performing a ritual dance.

She remained standing, picking up and setting down little glass bottles on top of a dresser. She'd loved all of these things. The whole house made it feel like it was there for her to play with. Even with cracks and layers of dirt, she still wouldn't want to be anywhere else. It hurt that Mike didn't think this place was like her.

"I love my family," she said. "They're part of who I am. So, in that sense, this place *is* me."

Mike stopped pacing at the side of the bed, nearly doubled over. He breathed hard. His skin was so flushed he almost looked translucent. He'd had anxiety attacks throughout the years over taxes and work. Over retirement funds and market crashes. Once over a Super Bowl loss. But this, this was different. Tatinelly had always been so certain that Mike loved every part of her. They were supposed to be the constant things in each other's lives. If he didn't like this part of her, could he truly keep loving her at all? Could he love their daughter?

She waddled over to him. She rubbed soothing circles on his back the way he liked. His muscles were so tight beneath. He turned and looked at her in that way of his, like he'd never seen anyone or anything so beautiful. Even if she wasn't, he made her feel that way.

"I'm sorry. Your grandmother — your family — this is a lot." He sat at the edge of the mattress.

She didn't want to mention that he was sitting on the same spot her aunts and grandmother had rested on in preparation for delivery. That they'd gripped the posters of the bed when contractions came. That their blood and embryonic fluid was the reason there was a permanent stain in the wood at their feet.

Then it occurred to her. Could they stay long enough for her to deliver her baby girl here? She was sure now that it would be a girl. It happened the moment they stepped out of the car at the top of the hill and she practically glided down the steep road. A breeze beheaded stubborn dandelions and took on a shape. The shape of a girl. Then the wind blew again, and the shape was gone.

"How are you not freaking out?" he asked. His hands were cupped in front of her, begging for an answer. "None of you are freaking out."

How was she supposed to explain her family? She shouldn't have to. "It's just — how things are."

"Your grandmother's feet are tree roots! You might as well have said 'open sesame' to get the door open. That entire family turned black and white. Not to mention your uncle Enrique is a dick."

"Well, yes, that's never happened before. The roots part. Uncle Enrique has always been . . . I want to say, difficult. So that's not so new."

"But other things have?"

She thought about the moments she never questioned while spending summers in this house. Once, a girl stuck a wad of gum in Tatinelly's hair at the Four Rivers community pool. Panicked, she cut it as close to the root as she could, but she had a bald patch right on the top of her head. Orquídea calmed her down. She expected Orquídea to tell her it was her own fault for trying to chase after people who didn't want to be friends with her. Instead, Orquídea went into the kitchen and Tatinelly followed. She pulled out glass bottles of oils and syrups with cork stoppers and poured the nasty smelling liquids into a bowl. Then she cut herbs from her garden. Smooshed cherries and an apple from the orchards. Covered all of Tatinelly's scalp with it. In the morning, the bald patch was gone, and her hair had been restored. Back then she didn't call it by what it was — magic. It was just how Orquídea was with her home remedies. Everyone had home remedies, didn't they? Everyone had brought secrets from the old worlds with them.

Not everyone had, alas. When she met Michael Sullivan's family, she realized they didn't have remedies or languages they spoke only in private. Everything the Sullivans ate came from a can or a frozen bag. They didn't use salt on anything, except a pinch in their food. They didn't suck the marrow from their chicken bones for health. They didn't have stories of ghosts or duendes or cucos hiding underneath the bed. Their grandmothers lived far away in old people homes and, though he had cousins, Mike could go his whole life without ever seeing another Sullivan and be all right with it. Tatinelly was starting to make herself fit into Mike's family because he had been so good to her and he loved her so much. But being back at the ranch made her feel like she had been missing something. If not for her, then for her child. She wanted her daughter to know there was magic in the world.

"I'll go get you some water," Tatinelly told Mike. She brushed his thinning hair back and kissed the sweat on his forehead. She didn't think he could handle much more of this.

"Maybe something stronger." He kissed the back of her hand, worshipped her boney knuckles with his lips. "Please."

Tatinelly smiled. Her smile had made Mike dizzy when they first met; and even now, when he was confused and a little scared. She had Orquídea's smile. So would their daughter.

"I'll be right back," she said. When she touched the wall, a rose petal fluttered under her fingertip.

Downstairs in the library parlor, Marimar opened every window and every shutter.

She swept dirt and dust out the door. Rey and Penny followed with mops and buckets full of Orquídea's homemade cleaning liquids.

"That's all of it," Rey said, turning the bottle on its head until only droplets fell out.

"There's no salt," Penny said, holding up a burlap bag.

"What do you mean there's no salt?" Marimar asked. She gently picked up the bag, needing to feel its featherweight in order to believe it. She hurried into the hall and yanked open the pantry. The jars were empty, too. The metal bin, usually full of coffee beans only had a handful of kernels.

"This is all that's left after they took what was needed for cooking," Penny said, gnawing on the inside of her lips. "This is bad, right? I mean, I know we're avoiding Mamá Orquídea turning into a tree but, like, I feel we should all admit that this is bad."

Rey pulled their cousin into a hug and brushed wisps of hair away from her face. "We'll do without. Why don't you see if your mom needs help?"

Penny ran off, leaving Rey and Marimar alone in the hall.

"What do we do?" Rey hissed. He was out of cigarettes and had moved on to the rum.

Oddly enough, the liquor in the house was still well stocked.

Marimar pushed down her anxiety. The house was too big to fix in time for dinner. She reminded herself that Orquídea didn't have long and didn't need a clean house anymore. Admitting that to herself, even in her own thoughts, filled her with a deep melancholy she'd been trying to avoid. What would her mother have done if she was alive and among them? She'd put on one of Orquídea's records and pretend like it was all a game. The first one to find something silver, something red, and something made of glass would win. Marimar would polish the silver, oil a red leather footstool, shine Orquídea's menagerie of tiny crystal animals. For a moment, Marimar heard the echo of her own childlike laughter, the blur of her and Rey running down the same corridor and playing in the same parlor. She ached for a time that was long gone and for things she could never get back. She scratched at the hollow of her throat wishing she could carve out the emotion.

Then, a skinny rooster clucked through the front door leaving a trail of blue feathers.

"Gabo!" Marimar shouted, unable to believe the creature was still alive.

The twins trailed in after. "Come back here!"

"You're supposed to be making up the dining room." Marimar felt a hundred years old as the words left her mouth.

"I'm *trying* to save him," Gastón explained. Or maybe Juan Luis. She never could tell them apart.

"Yeah, Ma wants to cook him. Says it's a mercy kill since otherwise he'll be left all alone when Orquídea is gone."

The bird cocked his head to the side like it knew they were talking about him. He was little more than skin and feathers, and Marimar wondered if, like the protections and wards around the house, Gabo the rooster was just another thing that had protected Orquídea and her valley.

"I need a refill," Rey said as he leaned the mop against the wall and left the hall, laughing.

"Okay, take Gabo and leave him in the shed," Marimar suggested.

"That's where dad's killing the pig!" Twin One said.

"Right," she said. "Put him in the guest room upstairs. No one would bother Mike."

"Probably because he looks like a blobfish," Twin Two said.

"No, blobfish are round and pink. He's

like if a blobfish and a giraffe had a baby," Twin One said.

Marimar spotted her very pregnant cousin waddling down the stairs. If she heard the twins talking about her husband, she didn't comment.

Juan Luis and Gastón made the sound of a scratched record. They snatched up the ancient rooster and Juan Luis (probably) cradled it like a baby.

"Tati, hey," Marimar said.

"I was just coming down to get Mike something to drink. He —"

She stopped in front of Marimar and faltered, unable to find the right words. He can't handle this? He can't handle us?

"Yeah," Marimar finished for her.

At that moment, Rey stepped back into the hall with a crystal highball glass in hand, complete with a sprig of rosemary and ice. Marimar snatched the drink and ignored the incredulity dawning on his face.

"Mike can have this one," Marimar said. She handed it to the twin who wasn't holding the rooster and winked at them both. "Take this up to Tati's husband. And keep Gabo safe."

They shared the Montoya grin that held a thousand secrets.

"I guess I'd better go and make a *new*

drink," Rey said. He extended his arm to Tati. "Orquídea wants to see you."

Marimar took a step back when she saw the outline of a foot pushing right through her cousin's shirt.

Tati rubbed her belly. "Oh! I thought she was talking to Enrique."

"He's off somewhere being an anthropomorphized bag of dicks," Rey said.

With Rey and Tatinelly off to see their grandmother, the twins trying to protect the family pet, and the others cooking up a storm, Marimar needed to do her part. She needed to get to work.

For a long time after moving to New York, all Marimar wanted was to push away memories of the house and Orquídea Divina. The brutal love of the city served as a barrier to the constant reminder of her mother's tragic drowning, or the valley and the orchards with their glistening ever-ripe fruit. But the memories inevitably found her, because putting Four Rivers out of her mind and heart was like trying to live day to day with a blindfold and her hands tied behind her back. Marimar thought she was done with Four Rivers, but Four Rivers wasn't done with her.

Now that she was here, she couldn't avoid it. Marimar remembered splitting her nail down the center trying to claw out the laurel leaves on the door. "This is your fault!" she'd screamed, blood spilling on the floorboards. "You didn't protect her. You killed her." Marimar remembered the way Orquídea's palm had stung against her cheek, and the stillness, the silence of the house as Orquídea sat in her goddamned chair and drank her goddamned whiskey and settled into that deafening silence that could last for days. They never even said goodbye.

Pena Montoya had drowned. Marimar accepted that now, but she hadn't wanted to believe it then. She'd needed someone to blame, and that was Orquídea. She'd loved her grandmother. Wanted to possess her magic, too. She'd wasted seven years simmering in her anger and all it took was a few hours breathing in the dusty air, seeing her grandmother in this state, and she was homesick enough to forgive.

She wondered, did everyone have such a fraught relationship with the places they came from? Did anyone else have a grandmother who might as well have been a legend, a myth, a series of miracles that took the shape of an old woman?

Orquídea wasn't an old woman anymore. She was transforming, and Marimar couldn't help wondering if that meant she would transform, too, one day.

She picked up a broomstick and swept away the layers of dust and decay that gathered in every corner of the downstairs rooms. Green and brown-striped snakes nestled in ceramic bowls and on the carpet, faded from exposure to the sun. She remembered Rey saying that he'd been bitten by one.

"Shoo!" she hollered.

Their eyes snapped open at her like *Marimar* was the bother and hissed as they slithered outside through the holes in the walls created by Orquídea's vines.

Silvery spiderwebs glistened, entire arachnid cities stretching along the banister, up the stairs, and across the ceiling. Marimar ran the broom along those surfaces, and the spiders crawled out in quick succession. She shivered when she thought she heard them speak. But then she realized she was hearing loud chatter and laughter that came from the kitchen.

Rey returned then, with two glasses in hand. "I brought two just in case you decided to give my things away again."

Marimar traded her broom for his cocktail. When she sipped the rum, the air carried with it the smell of burned sugar. It was strong and sweet on her tongue. "What did Orquídea want with Tatinelly?"

"I'd *never* eavesdrop."

She hummed her incredulity and took another sip. "Sure."

"I truly stopped paying attention after I realized they were going through baby names."

"I hope she doesn't name the kid Orquídea."

"If grandma is handing out fortunes, *I'd* change my name to Orquídea."

Marimar rolled her eyes and carried her drink and broom back down the hall. Rey followed her into the parlor where Orquídea would listen to old records. Martin would sing along to Billie Holiday or the Buena Vista Social Club, and Marimar would play with her dolls while Rey complained that the music was old, and tried to pick the lock to the closet no one could get open.

Marimar bent down in front of the wooden chest that contained all the records. The paper was worn, but the shiny vinyl was still intact. She blew on the surface and set the needle. The record player warbled and scratched, like it was remembering that it still worked after all these years. The sounds of El Gran Combo de Puerto Rico filled the room, down the halls. Orquídea never danced — not in front of Marimar, at least — but she used to wag her foot to the beat, the congas, the brass.

Now, they cleaned and sang along, putting all the weirdness of the day into the cathartic rhythm of a song whose words they only understood tangentially. It felt like a ritual, preparing the body of the house for burial. When the record reached the crackling end, they sat on the floor and finished lukewarm drinks.

"How long do you think it's been like this?" Rey whispered.

"A long time," she said with certainty.

"Don't you start feeling guilty." Rey rested his head against the wall, slurring his words a bit. "*We* didn't do this. *We* didn't make her do this. She came this way. In fact, *she's* the reason we're like this."

"Like what?" she asked, but she knew.

"Broken, Marimar. Missing pieces."

"Maybe you should ease up on the rum."

"Maybe you should learn to sweep. You missed a spot."

She shoved him and he fell over laughing. A sound reverberated in the room. They looked at the record player, but the needle was raised. They looked out into the hall, but there was no one there. They were used to the strange noises of the house, the metal joints that needed to be greased, the crickets and birds that liked to gather too close. But this sound was a heavy thump. A fist against a door. It seemed to come from the locked closet in the music parlor.

They listened, just to be sure.

The sound in the room was hollow, like negative space. Like the end of the vinyl record searching for more music to play.

And the fist thumped again.

"One time she caught me trying to pick the lock," Rey said. "Orquídea told me that was where her monster lived and if I kept bothering it, the thing would use its nails to poke my brain through the keyhole."

"Charming." Marimar took a deep breath, got up, and went to the closet door. It was locked, just as it had always been.

"I know there's a key. I just never found it." Rey started opening drawers, rummaging through tiny ceramic bowls containing everything from bits of yarn to a coyote skull and dried husks of purple corn. Marimar couldn't recall a time her grandmother had ever knitted anything, so yarn, out of everything in the entire house, was the strangest thing they'd found so far.

"Actually," Rey said, pointing at a blue vase in the dusty cabinet. "This thing is supposed to contain a duende who liked to steal our dreams at night."

As a little girl, Marimar believed that the house had duendes living in the closets, making all of the sweets disappear. In her mind, the mischievous spirits had been the sworn enemies of the good fairies that lived in the tall grass of the valley.

Marimar grabbed the blue vase and stuck her hand in. She wiggled her fingers and felt nothing. Then, something metal and cold rattled against the ceramic. She fished out a skeleton key and brandished it to her cousin.

"Look at that," she marveled.

"I'm personally hoping whatever is behind that door is a beautiful man with a never-ending supply of booze."

Marimar considered it. "You have to be specific. Is he holding the booze or is it coming from him?"

Rey was stumped. "I actually don't know what I'd prefer."

Marimar laughed nervously, turning the key between her fingers. What did Marimar hope was behind that door? A tunnel to another world? They were too old for stories like that now, but belief in the impossible never truly went away. Did it? She remembered wishing on Orquídea's altar. Shutting her eyes so tightly she saw pinpricks of light behind her lids. She'd wished for good grades. She'd wished to meet the father that had abandoned them. She'd wished to be as magical and impossible as her grandmother.

She unlocked the door and, like so many parts of the house, it wheezed as it opened. She pulled on the chain hanging from the ceiling, while Rey peered over her shoulder and gasped.

Marimar felt heat behind her eyelids, the sting of tears that she wished she could keep back.

There were boxes and boxes, each one labeled with handwritten names — Pena. Parcha. Félix. Florecida. Silvia. Enrique. Ernesta. Caleb Jr.

Orquídea had always said that she gave her mother's things away. Marimar had seen the local church ladies drive over to collect boxes of donations. Orquídea wasn't sentimental about things like booties and baby clothes. But as Marimar rummaged through the eighties prom dresses and little league jerseys and cleats too small to fit even Juan Luis and Gastón, she considered that perhaps her grandmother was an ocean of sentiment. She just didn't want anyone to see it.

"Well, she never fails to surprise." Rey

yanked a photo album from his mom's box and sat in Orquídea's favorite chair. "Yes! Embarrassing photos."

When he flipped to the first page, there was only a tan residue where photos had been stuck once and the crinkle of a sheer plastic protector. He flipped and flipped. There was nothing for a few pages until he landed on a grainy photograph.

"Is that —" Marimar sat on the arm of the chair and stared at the picture. Pena and Parcha Montoya were so young, possibly nineteen or eighteen. Cheesy smiles, cropped halter tops, high-waisted jeans, and big hoop earrings.

"Your mom never changed," Marimar said to Rey.

He traced his finger across the bright spot beside them. A light that cast them in an incandescent glow. There were more pictures on the following pages, each one with an overexposed flash taking up space. They were at a local carnival, the one the church and high school always put on to raise money over the summer.

"Is that a double date?" Rey laughed. "This is definitely my dad. Holy fuck, why haven't I ever seen this one before?"

"Wait." Marimar plucked the picture off the sticky sheet and peered closer. Beneath the flash was a fourth person. Obstructed. But he was there, an arm wrapped around her mother's shoulder. The blurry outline of a hand, a silver ring with an eight-pointed star engraved at the center.

"Is that — ?" Rey started to ask.

The pressure behind Marimar's belly button returned, then extended across her skin, wound around her muscles. She was being pulled apart. After nineteen years, this photo, developed at the Four Rivers drug store and stored in a box, was all she had of the man she'd never met.

"I think that's my father."

9
THE GIRL AND THE
MOONLIT PATH

After Isabela's wedding to Wilhelm Buenasuerte, Orquídea's life changed, just as her
mother had promised. The entire city was
changing, too. Every time Orquídea walked
to school there was new construction. New
bridges and ramps. Ships in the Guayaquil
harbor loading thousands and thousands of
bananas for export.

Wilhelm Buenasuerte led the charge to
developing La Atarazana, starting with the
single-road town where he'd first met
Orquídea and fallen in love at first sight
with Isabela. A contract with the city had
allowed him to modernize and pave the
streets. Isabela had turned over the modest
plot of land she'd bought when she had no
one but her daughter, and Wilhelm used
that land to build a great big house with a
courtyard, and two levels that overlooked
the river. He pushed out smaller, poorer
families, but there were some who stayed

put. Who'd empty out their bedpans full of shit and urine every time the "German Engineer" swung by. But Wilhelm would not give up his new claim on the neighborhood and he was a patient man.

Despite all the changes, La Atarazana still felt like it belonged to Orquídea. She'd carved her name on a small boulder on the river shore and it was her name that the locals acknowledged when she went on strolls with her pregnant mother and stepfather, a fact that gave Wilhelm Buenasuerte a permanent scowl between his brows.

Orquídea had been forbidden from fishing or swimming in the river, especially by herself. But the fishermen knew her. They protected her more than the Buenasuertes did. And besides, she was still the only one in her little pier who could catch the most fish. Sometimes she snuck the fish home and handed them to Jefita, the housekeeper. But mostly, she took her pail down the row of shanty houses and offered her catch to la viuda Villareal, to Jacinto, who'd lost his leg at the border war with Peru, to Gabriela, whose husband left her too bruised and beaten to leave the house. They didn't care that she smelled like fish and mud. They blessed her, but not even those blessings could counteract Orquídea's cosmic bad luck, or the treatment she endured in the Buenasuerte house.

Once a week, without fail, Wilhelm and Isabela Buenasuerte hosted the elite of the city. Lawyers and doctors. Actors and soccer players. Ambassadors and artists. They opened their home to host brilliant minds. There was Alberto Wong, a philosopher who'd spend an entire month with the Buenasuertes theorizing on the happiness quotient in coastal populations versus those of the colder regions. There was a socialist poet from Bolivia who spent every dinner shouting with Wilhelm, and then laughing between puffs of cigars late into the night. It was the summer of Orquídea's fifteenth birthday when he'd shared his cigars with her and written several poems about her skin, her hair, her lips. Her mother had locked her in every night, and even though Orquídea had no interest in men yet, she did as her mother said and occupied her time caring for her four siblings.

The Buenasuerte-Montoyas were a large brood. Isabela got pregnant on her wedding night and didn't stop being pregnant until her sixth child, Ana Cruz, was born prematurely, and her uterus slithered out of her body with the baby.

By the sixth child, Isabela had settled well

into the role of a celebrated engineer's wife. She was still a beauty, turned plump and delicate like the macarons Wilhelm surprised her with on his returns from Paris. She never corrected her guests when they assumed Orquídea was another housemaid. She never let Orquídea sit at large banquets or put her in too-pretty dresses so that men wouldn't leer at her. Perhaps in some way, Isabela believed she was protecting her first daughter from the cruelty of the world she'd become a part of. But the first cruelties Orquídea learned were the ones Isabela doled out herself.

When Orquídea was fourteen, she wouldn't stop going to the river, so her mother marched to the shore, ripped the net out of her hands, and heaved it into the water, where it sank and snagged on a tangle of reeds. Orquídea still went to the river's edge and stood by the pier, but she didn't fish. She talked to no one. She simply watched the canoes, the ships in the distance, and the clouds swallowing the skyline of Guayaquil and Durán across the way.

The summer when her mother had Ana Cruz, and lost her uterus, Wilhelm's family came to stay, and Orquídea lost any chance she had to visit the river. Instead, her days were occupied with tending to the colicky

Ana Cruz. She'd had to give up her room to the guests and sleep on a cot in the nursery. When she wasn't caring for the baby, she was helping Jefita do everything from peel potatoes to slaughter two dozen turkeys. She cleaned every part of the house, but as soon as she was finished mopping, the Buenasuerte cousins — Mila and Marie — would stomp around with muddy shoes. They threw bloody underwear to be laundered when they caught her in the courtyard. They taught little Wilhelm Jr. and Maricela that Orquídea's skin was made out of polished wood, like a marionette, and couldn't bleed, and so they tested that theory by pinching her so hard they drew blood with their jagged, bitten nails. Mila and Marie stayed for two years.

Some people were born evil, some people were taught. Her siblings were both. Orquídea had been born cursed and adrift, but at least she hadn't been born evil. She still had that. Her siblings — though they were only between the ages of six and one — were her own personal demons. They ran wild, red-faced from the heat, trailing after German-speaking cousins and repeating every insult they could toward their half-sister.

Once, when Wilhelm Jr. refused to get dressed for school, he shoved Orquídea

163

down the stairs. The doctor who came to the house told her she had a concussion and a sprained ankle and needed to stay off it. Isabela told her to be less clumsy. They had a feast in a month's time to prepare for. During the two weeks she spent off her feet, Wilhelm was tasked with taking food up to his sister.

"She's not my sister." He'd repeat the words he'd heard his father use: "She's a bastard."

But the little boy went anyway. He'd leave her food outside the nursery door, and in his pure childish boredom decided to make things more interesting. He found the raw carcass of a fish in the garbage and added it to her soup as a garnish.

After that, Orquídea got her own meals, limping her way to the kitchen three times a day. She didn't mind because that way she could sit in the courtyard gardens. There, in Orquídea's arms, while swinging back and forth in the hammock with a radio crackling the latest boleros, it was the only time Ana Cruz didn't cry.

On October 9, Guayaquil's Independence Day, the streets were flooded with parades of cars and revelers. Fireworks burst from alleyways and street corners. The pale blue and white of Guayaquil's flag waved proudly from the front of the Buenavista home. Anyone who was anyone in the city attended the feast.

Up in the nursery, after cooking, cleaning, and bathing Ana Cruz, Orquídea put the finishing touches to a dress she'd spent weeks crafting. She'd used her mother's old sewing machine and dress pattern. Orquídea had used most of her savings to purchase the fabric from a seamstress over in Las Peñas. The satin was a deep peacock blue that gleamed in the candlelight. She sewed crystal beads in the shape of stars around the waist to look like a sash. She swept her curls back into an elegant bun like a prima ballerina, buffed her nails, and lotioned her toned arms and calves. When she spun around in her room, Orquídea felt like the night sky. She could hear the music and imagined batting her lashes at a young officer, dancing with the mayor himself. If everyone, even Jefita's family, was allowed to have fun, then so would she.

One day. All she wanted was one day to feel happy.

Jefita knocked on the door and gasped at Orquídea. "You look like a movie star! Beautiful like Sara Montiel in *Ella, Lucifer y yo.*" Then she made the symbol of the holy cross over her body. A woman of superstition and faith, Jefita was from Ambato, in the Tungurahua province. She'd come down to the coast for work after she lost everything at thirteen in the earthquake of 1949 and found it in the Buenasuerte household. She loved bitter chocolate, feeding the iguanas in the park, boleros, and scandalous soap operas, even if she couldn't get through most seasons without hyperventilating.

"Are there a lot of people already?" Orquídea asked.

She snapped her fingers in the air and giggled. "The mayor's just arrived. His wife is wearing a *tiara*. If you ask me —"

"No one asked you, Jefita," Isabela interrupted. Dressed in an elegant blush pink gown, she looked like the whisper of a goddess, if a bit gaunt from her poor health.

Jefita bowed her head, her artfully coiled braids were threaded with gold and carnations. "I'm sorry, Mrs. Buenasuerte. We were just playing around. We promise to behave tonight."

Isabela looked past her head of house, and at her daughter. Orquídea was a vision in blue, her hourglass shape accentuated by the stars.

"What are you wearing?" Isabela asked.

"You don't like it?"

Isabela shut her eyes and pinched the

bridge of her nose. "You look like ripe fruit for men to snatch up. Is that what you want? Is it?"

"I —"

"Do you want to embarrass your father and me?"

"He's not my father."

Orquídea felt the hot sting of her mother's hand. It didn't stop until Orquídea was crying, setting off Ana Cruz's wailing. Jefita stood exactly where she'd been the whole time, staring at the floor.

"Ungrateful girl. Where would we be if Wilhelm hadn't been good to us? I've tried so hard, Orquídea, but you're a reminder of the mistake I made all those years ago."

Isabela was the first to gasp at her own words. Deep down, she didn't believe she'd meant it, but the words were spoken and could not be taken back.

"Perhaps it's best if you stay here and watch Ana Cruz until you calm down and put on something decent."

But Orquídea didn't change out of her dress. She didn't look cheap or easy. She looked and felt like a jewel, even if that might have been a diamond in the rough. She did not attend the party but watched from the top of the banister as the beautiful, wealthy families danced and laughed.

Men with thick mustaches and growing bellies orated toasts in the Buenasuerte name. Every man in the room formed a line to dance with Mila and Marie in their chiffon and tulle dresses that made Orquídea think of butterfly wings. Those were her dances, and her charming smiles. All she'd wanted was *one* day, but no matter how hard she worked, how well she behaved, how much she tried, it wasn't enough. She didn't belong there.

That night, while the guests were being serenaded by Julio Jaramillo, the Nightingale of America himself, she snuck out and went to visit the river. She lived so close and yet she'd been severed from it, the only place that had claimed her.

"Please," she begged. She wasn't sure if she was talking to the river monster, or some distant god, or the stars.

And then, beneath the lapping crush of the river, the cacophony of the Buenasuerte house, and the distant fireworks, she heard it — a murmur. The pulse of the sky. An earnest reply.

Find me.

"Who are you?" Orquídea asked, turning in place. There was no one near her. Further along the row of shanty houses, kids kicked a soccer ball in the dark. Others lingered

168

outside the Buenasuerte house waiting for the scraps the servants threw out.

Find me, the voice repeated.

Orquídea felt a pull. A sense of certainty. In that moment Orquídea realized that some people stay in certain places forever, even when they're miserable, and that is neither bad nor good. It's survival. She had learned that lesson too early because one day she'd grow comfortable in thinking the worst was behind her.

But in that moment, she walked toward the voice.

Find me.

It wasn't safe for girls to walk in the dark dressed in satin, her dress so blue it was like a soft bruise. Isn't that what her mother had called her? Ripe, bruised, spoiled fruit. But Orquídea felt protected. No, possessed. It was like the night had laid out a path for her to follow, and anyone who laid eyes on her could see that she was spoken for by fate.

Hours later, when the moon was swollen and tinted red, Orquídea came upon a lot where a carnival had been erected. A great white tent pierced the starless sky. Even though the sound of the voice was gone, she knew she was in the right place. Her feet hurt, but she crossed the parking lot, strewn in hay, and stopped in front of a woman draped in red velveteen and smoking a cigarette from a silver holder.

"Hello. Do you have work?" she asked.

The woman smiled with the burden of someone who knows too much. "My dear, you are just the thing we were looking for."

10
THE HUNGER OF THE LIVING

Marimar pressed the photograph against her chest. *Was* this sylph of light clutching Pena Montoya the father Marimar had never known? Her mouth could barely form the word. She usually went out of her way to avoid saying it out loud after over a decade of having to explain herself at school. Teachers were always either sympathetic or judgmental about her situation. One year, Marimar wasn't allowed to be exempt from the Father's Day card art project and resentfully glued some macaroni into the shape of a hand flipping the middle finger. She'd seen her tía Parcha do it all the time. When her mother had to be called into the school to pick her up for being rude and disrespectful, Marimar asked, for the hundredth time, where her father was.

Pena Montoya had a smile that stopped traffic, and it often did when she took long walks into town. But on that day, she didn't smile. She raked her long waves back and gnawed on her bottom lip. She looked up at the sky and Marimar swore that her mom was asking it for help.

Pena got on her knee to be eye level with her daughter. "He's gone, Marimar. He had to go."

She'd sounded so sad, and even at seven years old, Marimar knew not to press. For some time Marimar figured that "gone" meant that he was dead. But there were so many ways for a person to be gone that had nothing to do with their mortality. Was he dead the way Rey's father was dead? The way Orquídea's husbands were dead? Or just gone like how Vanessa Redwood's dad had left in the middle of the night and everyone in Four Rivers knew it?

Now, Marimar ran out into the hall in search of answers, clutching the photograph like a compass. Sweat pooled between her breasts and ran down her spine. Her heart thundered as she stormed into the living room. They'd moved the table in here, set for sixteen. Silver cutlery, candelabras, and porcelain dishes glinted in the evening light. Red embers peered from the fireplace like tiny blinking eyes.

"What is this?" Marimar asked, holding up the picture in her grandmother's face.

Orquídea stirred the ice in her drink with her index finger. The nail had turned into a slender branch, like the new buds of spring. "It's a picture, Marimar."

Marimar grunted. She'd walked into that one. The only way to get real answers from her grandmother was to ask yes or no questions.

"Light the fire, Marimar," Orquídea said softly. Wrinkles deepened around her lips, the color of her eyes fluctuated between black and milky gray.

"I will if you answer me." Then, because she knew she'd do it anyway, Marimar added a strangled, "Please."

"The transformation makes me cold."

"Transform" was a prettier way to say die. But she couldn't deny her, even if she was angry with her. Marimar left the photograph on the table and hauled two logs from the iron rack in the corner. She threw in a fire starter, lit four matches at the same time, and waited for the flames to catch. She took the empty seat in front of Orquídea and once again picked up the old photograph.

"Is this my father?"

Orquídea tipped her glass back. She reminded Marimar so much of Rey in that moment. Or Tía Florecida, with the dimple in her cheek that only the two of them shared. The spark of secrecy, though. That was Orquídea's alone.

"Are you sure you want to know?"

No, she wasn't, but she still said, "Yes."

New shoots sprouted at her grandmother's knuckles, her wrists. She took in a deep breath like it hurt and then said, "That's him."

"You knew what this would have meant to me." Marimar trembled. She looked at the photo again. Her mother's head tilted toward the man like a flower toward the sun. Her father. The lights of the Ferris wheel in the background were blurred. She could practically hear her mother's infectious laughter. The stark joy on Pena's face meant that they'd been happy once — then what happened?

"What did you want me to do? Give you an old photo of a flash? What would you have done with that?"

"You're not telling me the truth. Why is that so hard for you?"

"Because I can't speak his name, Marimar!" Orquídea shouted, her breathing was short, jagged. She coughed and coughed. She covered her mouth and tiny bits of dry dirt appeared on her palm.

Marimar went to get water, but Orquídea shook her head. Marimar picked up the

174

bottle of bourbon instead and refilled Orquídea's glass. She took it in shaking hands and drank. Cleared her throat until her voice regained its even alto.

"There are so many things that I can't speak," Orquídea said bitterly.

"Why?"

"Because I made a choice, long ago." She grabbed Marimar's hand and squeezed. The beautiful dark brown of her eyes faded again. "I thought we'd be safe here, but I didn't see the danger until it was too late. And then he took her —"

Orquídea leaned forward. She dropped her glass and it shattered. Marimar could see the strain at her grandmother's throat as she coughed up more dirt. This time it took longer for her airways to clear.

And then he took her. Despite the roaring fire, Marimar felt cold. She stepped away from her grandmother, who rested her head against the high-backed chair, staring at Marimar.

"Did my mother really drown?"

"Yes."

"Did my father have something to do with it?"

When Orquídea breathed she made a terrible wheezing sound. So she only nodded, but even that motion hurt her. It cost her.

There were hundreds of things Marimar wanted to know. Why is this happening? Why can't we stop it? Why didn't you try to tell me sooner? Who are you? Why do this? What broke your heart so completely that its splinters found their way through generations?

But Marimar knew she had inherited her grandmother's silence, and said nothing else as she walked out of the room.

She took a right at the hallway and cut through the kitchen. Teal and white tiles covered the walls, vines snaking their way in through breaks in the windows. Her aunts and uncle Félix were busy peeling potatoes, splitting the husks of green plantains, dicing so many onions that they sang along to the music in order to combat the salt of their tears. Tía Silvia blew a strand of hair out of her face as she poured half a bag of rice into a giant steel pot and shouted, "Juan Luis, you better bring that rooster down here!"

Marimar stormed out the side entrance, past the smelly chicken coop. Past the shed bloodied from the pig Tío Félix killed earlier. Past the dead orchards with leaves and bark crumbling into ash.

She stopped at the cemetery, overgrown with yellow weeds and dead flowers. She wasn't going to get answers from the dead, either, but at least here she would have quiet. Her father had been responsible for her mother's drowning. The momentary elation she'd felt at the prospect of knowing his name was gone. She wanted to scour the earth for him. And what? Introduce herself as his daughter and then ask Sheriff Palladino to arrest him? Kill him herself, perhaps.

She wanted to scream.

Marimar was so full of want for things she couldn't put to words. She wanted a magic that had always existed at her fingertips. Every time she thought she got closer, it drifted away. She wanted her mother alive. She wanted her grandmother's love. She wanted simpler things, too. A good job. A home of her own. She wanted truth.

"You should be here," Marimar said to her mother. She brushed the simple, marble headstone. She traced the letters, Pena Lucero Montoya Galarza. Sometimes, when she was starting to forget her mother's smile or laugh, Marimar remembered the little things. Her mother was the wildflowers blowing in the breeze. For someone who had rarely left Four Rivers, who had worked at the local vegetable farms and the video stores, Pena Montoya had gone through the

177

world like she'd already seen it all and loved every second of it. She burned with light. Effervescent. And then she drowned. She was murdered.

"You should be here." This time, the hollow space in Marimar's chest felt like it echoed. She heard a susurration in the sunset air, the cicadas and crickets nearby. When she was a little girl, her mom and Tía Parcha liked to say that they could hear the stars speaking to them. That's why they spent so much time outdoors. Marimar could never hear stars speak. But for a moment, there was something out there. It felt like a voice calling to her.

"You should be here." Marimar only said it once more before moving on to tug at the wilted weeds growing around the headstones. She moved on to her grandfather, Luis Osvaldo Galarza Pincay. Tía Parcha, whose headstone was purely decorative since she was buried in Woodlawn Cemetery. Then Héctor Trujillo-Chen. Caleb Soledad. Martin Harrison. By the time she was done, the sun was nearly finished setting, and her anger had ebbed.

Marimar noticed a glittering stone sticking out of the dirt. She crawled on her hands and knees to get closer. It almost looked like bone, but bone didn't gleam.

She brushed the earth away, digging her fingers around the object. It was stuck. She found a flat rock and used it as a pick and shovel. She looked up to see fireflies surrounding her, illuminating as she dug deeper and uncovered the artifact.

It was a baby the size of a watermelon made entirely of moonstone. How many more of her grandmother's secrets would she find that night?

Marimar picked up the moonstone baby and held it in her arms. It was cold to the touch, but she traced its smooth forehead, its closed eyes and round little nose. Strange as it was, it looked peaceful. Whoever had carved it had done so to perfection.

Sitting on her knees, Marimar glanced back at the house, all lit up to celebrate a death. As she trudged back, the statue in hand, she noticed Gabo flap his blue and red feathers on the roof, chest puffed up like he was ready and waiting to crow at the waning moon.

Rey couldn't find Marimar anywhere. He'd half expected to see her running up the main road, but he remembered that if she was going to steal his truck, she'd need the key in his pocket. He decided to be mad at her later when they were on their way home.

She'd left him all alone to finish helping in the kitchen.

He didn't want to be the guy who got drunk in order to deal with his family, but as Tío Félix told Rey of his detailed plans to retire super early and take a fishing road trip across the States, Rey fixed himself another drink. He was good at listening. His mom told him once that he had a tender heart and a sincere face and needed to protect himself. He'd been ten, and it wasn't the strangest thing his mother, who liked to dance barefoot on full moons in Coney Island, had ever said.

In a few hours, he was caught up with everything the Montoyas were up to. Tía Florecida had just had a divorce party, which no one in the family had known about until Rey asked about the tan line on her ring finger. Penny was living with her dad most of the time, since he got to keep the house, and Flor was having a second coming of age in San Diego. Ernesta had gone into marine biology and spent her time in Florida and labs because she was better at talking to sea life than to people. Caleb Jr. was busy smelling great and making designer perfumes. Silvia was an ob-gyn and every spare moment was dedicated to making sure her twins didn't accidentally burn the house down with their pranks. Honestly, Rey didn't see what the big deal was. When his mom was still alive, she'd left Rey and Marimar alone all the time, and between her smelly sage and his cigarettes *they'd* never burned down the apartment. Everyone seemed to be doing just fine.

"How's work treating you?" Félix asked as he cut a sliver of crackling pork skin and crunched down on it.

"Good. Got a promosh. Totes fulfilling." He didn't *want* to talk like the bros in his office who abbreviated every word, but it just slipped out when he was nervous or if he didn't want to have a conversation and deflected. "Actually, I forgot I had to refill grandma's drink."

Rey carried a bucket of ice back down the hall, taking in the deep scent of dirt and lemon cleaner. First, he stopped in the parlor to key up another record — Buena Vista Social Club, Martin's favorite. Rey danced by himself, determined to keep a hold on his bright mood. But this house was a memory capsule that refused to remain buried. He traced a finger along the rows of records that had been the only music allowed in the house. Pushed aside the rug to see if the stain was still there from the time he and Marimar had tried to make paint out of berries and crushed insects. He moved out into the hall and stopped at the bannister leading upstairs. Instead of marking his height with a marker like other mothers, Parcha had made little cuts into the grain of the wood panel. She said it was so the house could remember his height, but now that Orquídea was passing on, who would get the house? Who would remember the boy he'd been?

As he danced, he kept thinking of his mother. He'd wanted to be like his mom for a time, unworried and carefree in a way so few people get to be. When he was a little boy, Rey had wanted to be a brujo. Conjure spirits from the ether. He wanted to pull gold right out of the earth, meld it with his bare hands just as Orquídea had done in her stories explaining what she had once done to pay for her journey to come to America. He wanted to speak to the stars like his mother, before the stars stopped speaking back and she wasn't strong enough to bear the silence after his dad died. That was when she moved them to the loudest place in the world. Turns out New York couldn't drown out her emptiness, but she found a way to keep going. She raised Rey and Marimar and got a job as a teller at the Met, and everyone knew her as Parcha, the lady with the weird name and big laugh, who made cookies for everybody just because. Who was always in a good mood and brought her scrawny little son around to be bored while he waited after school for her shift to be over. He liked to wander around and pretend the Temple of Dendur was his backyard. He'd stare at boys his age huddle in whispers and dare each other to reach into the water and fish out the shiny pennies from the reflecting pool that was supposed to be the Nile River. He wanted to tell them what Orquídea once had — that you shouldn't steal other people's wishes because that's when everything goes wrong. But so far away from his grandmother's reach, Rey knew how that sounded. He was too old for that shit. Too old to believe he could do anything more than sit at a desk and count numbers.

The security guards all got to know him, too, and the tour guides let him hover at the fringe of their groups like a little lost planet trying to find its orbit. Like his mother, he'd lost a small part of himself when his father died in a motorcycle accident. Rey stopped wanting to be a brujo. But inside the hallowed halls of the Metropolitan Museum of Art, he'd flirted with the idea of being an artist. Everyone mistook his silence for boredom when actually Rey was manifesting a wish. He knew from Orquídea that wishes didn't grow on trees. They had to be nurtured, carefully constructed like houses so you got exactly what you wanted. Orquídea had an altar with candles and crystals and pictures of forgotten saints, bones and safety pins, dry roses and seashells. Rey didn't have an altar. He had a penny that he kept in his pocket. He held it for years, rubbing it between his thumb and index finger while he stood in front of paintings and imagined his own hands at work. He'd rubbed it for so long, Abraham Lincoln's face was smooth. And when he finally flicked it into the water to make his wish, his mother died from an aneurism, triggered a day after she hit her head in the subway.

Everything had happened so quickly. The funeral in the Bronx. He hadn't even been mad at the other Montoyas for not dropping everything to show up. He hadn't cared as long as Marimar was there. A year from turning eighteen, he'd forged every signature necessary and lied about his age to make sure he and Marimar didn't lose the apartment or were made to stay in foster homes or had to go back to Four Rivers.

He turned his wish of becoming an artist

184

into the desire to survive. Everyone said New York City was for creatives, for artists, but that was a washed-up remnant of the past. New York wasn't for artists anymore. It was for steel and glass and suits. It was for fifteen-million-dollar Central Park apartments that remained empty all year round, ghost homes, tax shelter homes. Artists were as common as subway rats, except subway rats had free food options. New York gutted artists, used them as food, sucking out their marrow to make the glamour stronger.

So he'd become an accountant and he'd been all right with that, you know? It was no one's fault but his. Not New York, not his mom, not his grandmother, not his cousins, not the magic. It always came back to the magic. How could something that had never been his leave a hunger nothing else could fill?

As he danced alone in the parlor, the sun was a bloody red thing sinking behind the clouds, streaks of furious pinks and oranges creating the illusion of fire behind the valley. The last song of the record was followed by the hollowness of the end. Sometimes he wondered if that's what the afterlife sounded like. Those few seconds at the end of the vinyl where there's sound but no music, just a crackle, a warped scratch. He pushed the records apart and found one of Orquídea's records, the one full of pasillos she played on blue moons while she sat on the porch swing with a glass of bourbon and salt crusted on her face. His mom used to say that it was music people listened to when they wanted to be sad, and back then Rey had never really understood why anyone would choose to be sad.

But now, he danced with the melancholy out the hall. The front door was still open. *Now,* he could hear the night, an incandescent whisper that only ever happened once after his dad died. He heard the stars.

Or were those crickets?

Rey made his way into the living room where Gastón, Penny, and Juan Luis were setting the table while Orquídea grinned at the music. He picked up a red ceramic plate dotted in gold. None of the pieces matched, like they were missing parts of several sets.

"Watch it!" Penny said, arranging the center pieces of dried flowers in colored glass vases. "I'm not finished yet."

Orquídea turned her head in Rey's direction, the movement slow, like it pained her. "Pour me a drink, niño mío."

Rey wasn't a little boy, but he thought it was okay if he was *her* little boy for the rest of the night. For always. He went to the bar cart and fixed both of them drinks.

"What's your poison tonight, Mamá Orquídea?"

"Bourbon, neat."

He poured generously into two glasses and his grandmother accepted his offering. In the time he'd been cleaning the parlor, Orquídea's roots had spread, growing thicker. She was like a mermaid whose legs were being bound together, only with bark instead of scales.

"Is it painful?" he asked.

"Not any worse than it was giving birth," she said.

He almost pointed out that this would be like giving birth to herself, and how gross that image was, so for once, he kept that comment to himself.

"How's your art?" Orquídea asked.

"I haven't done anything since I sent you that painting," he said, gaze traveling to the one hanging over the fireplace. Part of him had imagined that she'd put it in the shed or something. How funny that Orquídea would ask about his art, something he hadn't let himself want in years.

"It's my favorite. Make another."

It was a portrait of Orquídea as she'd been as a young girl. Her hair was long and curly, and she wore a white dress. In her hand a fish and in the other a net. He'd found the picture between the pages of her favorite novel. Now he wondered if, like the photo of Marimar's father, she'd *let* Rey find it.

"Work is crazy," he said by way of explanation. "This one was a fluke."

She let loose a gravely laugh. "Was it a fluke or was it that you couldn't stop yourself?"

Rey shrugged. He remembered painting that over a week, locked in his room the summer after his first year at college. He'd been sick with adrenaline, red-eyed from not sleeping for days. Marimar was ready to break down the door, but he said he was fine. He ate the food she left at his door. And when he emerged, the painting was finished, he slept for another week and said *never again.*

"Why am I not surprised that you already know?"

"I only mean that you made a beautiful thing." She looked into her glass, then at him. He tried not to jump when her eyes went milky-gray and then coffee-black. "Why did you choose that picture?"

He'd blacked out the event, but he did recall one thing. He'd walked all the way home from his last day of classes and stopped at the Met. He'd paid a one dollar suggested entry because he had to pee, and it was a cleaner bathroom than the ones in the park. He meant to go in and out, but he couldn't help himself. He went to the reflecting pool in front of the Temple of Dendur and stared at the pennies in the water and even though it was impossible, he spotted his, bright and hopeful and unspent. On his way home, he stopped at an art supply store, bought a canvas, brushes, and paint at random, sweating like he was going home to assemble a bomb.

But as for *why* Rey had chosen that picture — He took a big drink and licked his lips. He scratched at the inside of his wrist and flashed a smile at his grandmother.

"You told us a story once about catching a river monster. It always stuck with me, I guess."

She smiled and her wrinkles deepened. "He's not a monster. The monsters look like us. He outlived me, so what does that say?"

"It says I need another drink."

She reached out and grabbed his wrist. Her hand felt like rough, ridged bark. One of the stems protruding from her wrist was showing pink petals beneath the green, like it was going to start blooming.

"Paint me another."

He shook his head and a sensation like a vise clutched his heart.

"Your heart is trapped, and this is the way it will be free. Mine was, too. That is why — It's too late for me but not for you."

"Mamá —"

"Promise, mi niño."

"I will," he promised then. "I will."

It was a momentary relief when Penny ran back into the living room. "Mom says you need to light the candles because you smoke that *trash* porquería."

"Charming," he muttered, but dug his metal lighter from his back pocket. Did they need so many candles? He went through them one by one, running down the line of the dining table, lighting the ones on the windowsills.

"Don't forget the altar," Orquídea said.

So he lit those, too. The altar had changed slightly. There were more pictures of her family. Usually, people put up the photos of the people who were dead, but Orquídea had her whole family. Old Polaroids, new glossy photos developed at the pharmacy, and graduation portraits beside small sepia portraits of faces he didn't recognize. A ticket drew his eye. Rey had stood before this altar a million times. He'd memorized the placement of every trinket. Tatinelly's wedding announcement and Caleb Jr.'s ad in *Vogue* were new additions, but so was this ticket. Rectangular, like from an old-timey theater. The ink was faded but he made out the word *Spectacular*! And an eight-pointed star.

Where was Marimar? he wondered.

But then came the war cry from Tía Silvia. "¡A comer! Don't make me go look for you."

Tío Félix and his wife Reina brought in the roasted pig while the others carried bowls of crisp salsa topped with cilantro. An ají that made Rey's eyes water even from across the table. Heaping towers of patacones and maduros. A mountain of arroz con gandules. Yuca frita stacked like a Jenga tower. Camarones apanados. Whole avocados ready to be cut.

One by one, the Montoyas took their seats. They congratulated Penny on the table setting and scolded the twins for hiding Gabo. But they were forgiven, with their easy smiles of sweet preteen boys. Those smiles would get them in trouble with women and men in the years to come.

Rey wanted to change the record but was pulled into a conversation with Tía Silvia's husband Frederico to give tax advice, which was as delightful as the time Frederico had gone off on a homophobic Christmas rant. Ernesta was trying to convince Caleb Jr. that he'd be rich if he found a way to synthesize the smell of the ocean. Tatinelly held Mike's hand and rubbed her belly as she gave her medical history to Tía Silvia, who was measuring the size of the belly with some concern, as Tati was well over the six-ish months she claimed. Penny whispered to her mom that she heard Rey say that he'd done the painting of their grandmother hanging over the mantel. All of a sudden, they were taking pictures of it. Even Tío Félix took out the photo from his wedding day. "Paint me this way," he said. "I want to be just like I was in this moment."

Rey agreed, mostly because he wasn't sure when he'd see his uncle next, and therefore probably wouldn't have to keep his promise. He'd say anything to get through the night. When this was over, he had to go home. Make sure his boss hadn't given his tiny desk to Paul the Intern. He had to continue on the path he'd carved out for himself.

Rey wanted Marimar to hurry back. If he was getting through this, then so could she. He needed to tell her about the ticket he found on the altar, conveniently now in his pocket. He wondered where Enrique was, but he didn't really care to know the answer.

Gabo let out a long, screeching cry from somewhere outside.

"How is that bird still alive?" Félix asked, holding a fork and knife in each fist, ready to dive into the crackling pig skin and juicy meat.

"He's come back to life twice," Orquídea said.

To which the twins responded with, "ZOMBIE CHICKEN."

"Zombie *rooster,*" Penny muttered, but only Rey paid attention to her.

"Right you are." He raised his drink in acknowledgement.

"It's a shame the Buenasuertes didn't stay for dinner," Florecida said, twisting a wine opener into the cork of a red bottle. "It might have been nice to know about Mom's other side of the family."

"Nice like getting a root canal, maybe," Rey said.

He felt someone pinch him but couldn't tell which of his aunts it was. He rubbed the side of his arm and was determined to stay quiet. To enjoy these last hours with his family. Listen to Félix detail travel destinations he'd never get to see because he was a dreamer, not a doer. Wait for Silvia to force the twins to sing while Penny played the guitar.

Unfortunately, Enrique finally stalked into the dining room. His dress shirt was unbuttoned to the middle, like wherever he'd been he'd worked up a sweat and had stripped to his white tank. There was what looked like a snake bite on the veiny top of his hand. His fingers were smudged and there was a cobweb in his hair, which his twin Ernesta plucked and threw away as he sat.

His uncle had been searching for something. Rey was sure of it. By his foul mood, he hadn't found it.

Enrique poured himself a glass of wine and leaned back. "I thought this was your funeral, but you're still looking well, Mother."

"About as well as you," she said, eyeing the bite on his hand, then held out her glass in the air. "Marimar is on her way, but I want to start off with a toast."

"Come on, Mom," Enrique said, drumming his fingers on the table. "Do we have to sit through this? You wanted us to come back to give us our inheritance, so do it. We all know this land is mine by right."

"We do?" Rey laughed.

"Excuse me, you little shit, but there are plenty of your brothers and sisters who are

194

older than you and less entitled," Florecida said.

"The food's going to get cold," Tatinelly said softly.

"Wait a minute," Félix said, his bushy eyebrows knitted like two kissing caterpillars. "I don't want the land. I wanted to see my mother. My brothers and sisters. We'll figure out what to do with the valley later."

"You *would* say that." Enrique scoffed. His green eyes were taking on the pale shade of water poured into absinthe. "The oldest brother trying to keep the peace."

"Actually, Pedrito is the oldest," Orquídea said. It was so low, and it didn't carry. But Rey followed her line of sight to the empty chair where Marimar should be. A cold sensation snaked around his throat. It prickled the hairs on the back of his neck. Who was Pedrito?

"No more ghosts, no more stories," Enrique said, raising the baritone of his voice. "Just — where is the paperwork?"

Orquídea Divina looked at him. She bit down and froze, like the words she really wanted to speak were caged by her teeth. Instead she said, "I tried to do the best I could. I failed. I knew the price."

Enrique barked a laugh, his eyes incandescent with anger and jealousy. "The price of what? Why can't you ever just say what you mean? Where is the paperwork?"

"Upstairs. Second drawer on my nightstand."

He got up. The chair smacked to the floor. He took only his drink with him. But before Enrique could leave, Marimar appeared at the threshold. Her hair was windswept, tears carved away a pattern on her dirty cheeks. At first, he didn't understand what she was carrying in her arms. A white pumpkin? He wouldn't put it past her to have found an albino fox, but the thing didn't move. In her arms was a baby carved entirely of moonstone, and gathered behind her were the ephemeral outlines of six ghosts.

11
THE FEEDING OF FIFTEEN LIVING HOUSEGUESTS AND SIX GHOSTS

No one moved. No one spoke. Rey was positive no one even breathed for several moments.

"Dad," Enrique said breathlessly.

That word was said over and over. Dad. Daddy. Papá. All four of Orquídea's dead husbands moved into the room. They were not the way Rey had thought ghosts would look like. He'd always imagined see-through white figures, outlines of what they used to be. But these people — these phantasms — did have touches of color. His grandfather Luis's brown skin gave him the impression of being alive. The only thing that marked him as dead was the way he flickered as he walked through the table and across the room to embrace Orquídea. For the first time in his entire life, he saw a tear run down her face. It shimmered, like tree sap.

Rey looked for her and there she was. His heartbeat fluttered as his mother appeared in front of him. Parcha was faded except for her rose red lipstick, the one she always wore because she said that roses were the most beautiful flower and everyone else was out of their goddamn mind to think otherwise. He trembled all over as she kissed his whole face. It felt like the first snowflakes that signal a blizzard.

Tía Pena glided like the wild breeze she was, like she was still underwater. She traced her daughter's face and tried to talk. But when she opened her mouth no sound came out. Pena drifted across the room to her mother, holding her delicate throat.

"Pena, mi Pena." Orquídea wept glittering tears. Caleb Sr. and Héctor and Martin followed suit, kissing her cheeks, her forehead, then joining the others around her, waiting like reapers.

Orquídea extended her arms, which were sprouting branches of their own. Green nubs edged their way out as they started to become leaves. "Marimar, sit here, bring me Pedrito."

Marimar took the seat left open for her beside Rey. She handed over the baby like he was made of tender flesh and blood. "What happened to him?"

Orquídea held the moonstone baby in her arms, right against her heart, like she could make him a part of her if she tried hard enough. "He was my first son. There was a terrible accident that also took my first husband back in Ecuador. I couldn't save Pedrito. It was all my fault."

"Why didn't you ever say anything?" Félix asked.

"There is so much I can't say. I can't. Long ago, I made a bargain. Everything I have, everything I've ever given to you came at a cost. Even this house." Orquídea, surrounded by the living and the dead, smiled as the clock rang the ninth hour. "Please, let's eat. I'm running out of time."

"That's it?" Enrique asked harshly. "That's all you're going to say?"

"Why are you doing this?" Marimar asked. "What *can't* you say?"

"For you. For all of you. We become what we need to in order to survive and I need to make sure that you are all protected."

A knot formed in Rey's throat.

"It's not what you all want to hear, or what I want to say. But it is what I can manage." Orquídea shut her eyes. Her thumb, which was now twisted at the tip like two vines intertwining, brushed the back of Pedrito's head.

"You never give a straight answer," Enrique said.

"You never ask the right questions."

Enrique stormed out of the room, stopping for a moment in front of his father. It was like looking into a mirror that revealed your future self. But not even Caleb Soledad could staunch Enrique's rage, and he barreled through his father's ghost.

"He'll get over it," Félix said.

"He won't, but you heard what Ma said. Eat." Tía Silvia, whose tears ran down her face in glittering rivers, piled food on plates. Goblets brimmed with the deepest red wine. The spirits ate and ate. The living hurried to tell their stories, their accomplishments, their wins, their progeny. Martin vanished for a moment, then returned and the sounds of Orquídea's favorite songs filled the house, which had been empty and silent for too long.

Gabo's cry cut through the music, the chatter of voices from the living and dead. Orquídea looked out the window at the moon, perfectly aligned to her needs. She was running out of time. She had wasted so much time.

Marimar turned to her grandmother. "You can't leave yet."

"Oh, Marimar. You're a bright, wonderful being. Do you know what I love about you?"

Marimar shook her head.

"I love that you care about people. You know how to love. I taught myself not to. Someone in my bloodline had to make up for everything I lacked."

"How could you not know how to love?" Penny asked. "You were married five times."

Penny's words, innocent if rude, made everyone laugh. Orquídea sipped her bourbon, and it burned the whole way down. Her movements were getting slower. Her bones ached as they transformed into someone different. Something else. But she held on tight to her firstborn son and said what she had to say.

"Love and companionship are different things, Penny. I have made mistakes out of fear. But this?" Her eyes roamed the room to look at each and every member of her family. "This was not one of them."

"What mistakes did you make?" Gastón asked.

"The bargain," she said. "Forty-eight years ago, I made a bargain and it cost so much more than my silence. This is the only way I can protect you from him."

"From *who*?" Rey asked.

A hard wind snuffed out the lights on the windowsills as dozens of dragonflies and fireflies flew in. They were followed by hummingbirds, blue jays, and larks. Frogs and newts. Snakes and lizards. Field mice and rabbits. They came all at once, filling the room. Some crawled into empty bowls, others perched on chandeliers and wine goblets. Penny gathered a rabbit to pet between its ears. The twins sprung out of their seats trying to catch snakes.

Florecida, who had a fear of mice, hopped up on her seat. Tati tried to calm her down, but Mike Sullivan had gone faint and fallen over his chair. Silvia sprang into action, checking his pulse and shining a light in his eyes. Penny gathered the mice out of the room. Meanwhile, Gabo crowed again, and the spirit of Luis Galarza Pincay danced with his daughters to the plucking sounds of guitars and boleros. Marimar wondered if they were truly ghosts, or if they were impressions created by Orquídea's sadness. After all, if the dead could rise, then why hadn't her mother come to her sooner?

Juan Luis and Gastón began to choke. They raised their hands in the air and Rey hit their backs until they coughed up identical balls of hard phlegm.

"Cool," they said in unison and picked up the slimy things, as Rey muttered, "Disgusting."

Enrique thundered down the stairs and rushed into the living room. A sparrow flew at him, but he swatted it away with the papers in his fist. He held a finger to Marimar like a cocked gun. "You're leaving the house to her? She's a child!"

"Marimar is nineteen. Aren't you?"

"I am."

"This house belongs to *me*," Enrique said. "Why do you think we all came here? Because you were such a warm and loving mother? You show that stone thing you're holding more affection than you ever did any of us. I'm not leaving without what's mine. This land is rightfully mine."

"*Nothing* is yours, Enrique," Orquídea shouted. "You don't have the first clue of what I did to survive. To make something out of absolutely nothing. I did what you don't have the guts to do. You want to fight over a bit of dirt? It's too late. It's done."

The animals in the room buzzed and croaked and hissed louder. Tatinelly made a sharp gasping sound and the house shuddered, cutting off the electricity so that the only light came from the fireplace, the dripping candles along the center of the table, and the moon shining through the window.

"Why make us come here?" Enrique asked, breathless as he slumped into an empty chair. His father's ghost appeared beside him and rested a hand on his shoulder. "Why aren't the rest of you angry with her?"

"We are, I think. But we can't change her," Caleb Jr. said.

Everyone nodded. Félix yanked off the crunchy ear of the pig and Ernesta joined Rey in opening a new bottle of bourbon.

"To the Montoyas," they said, and clinked each other's glasses.

"If you look closer at the invitations, there is something for each of you," Orquídea said and gestured to the twins.

Gastón had picked up the phlegm they'd coughed up. On closer inspection, it wasn't phlegm at all. They were seeds.

Around them, more Montoyas doubled over and coughed and coughed until they spit up seeds of their own, glossy with saliva.

"It's done," Orquídea repeated. The next breath she took looked pained. "When I'm gone, you will have each other. Plant them. Take care of them. These seeds are your protection against the one person I cannot fight."

"Who?" Rey asked.

When she tried to speak, his grandmother coughed up mud. Shaking, she turned to the dead, and said, "Take me."

The ghosts walked through her, and then, one by one, they were gone.

"Perhaps now I'll finally have peace," Enrique said, angry tears streaming from his hungry eyes. He wiped at the corners of his mouth, got up, and threw his seed in the fire.

Orquídea stood as much as her legs would allow. Everyone, except for Enrique, moved to help her. They gathered around, but she wanted to do this on her own. At first, she wavered, her body attempting to balance on the roots that devoured her legs. When she was steady, she poured the last of her bourbon. She hummed the last line of the song. She turned to her family and raised her glass with one hand and clutched Pedrito with the other.

"All you have is each other. Protect your magic." She drank and then shattered the glass on the floor.

For a moment, there was only the buzz of thousands of wings, the crackle of fire, then the howl of every creature in the room. Beneath all of that, a series of heartbeats. Each one with its own unique rhythm of wishes and hopes and dreams. The symphony of Orquídea's death.

Tatinelly slammed her palm on the table, the other on her baby bump and the earth rumbled. Orquídea Divina Montoya stretched higher and higher. Her legs finished transforming into the base of a thick tree trunk, roots undulating through the floorboards like rivers carving their way through stone, pushing away the table, breaking through the nearest wall, the ceiling.

"My water broke," Tatinelly announced with a gentle gasp. She lifted her shirt, revealing the pearly stretchmarks across her belly. A rose grew out of her belly button. "My water broke!"

"Upstairs! Juan Luis, get the bag out of my car." Tía Silvia shooed everyone out of her way. "Someone, for God's sake, wake up that man from the floor and tell him he's about to miss the birth of his child. If you can't make yourself useful, stay here and clean up. That guest room better be spotless."

"It is," Tatinelly assured her, as they left the room. "It's like she knew. She knew."

After Rey called for help, he and Marimar pulled up a seat at the destroyed banquet.

"Did you cough up any magic beans?" Rey asked.

"Nope. I just get this house, apparently," Marimar said. Most of the glasses were shattered, so she drank straight from the bourbon bottle and grimaced.

Upstairs Tatinelly's screams were piercing,

competing for attention with Gabo. She could hear Tati's frantic pulse in her ears, plus a second heartbeat — the baby's. Marimar's own blood was like fire beneath her skin. Something hot and piercing stabbed at the notch between her clavicles. But she ignored it as Enrique stood before her.

"You always were her favorites," Enrique said, his eyes pale, ensorcelled by his own hate. "Sign over the deed, Marimar. You don't know the first thing about fixing this house. It'll be worthless once she's done."

The house groaned around them. The tree still growing. At its center was a smooth heart made of moonstone.

"You're wasting your time," Marimar said. "I'm not signing over anything to you."

Rey got between them and shoved Enrique. "Leave. You didn't want to be here in the first place."

Enrique threw the first punch and Rey was slow with drink, but he punched back. Marimar shouted around them to stop. Orquídea was dead and Tatinelly was giving birth upstairs. There was no time for this. She picked up an empty bottle and hit her uncle across the head. He fell to his knees, nursing the spot. His eyes regained their jade color. He watched in horror at the sight of his mother's tree, then turned to the open windows.

A storm of dragonflies clustered around him, their tiny arms and legs crawling all over his face, his eyes. A frog leapt into his mouth when he screamed, and a snake wrapped around his throat. He tried to pick himself up but yanked on the tablecloth, knocking over candelabras.

The fire caught fast. It spread along the tablecloths. The stuffing inside Orquídea's favorite upholstered chair. The alcohol-drenched rug and the floorboards.

Upstairs a newborn's cry pierced the night.

Tatinelly got her wish. She didn't know why but, despite the pain of the delivery, she was overcome with a certainty that her daughter would be okay. Even though she'd grown up to do ordinary things, she would have an extraordinary daughter. She promised to tell her stories of her Mamá Orquídea who built her own house in a magic valley. Mamá Orquídea, who was strong and angry and silent, but saved her real love for when it mattered.

Earlier that day, Orquídea had called her in.

"Tatinelly," Orquídea had said. "Let's see you. Come."

Tatinelly waddled around the table and took the upholstered seat Enrique had vacated. "How are you, Gran?"

"My bones are weary. But I'm happy you came. It's been so long since we've had a baby in the house. The last ones born here were Juan Luis and Gastón."

When Tatinelly sat, her shirt rose up a bit. Her belly button looked like the bud of a rose.

Orquídea held her hand out. "¿Puedo?"

"Of course," she said.

Orquídea placed her free hand on the top of the belly and closed her eyes, as if her fragile bones could protect that child from the world. She listened. What was she listening for? Could she hear the stars in her womb? Were they whispering now? Just then, Orquídea Divina's hand grew a single white rosebud in the fleshy web where her index finger met her thumb. The old woman took a deep breath and a deeper drink of bourbon.

"A girl. Good. Be good to her," Orquídea Divina said. "Let her run free."

"Thank you, Gran," Tatinelly said. "I'm sorry I didn't get to visit more. I always meant to and then things just got in the way."

But the old woman dispelled the apology

with a wave of her hand and the blooming rose that had grown so quickly, withered into dust seconds later.

Then, Tatinelly felt a kick, a sharp pain. The sensation gathered at her belly button, where a quarter-sized flower bud had sprouted. She looked into Orquídea's eyes, sparkling and black and wet, and didn't have enough words for what her grandmother had just given her. A gift for her daughter. Something extraordinary.

"Do you have a name yet?"

"I do. It's —"

"Don't tell me! I want to be surprised, too."

As Rhiannon Rose Sullivan Montoya came into this world, twenty-eight days early, and was placed in her arms, Tatinelly was sure of two things.

The first was that her daughter was special. All kids are special to their parents, she supposed. Tatinelly hadn't been special. She'd been ordinary like her mom and dad. But not Rhiannon. The quarter-sized bud that had sprung from Tatinelly's belly button now blossomed at the center of Rhiannon's forehead. It was the most beautiful thing she'd ever seen. A tiny, fairy creature that she'd made. The women around them cooed and awed at her. She had the doe brown skin of her mother, and a full head of light brown hair.

Mike didn't want to hold her, worried that something had gone wrong, that there was a cursed mark on his daughter. But Tatinelly knew that he would come around.

The second thing she realized was that somewhere in the house, there was a fire.

Marimar and Rey ran into the room to warn them, but the flames had raced up the stairs and now blocked their way out. Rey went to the window, but it was too dangerous to jump. Marimar threw herself on the ground, yanking at the carpet under their feet. She was knocking, keeping her head to the floorboards.

"What do we do?" Reina asked.

Tatinelly smoothed Rhiannon's sticky hair. A smile tugged at her lips. She shouldn't have felt that calm, but that's how she was, the eye of a hurricane.

"Got it!" Marimar shouted as she pressed down and a latch opened on the floorboards. The way was dark, with old stairs leading down into who knew where.

"Mom said this is how she used to sneak out," Marimar said, and waited for the others to file in. "Tati, you first."

"I will slow everyone down," she said. She

handed Rhiannon over to her cousin. Marimar was terrified, but she gave her a reassuring nod and went.

"Go!" Tía Silvia shouted. Her hands were still covered in blood, so bright it looked like she was wearing gloves.

They went, one by one. Tatinelly wasn't sure where she found her strength, but she got downstairs. Mike held her hand. He was terrified into silence, shaking, craning his neck to see the end of the passageway. Rhiannon didn't cry out despite the roar of the flames or the scared hiccups Penny was letting out. The stairs were dark, illuminated by glowing dragonflies and lightning bugs. They zoomed back and forth, and Tatinelly knew that they were here to make sure Rhiannon was safe.

When they got to the bottom, they realized they were in the walk-in pantry, empty for the first time since the house came to be. The fire hadn't reached the kitchen, and they hurried out through the yard and back around.

In the distance, Enrique was running away from the house, trudging uphill just as an ambulance and the sheriff's Lincoln were speeding downhill. The volunteer fire department was two towns over and on their way, but they all knew it was too late. The stench of rot and decay around the house was replaced with smoke. Tatinelly stood downwind of it, covered in jackets and sweaters and anything her family could take off. If she closed her eyes she could imagine sitting around a fireplace, with the kind of family that was bonded by blood and roots and magic.

After hours of being unable to stop the flames, they simply watched it burn. Bathed in morning light, the house was nothing but a pile of ash and debris around a great tree with branches that reached for the heavens, surrounded by thousands of incandescent creatures.

Marimar was barefoot again and she still couldn't tear herself away from the front of the house. It was the spark of Rey's lighter that brought her back to the present.

Sheriff Palladino stepped out of his car and took in the scene. He had aged well, Marimar thought. The paramedics were on Tatinelly at once, taking her blood pressure and giving her and Rhiannon oxygen.

Marimar and Rey stayed close.

Sheriff Palladino approached the three of them. His bright blue eyes went from Rhiannon's forehead, to Rey's hand where a red, red rose had sprouted between his thumb and index finger. Marimar, too, had a green bud at her clavicle. Marimar didn't have time to wonder why her flower hadn't bloomed like the baby's and Rey's. She watched Sheriff Palladino stare at the flowers, but he was used to Orquídea's inexplicable life in Four Rivers and he did not ask questions they couldn't answer.

They gave statements, and he took off his hat at the news that Orquídea had perished in the fire. He looked at the tall tree that had appeared straight through the center of the house. Its species, a ceiba common in the Amazon rainforest, did not belong in the hills of Four Rivers. But just like the house that had appeared one day from thin air, he could not refute its existence.

As they readied to load Tatinelly in the ambulance, she looked at her cousins. "What are you going to do?"

Marimar surveyed the damage. She ran her fingers through her hair. A hummingbird appeared, and flew close to her throat, then disappeared into the night.

"I don't know, yet," she said, but Marimar felt it. The familiar pull of the night, the whisper of the earth. Those times her grandmother had told her to find fairies in the hills, to listen to the stars, Marimar had always come home defeated. Now she knew she hadn't been listening. They had been with her all along. The dragonflies shimmered with light, rising all around the twilight valley, with the magic of fading stars and the wild mountains.

They were here for her.

They screamed at her, and Marimar did what she'd wanted to do since she returned home. She screamed back.

12
Orquídea Montoya Becomes Orquídea Divina

■ ■ ■ ■

PART II
HIBERNATION

■ ■ ■ ■

13
La Vie en Rose

When Orquídea Divina arrived at the Lon-doño Spectacular Spectacular, she was of-fered a single ticket and a seat with an obstructed view. She'd never been to the circus before, though the Buenasuertes had gone every time one rolled around. Wilhelm Jr. loved the elephants and Greta would save her candied apple and eat it little by little, like a rabbit gnawing away at a carrot too big for its size.

When the lights inside the tent dimmed, the barking chatter from the crowd ceased. There were whispers. Children getting in their last curious questions. *Is that a real lion? When does the flying woman come out? Do they really have a living star?*

Orquídea wondered all of those things. Leggy women danced in a line. They looked like a row of marionettes moving as if the same person was pulling the strings. They were followed by clowns on bicycles, which

219

she hated because the heat was making the diamonds painted around their eyes run. There was an elephant that ran around like a dog, and she felt his heavy steps deep down within her. She was most fascinated by the long-legged woman who walked across a tightrope. Orquídea held her breath until the young woman crossed to the other side, and all she could think was that she had finally witnessed the living embodiment of what it was like growing up in La Atarazana to walk that long road to and from the river. Hadn't she done her best to be a good girl? Hadn't she tried to do right by herself and her mother? Orquídea imagined herself in the bodysuit covered in rhinestones, her hair pulled back into an elegant bun. She pictured herself walking across the high wire without a net.

The Spectacular Spectacular went on into the night, but it felt like no time had passed at all. She laughed at the jugglers who dropped their things on top of each other, the men lusting after the woman who swallowed swords. Watched mothers cover the eyes of their children as a mermaid was brought out to the center of the stage in the bed of a giant pink clam. She had long braids piled up like a crown atop her head and pearls that dripped over her shoulders and across her chest, covering her nipples but nothing else. Her abdomen was soft, and the tail that she was wearing created the illusion that she was truly half woman, half fish. Boys dressed like sailors pushed her around the circus grounds so that everyone could witness her. Orquídea and the mermaid made eye contact. She was sure of it, even if it was dark and Orquídea's face was just one among hundreds.

When the stage had been cleared, a spotlight shone down on a man. Orquídea felt a pang under her ribcage, a twisting sensation that she'd never had in her life, because she'd never seen a man like this before. He wore a blue velvet tailcoat trimmed in gold. His trousers hugged the thick muscles of his thighs and calves. When he removed his matching blue top hat and held it over his chest, there was a murmur of pleasure. Orquídea had not been the only one to notice his beauty. Black waves slicked back in a way that made him appear polished, but not manicured. His beard was neat, trimmed in clean lines around a sharp jaw. He looked like the Devil himself had come to Ecuador to find her. Maybe that had been the voice she'd heard. Maybe, because he was watching her with sapphire eyes framed by thick black brows. She peered over her shoulder, but when she looked back, he flashed a smile that gutted her.

"Ladies and gentlemen! People of the center of the world!" His voice was deep and booming, melodic in a way that made the audience answer with delighted cries. Orquídea found herself sticking her thumb and index finger against her teeth and letting out a sharp whistle that cut through the reverie. He noticed her again and this time he floundered, for a breath of a second. He looked like he'd forgotten where he was or what he was supposed to say next, and all he could do was look at her, Orquídea Montoya.

When he recovered, he said, "The Londoño Spectacular Spectacular has been all over the world and I'm here to tell you that no crowd had shown us as much love as you have tonight." He pressed his hand over his heart and accepted the applause, the kernels of popcorn, and even a lace brassiere.

He chuckled, like he was flattered, and gave that general direction a wink. "This is our first event since my father, the great Pedro Bolívar Londoño Asturias II, left God's green earth. I don't think I will ever fill my father's very large shoes, but by God, I will try. We are a family. For decades my father has brought together the most marvelous, curious, inexplicable people from around the globe. But tonight . . . tonight we bring you something from the heavens." He paused and waited for the crowd to lean in, just a little bit more. "I present to you — the Living Star!"

The tent went pitch black. So dark, Orquídea couldn't even see her own hand in front of her. There were yelps of fear and excitement. She'd seen the advertisement outside, but she hadn't known what to expect.

A living star.

Before she could think about how in the world that would be possible, a pulse of light shone from the center of the circular stage. It looked like a heartbeat made of light. A firefly alone in the dark. Then it grew brighter and brighter, filling the entire tent. It was so bright that every single person in the room averted their eyes, looking away because, for a very real moment, it felt like they had looked at the sun.

Orquídea chanced another glance, and this time, she stood. She rubbed her eyelids to get rid of the dancing red light in front of them.

The outline of a person appeared from the shadows. She thought of the times she made her own dolls by taking two panels of cloth and snipped the outline of a person, then she'd stuff it with dry lentils or cotton and sew it shut. That's what this was, the shape of a person made of light, and when the star moved, it rippled with a prism of color.

She looked for the wires, the tricks, the magician's precision that was needed in order to make them all see this. It wasn't possible, but there it was. The crowd roared its approval, its fascination and wonder.

After, the audience rushed out to the fairgrounds, to the fortuneteller tables and games and popcorn stands. Orquídea sat alone in her gifted seat and replayed the last hours.

"Did you enjoy yourself?"

She turned around at the rich sound of his voice. It was really him, the master of ceremonies, still dressed in blue velvet. Up close, she could see that he wasn't perfect at all. There was a scar that cut across his right eyebrow and his roman nose was wide at the bridge, like it had been broken, then broken again.

"I've never seen anything like this," she said. "I didn't know it was here. I went for a walk, and here it was."

"What's your name?"

"Orquídea."

"Bolívar Londoño, at your service." He approached her slowly, the way the lion tamer had done to the lioness not a few hours ago. Like he thought she might bite. She was suddenly aware of her battered shoes, her eyes puffy from crying.

"The Widow said you were looking for work."

A rush of hope came at her quickly. She pressed the ticket against her stomach. "I am — I can learn anything."

"Do you have any talents?" he asked with a coy smile.

"Fishing."

He started to chuckle, but then he realized she was serious. He ran his fingers along his beard. There was a striking ring with a coat of arms on his middle digit. "La Sirena Caribeña is retiring today. We need a replacement. We're leaving for our European tour tomorrow."

Orquídea felt her neck heat up as his eyes took in her collarbone, the swell of her breasts, her small waist, and the bloom of her hips. He looked at her like she was someone who should not be ignored. He looked at her like he wanted to be consumed by her.

"I —" Hadn't she wanted this? It was so easy to fantasize while she was watching, to put herself in the role of these women dressed in fantastical clothes, performing miracles, defeating the laws of gravity. Dressing up as a mermaid who got pushed around on stage wouldn't require anything from her except putting on a costume. Being another person. In Europe, no less!

She could escape.

All she would have to do was live with the circus. Any time her mother had returned home from a circus, after the night's fun had been had and the spell of it washed away, she'd remark on the women who walked around nearly naked. Whores with loose morals and looser legs. After that night, Orquídea knew what her mother thought of her. What would be the difference?

She could be someone new.

The oddities that were spurned by God and creation.

She could *be*.

It was a dream, that's all. Every insult and cruel word that had been thrown her way like arrows pierced into her skin. What would she have without her mother? She remembered her old friend from the river who had called her the Bastard Daughter of the Waves. If she went home now, perhaps her mother wouldn't notice that she'd run away for the night. Perhaps there was time to fix things.

"I can't go with you. I'm sorry."

"We're leaving for Paris tomorrow morning," Bolívar said, flipping his top hat between deft fingers before securing it on his head. He took her hand in his and the skin-on-skin contact tightened a cord around her heart. His soft mouth brushed against her knuckles, then the inside of her wrists. "Ship leaves at four in the morning, if you change your mind."

That night, Orquídea ran home with the intention of apologizing to her mother, to Mr. Buenasuerte. But when she stepped in the house, she felt like an intruder, slinking around the dark. The party had long finished, and everyone seemed to be asleep. They didn't even know she was gone.

She did not belong in her mother's new life with her new husband and new kids. She had no father to turn to. When she crawled into her narrow bed, she thought of Bolívar Londoño's stare, the way he made her skin feel hot, like molten sugar turning, transforming into something to sink teeth into. She ran a thumb over and over her knuckles, the place where he'd kissed her. Had he meant it?

She gave up on sleep and packed a bag.

She owned very little, but she took what would fit in her leather school backpack. Three cotton dresses, a hand-me-down robe, slippers, two pairs of stockings two shades too light for her skin, a pair of socks, three hundred sucres, and a photo of her mother — black and white and faded at the edges. She thought about going to say goodbye to Ana Cruz, but didn't want to chance the baby waking up and alerting the whole house. When she whirled around to go, Orquídea saw she was not alone anymore.

"Don't go, niña," Jefita said. "I'll have no one if you go."

Jefita. She'd had Jefita. She held her friend in her arms and allowed herself to cry for the life that was never hers. The one she'd leave behind without a trace.

Orquídea arrived at the port breathless, eyes scanning for him.

There he was, dressed in a dapper green suit. He stood apart from his crew, like he'd been waiting for her. When their eyes met, Orquídea felt that tug beneath her ribs. This was her present, her future. Hadn't that been her destiny all along? The girl who'd been born unlucky, a soul lost to the seas.

Damn the stars and damn luck. Damn

everyone and anything who thought her insignificant. Orquídea Montoya was going to rewrite her fate.

14
EPHEMERAL BEINGS

After the fire died down and the ambulances took the Sullivans to the big hospital in the next town, and the animals returned to their hiding places in the valley, after the Montoyas dispersed once again across the country, and Enrique called to remind her that this wasn't over, Marimar stood among the rubble with Rey.

Orquídea had not prepared them.

"What are we supposed to do?" Rey asked. He was out of cigarettes and out of booze and the moment wouldn't allow him to go in search for either for a while. "You heard what Orquídea said. She was hiding from someone. Scared. Do we tell Sheriff Palladino?"

"And say what? File a report for a man with no name who *might* be a danger?"

Rey deflated with a frustrated sigh. "I don't know, Mari. Maybe this is why Orquídea never left Four Rivers. Maybe we would have been safe if we had stayed."

"If she had been safe, she wouldn't have become this."

They turned in the direction of the ceiba tree among the rubble. The valley whistled, carrying away ash and embers in a strong breeze.

"I'm open to suggestions," Rey said.

There was only one thing to do, Marimar knew. "Clean, like Tía Silvia told us to."

"Have you heard from anyone? Nice of them to leave us with the mess."

Marimar shrugged. She didn't remind him that Orquídea had left her the house and so this was her mess. She was afraid if she did, he might leave, even though she knew he wouldn't. She had one text message from Juan Luis that said, "Sick funeral." And one from Tatinelly reminding her to keep in touch. What would her in-laws say when she showed up with her baby girl, a pert little flower growing out of her forehead? Florecida gave her an invitation to come live temporarily in Key West, but Marimar had declined.

"It's just you and me, kid," she said, and he grinned. That was the same thing he'd said the day after his mother's funeral when they sat in the living room with a bunch of sympathy food from neighbors and coworkers. *Just you and me.*

Rey would leave five months later, but he stayed for her. He stayed because he couldn't bear the idea of going back to New York and trying to work at his desk and tally up numbers and yell at clients for trying to expense their third jacuzzi. He just couldn't, and Marimar saw that, too. She was afraid of being alone eventually, and so, to make her cousin stay as long as possible, she went to get provisions.

While he was renting a tractor from old man Skillen twenty miles down the road, Marimar went out and bought a case of wine, three bottles of bourbon, six cases of cherry soda, a college student's semester supply of 30-cent ramen packets, and locally made bison jerky.

Rey brought his own provisions. He returned with two men, a tractor, and an industrial-sized garbage bin. "Bitch, you owe me *two* cases of wine."

The men in question were Christian Sandoval and Kalvin Stanley, two boys she'd gone to middle school with. Even though Chris had been two years older, she'd dropped a Valentine's Day card in his locker and by lunch he'd been shoving his tongue down one of the Mary Somethings right in the hall for everyone to see. It wasn't a heartbreak for Marimar, more like prickling herself on a sewing needle, but it still stung.

Typical of Four Rivers, Christian and Kalvin hadn't wanted to go anywhere after graduation. There was nothing wrong with the community college in the next town, and Four Rivers had everything they needed. A house. Work. Free pie from the diner, though that would get old in a few years, when their looks went and the world beat the charming out of them, whatever small quantity they possessed.

Chris and Kalvin spent most of their days alternating between the Home Depot and the salvage yard. At twenty-one, they were all corded muscle that came from hauling sheetrock and steel and lumber. They were just as dumb and beautiful as they'd been in school, but now that they had nowhere to go, they actually made small talk with Marimar and Rey. *Tragedy. Wow, New York? What's it like? Wow, no way. Wow, so you're like* back *back? You hear about Coach Vincent? Talk about tragedies.*

As the Wow Guys began removing the scorched rubble, the remaining Montoya cousins sifted for anything salvageable. Even in the afterlife, Orquídea Divina was making them sort through her things to find answers.

"*So,* while I was in town," Rey said, "I discovered that the girl who tormented you in elementary school is now on her third child and her baby daddy just got picked up for indecent exposure at the mall two towns over."

"Is that supposed to make me happy?" Marimar asked, towing away a charred piece of bone. Upon closer inspection, it was the roasted pig.

"Well, the two beefcakes I picked out for you aren't helping. We have alcohol, an empty valley, and I'm pretty sure one of them is gay, so we could find out which."

She laughed, but it didn't quite reach deep inside. "You know how much I want to support and enforce the gay agenda, but I don't think that hooking up with the guy who once called me a Smelly Satan Worshipper is going to make me feel better. Plus, Orquídea is right there."

Rey lit a cigarette and looked down, already done with work even though they'd just started. "She's a tree."

"The tree is alive."

They went on like that for days. Marimar going through the motions; Rey trying to cheer her up. Marimar saying three things to the crew: Hello, do you want something to drink?, and see you tomorrow.

Rey tasked himself with finding out every detail of their lives. Chris was allergic to poison ivy and failed at being a Boy Scout because he wound up in the hospital after falling into a pit of the stuff. Kalvin was the seventh kid in a giant family, so another reason he hadn't gone off to college is because, by the time they got to the third kid, his parents had run out of money. Chris sang to the classic rock station he set up in his car and was full of semi-useless information about the sex lives of rock stars, but he killed at trivia nights at the pub. Kalvin had donated a kidney to his older sister two years ago. Chris tried to pull Marimar into conversation, but she mostly just smiled politely and tucked her hair behind her ear and pushed down the fluttering sensation beneath her skin when he looked at her that way.

Marimar had found camping gear in one of the sheds from when Caleb Jr. had discovered John Muir and had wanted to hike in every National Park. He'd gone to Yosemite once and returned home the next day. His tents and sleeping bags still smelled new.

She turned the camp they set up into a little home. Kept the firepit roaring when she couldn't sleep, and the sound of dragon-flies and frogs kept her up at night. Marimar discovered it was Kalvin who was gay when she was roaming through the orchards and found him and Rey kissing among the dead trees. Part of her wished that she wanted that. But she mostly wanted to be alone. To figure out why the flower bud at her throat hadn't bloomed but Rhiannon's and Rey's had. It was the part of him that Kalvin kept touching.

A week after the fire, when Rey was still asleep with Kalvin in his tent, Marimar worked up the nerve to try and talk to Orquídea.

"You owe me more than this." She pressed her hand to the undulating roots that could have only belonged to a tree that had been in the same place for hundreds of years. Bright green leaves rustled in the summer breeze. The moonstone center gleamed against the night. Pedrito's serene, sleeping face haunted her even when she was awake. "What happened to you?"

But Marimar got no answers.

She put the anger toward her grandmother into her work, going through the destruction of the house like she was looking for a passage to the other side of the earth. Three weeks later, there were two piles — salvageable and not.

Among the things that could be saved were several stone mortars and pestles, bottles of herbs and seeds carefully labeled and protected in a metal box. Part of the portrait that Reymundo had gifted his grandmother; only the bottom half had burned. A photo album that Orquídea had kept in her room. The deed to the house and land. A tin box of letters with paper so thin, Marimar thought it was a miracle it hadn't burned. Not a miracle. Magic. Then there was the Virgin Mary statue from the altar, the one where she's depicted with brown skin and three crowns of stars. Orquídea's favorite pen. And, to Rey's joy, a trunk of records.

It didn't feel like enough, but it was what was left. How could her grandmother's entire life be reduced to these memories? She'd come to touch the green bud at her throat every time she was pensive, and she was growing used to the new appendage.

Gabo the rooster, whose feathers had turned an unnatural cobalt blue, had survived, too. If Orquídea had been telling the truth, then this made it Gabo's third resurrection. Rey found him walking around through the ash, devouring fire beetles and trying to nest in a small crook of Orquídea's roots. Sometimes Gabo walked along-side Marimar and Rey on crisp mornings when the fire pit wasn't enough to keep them warm, so they took to heating up by walking up the steep hills.

"I'm going to get a record player," Rey announced.

"You should try the antique shop on Main."

"Kalvin's sister works there. Maybe she'll give me a discount."

"But where are you going to plug it in? We don't have electricity."

"We will." He sounded sure, bright. "You know what's weird? That's all I can hear. Even now. An earworm. Those songs that I played at the funeral. Or was it a wake? Or Shiva?"

"We're not Jewish."

"Caleb Soledad was."

"Don't invoke them. Enrique might show up."

"Fuck Enrique. Also, we haven't discussed the fact that our grandmother had five husbands. Five. I mean, get it, Grandma, but why wouldn't she tell anyone about the first husband? Who do you think he was?"

Marimar shook her head. "I don't know, but his ghost wasn't there."

She told Rey her theory, that those hadn't

been ghosts but something more, but he brushed it away. Maybe he wanted to think that their mothers had come to see them, that the dead had risen to give Orquídea a glorious send off. But they weren't taking her anyway. She was still here, living, but transformed.

"Maybe he's in the photo album or her letters," Rey suggested.

They did not get a record player. But they did investigate the matter of Orquídea's secret first husband. Marimar had an idea to invite the Montoyas back when everything was clear and the house rebuilt. But this couldn't wait. The salvaged items were kept in one of the sheds. They found pictures of their cousins' graduations, Tatinelly's wedding, baptisms. Rey held up a memorial card with a prayer on the back. "This is from my mom's funeral. My dad's sister must have sent one."

"*I* don't even have one."

"You don't have an altar, you heathen. It's like she kept the moments she never got to attend because she wouldn't leave Four Rivers."

"*Couldn't* leave," Marimar reminded him.

"What about this one?" Rey pointed at a handsome Black man in Marine dress blues. "It looks aged."

"It's a photo, not cheese." But still she flipped the photo to read a name on the back. "Holy shit, that's Martin. What's he, like eighteen? I barely recognized him without the sensible jean shirt and Cowboys baseball cap."

For each husband, Orquídea had a photo from when they were young, and another from their weddings. She'd worn a different dress every time, which Rey respected and Marimar thought impractical for the grandmother she knew. She looked happiest in her fifth wedding, though, and Marimar gathered the photos back into the box for safe keeping. But as she closed the box, she noticed the lining paper peeling.

Carefully, Marimar tugged the paper back so as not to rip anything. There, pressed tightly against the metal tin was a photograph torn in half. There was Orquídea, so young and beautiful. A man's hand gripped her tightly, possessively. It was all that was left of him.

"Found something."

Rey looked at the black-and-white photo for what felt like hours, tracing the seam where the rip was. "There's that."

There's that. A torn photograph from her first wedding and nothing more. Marimar had also hoped to find more pictures of her dad. But those two men had been completely removed from the family, like they'd been cut with an X-Acto knife. Or maybe they were amputated. Remove a limb to save the whole organism. She wondered, is that what Orquídea had done to herself? She'd said that she was doing this for her family, to protect them. They had to protect their magic. But from what? From whom? Who could possibly want this curse?

After a month of clearing the debris, Kalvin and Chris took away the industrial garbage bins. Everything Orquídea had built was gone. The land was clear save for the ceiba tree.

Three months after that, Rey woke up to Gabo's crow and announced, "I need to leave."

"I know." Marimar said. They sat at the top of the hill like they did most days at sunset. Rey with his cigarette and Marimar with her can of cherry soda. "Do you think they're going to take you back at the firm?"

Rey shook his head. "You don't really get a six-month bereavement when your grandmother dies."

"She's not dead."

"She's a tree."

"The tree is alive."

He took a drag and sighed. The rose at

the crook of his thumb was a sharp red that beautifully contrasted against his light-brown skin. Sometimes, when he just sat there, he'd touch it the way Marimar would twirl a strand of hair or bite her fingernails. Like it was an extension of himself that had always been there. Maybe it had and they had only ever just noticed it after Orquídea's transformation.

"So, what are you going to do?"

"I don't know," he said, shoving his hand in the pocket of his jeans. "I made her a promise. I hadn't intended on keeping it but I'm more afraid of her finding me post-mortem."

"Use my old room as a studio."

"Come with me," he said, wavering in his resolve. She felt it too. They hadn't been apart since she was thirteen and showed up at the apartment with a duffle bag. "We should stay together."

"I think I need to be here right now." Her cheeks were cold, and she felt a pressure behind her eyelids.

"I wish I could be in two places at once."

She rested her head on Rey's shoulder. "Are you going to call Shane and try to get back together?"

"He didn't understand why I had to stay for so long. He won't understand me now."

He flashed his straight white teeth. Marimar thought that he had his mother's smile. She thought that maybe they were going to be okay.

As he got in his truck and dug in his back pocket for his lighter, he gasped so loud his cigarette fell out of his mouth. "Fuck, fuck, fuck. I can't believe I forgot this."

"What?"

"I wanted to show you this the night —" But he didn't finish, only handed Marimar the old theater ticket. She didn't see why it was important, the ink had long faded leaving behind the ghost of the word *Spectacular!* and an eight-pointed star, just like her father's ring.

"It was on her altar," Rey explained.

"What does it mean?" But even as she asked her mouth felt bitter with all the things she did not know.

"I'm sorry." He kissed her forehead and started the engine.

Don't leave me, she thought, but she couldn't bring herself to say it out loud.

After Rey left, the fall chill rolled in. Marimar drove into town for supplies: food, water-cooler barrels of water, underwear, sweaters from the thrift store, and new sheets. She hired Chris to put in insulation

243

and fix the shed door and roof. When Chris told his uncle that a Montoya was staying behind after the fire, he and two of the local farmers came by and put in a small wood-burning stove to keep her warm during the winter. They'd come by when she was clearing away the dead leaves in the orchard, and they'd gone without saying a word.

The kind gesture undid her.

"Don't cry," Chris told her. He was bashful in a way he hadn't been when they were in school. It was like being in the real world had put a permanent crack in his confidence. He raked his fingers through dark waves and searched the valley for help because he didn't know what to do when a girl was crying. "It was supposed to be a good surprise."

She thanked him, and then she kissed him. She hadn't planned on doing so, but he was there, and he was beautiful. He took off his T-shirt and they walked back into her refurbished shed. It didn't smell like pigs' blood and iron anymore. It smelled like sawdust and clean linens. She pushed him onto her air mattress, which squeaked. It made her laugh, which made him snort. They kissed for hours. Fast at first, like she wanted to devour his goodness. Then slowly, tracing the length of his neck, his torso.

They kissed until she was familiar with the places that made him hiss or grunt. Until she was clawing at his back and an urgency snapped within her, a heady need to lose herself in someone. To be needed.

They'd slept curled against each other, under a wool blanket she'd bought at the general store with grizzlies and horses on it. Chris's calloused finger traced her shoulder bone, but he always stopped just shy of touching the very alien part of her that existed at the base of her throat. He didn't ask about it. This thing that felt more intimate than sex.

But he was working up the nerve, she could tell. He left in the morning when she'd pretended to be asleep to avoid any awkward conversation. When he was out the door and driving up the hill, she got up to do her chores.

Marimar had never so much as had a plant in the City, and now she had a valley to tend to. A house to rebuild. She made her rounds, and when everything became overwhelming, she'd climb up on the massive roots of Orquídea's tree and sit a while, listening to the breath of the land, the flutter of wings.

That night, Chris surprised her with dinner because he'd noticed that she always forgot to eat. And she let him in because she'd liked the feel of his lips on hers. They ate burgers from the diner, and he dunked his fries in mustard, which made her wrinkle her nose. She was relieved that he did most of the talking, and when he asked things she didn't want to answer, like about her mother's drowning accident or what had started the fire, he didn't press.

He'd only approach her slowly, like she was a deer he didn't want to scare off. But she didn't feel like the doe. She wasn't even the hunter. She was something else. A spider, perhaps, letting him tangle himself in her.

In the morning she pretended to be asleep again, and he pressed a kiss on her naked shoulder before leaving. She thought that he knew what she was doing, and she wondered if he was genuinely giving her time and space or if he was perhaps a little more clueless than she thought.

The next day, after she'd set fire to the heaping pile of mulch, she grinned at the sound of his giant truck ambling down the hill. Her heart gave a tiny flutter when he stepped out of it, jean shirt open over a tight white T-shirt. She pulled him onto the grass and they fucked right there on the side of the hill. Every day he arrived a little earlier, always bringing food. Drinks. A crate of used books to keep her entertained, even if she didn't want stories or music or movies. She wanted him and silence.

Eventually, he'd stay completely, and she couldn't pretend to be asleep in the morning. He'd wake up and make coffee and start her chores. They'd bathe in the freezing cold lake and warm up in her shed. When he'd suggest that she could stay at his house, that his parents would love her, she'd go quiet again.

Marimar knew she needed to end things with Chris. That she hadn't healed enough yet to give him what he needed. That she didn't even consider what *she* wanted. But he was beautiful and charming, and he felt good inside her.

"Is this a family thing?" he finally asked. They'd brought a blanket out to the clearing near the orchard. The trees looked like witch claws coming out of the dirt, but Chris said they looked more like chicken feet. He made a fire and then they lay side by side to watch a meteor shower. He propped himself on his elbow and traced the collar of her sweater, careful not to touch the flower bud at the base of her throat.

"Sort of," Marimar said. The fire crackled

and she rested her head on his bare shoulder. He had a leopard tattoo on his side. It was shoddy work and faded.

"Some of my cousins have webbed feet," he said. "And I have the same mole on my belly button that every one of my brothers and sisters have. You should meet them one day."

"This one?" she asked, dragging her finger around the beauty mark. He shut his eyes and lost himself to the sensation of her on his abdomen, his erection, his entire being. She was going to run out of excuses to not drive twenty minutes to meet his family, who sent her food and socks to make sure she was warm in that little shed of hers. The Sandovals were Mexican before there was an America and new borders to modify their identity as Mexican American. Like her, they didn't speak Spanish either. But there was something warm and familiar. Familiar enough that she should have wanted what Chris was offering her.

She would have given in, too, if she hadn't scared herself that night when she was astride him, his fingers digging into her hips harder than he'd ever done before, so hard she felt the indentations they'd leave. She reeled her head back and looked at the shower of stars, felt his hands wrap around her throat. The sweet, bright pain of it unraveled something within her, and when she opened her eyes Chris was screaming and pulling out of her. Thick vines of ivy had wrapped around his ankles and up around his muscular calves, all the way to his inner thighs and his perineum. Needles prickled at her throat and when she touched the bud, she felt it opening.

"What the fuck?" Chris breathed hard and scrambled for his pocketknife on the floor to cut the vines off. The skin was instantly red, and yellow pustules bloomed where the poison leaves had touched him.

She drove him to the hospital with him lying on his belly in the bed of his truck because he was too tall and wouldn't fit anywhere else and she couldn't stop crying as several people had to get him on a gurney. Without having to ask, he lied and told the doctor he was clearing a patch in the valley, even though no one gardened in the middle of the night while naked. And if they did, it certainly wouldn't have been the pint of vanilla ice cream that was Christian Sandoval. The doctor cocked his brow at Marimar, mouth still swollen from kissing him. He wasn't a complete idiot, but it was like he'd decided he didn't want to know the truth when a Montoya was involved.

Chris got a shot and some cream and slept in his own house after dropping Marimar off.

She called Rey right away. "Has anything weird happened?"

"Define weird."

She hesitated, shoving a log into her stove. Then she told him everything. Marimar hadn't known what to expect from Rey. A mild joke. Gratitude for having brought Chris into her life in the first place. Anything but unadulterated laughter. She'd watched cartoon witches laugh with less glee.

"Oh, Mari," he mused.

"Fuck you."

"I'm serious, you have mildly rough hetero sex, and you try to kill the guy."

"I hate you."

"You love me. And miss me. Though I'm glad I'm not there for your sexcapades." She heard him sigh. A clatter like he dropped brushes or something. "Do you need me to come out there?"

"Where are you?"

"Enrolled in an art class at Hunter. I hate the teachers, but I'll give it a shot."

"No, I'll be fine. Just let me know if anything weird happens to you."

"My sex is always weird, Marimar."

"Goodbye," she said and fell into a deep,

dreamless sleep. The bud at her throat shut once again.

Six days later, Chris showed up again, even though it clearly pained him to get out of his truck. She took one look at his crooked smile, pressed her hand against his chest. He was ready to forgive her, to turn the occurrence into a funny, strange story he might tell at a bar one day. She didn't want that, she'd decided. Before he said anything, she ended it, and he left quietly and softly. His sad smile was imprinted in her, like the heat of the kiss he left on her shoulder every morning for a month and day.

She watched him disappear up the hill and turn onto the road. Orquídea had warned her to not make the same mistakes. To love. But she'd also warned her to protect her magic. How could she do both, if letting Chris near her meant unraveling a part of herself she wasn't ready to face? Maybe not ever.

She stood at the bottom of the hill so long she was startled by the first flurries of snow dotting her cheeks where her tears should have been. But she didn't cry for Christian Sandoval. She smelled winter approaching and got to work instead.

Marimar found an axe and hacked up the

dead trees for firewood. Stacked the logs neatly in the corner of her shed. She left the window open to air out the scent of leather and sandalwood that Chris had left behind. She hung her sheets in a line, and they smelled like unseasonable lavender that had sprung up in the valley over the last month.

When it was so quiet that she couldn't bear her own thoughts, so quiet not even Gabo doled out a song, Marimar tried to talk to the ceiba tree that used to be her grandmother. She pressed her palms against the bark. She begged, first in quiet whispers.

"Please, what am I supposed to do?"

Then in screams. "Tell me what it all means! What am I supposed to do with a fucking *flower* growing out of my throat?"

When her questions continued to go unanswered, Marimar started talking to her instead. Confessing things she never would have as a girl. Sneaking out with Rey and going into town to watch movies with the other kids. Drinking Orquídea's liquor stash in junior high. It occurred to Marimar that Orquídea must have known all of those things and more. She talked to a tree because it was easier than calling one of the Montoyas. And saying what? Nothing has changed. *Some progress on the house. I think*

I broke a good man's heart. Our magic hurt him.

She waited for the miraculous things that Orquídea had once made happen — calling down the rain. A house appearing where there hadn't been one before. Summoning spirits. But Marimar was not Orquídea Divina. She was just alone.

One day, Marimar found a pocketknife on the floor made of steel and some sort of animal bone. Chris's knife, the one he'd used that night. She used it to try and cut off the flower at her throat, but she passed out from the pain. When she woke up, her sheets were covered in blood and the stem that protruded from her flesh grew a lone green thorn instead.

She would not try this again for a while.

When the first heavy snow fell in Four Rivers, the leaves of the ceiba tree never turned. They remained a strange sharp green as snow fell all around them. Eventually, Marimar gave up talking to Orquídea, and there was nothing she could do on the property until spring. She felt like she had slowly transformed into a bear, ready for hibernation. All the grief she hadn't let herself feel when her mother and aunt died washed over her threefold. Even though she hadn't lost Rey, she missed him. She even missed Tatinelly, though they had never been as close. The hollow shape within her heart seemed to grow. That wasn't the point of having come back here. That wasn't the point of having stayed. Marimar was like the earth covered by layers of ice and snow. She needed rest. She needed to heal.

She slept for six months.

During her time under, she dreamed. Most of the time she was floating in outer space with the stars. She could see her mother but at a distance, so far away. Then she would just fade. Once, only once, she heard an echo, faint, but there. "Find me."

When she woke up, it was spring. The earth around her was green. Wild. Orquidea's tree had grown white cotton-like flowers. She was ready. The valley was ready.

Marimar hired a local contractor, but she insisted on carrying wooden planks and hammering nails along with them. It would take seven years to build her new house, because something always stopped construction. Once, it rained for so long the valley flooded. Marimar slept in her tent at the top of the hill until the water receded. Then there were electrical failures. Several townsfolk had petitioned to see evidence that Marimar owned the deed to the land. It was five more months before she was cleared to put in a work order, and when she did, the dragonflies and grasshoppers of the valley descended on the construction workers. They left of their own accord, and the workers that followed discovered several code violations and they had to redo it all anyway. One day, that entire team quit on account of ghosts and the zombie rooster that wouldn't stop crowing. When the foundation was finally solidly built, Marimar decided to finish the rest herself. It would be hers, through and through. Her house was positioned right beside Orquídea's tree. The ceiba that did not belong but had made a home there regardless.

Marimar kept moving. She enrolled in community college, but couldn't quite find something to love, something that made her feel settled. Still, she went to classes and graduated. She'd see Chris at the farmer's market or the hardware store, and he'd give a short wave before putting distance between them. He had met a nice girl, a baker, and they'd go on to have three kids, each named after famous baseball players. But before that, she noticed a new tattoo on the inside of his wrist. A twist of ivy.

Then, Marimar discovered she was good at something. Making things grow. She fixed the greenhouse. Even if she couldn't figure out how to get her own flower bud to bloom, she had a green thumb. Those seeds that had survived the fire were still in their bottles. Roses. Orchids. Tulips. Geraniums. Carnations. Hyacinths. Foxglove. Baby's breath. Daisies. Sunflowers. She made a garden of her own. She sold her flowers at the farmer's market and more people knew her as Montoya than Marimar. She was the only one in Four Rivers, after all.

She called her family once a week, then once a month, then every other couple of months. She found that, after months of silence, she liked being alone too much. For a while she was okay with that. Silvia and the twins visited once. They'd never planted the seeds Orquídea had given them and chose to do it on the third anniversary of her transformation. Everyone visited once or twice, but never together. Never staying more than a couple of days or so. Enrique never came.

Seven years after the fire, Marimar sat down to have her eggs and black coffee for breakfast. Her rosebud still hadn't bloomed, but her house was complete.

On what should have been another morning, the phone rang. The voice on the other line came rushed, urgent, weary.

"Tati, I can't — slow down."

"I'm sorry," Tatinelly said. "It's going to sound crazy."

Marimar bit the side of her thumb. She looked out the window at her grandmother's branches moving in the breeze. She absently pressed the pad of her thumb against the thorn on her flower bud.

"Try me."

"I think someone is following us." Tati made a strangled sound. "I shouldn't even be saying this on the phone. Do you think I should?"

"Start over. What makes you think that someone is following you?"

"Mike thinks I'm being crazy but there are times I see this man standing at the end of our block. When I go point him out, he's gone. But Rhiannon sees him too. She says that he said hi to her once. I don't know. I've just been thinking lately about how everything happened all those years ago. And we just left you, Marimar. We just left and we should have stayed and every time I wanted to call you I'd get scared that you were mad. Are you mad at me?"

"I'm not mad at you," Marimar said, trying her best to sound gentle. "Have you called the police?"

Tati's laugh verged on hysterical. "They agree with Mike. I explained to them about

257

how Mamá Orquídea said we needed to protect — you know — but they looked at me like I should be institutionalized. I told Mike to tell them I'm not lying, but he said he can't remember *that day* because he passed out before the fire. He thinks he dreamed it. I just — Can we come visit? Please? Please, Marimar."

"Of course, you can come here," Marimar said. "Stay as long as you need."

Marimar took a sip of her coffee and let out a slow breath. She tried to go through her catalog of memories. Remembered calling Rey all those years ago and asking if anything weird had happened to him. For the Montoyas, weird was their normal. She couldn't think of anything that stood out, but if she was honest with herself, she'd stopped searching. She didn't care about unearthing Orquídea's past, and she didn't care to know who her birth father was, and she just wanted to tend to her flowers and work on maintaining the valley. She'd gotten what she'd asked for, mostly. Peace. Home.

Something was coming that was going to disrupt that. She felt it in the chill of the air. The hard breeze slammed the shutters closed. Gabo screeched louder than he'd done in ages. The phone rang again.

"Tati?" she answered.

A sound broke through, but it wasn't Tati-nelly. It was white noise, the crackle of a dead radio station, a voice she'd heard once in her dream during her hibernation, and he said, "Open the door, Marimar."

15

THE KING OF THE EARTH

The first lie Rey told himself upon returning to New York City was that he was only
doing this to keep his promise to Orquídea.
You can't lie to the dead. Although Marimar insisted that Orquídea wasn't *dead*
dead. She was still gone, and they were still
fucked.

On his first day of classes, people had
stared. For once, it was nice not to wear a
sensible blazer or colors that made him look
like he'd fade into the muted shades of a
mountain side. It was winter and he'd opted
for cashmere sweaters in emerald green, the
bloody red of pomegranates ripped in half.
He didn't want to be one of those New
Yorkers who always wore black, mostly
because he wasn't a New Yorker. He was
from Four Rivers, the product of women
who were transmutable. First mortal, then
divine.

Rey had told Marimar that he hated his

teachers. Each one possessed an air of boredom. They walked around the studio checking in on his progress. Too slow. Too sloppy. Was that supposed to be modernism? He didn't understand terms or categories. He was the oldest one in each of his classes filled with unkempt freshmen who smelled of marijuana and three-day-old arm pits. Once, while eating slices of pizza in the glass walkways that bridged the different buildings of Hunter College, one of the girls from his class had sat beside him. Her hair was blonde at the bottom and dark at the roots from excess oil.

"Can I touch it?" she asked.

He'd nearly choked on his pizza. "Pardon?"

"The flower." She looked at him as if he should have known. "Is it real?"

"It's real, and no, you can't."

She rolled her eyes and got to her feet like a child who'd been denied something. As he went to take another bite of his pizza, she grabbed his wrist. Tugged on a petal. He remembered the time his mother had dragged him out of school by his ear for fighting. Only it was a thousand times worse. He'd never had a piece of himself ripped out so violently.

When he screamed and people started

looking, she let go. He lay on the ground for half an hour before someone checked on him, and another half an hour before one of the security guards told him he was bleeding on the floor.

He hadn't even gotten to finish his pizza.

Hence, Rey hated going to art classes at Hunter College. He didn't see the girl in his class anymore, but he imagined what he'd say if he did. He couldn't very well punch a girl, even if she'd assaulted him. He couldn't call the police or explain his rose.

Orquídea's voice came to him in those moments. *Protect your magic.*

Had his grandmother really been envisioning a dirty art student when she uttered those final words?

Ever since then, Rey was more careful. He made do with those ungodly long-sleeve sweaters with the holes in the sleeve. He felt like an emo kid who'd gotten lost on the way to a My Chemical Romance music video. Or a housewife from Manhattan putting on athleisure wear. The intersection of that particular clothing item did not make Rey feel settled, but it was a necessary precaution.

He told himself he could drop out. He already had a degree. He'd already humored his grandmother. But there was a moment when he stood at his easel, when he put on his headphones, when he rolled up his sleeves, when he was alone in the studio — well, it didn't all suck.

He didn't stop painting. Couldn't stop. Part of him was chasing the high he'd felt that first time when he'd locked himself in his room and worked on the portrait of Orquídea as a young girl. He was stubborn, kept to himself, and didn't listen to his professors. He barely had a 3.0 average.

But during the end of the semester student showcase, when anyone walked past his paintings, they stopped. They looked. Some even wept. That attention was too much. Rey had been searching for a reprieve from the crowded show, and made the mistake of winding up in a small corner. He didn't notice that someone had followed him, and he didn't notice the guy block him in until it was too late. The stranger was in his early twenties, broad chested, and taller than Rey. His cheeks were pink from the box wine being served.

"I've been looking at you all night," the stranger said, so close Rey smelled the sour milk breath on him.

"Good for you," Rey said and did the only thing he could. He tried to push past him.

The stranger pressed Rey against the wall with the spread of his forearm. Rey's mouth went dry, muscles soft as jelly. He'd been in so many fights, clawed his way out of groups of boys who tried to get him to *man up.* He thought of his father teaching him how to punch, how to take a hit and let it roll off so you could get away. But that was all before.

The stranger traced Rey's arm and brushed a thumb across the soft rose petals. Rey thought of how Marimar said that poison ivy had attacked her boyfriend when he got a little passionate with her. He'd laughed but here, as panic paralyzed the drop of common sense he usually had, he was mad. Mad that he was surrounded by marble and glass and cement instead of dirt and grass and hills.

His attacker's grip tightened and this time, he cried out. Rey felt the warm trickle of blood before he saw it. A dozen thorns, each one half an inch long, had protruded from his skin.

"What's wrong with you, freak?" the drunk stranger yelled, staring at the blood running out of his palms from perfect tiny punctures.

"What's going on here?" someone shouted. Professor Something, Rey realized.

The attacker shoved his bloody hand in his pocket. "Just congratulating Rey on a good show."

"Is that right?" the professor asked Rey, who cradled his flowered hand against his chest.

He nodded. Again, who would believe him?

The stranger scurried off, but the professor remained. He was of average height and build. A full head of hair gone completely silver and forget-me-not blue eyes. No, hyacinth blue. Pretty fucking flower blue. Despite his coloring, his face was young. He wore an emerald blazer and a tiepin with a garnet on it, and jeans to throw off his wealth. He kept his distance, but homed his gaze on Rey, whose heart was a sledgehammer against his ribs.

"Can I call you a cab?"

At that, Rey laughed. He felt like a diffused time bomb as he said, "Actually, I prefer to be called Rey. Professor —"

"Edward Knight."

Edward Knight, an art critic who doubled as a professor, took Rey under his wing and into his bed.

Rey, with his beautiful smile and honey brown eyes. The body he'd carved like

Michelangelo did David. Eddie had swept into Rey's life the night of the party and hadn't left his side since. Rey gave art school one last semester, but his heart told him it wasn't for him. While Eddie was never Rey's teacher, he made time to stop by Rey's apartment every day and see his progress.

Sometimes he had nothing to say, simply sat on a chair and watched Rey work. Stroke by stroke until the painting was finished.

"Why do you look so shocked?" Rey asked one night.

"Not shocked. Fascinated."

"Because of my rose?"

"Because you don't hesitate. From the first moment your brush touches canvas, you don't stop. You barely even eat. It's like you're —"

"I'm inspired," Rey interrupted, because he didn't like the word *possessed*.

Rey worked on what he called weird shit, but Eddie preferred to call surrealism, even though surrealism was passé now. Rey didn't know the names of famous artists or movements. He used his art history text-books as palettes if his palette paper ran out. When Eddie took him to a real gallery show, Rey mostly smiled and drank champagne while all of Eddie's friends spoke in rapid-fire French. He was surprised to find that none of them touched him, not even a casual tap on the shoulder. It almost felt like they'd been warned. That Eddie was his shield against the art scene that felt so foreign. After all, no matter how much schooling he'd had, his degree, how long he'd lived in New York City, when he was in the escargot-filled belly of art critics, Rey still felt like a townie from the middle of nowhere.

Slowly, he learned the right things to say. The right clothes to wear. He learned that people didn't always want to talk to you, they wanted to simply be near you, just in case you were the next big thing. He'd become a story people might tell at Labor Day barbecues or happy hour. "Oh Reymundo Montoya? I was at his very first show. And yes, *it's* real."

Eddie insisted that everyone call him Reymundo. Rey was too sweet, too causal. Why be Rey? Something that meant king, when his mother had intended for him to be the king of the earth. Why be less when he was so much more?

Over the years Rey kept up with Marimar. He kept encouraging her to snatch up an eligible cowboy from town, but she was happy in her garden, still hibernating her heart though winter was long gone. The rest of the Montoyas, at least, were thriving. Caleb Jr. had come to the city for a partnership with some flashy designer, and Rey'd dropped thousands of Eddie's money at New York Dolls on Murray Street just to show his uncle a good time. They'd visited Florecida in Key West and taken her on a booze cruise where she met her second husband. Eddie had even sat with Rey in the rain at the Jones Beach concert arena just to watch Juan Luis and Gastón be the opening act of a new boy band.

Knowing his family was safe, that he'd worried for nothing, he kept painting. He rolled his eyes at Marimar when she called him a sugar baby. She didn't know how much Eddie protected him from the vultures of their world. Sometimes he worried that people were there to want him, to be close to the rose on his wrist, which he'd stopped hiding. That was when he locked himself away and didn't emerge until he'd had a new batch of portraits. Florecida watching the sunset at the furthest most point of the United States. Marimar in her poison garden. Rhiannon with her pretty flower on her forehead, always changing.

A buyer once asked him, "Where did these come from?"

She pointed to the flowers growing out of Marimar's throat and Rhiannon's brow. She meant the one on his hand. She meant to ask how real he was, how authentic he was down to his bones.

"It's a family curse," he said, and he thought he meant it as a lie, but sometimes he wasn't certain. But if people were going to stare and ask and want to touch, he might as well put on a show.

At that same show, a young woman buying art for some rich Brit approached Rey. She knew to stay at least six paces away, to keep her arms at her sides where Rey could see them. Eddie had done his job training the world on how to approach him, and sometimes, Rey was bitter he could not do it himself.

"One million dollars," she said.

Rey was confused. He was standing in front of his favorite painting of Marimar. She was looking up at the night sky and stars were falling. The hummingbird he drew was so lifelike, if you moved, the creature seemed to flit back and forth. The most his paintings had sold for were thirty thousand, but Eddie had assured him his value would only increase. "I'm sorry, there must be a mistake."

The young woman was dressed in all jagged black. She looked around and carefully took another step closer. "I'm buying for a very reclusive client."

"Is that why he's not here?"

"My name is Finola Doyle. I've attempted to get a hold of your manager, but alas." She handed Rey a card made of the thickest cardstock. It had a coat of arms with a knight and heraldic lions. "Like I said. The offer is one million."

Rey looked around at the noisy room, the clusters of people gathered around his pieces. He'd spent sleepless, hungry nights making them. "For the painting?"

"For you." She blushed.

Rey let loose a soft chuckle. He touched the card in his hands, looked at Eddie on the other end of the room. His silver knight.

Rey did the only thing he could do. He went home, because if he stayed another minute longer, he'd be tempted to say yes.

People weren't happy just looking at his art. No, they wanted to look at him. To rip off pieces and take them home. The bigger his profile became, the more people wanted to cut him open, down to the bone. He could never give a satisfactory answer to the flower on his hand. Was it a modification, the way some people split their tongues to hiss like snakes or the way some people surgically point their ears to make them look elf-like or the way people got diamonds embedded into their skin?

Though it was exhausting, after a while, being touched and tugged at like he was a doll became something he was used to, as long as they bought something. Even Eddie kept him like a toy.

Rey went out less. Didn't return calls. Every moment outside of his studio felt like a moment he was wasting. Creating something out of nothing came at a cost. Seven years after the fire he could still remember his grandmother telling him that. There was a cost. A price. Why did some people have to pay a price and others didn't?

Take Eddie. Eddie was the kind of rich that came with a Connecticut *and* a Hamptons vacation house. Fuck-you money that had paid for art school and years in Eastern Europe, where he went to find himself even though he hadn't been lost in the first place. He'd stumbled into being an art teacher because he liked colors and judging other people, mostly. Eddie's whole life, when he recounted it to Rey, felt like a fever dream. The kind he'd only ever seen in Baz Luhrmann movies. What was Eddie's cost other than a beautiful young lover he could put on display and then take home and fuck?

Rey didn't like thinking that way, but one day, that carousel of thoughts set in and never stopped. On top of that, he couldn't shake the feeling that someone was watching him. It started in his new apartment, a brownstone he'd bought in Harlem. He stood in front of the window and thought there was a shape on the other side. His room was on the third floor and so there shouldn't have been anyone. He convinced himself that he was looking at his reflection, but the shape was not his own. It was a taller man, with long hair. He couldn't make out much, just the glare of the sun hitting the glass.

Rey stumbled back, his heart hammering in his chest. The memory of ghosts, of his mother's disembodied spirit, replaced any thought of his encounter.

Eddie came up behind him, resting a hand on either side of his muscular arms as if Rey was just having another moment of creative doubt. "What's wrong?"

"Nothing. Working too long."

Eddie kissed Rey's naked shoulder. "Come to bed, then."

"It's daylight and I have to work."

"You have been nonstop since I met you, baby. Take a break. What's the worst that could happen?"

Rey laughed, but didn't answer.

The next couple of nights, it happened again. The shape was at the window, in the puddle on his walk to clear his head, in the mirror. He never saw a face and sometimes not even a body. Once, the figure got so close that Rey could see glowing eyes staring back at him.

He called Marimar, but she didn't answer. He convinced himself that his mind was rebelling from not sleeping, too many cigarettes, and copious amounts of wine. What was she going to do anyway, hundreds of miles away as she was?

He focused on painting instead. But even in his paintings, he began to capture the figure that haunted him — a man who was like the negative of a roll of film. All of his insides filled in with the colors of a supernova. Rey painted another, and that time, it was black paint with a human-shaped prism at the center. Another, and it was a violent flash of light gutting the night sky.

These were not his usual neosurrealist paintings in saturated colors. These were not going to impress his agent. Although, if the universe had a sense of humor, he'd probably sell these for a million dollars.

Then he could have his own fuck-you money.

When he showed them to Eddie, all he'd said was, "Interesting direction," in a way that made it seem he was both confused and a little scared.

How could Rey explain that he wasn't in control of his own hands? He wouldn't tell his own boyfriend, but some nights he blacked out. When he would wake, three days had passed, and the painting was finished. He touched the rose on his hand and remembered his grandmother's words. *Paint me another.* He'd been painting for the last seven years, so why was this happening to him now?

He needed to get out of the house. The air was unseasonably cold, but he zipped up a hoodie and jammed his earbuds in. Music and audiobooks helped block the outside world. The cold humid air seeped into his clothes and into his bones as he trekked from 125th and Fifth Avenue, and straight down Central Park. He liked to catch the sunset over the reservoir.

But when he went to turn on Ninety-Second Street, the tall figure he'd seen at his window was standing at the corner. Rey broke into a run, shoving aside runners and tourists, and kicking up gravel. He sprinted with the calm murky water to his left and shadows taking up his peripherals. Where could he run to? *Four Rivers,* he thought, but even as he conjured the words, he opened his mouth to laugh and only a scream came out. Rey glanced back and saw the prism of light at the heart of the shadow, then leaped out of the running track to cut to the West Side. His thighs burned and the soles of his sneakers began to smoke. He blacked out again and when he opened his eyes, he was in the middle of traffic with cars honking incessantly. A police officer on horseback galloped in his direction. Rey couldn't hear anything other than sirens and blaring horns. The officer lost control of his horse and the creature bucked, kicking Rey in the chest.

Rey woke up in the hospital for the first time in his life. He touched his rose, fearing that they'd done something to it. Fearing that if it was gone, he would also lose his art, and Eddie, and the nameless faces who wanted — needed him.

But it was still there.

Eddie was frantic at his bedside. His hair looked grayer than silver as he alternated between, "What were you thinking?" and "I'm going to call my therapist. He can prescribe you the good stuff," and "Baby, are you sure you're okay?"

"I swear, I don't remember how I got there," he said, and he meant it.

Eddie sighed deeply. "Well, I don't know your password and your phone has been blowing up for the last few hours."

Rey felt a pang of guilt in his gut. There were twenty-three missed calls from Marimar, all in quick succession. The cold spread from the center of his chest outward as he drew up the phone to his ear. Even just the sound of her voice brought him to tears.

"Hey, Tatinelly has a stalker and she's driving over here with Mike and Rhiannon. I know! You should stop being a celebrated artist and come to the sticks to hang out with your cousins. Love you, loser."

Relief flooded him. She was fine. They were fine. He played the next message.

"Uhm . . . Tío Félix is dead." He heard the static silence as she searched for something. "Car crash. I'll call you back."

"Rey — Tía Florecida is gone," the next one said. That time her voice cracked. "She drowned in her bathtub. Fell asleep. Penny found her. I'm trying to get in touch with her. Juan Luis — that's him on the other line."

Rey quickly pressed the button for the

next message. He had to hear her voice. He clung to it even as Eddie tried to insert himself, asking more and more questions.

"Penny," Marimar said, so softly he had to replay the message again and again just to be sure he understood.

Another call. "Tatinelly just got here."

Then another. "Please tell me you're not picking up because you're a famous dick and not because something happened. Okay."

And finally, just, "Rey."

He was not okay. He was not going to be okay. He checked the time stamp of each message and they were all today. All while he'd been ignoring his phone and had somehow wound up in the middle of a street running away from some *thing.* Is that what Orquídea had warned them about? Was it finally here?

"Wait, where are you going?" Eddie asked. When he was worried, the wrinkles around his eyes and lips became more pronounced. He hovered as Rey quietly got dressed and then barricaded the door with his own body. "Rey, talk to me."

"I can't explain. I have to go home." He meant a different home, of course.

Eddie went home to their Harlem brownstone, but he wouldn't find his Reymundo there. Rey went straight to the airport and kept going, couldn't stop moving until he was back in Four Rivers, because he wasn't sure what would happen to him if he stopped.

16
MUSINGS OF A FAIRY CHILD

Mike Sullivan remembered the first time he'd set foot in Four Rivers. He didn't want to offend Tatinelly, but he hadn't understood why her family had made such a commotion that the whole place had caught on fire. The house, though impressive, had been in need of a renovation, stat. The fire was a blessing in disguise, if anyone asked him. No one did.

Families were not supposed to be dysfunctional the way the Montoyas were. Thankfully, their little unit was perfect. Tatinelly, Rhiri, and himself. Though he preferred that they spend holidays just the three of them, they alternated years visiting his parents and hers in Texas. He didn't think he could handle another full-blown family reunion. But Tatinelly had been stressed all week, what with the news making her feel like she was being followed. He'd told her not to watch it before bed, but she insisted. They lived in the most secure neighborhood in Anywhere, USA. There was no possible way she was being followed.

Still, there was a snowstorm blowing in on the Pacific Northwest, and he had a few vacation days he wanted to spend with his best girls. Four Rivers wouldn't have been his first choice. In fact, he'd intended on driving right past Four Rivers to the Gulf Coast for better weather, but then they got those terrible calls.

At the sight of the tree, Mike felt a deep shudder in his bones. How could a person have become a tree? Even though he'd seen it with his own two eyes, part of him didn't want to believe it had happened. He'd said he was asleep, but he lied. He had to lie. How could he go on record saying that he'd seen what he saw? It wasn't natural. The Montoyas could keep their crazy. At least now that Orquídea had passed, rest in peace, the whole family could move on from their myths and superstitions.

But then he looked at Rhiannon in the rearview mirror, nearly bouncing out of her seat as their pink Beetle crested the engine-killing hill. She should know her family, no matter how odd and off-putting Mike found them. Rhiannon was perfect. He'd even come to love the small pink rose growing out of the center of her forehead. She got her sweetheart shaped face and high cheek-bones from her mother. Truth be told, the only part that she got from her father was her hair's wheat-brown shade, when he'd had hair. After the fire, he'd woken up with it ashen. Then, a few days later, every single strand had fallen off, like a tree gone barren after a good howling wind.

Rhiannon pointed out the window and said, "It's her! It's Mamá!"

Tatinelly smiled, though every part of her hurt. They didn't understand what caused her pain. When she went to the doctor, they told her she was well. She was imagining things. But when she moved, she felt like she was made out of rusted and forgotten metal parts. As if health issues weren't bad enough, Tatinelly claimed to have her very own stalker. No one seemed to believe that either. But now that they were in Four Rivers, with the wildflower-scented air, she felt settled. She wished they'd come during a happier time. She wished she'd been able to call her daddy earlier in the day. Maybe she would have made him late for work and he wouldn't have gotten clipped by that truck. Tears ran down her cheeks again, but the cool breeze kissed them away.

She reached out a hand to Rhiannon.

"Yes, baby girl. That's Mamá Orquídea."

Rhiannon's voice was like a bell chime trilling in the wind. Dragonflies flitted into the car, nudging at her rose, walking across her shoulders, nesting in the curls of her hair like she was a fairy changeling coming home.

The Sullivans parked outside of the house where Reymundo and Marimar were waiting on the porch. The tree beside it cast a long shadow. When they parked, the dragonflies left them for the tall grass in the hills.

"It's good to see you," Tatinelly said, hugging her cousins tightly. She regained some of her strength, as if Reymundo were giving her some of his and Marimar was holding her up.

There was no time to regret how little they'd seen of each other over the years. How unfortunate the circumstances were. Rhiannon leaped from the car. Her dress was a sharp green, the color of new leaves, the color of the tight rosebud at Marimar's clavicle that had never blossomed.

Marimar couldn't help but laugh as the girl hugged her legs. She spoke at about a thousand words per minute. Her favorite color was leaf-green, and she was in the second grade. Her best subjects were science and reading. Her favorite stories were the fairy tales her mother liked to make up, stories about magic hills and river monsters and a place that neither of them had ever been to. She was afraid of the dark, but only when she was alone. She wished that she was tall enough to touch the flowers on the big tree. She could hear the tree crying. Could any of *them* hear the tree? Was there someone inside of it?

"You can *hear* the tree?" Rey asked, but his clipped tone wasn't disbelief. It bordered on jealousy. "We never heard anything and we *cleaned up* this mess."

Mike ruffled his daughter's head. "She thinks all the trees talk to her. Such an imagination."

Rey feigned a smile. "Such."

But Rhiannon had already lost interest in her cousins. She pointed at the blue rooster and asked, "Mommy, what is that rooster doing?"

"Gabo is laying an egg, honey."

"Actually his name is Jameson now," Marimar said.

Rhiannon cocked her head up at Orquídea's tree, waited as if listening, and giggled. "Mamá Orquídea doesn't like that you changed his name."

Marimar blanched. "What?"

"Why did you rename Gabo?" Rey asked.

283

Marimar shrugged defensively. "He drank a whole bottle of Jameson and croaked. I buried him, even, but there he was the next day, roosting in Orquídea's roots."

"Does he have nine lives? Like a cat?" Rhiannon asked.

"Yes, honey," Tatinelly said, because the chances were highly likely. "He is on his fourth or fifth resurrection."

"I'm going to regret asking this," Mike said, shoving his hands in his pockets. He was sweating despite the cool breeze. "But how is that rooster laying an egg?"

"Yeah, after the fire, Jameson turned completely blue and started laying eggs," Marimar said. "I don't have to buy eggs anymore though. The yolks are green, but you get used to it."

"Do you, though?" Mike laughed nervously, and scratched a dry patch on his scalp.

"Come inside," Marimar offered. "I called everyone and they should be arriving soon."

As the Sullivans followed her inside the house, Mike noted that Marimar looked the same as she had when she was nineteen. Though she had traded her ripped jeans for cotton dresses that made her look like a wind spirit among the tall grass, she still wore her heavy leather boots, which she took off at the front door. Reymundo was different, though. More muscular, beautiful in a way that made Mike stare, pink cheeked and embarrassed.

Marimar brought out coffee for everyone in the new sitting room. Everything about the house felt new. New trim. New paint. New wallpaper. There were some things that had survived the fire, but barely. Records and photographs Marimar had framed across an entire wall. Tatinelly smiled at the painting that hung over the fireplace, a scorch mark on the bottom half. She thought that the stain resembled the face of a man, but perhaps it was like those shrink inkblots. She poured fat sugar cubes into her coffee and milk that tasted thick and fresh. The coffee itself was different. She shouldn't have expected Orquídea's smells and flavors when Orquídea was not here.

"I'm sorry about your dad," Reymundo said, pouring bourbon into his coffee.

"I'm sorry about everyone," Tatinelly lamented. "My dad's will says he wants to be cremated and scattered in the river where Orquídea went fishing as a little girl."

Marimar frowned, confused. "I remember one Thanksgiving when your dad said fishing was the reason grandma was so mean."

"It's what he wanted." Tatinelly chuckled.

She was at ease and the pain in her bones dampened. So much so that she wondered if her sudden aches had been caused by her fear and anxiety. By being so tense that her body revolted against her. "What about Tía Florecida and Penny?"

"They'll be buried here in the family cemetery," Marimar explained.

Tatinelly nodded. She turned to the sharp scream coming from the open window. Rhiannon ran across the wild grass chasing Jameson and the dragonflies.

"I'll go keep her company," Mike announced, and excused himself, leaving his empty, untouched cup behind.

Tatinelly watched him leave, accepting the caress of his hand as he walked past. Then her face turned serious, conspiratorial as she hooked her finger in the direction of her cousins and reeled them in. "What are we going to do?"

"I don't know," Marimar said, biting the red skin of her thumbnail.

"Mike doesn't believe me. But I've seen a man following me."

"We believe you," Rey said, sipping from his cup, etched in gold and dotted with a moon and stars. "I've seen him. The figure. I'm not sure what it is."

"Did he — I don't know — shine?" Tatinelly let go of an anxious breath.

Rey nodded. How could that figure be at two opposite sides of the country at once? "What does it want?"

Marimar touched her flower bud absently. "The bargain Orquídea made. It's coming back for us."

"But what was it? How do we suppose we find out the details?" Rey asked. "We looked. You know we looked. A few pictures. A theater ticket. She couldn't say it when she was alive, how can she say it now that she's — transformed?"

"Have you tried to *talk* to Orquídea?" Tatinelly asked.

Marimar scoffed. "She's as responsive as she was when she was alive. Though apparently Rhiannon can hear her."

"So, you haven't seen anything?" Tatinelly asked.

"I heard a voice. It told me to open the door."

"What did you do?" Tati asked.

She laughed. "Washed the floors with lemon and salt. Made an altar. Felt ridiculous because nothing happened after that. For a minute I thought it was Enrique being a dickbag."

"I mean, he sort of is," Tati said. "But my mom said he had a run of bad luck. Fraud.

Bankruptcy. His wife took everything."

"He got *married*?" Marimar asked and was surprised that it bothered her not to know.

"Sure, we went to the wedding. She left him for some Saudi prince. He's living in Ernesta's basement after she took pity on him because he was sleeping in his car. He's still family. Anyway, I don't think he'd have the energy to prank-call, or the money to fly out and scare us. It's someone else."

Rey drained his glass, then poured another. "How do we do the opposite of find out?"

"Why would we do that?" Tatinelly asked.

"We're safe here," Rey said, clearing any lingering fear from his voice. "Besides, Marimar could use the company."

"I would?" She asked.

Rey winked. "Admit it, you missed us."

She did. She missed his laugh. Tatinelly's calming presence. Even the others. The twins signing and trying to burn everything in sight. The way Caleb Jr. and Ernesta competed with their knowledge of useless trivia.

"I don't know." Marimar crossed the room and stood at the window. Seven years. She'd lived a quiet, good life. Now three of her family members were dead and two were being followed around by a figure only the two of them could see. She didn't want this. She didn't ask for this. But neither had they. She thought of something happening to Rey and it made her feel weak. She'd worked too hard to have this life and she'd do everything she could to hang on to it.

"Orquídea always said that bad things keep on coming when you're a Montoya."

"I thought it was bad things come in threes," Rey said.

Tati traced the edges of her mug with her index finger, her eyes fixed to where her daughter ran around the valley like a wild thing, and said, "I've always accepted that I'm ordinary and plain, you know. But I can't ignore this feeling right here. It's never been there before. It's telling me that something is coming for us."

"Baby, you're anything but plain," Rey assured her. He almost wished he hadn't said anything, because she broke down crying.

Protect your magic. Those were their grandmother's collective parting words. Instructions. But how were they supposed to protect something they didn't know how to wield? How were they supposed to fight a man whose face they hadn't seen?

"I've tried talking to the tree," Marimar said. "And raising her ghost. Where else do you keep secrets?"

Rey shrugged. "What's the last place your family would think to look?"

"I keep them in a butter cookie tin and then I get sad when I open the tin and there aren't any cookies inside," Tati said.

Rey choked on his coffee and for a ludicrous, delirious moment, they had a good laugh. They laughed so hard it hurt, so hard it cycled back to tears and then crying again. Manic, cathartic sort of laughter.

When they were done, Marimar was drawn by Jameson's crow. Several cars were making the way down the packed-dirt road she'd had fixed. Marimar filled the kettle and then went to greet everyone.

There were two caskets — one for Florecida, one for Penny. A bereaved Aunt Reina carried the silver urn that held Félix's ashes. Marimar, Rey, Juan Luis, and Gastón dug the graves. In Four Rivers, which wasn't considered a town on its own anymore, most families kept their own plots on their land. Marimar hadn't considered that they'd have to add more bodies so soon.

The spring dirt was soft, giving way to their shovels. Marimar felt every strike shoot up her arms. Insects gathered, but it wasn't like before. They simply waited for their dinner. She hit roots, and realized that the hole wasn't big enough. She cursed, then apologized even though she wasn't sorry. She just knew she wasn't supposed to swear in front of the dead. She hit and hit the ground, trying to dig through the tangle of roots in the way. Rey hit a wall and slumped to the ground.

Then, a set of hands took the shovel from her. She followed the calloused hands all the way to Enrique's face. The wrinkles at the corners of his eyes looked like spiderwebs. His jade eyes were rimmed red. Dressed in a simple sweater and jeans that hung off his slender figure, he began to dig.

Marimar opened her mouth to protest. Didn't he remember what he'd said to her? What he'd said to all of them?

"Please, Marimar," he pleaded. "Let me."

And so, she let him dig, and dig, and dig.

When it was all over, they sat down to eat the catering she'd ordered from Uncle Nino's restaurant. Unlike the day of Orquídea's passing, there was no cooking, no music, no ghosts. The Montoyas wept in silence and listened to the sounds of the night.

Marimar could feel their fear. It vibrated from them and into her bones. She had to do something. She had to get answers.

"Mamá Orquídea is crying too," Rhiannon said after a while.

They were in the sitting room, which had once been the old parlor. The other Montoyas, who hadn't truly noticed the fairy child among them, stared curiously.

"You can hear her?" Enrique asked.

Rhiannon nodded. "She said you're supposed to play music to celebrate the dead. Rey knows the songs."

"Ask her if she has anything actually helpful to contribute," Rey said, slurring his words and ignoring his aunts glaring at him.

But Rhiannon relayed the comment through her faint connection to Orquídea's tree. To everyone it just looked like the fairy child was listening to a distant sound. "She's far away, I think. She said she can't help."

Rey shook his head, but said, "As expected."

"Wait!" Rhiannon chirped. "She said you forgot everything she told you."

Tatinelly pulled Rhiannon closer. "What did we forget?"

"The laurel leaves," Enrique answered, his voice like the scratch of a record. "You never replaced them."

Marimar walked out of the room and out the front porch. She took in her house, the labor she'd put into finishing it after so many starts and stops. She could see the silhouettes of her family members in the sitting room. She'd never been afraid of the dark before, not out here. But on that night, moonless, cold, with grave dirt still packed under her fingernails, Marimar Montoya was afraid.

She wondered if that was what her grandmother had felt during her trek from Guayaquil to Four Rivers. If fear was the key to every decision her grandmother had ever made. Why else put her children on a path that could lead to their deaths? Why keep them locked in a house they'd rebel from?

Marimar wasn't Orquídea, but she didn't have to be. The Montoyas were now hers to protect and it started with the house. She remembered that sensation she'd only truly felt once. That night with Christian Sandoval, when her flower bud had nearly opened. It had reacted to the perceived threat, even for a moment.

Her muscles still ached from digging the graves, and her heart hurt worse from the things she couldn't change. She pressed her palm against the front of the door. She'd painted it a deep teal, the color of peacock feathers. She'd bloodied her knuckles sanding the wood beneath. She felt the heat at the core of her palm, and when she withdrew her hand back, there it was. A gold laurel leaf etched into the grain.

Marimar knew what they had to do, even if it would be difficult. The wind howled as she stepped back in and shut the door behind her. In the sitting room, she looked up at Orquídea Divina Montoya, watching them from the half of the painting that had survived the fire. That little girl had grown up. She'd had five husbands and nine children. Even when they thought her heartless and cold, she had given them these gifts. Marimar touched the closed flower bud at her throat. The thorn it grew to fight back against her. There was only one place they could go to learn their grandmother's secrets.

■ ■ ■ ■

PART III
THE HUNT FOR
THE LIVING STAR

■ ■ ■ ■

17

THE LONDOÑO SPECTACULAR SPECTACULAR FEATURING WOLF GIRL, ORQUÍDEA DIVINA, AND THE LIVING STAR!

Bolívar Londoño III wanted Orquídea Montoya more than anything. But he would take his time. First, he needed to see if she was cut out for this life. The travel made the body weary. His own mother hadn't been suited for it. His father, Bolívar Londoño II had turned a backwater country magician act into something spectacular. The first Londoño Spectacular had been nothing but a con because the very first Bolívar Londoño had been a conman.

Born to a Galician mother and a mestizo father from Cartagena, that first Bolívar was orphaned after a fever swept through their town one particularly nasty rainy season. His father's estranged brother had taken charge of the finances after the funeral, abandoned Bolívar in a dingy little tavern called San Erasmo, then he boarded a ship to Santo Domingo and never looked back.

Bolívar had nothing but the clothes he was

wearing as his uncle had taken everything including their last names. Celia Londoño, the barmaid who found him searching for food in the alley, took him home. Gave him her name, because she'd never had a partner or children of her own. She raised Bolívar in the tavern, and when he got old enough, he was put to work scrubbing the floors and keeping the liquor bottles stocked. He had a knack for fighting and for card tricks, but soon enough the card tricks would have a knack for him.

After Celia died, he stopped working at San Erasmo and made his fortune cheating at cards. The older he got, and the more money he earned, the more he spent on women, liquor, and gambling. When he lost it all, because he always lost it all, he'd go back and make more. Bolívar would have been devastatingly handsome if he bathed, but there was still something about him. Reckless, easy to provoke into defending his honor, if he'd actually had any. The women who had the misfortune of loving him said there was something of Satan himself in that smile, the jeweled blue of his eyes. He was always half sober, and migrating across the city, coming hard and fast and ruinous as a hurricane.

Bolívar Londoño never married but fathered a boy, whom he trained in the art of cards. One night, after cheating a merchant out of a small fortune, and even later that night taking the merchant's wife to bed, Bolívar had a price on his head. A two-wagon traveling variety act called The Spectacular rolled through town the next day, and Bolívar and his boy left Cartagena with them as a father-and-son act who were so clever, so deft at sleight of hand, they were often accused of witchcraft. What the audiences didn't see was that Bolívar II was so practiced because if he wasn't, if he fumbled, the father would beat his son within an inch of his life. After the beatings, he'd have to go back out and perform.

Bolívar, the first one, could have been great. He had the seeds of potential, but there truly was something about him. Not the devilish grin. Not the misfortune or loss. There were some kind of men who could turn a gift into ruin if they weren't careful, and that was Bolívar. When the Spectacular returned to Cartagena years later, the city remembered Bolívar's crimes because, even when men don't remember, the earth does. He was found dead exactly where he was left orphaned all those years ago, only this time there was a dagger in his back. His son, who hadn't shed a tear, not a single one, for his father, left with the Spectacular, only to inherit it and rename it the Londoño Spectacular.

Bolívar II was just as handsome as his father. But where his father had cared only about his own needs, Bolívar II cared too much about everyone else's. He gave too much. Too much of his profit. Too much of himself. A happy drunk. Funny. Gullible. Soft. The Londoño Spectacular was his gift to the towns and cities they traveled to, and he would have rather earned the smile on a child's face than a dime. But all would change with *his* son.

Bolívar Londoño III trained his whole life to be a performer, watching his father's sideshow turn into a full-blown circus. But he'd always longed for more. He learned how to use alchemy in a way most people could only dream of. He discovered how to make those dreams transmutable, tangible. Under his reign, he transformed the show he inherited into the Londoño *Spectacular* Spectacular.

From a very early age, Agustina, the fortune-teller from Málaga, predicted his future. He'd live to be eighty-seven and father one son, but the Londoño line would end with him. Still, he'd be adored by audiences around the world. Just like his father, and his father before him, Bolívar III had the same devil in his smile. Sapphire eyes. A jawline that could have been engraved on a coin. He'd shatter hearts in every continent, and on several seas. He'd grow to be charismatic beyond belief, and well endowed, though some would say *too* well endowed, and even then, others might say it was really a matter of endurance. Bolívar III's good fortune would only be marred by a small flaw, his Achilles' heel, and that was his weak heart. Not fragile, but brittle. Incapable of carrying the weight of love, even when he wanted it to.

When he met Orquídea, he desperately wanted it to.

He loved everything about her. The shape of her legs, the burnt sienna of her skin, the way her innocent smile made him want to stop breathing. So enchanted was he by Orquídea Montoya, that he smuggled her on the ship to Paris, and figured out a way to procure her documents. She'd had a small backpack to her name, carried her birth certificate folded into a little square. She had no passport, no family. She had no table manners, and swore like the stable boys, but none of that mattered.

On her first night as La Sirena del Ecuador, he missed his cues several times. Only his crew noticed, of course. Bolívar III didn't make it a habit of bedding the new performers. The idea of having a family felt like something better suited for other men. After all, he was left in his own father's dressing room after his mother ran off with the Ukrainian contortionist. Before that, his father had been orphaned. And before that, his grandfather had been abandoned. He knew there was a weakness in his heart — his lineage — and took great care to not spill his seed where he did not want it to grow. Not after the Italian Knife Thrower had nearly bludgeoned him to death when their tryst fizzled. And so, he did his best not to linger at Orquídea's set.

He failed. He looked hard and long. If he'd been a simple man, he'd have accused her of bewitching him. As she glittered under the spotlight, he felt himself stop breathing. More humiliating was Horacio the Hunchback snickering as he walked past him backstage. Bolívar hadn't been sure why the stagehands were snickering until he looked down. He adjusted his erection straining against the buttons of his tailored slacks. He took a lap. Splashed cold water on his face from the stable troth. Ran a wet hand against the back of his neck and returned to see the end of Orquídea's set.

He wasn't sure if the show was made more radiant because of her, but when the pink clam shell opened and she danced and moved her body like she was suspended on a wave, it was over for him.

He complimented Mirabella, the seamstress, for tailoring Orquídea's scalloped mermaid tail and matching the sheer materials to her perfect skin.

When he showed up at the cabin that she shared with Wolf Girl and Agustina, he purposely avoided the old fortune-telling witch's eyes. Bruja, she was. Always filling his head with nonsense about being careful of destiny. What did he need destiny for when he had stumbled on the greatest power known to man?

"Señorita Montoya," he said. "Would you do me the honor of accompanying me to the opera tomorrow night?"

She said no.

And he wanted her more.

Orquídea knew to be wary of men. Bolívar had been kind to her. Helped her escape the Buenasuerte house. But he was also too beautiful to belong to anyone. Not truly. It was a funny thing that people warned of the dangers of pretty women, that there was power in beauty. But Orquídea thought beautiful men were even more dangerous.

Men were already born with power. Why did they need more? She'd been witness to girls in her school and neighborhood who fell prey to those men. They ended up the same — pregnant and penniless. Like her mother. She did her very best to resist his charm.

Still, when she was near him, she perked up like a flower toward the sun. Bolívar Londoño III could have had anyone in the circus, but he wanted *her* when no one else had. Didn't that mean something? When he looked at her, she felt every brick she'd built around her heart come crumbling down.

Until finally, she said yes.

Bolívar was going to be patient when it came to her. If she wanted, she could have whatever she wished. He would turn himself into a fucking genie just to make her happy. When she'd appeared at dawn, after he'd asked the heavens for his true love, she felt like the answer to every prayer he'd ever made. Fuck destiny and fuck Agustina for saying that his heart was brittle. When he was with Orquídea, it had never felt stronger. Beat harder, faster.

Everyone in the carnival loved her. She helped Wolf Girl brush the tangles out of her hair. She made teas for Strong Man's muscle aches. She went swimming with the

Seal Boy when no one else wanted to. She listened to Agustina's predictions without laughing. Unlike the others, she never asked for her own future to be unveiled. He wasn't sure if she didn't believe, or if she didn't care. He eavesdropped one night and heard Orquídea say she didn't need a psychic to remind her she'd been born cursed. His Orquídea. His whole heart. Cursed? He'd have none of it.

One night, as they traveled along the French Riviera, she rode with Bolívar in his train compartment. The other performers were stuffed in cargo holds. He assured her she should not feel guilty. Her bare feet dug into the plush rugs and he filled her glass with champagne. He wanted nothing more than to kiss her. The want of it all was the biggest rush he'd felt next to performing, and he would wait. He let her ask everything her curious, clever mind wanted to know. It was like she could see through him. She knew Pedro Bolívar Londoño Asturias was a ruse, a story he'd concocted because it was what people wanted to hear. He'd come up with the name Asturias after looking at a map of Spain. He'd added the name Pedro because it sounded old, established. He wove words together that turned into mirages, but only Orquídea seemed to recognize the truth behind it. She wanted to pull his curtains back and see the fibers of his being. She prodded at him with her questions. She'd never known her father's name, and legacy made her curious. What happened to his mother? Did he ever wonder where she was? What did he love, truly love, about this life he'd built? And he felt, for the first time, that when he gave her the answers she asked for, he couldn't lie.

Orquídea took in the gold painting trim, the prisms of the crystal glasses. She tucked her fine legs up on the settee. She'd begun the night on the other end, and she was slowly moving toward him like the tide.

"How did you attain all of this?" she asked.

"My father." He told the story of his father and grandfather. He'd turned their misfortunes into something that could not be ignored. Something the public wanted to witness. And he'd done it all by the age of thirty. "I show people that there are true marvels in the world."

"I'm a marvel?"

"No. You are divine. My Orquídea divina."

With her, in the privacy of his room, he was just a man. There was nothing special about the silver buttons on his shirt, there was no wax in his beard or oil in his hair. It was as vulnerable as he allowed himself to be.

Then she closed the distance between them and kissed him. Bolívar had never been kissed this way. Slowly, carefully, as if he were the one who needed the soft touch. Like she had peered into his brittle heart and wanted to have care. She undid the silver buttons of his shirt that had always appeared like blinking stars when he was on stage. Her warm palm rested between his pectorals.

"What's this star on your ring mean? It's everywhere in the Spectacular."

She ran her fingers along his bicep and forearm until she touched the signet ring snug on his finger. An eight-pointed star, like a compass rose.

He hesitated, then said, "A family sigil."

"I've never seen silver so lustrous."

He could have lied. Said it was white gold. Platinum. But he couldn't seem to lie to her. Not in the beginning, at least. "It's from a star."

She playfully rolled her eyes. She didn't believe him and that was all right. Maybe that was best. Letting his hand rest against the dark hair of his chest, she continued to explore him, and he sat there, a table set for her hunger. He'd never been so aware of his every breath, the uneven murmur of his heartbeat.

"You look afraid," she said, kneeling on the furs.

"I'm not." His laughter was a dark rumble because it wasn't quite true. Bolívar had never been afraid of anything, or anyone. He couldn't quite figure out what it was about this young woman, this girl who had never been anywhere before she'd met him. He'd watch her stand still when the lioness roared in her cage. He'd watch her laugh with glee at the storm that set upon their ship across the Atlantic. Now, with her mouth on his swollen erection, she was a lightning rod splitting him in half. And he realized that it wasn't Orquídea he feared, but the way he lost control when they were together.

Bolívar yanked her on top of him, pushing up her dress. His drink spilled over her and he drank it off her skin. He thought he was consuming her, but it was she who was taking from him until they were naked and tangled on the floor among the fringe and furs.

He pulled a cushion under his chest and turned to the side to look at her. She filled her glass with what was left in the champagne bottle. Traced a cold finger along the scars on his bicep, the hard muscles of his back.

"But *how* did you find all your marvels?" she asked.

He rolled over on his back and rested a hand on his chest, grazed her leg with the other. "My father wished for them."

She frowned and pinched the taut skin of his abdomen. "I may be from a small country, but I'm not stupid."

"Can I trust you?"

"It's not whether or not you can trust me. It's whether you want to. If you have secrets, I swear I would never tell."

Bolívar weighed her words. He made a choice. "One day, my father saw a shooting star. He saw where it fell near our camp and we went in search of it. But what we found instead was a boy. A living star."

"Are you trying to convince me that the Living Star is real? Bolívar —"

"The ground around him had turned into a small crater, and everything was covered in what looked like glass. Even in the night, it lit up like a prism, like water on an oil slick. I cut my finger on it." He held up his index finger, where there was a thick scar across the pad. She kissed it.

"Am I supposed to believe you?"

"It's not whether or not you can believe

me. It's whether you want to." He climbed on top of her, caging her with his forearms. He kissed her deeply, until she unfurled her knees for him. Kissed the brown skin of her nipples, the hollow between her breasts. He wanted to consume her heart as she had done his.

"I thought that it was a trick. Like the magicians who pull animals out of their jackets and get sawed in half. Like how you made me a mermaid."

He nuzzled his face into her shoulder and sank into her. He couldn't think clearly. He wanted to drown in her. His siren. His mermaid. His answered wish of true love. "Real as you and me, mi divina."

She sighed. "But how?"

"He just fell right out of the sky."

18
WAIT, DO ASHES COUNT AS ORGANIC MATTER?

Leaving Eddie and New York City further behind was easier than Rey had expected. Although, Rey had come to hate international travel. His new career had taken him to most countries in Europe where he always felt like *he* was the one on display rather than his paintings. Mexico and Argentina had been better, but there was an expectation, a judgement from the locals when they discovered that he didn't know how to speak any Spanish. Once, in Buenos Aires, an art critic slaughtered him in a review because Rey had said "español" instead of "castellano."

Going to Ecuador did excite him. Even if he, Marimar, and Rhiannon had to get private screenings on account of the flowers protruding from their skin. The TSA agents didn't have anything in the handbook for their peculiar body extensions, and it took five people to determine that their flowers were organic material and should be considered body modifications.

"Not the weirdest thing I've ever seen," said the TSA agent. "There was a woman with horns grafted into her skull. Hey, wait a minute. Aren't you the art guy from that magazine?"

"Yup."

A painting hanging at the MoMA, a front cover of *The New Yorker,* and this guy who might as well have been a mall cop called him "Art Guy." Rey needed to stay humble.

Their family occupied half of the first-class cabin, a small gift from the Art Guy. While the rest of them took the opportunity to sleep on the red-eye flight, he watched the tiny screen in front of him, tracking the flight path across state and country lines, over oceans and seas. Even though his life had changed since that great and terrible day at Four Rivers, mostly for the better, he didn't want to be the kind of person who ever took this for granted.

Orquídea had never gotten on a plane. She'd said she walked all the way from Ecuador to the United States, but never stopped to see the sights or relax at a restaurant. "I kept going because stopping was not an option," she'd said. She couldn't be the kind of person who might say "I see myself living here" for fun or out of ennui. One trip had been enough for her. But Rey — he'd inherited the wanderlust she didn't get to savor.

She'd stayed in the valley that had seemed destined for her, and people came to her. Before he finally fell asleep, he stared out of the airplane window at the pitch-black sky, the silhouette of gray clouds, and wondered if his grandmother had ever regretted staying, because now she was rooted there, unable to go anywhere. He pictured her tree. Then a woman of twenty with a husband and a rooster charting a path that spanned thousands of miles. Why had he never before wondered who had been chasing her, and why, after everything, had he not believed that it might come for him, too?

Their flight landed in Guayaquil, Ecuador's Aeropuerto Internacional José Joaquín de Olmedo. Even though Rey was the one who had actual travel experience, he and the Sullivans followed Marimar's lead. They disembarked and followed the crowds of crying children and tired adults, the men in canary yellow soccer jerseys, the small women in black hats and long braids, the white tourists in open-toed sandals and overstuffed backpacks with hand-sewn patches that boasted of open borders and open minds, but their money was strapped to their torsos.

Marimar watched them all and wondered if this was their first or last destination. How many were returning for good and how many were coming to visit. She was someone who had never had to go anywhere and now she was in the country where Orquídea had come from. She felt like a stranger.

As they followed the crowd through Immigration and Customs, Marimar became more and more aware that her dead uncle's remains were in her backpack. That Tío Félix had not enjoyed the bottomless wine service and microwaved dinner and dessert. He'd wanted to be scattered, not with his mother, not where his wife and daughter would eventually be buried, but in a country he'd never set foot in. Who was she to question his final wish?

At Customs, Marimar stumbled her way through the questions volleyed at her by a short agent with shrewd eyes —

Are you all traveling together? All of you? *Yes, we are all one family going to the same hotel.*

Where are you staying? *The hotel Oro Verde.*

How long are you staying? *Three days.*

Three? What is the reason for your visit? *A funeral.*

Do you have anything to declare? *Wait, do ashes count as organic matter?*

Do you have the body of the deceased? *In my backpack.*

That made the woman pause. Cremations weren't common in Ecuador, apparently.

Do you have the permits? *Yes.*

The airport was a maze of its own with empty designer shops, cheap souvenirs. Families hauling mountains of luggage and screaming children. Marimar didn't quite feel like she was in another country yet. She remembered being very little and her teacher asking them to color in the map all the places their families had traveled to. She was too young to know that there had been a before place for Orquídea, and that's how she'd thought of Ecuador for so long. The Before place. Getting details of the Before was worse than pulling teeth. At least teeth came out eventually. This was more like trying to dislodge something buried in cement.

She'd asked, "What was it like, Mamá Orquídea?"

"Hot."

"Why did you leave?"

"I had to go."

"Will you take me?"

315

"I'll make you a deal. If you can catch a hummingbird with your bare hands, then we'll go together."

"Why a hummingbird?"

"Do you want to make a deal or not?"

Marimar did want to make a deal. As she tried, she could never catch one.

Now, she thought she heard the buzz of wings by her ear, but when she whirled around, it was just a fan. Mike held on tightly to Rhiannon's hand and she pushed her own roller suitcase, pink with several butterflies printed on the plastic shell. Sweat spread around his armpits and the center of his shirt. He covered his mouth and coughed.

"Did you get the taxi confirmation?" he asked Marimar.

"Tía Silvia sent it to me," she repeated tightly. He'd been asking about the itinerary since they transferred in Houston. "She made all the reservations."

As they passed baggage claim, several porters tried to flag them down and get their attention, but they kept walking.

Outside the terminal there were dozens — no, hundreds — of people waiting behind the arrivals gate. They held balloons and "¡Bienvenido!" signs. A woman holding a baby screamed as her husband dropped all of his bags and ran to them. Grandmothers were swallowed up into waiting arms, and couples devoured each other. Marimar felt a twinge in her stomach.

"This makes me think of the time everyone at school got singing telegrams for Friendship Day except you and me," Rey said.

As they waded through the crowds, Marimar tried to pull up the taxi email on her phone. She felt people turn toward them, like a slow wave. A little boy ran up to Rhiannon and tried to yank the flower from her forehead. Marimar swatted him away and he ran screaming back to his mother, who glowered at them and made the symbol of the cross over her entire body.

"Do you think they're wary because we didn't bring more than carry-ons?" Rey laughed, putting on his sunglasses even though it was three in the morning.

"Hilarious." She stopped short of throwing her phone against the glass walls. "Roaming isn't kicking in. Look for a sign that says Oro Verde," she told them.

But they weren't exactly listening. Tatinelly was trying to help Mike with the tangled straps of his backpack and Rey was taking a selfie. Rhiannon chased after a stray balloon and Marimar ran after her. Someone asked to join Rey's selfie and soon it was a swarm. If this was how the rest of the trip was going to go, then they would not survive. Marimar caught up to Rhiannon before she got lost in the crowds.

"Hey, baby girl, don't run off, okay?" Marimar said, brushing Rhiannon's hair back. The delicate pink rose looked different. The petals' edges were saturated pink, the color leeching from the center. "Are you all right?"

"I'm sleepy." Rhiannon scratched at her forehead and watched the red heart-shaped balloon drift up and get stuck in the ceiling.

"Come, we'll be home soon." Marimar hadn't meant to say home, but the kid wasn't the only one who'd slept uneasily on the flight. The rest of the Montoyas were back at Four Rivers waiting for them to lay Uncle Félix to rest, and her mind created scenarios that told her the little gold laurel that had taken so much of her energy was not enough to protect her family. She did not believe in God, but she had always believed in her grandmother, and the prayer that passed through her lips was for her.

Rhiannon clung to Marimar and they zigzagged through the porters, families taping boxes that had been gutted by Customs. Bodies moved around them like waves, and if they weren't careful, they were going to get separated or carried away by the current.

"Auntie Mari, there's a lady looking at us," Rhiannon said. Her clear, soprano voice cut right through Marimar's thoughts as she focused on the petite woman standing feet from their cloister.

She had cat-green eyes and brown hair. The sign in her hand read: Montoya.

Marimar let go of an anxious breath. She waved, then extended her hand in greeting. "Hi, I'm Marimar Montoya —"

"Of course! I'm Ana Cruz. I'm sorry I'm late," she said and pushed aside Marimar's hand to better pull her into a tight embrace. Rey also allowed himself to be pulled into a hug and kissed, followed by the Sullivans.

The woman's name sounded familiar, but Marimar couldn't place it. Her body needed sleep, but she knew enough that the taxi reservation had a man's name on it.

"Your Tía Silvia got the time wrong on your flight," Ana Cruz said quickly in her lilting, accented English. "She didn't account for the time difference. But it's a good thing I checked the arrival board. You must be exhausted. Your rooms at the house are ready and waiting."

"I'm confused. Are you from the hotel?"

319

Ana Cruz laughed and waved her many-ringed fingers in the air like she was swatting a fly. "I'm sorry, you've never met me so of course you look surprised. Orquídea was my sister. I'm your grand aunt. Or is it great-aunt? I don't remember how it goes. Here we say, tía abuela."

Then it clicked. Ana Cruz Buenasuerte. Marimar remembered being in the old house's dining room when the Buenasuertes arrived. Learning of Orquídea's first secret family had been the least surprising moment of that night. Orquídea had asked for Ana Cruz, but she couldn't remember why she'd stayed behind.

"Wow! You didn't have to come all the way here. There's a shuttle taxi coming from the hotel."

"As soon as Silvia called and said that you were staying at a hotel I said, no way. You're family. You're Orquídea's babies. So, she cancelled your reservation and you're going to stay with me."

"Oh, how lovely," Tatinelly said. She kissed Mike's cheek. The trip had drained him, pronouncing the circles under his eyes. "Isn't that nice?"

Nice is one way of putting it, Marimar thought. "When did you talk to her?"

"While you were flying. My sister has been

on my mind lately and I reached out on a whim to connect," Ana Cruz said, and stacked her hands against her heart, like she was praying. "I know, it's a little bit strange. But family is strange. I wish I had been there to see her one more time. But I'm the youngest of my siblings, and I had to stay with my father. I couldn't be there for her then, but I hope I can be with you now."

"Thank you, but —" Marimar began to say before getting cut off by Rey.

"Give us a moment, Ana Cruz."

The Montoyas and Sullivans huddled together.

"Before you say anything, Mari," Rey continued, "I'm tired. I'm hungry. We have human remains in our bag. But remember we're here to learn more about Orquídea. Doesn't this feel like —"

"If you say destiny, I swear to god."

Rey winked at Rhiannon who giggled at Marimar's threat. "Fine. Doesn't this feel like a highly improbable but welcome coincidence?"

"It would be nice to have some help," Tati suggested.

Then it was agreed. They were going with Ana Cruz to the Buenasuerte house. Marimar put her phone away. The automatic doors hissed. She heard the rapid flutter of wings again, and this time she saw them. Hummingbirds flitting around them, welcoming them. They hovered by Rey's hand, Rhiannon's brow, her throat, and then they were gone before she could gasp.

Marimar noticed the humidity first. It clung to her skin. Curled the ends of her hair right away. Clouds rolled in across the twilight sky. Even though sunrise was fast approaching, stars blinked for attention. They cut across the full parking lot, and Rey handed his roller bag and duffle to Mike, before getting in the front seat with a cheerful, "Shotgun!"

"I'm so glad Rhiannon has a playmate her own age," Marimar mumbled as she climbed in behind the driver's seat.

When they were all buckled in, Ana Cruz peeled out of the lot, stopping only once to pay for her parking ticket.

"Sorry, I drive fast. I want to beat traffic and make sure you all get some sleep before everything you have to do."

"Speed demon, I love it," Rey said.

As they drove, they kept the windows rolled down. Guayaquil was alive despite the hour. When Ana Cruz warned about her driving, Marimar could understand why. Cars sped against each other, sometimes foregoing turn signals entirely. It was twice as heart-stopping as a drag race through Times Square. Highway lamps cast an amber glow along the roads. The yellow, blue, and red flag of Ecuador waved beside a pale blue and white one. What Orquídea hadn't taught her, Marimar had learned by doing her own research. But the sight that drew her eye was the colorful houses layered on top of each other like the world's brightest cake. If she stood still and tried to count the number of houses or floors, she'd never get close. Something at the very top sparkled with light, and Ana Cruz pointed out the lighthouse at the top of the cerro Santa Ana.

They went through a tunnel. In the back seat, Mike was asleep, but the others had gotten their second wind. When the car emerged from the other side, the city came alive with the rising sun.

"Who's that?" Rhiannon pointed at a monument of two indigenous figures nestled at a traffic circle. The man held a spear and rested a hand on the woman's back. She was topless and clutched a baby in her arms. A jaguar crept at their feet like a giant house cat.

"That's Guayas and Quil," Ana Cruz said. "They were leaders of this territory. My father used to say they were Inca royalty, but when I went to school, they taught us they were Huancavilca indians. They fought the Incas and the Spanish, too. Legend says Guayas killed Quil and later himself so they wouldn't be captured, and the city was named after them, but there are so many stories. It's impossible to say what is true and what is legend."

"How romantic, question mark?" Rey said.

"Daddy would have loved this. Is this Orquídea's river?" Tatinelly asked, her voice rising over the horns and wind.

"Sort of. Part of it. The Guayas River cuts down the coast of the city. Orquídea's old neighborhood is just a tiny part of it."

Rey inhaled deeply and turned around in his seat. "Take in the inspiration, Marimar."

She shot him a glare. She hadn't written a single thing since she dropped out of college and stayed in Four Rivers. He knew that, and still encouraged it.

"Silvia told me you have a very creative family. You with your art and her sons with their music career. All of my brothers and sisters just became civil engineers like my father. By the time I came along, no one cared what I did, so I became a kindergarten teacher."

"Are your parents still alive?" Rey asked.

"Grandma literally never mentioned them

until the day she died."

"No, they both passed a couple of years ago. I wish my mother were here. She used to tell me so many stories about Orquídea. It's a shame they never saw each other after Orquídea ran away."

"Uh, excuse me?" Rey nearly choked on his laugh. "Are we talking about the same person?"

"She ran away?" Tatinelly said softly. Hadn't Tati and Marimar done the same?

Ana Cruz met her eyes in the rearview mirror. "There's so much about your grandmother, my sister, that you didn't know. That I don't know. I will tell you what I can."

Guayaquil unfolded before them. The city was loud with air stinking of exhaust, not unlike Midtown traffic. The roads were all stacked on top of each other, creating underpasses. Some of them were lined with bright murals depicting the indigenous, African, and Spanish history that shaped the country. There were murals that called for peace and freedom. Some that said, "¡Primero Ecuador!" They passed rows of beautiful houses with red tiled roofs and manicured gardens, froyo stalls and sunrise joggers around parks. Then, a few streets over, there was a prostitute in high heels,

325

her dress bunched over her thighs as she bore down to urinate on the sidewalk. A few turns later, new stairs were being paved and modern apartment buildings erected.

Ana Cruz made a hard loop and drove up to a security check point at the base of a hill. She waved at the round guard drinking his coffee, and then maneuvered the mini-van up a street so steep they slid back every time she switched gears.

When they finally arrived, Marimar looked over the house with caution. Orquídea had run from the Buenasuertes and here they all were, unloading their suitcases.

The Buenasuerte house was two stories tall. The roofs were in the Spanish design, with red clay tiles and a cream cement wall that appeared freshly painted. The lip of the walls around the house were covered in sharp spikes. Ana Cruz told them that's how they kept thieves away. But in order to cover the gruesome appearance of the spikes, they'd tried to make vines and thin pink flowers grow like a curtain over them. The garage door opened onto a small courtyard. There was an angel statue and a tree with drooping branches. Marimar wondered if the others were thinking of Orquídea, too.

"Did Orquídea live here?" Rey asked.

Ana Cruz shook her head and dug in her

purse for her keys. "No, that old house is in La Atarazana where we grew up. It's sad what's happening to that neighborhood, but that's the way of things. I'm happy you get to see it before they demolish it."

"Demolish?" Marimar repeated.

"They're building new condominiums and extending the boardwalk. The whole neighborhood used to be full of Montoyas but after my father sold our plot of land to the city, a lot of people followed."

"What about your brothers and sisters?" Rey asked. "They were delightful."

Marimar elbowed him and was glad Ana Cruz didn't mind his sarcasm.

"Some moved to Hamburg. My sister Olga moved to Buenos Aires. Some people just seem to go."

Some people are forced to go, Marimar thought but didn't say.

Ana Cruz turned the key to several locks and offered Marimar a kind smile. As she stepped aside to let them enter she said, "This is my home. I have no reason to leave."

Lots of people had homes. Orquídea had a home with her mother once, too. Marimar wondered why some people left and others didn't. Is it just that you stay until someone forces you out? Until it becomes uninhabitable? Until it gets demolished to make room for others? There were people all over the world who probably would have wanted to stay home, but they couldn't. Something about Ana Cruz's answer, as honest and simple as it was, bothered her. Orquídea had run away. Knowing that, it put a previous conversation with her grandmother into perspective.

She'd asked Orquídea once. "Why did you leave Ecuador?"

"I didn't belong there anymore," Orquídea said dismissively.

"So where do you belong?"

Orquídea had sucked her teeth and said, "You ask too many questions, Marimar!"

Marimar had flashed a devious smile, the one she reserved for when she did and said things she wasn't supposed to. "I just want to *know.*"

"I belong wherever my bones will lie! Wherever my bones will lie."

19
DOWN BY THE RIVER

Tatinelly hadn't slept in weeks. Not since the shadow of that man appeared out of the corner of her eye and she was the only one who seemed to be able to notice he was there. He stood at the end of her street, in the park where Rhiannon liked to swing. Once, she'd seen him on the roof of her neighbor's home across the way. That was the only time that he had stared up at the sky instead of directly at her. Each time, Mike had talked her down from her fear. Anyone could stand on a street, in a park. That didn't mean anything.

"What about the roof? I'm going to call Bailey —"

Mike had taken the phone out of her hand, gently, like she'd been holding scissors or a knife instead. "Honey, there's no one on Bailey's roof."

But she'd sit at the living room window, the one that took up the entire wall so that they never felt cooped up inside. She watched for the stranger, her stalker. If no one believed her, then she'd prove it to them.

Of course, her stalker hadn't appeared since they drove to Four Rivers, and she felt better with Marimar and Rey. It was good for Rhiannon to be around family, since Mike's family never came by and seemed to forget to invite them to birthday parties and camping and barbecues.

The Buenasuerte house was lovely. Their guest room had family pictures. Paintings of birds and butterflies and mountains. Mike passed out without showering, but Tati wanted to wash the all-day travel from her skin, and made sure Rhiannon did, too.

Before she fell asleep, Tatinelly watched her two greatest loves. Mike's eyes fluttered rapidly under closed lids, and she gently kissed his forehead, wishing him sweeter dreams. Rhiannon was curled between them like a little nautilus shell, like she could wind herself into a fetal position and back into the womb. She brushed the silky petals of Rhiannon's rose, which had begun to change color. Tatinelly lay still. She convinced herself that things would be all right but, as she did, the heavy weight of panic settled into her bones, like she was being

330

pressed to death. Rhiannon curled closer to her mother, and then the dread went away.

"I won't let anything happen to you. I will give my whole life to make sure you are safe."

She wasn't sure where the words had come from, but she was overcome with the same sensation she'd felt all those years ago. The one that had led her to Mike in the first place. Purpose. Awakening. She would put her father to rest and enjoy the time she had with her cousins.

In the afternoon, everyone crept out of their rooms following the deliriously enticing scents coming from the kitchen downstairs. Mike had woken up with a bug and was still sleeping it off.

"¡Buenas tardes!" Ana Cruz said, folding her newspaper in half. "How did you all sleep?"

Rhiannon sidled up to a barstool at the counter and accepted a glass of juice from Ana Cruz. "Awesome. I was dreaming of the moon. Sometimes, it talks to me when I sleep."

"It was her favorite book when she was a baby," Tatinelly said, running her fingers through Rhiannon's thick light brown hair.

"*Goodnight, Moon* is *my* favorite book and I'm not a baby," Rey said, emerging from the stairs in black sleep shorts, a loose gray T-shirt, and a peacock-green silk sleeping robe.

Ana Cruz smiled deeply when she saw him. "Oh, qué fashion."

"I love you already," Rey said.

"You love anyone who compliments you," Marimar said in her deep, sleepy voice. She pulled up a chair to the kitchen island. "What smells amazing?"

"Jefita made something special for you," Ana Cruz said.

At the sound of her name, a woman stepped into the kitchen from the open courtyard. Jefita had deep brown skin and, despite her age, her ropes of straight hair were pitch black. Her dark eyes crinkled at the corners. She was crying.

"Jefita, these are Orquídea's grand-children, and one great-grandchild. Ya, no llores."

"Aww, don't cry," Rey said, letting the woman take his hand and turn it over. She cupped his face and said, "Qué bello."

But of course, Rey was beautiful. The most beautiful of the family, like Tía Parcha.

Jefita moved on to Marimar, Rhiannon, and Tatinelly. Lament, real lament, looked like this. An old woman who held the memory of someone after all this time. "Mi Orquídea. I remember the night she left like it was yesterday. I asked her not to leave me alone, but I knew she had to go. It was not a good place for her. I always wished that I could see her again. My poor unlucky girl."

Tatinelly thought that was a strange thing to call her grandmother. As far as she was concerned, Orquídea was one of the luckiest people she'd ever known. She had a giant house and a whole valley. She had five husbands who had loved her. Children. Grandchildren. She'd never been sick. She'd had food and plenty of it. What happened later — the fire, her transformation — was that luck or her choice?

"Jefita, save your tears for the funeral," Ana Cruz said, resting a hand on her hip.

Jefita made the sign of the cross over her body. Her words had a musical quality as she said, "I've never seen such a thing. A body in the river."

"Technically not a body anymore," Rey said, and Marimar swatted his arm.

"They're his ashes," Tatinelly explained.

"It's just not typical here," Ana Cruz clarified.

Rey sat next to Rhiannon and took up a glass of juice. "Speaking of inappropriate segues, what's for brunch?"

That seemed to be the magic words for Jefita to stop crying.

She had prepared a feast of roasted pork with thick, crackling skin; bowls of fat white corn kernels sprinkled with salt; yellow potato patties she called llapingachos. Rhiannon loved them the best and devoured them greedily. She repeated everything that Jefita said, and when she did, the rose on her forehead changed color. It grew into a more saturated pink than the pale powder one it had been.

Jefita made the symbol of the cross and pressed her hands together. "You are blessed."

"Does it always change color?" Ana Cruz asked more clinically than because she was awestruck with pious belief.

"One time," Rhiannon said at the same time as Tatinelly said "No."

They all turned to the little girl, content at her feast. "It was only for a moment. At the park, a man tried to talk to me, and my head felt itchy. My friend Devi said that my rose turned black, but I couldn't see it because it's on my forehead, but the man vanished into thin air."

They were all silent, a collective held breath until Tatinelly let loose a whimper. She held her daughter, squeezed her. "Why didn't you tell me?"

"Daddy didn't believe you, so I thought I was imagining things too. Besides, when I went home, my head wasn't itchy anymore, and my rose was back to normal."

"What man?" Ana Cruz asked, and Tatinelly and Rey told their stories of the stranger who'd appeared out of nowhere. "We have the best security here, I assure you. I won't leave your side."

"That's one of the reasons we came here together," Marimar said, absently pressing her thumb against the thorn at her throat. "We think this stranger was from our grandmother's past. Only we don't know anything about her past."

Jefita nodded reassuringly and held up a finger, like a threat to the universe. "No one will hurt Orquídea's babies. We will help, right, Ana Cruz?"

"Of course, although, it's been so long, the stories of my Orquídea feel like legends now. I'll dig through my mother's things."

"How did you meet Mamá Orquídea, Jefita?" Marimar asked.

"My mother and I worked for Señor Buenasuerte. They called her Jefa, and I became Jefita." The woman spoke with her hands, like she was making her fingers dance to her words. "We came down from the Tungurahua province after the earthquake. I almost considered leaving when Orquídea did, too, but I didn't know anyone. It was very scandalous. I remember the day she left because it was the city's independence day. In the morning, they sent out a search party and everything. The fishermen all combed the rivers even though no one would have believed she could have drowned. I alone knew she'd run away. I couldn't tell them, but I was nervous and Señor Buenasuerte saw that I knew more than I said. He told me I had to tell the truth or risk going to hell, and I knew Orquídea would understand that it was the price of my soul and she would forgive me. So, I told them. He beat me with the belt, but my mother reminded me that it was because I'd lied to our employer."

"That's horrible," Marimar said.

Rey's eyes cut to the austere older man whose face hung in a portrait. He'd contain his curses for later. "It's hard to imagine why our grandmother ever left."

"My father was a tough man to love," Ana Cruz said, sadly. "He was raised in different times."

Tatinelly wanted to say that it was no excuse for beating someone, but she was a guest and they'd be leaving soon.

336

"My father's discipline was violent with my siblings, but for Orquídea it was something more. I shouldn't remember this because I was so little, but when she held me, I felt how small she made herself because she thought she was trapped. I escaped my father's attention most of the time because I was the youngest. I was an accident, you see. Number six. He always said it would have been better if I were a boy. That the cost of my mother's health would have been worth it. So, I made myself scarce. I was only three when Orquídea left, but I always remembered her face. Her voice."

"You only stopped screaming when she sang to you," Jefita said.

Marimar cleared her throat, then forced a smile. "She never stopped singing."

After lunch, they got ready to take the ashes to the river. When Tatinelly went to check on Mike, he was warm to the touch. Beads of sweat dotted his pale forehead, like dew clinging to leaves. When he blinked around the room, he was unsettled. He didn't remember where they were or what time it was.

"We let you sleep in. It's time to scatter the ashes."

"I'm up." Mike tried to yank off the covers, but he was overcome with a bout of phlegmy coughing.

"You're not getting up. We can do it later," she said softly, but she could not hide the worry from her face.

He took the bottle of water she offered. "No, you should go. This is important. This is about you and Rhiannon. I must've caught something on the plane. Hand me my emergency kit. I'll be fine if I just rest a bit longer."

Tatinelly observed him for a minute. He looked a little pale. But she'd been with him all night. Why wasn't she sick? Or the others? "Are you sure?"

He squeezed her hand in his. "I promise."

The rest of them piled into the car. Tatinelly sat in the front clutching her father's urn. In the light of day, the city was brighter, livelier. Businesswomen walked quickly in sensible heels. Gaggles of students, all in uniform, flooded tiny cyber cafés and shops. Men, women, and children ran into stalled traffic to sell everything from bottled water to gum to phone chargers. Reels of green oranges and bags of candied popcorn. There were water fountains spouting from parks, and this time, when they passed by the Guayas y Quil monument, Tatinelly couldn't

338

help but think of their story. Tragic. Melancholic. She thought of Mike laid up in bed and held her father's urn tighter.

The minivan turned down a paved road that led to the river. The houses were run down and many of them had dark windows, boarded up. A team of surveyors watched them drive past, and Ana Cruz simply waved but didn't stop. Tatinelly tried to imagine her grandmother running down this unpaved road. She imagined Orquídea with her head held high. Those defiant, midnight eyes. She imagined that when these houses were torn down and new ones erected, that this road might be gone, and so would be another little piece of her grandmother.

They parked as close to the river as they could, and when they disembarked, local kids crept up around them, pointing at the flowers that always made people so curious. Jefita made quick work of snapping at the little ones, and though they scattered, they still lingered. Others walked over, recognizing Ana Cruz and wanting to shake hands with Orquídea's family. Tatinelly didn't understand everything they said, but she smiled, and it warmed her whole heart when these strangers said "¡Orquídea!" One of the middle-aged women grinned deeply.

"She always had a fish for us, so we'd have something to eat."

What a strange feeling it was, to learn about their grandmother in this way, as if they gathered enough anecdotes, enough smiles and memories, they'd be able to complete the pieces of Orquídea Divina Montoya.

The locals let the family get on their way, but not without offering prayers and well wishes. Tatinelly held Rhiannon's hand tightly as they walked up to a rickety pier. There were rusted canoes and wooden barges that were more splinters than vessels. Fishing nets covered in algae and muck. Bottles, cans, and broken glass littered the ground. But the view of the distant bright horizon, and the wide river was a beautiful thing.

"There's a monster in the water," Rhiannon whispered to Rey, who only patted her head and said, "That's nice, kid."

Tatinelly thought of the first time her dad had taken her fishing. He'd play his old songs, and dreamed of one day learning to sail, really sail. Félix Montoya's heart didn't belong on land with the others, but he'd never get to follow that dream. Not living, at least. Her father had given her so much love. He'd taught her how to fish, how to be patient. He taught her that one love was enough. That when she found it, she should reel it in, not rush it, hold it tight. When she'd left home so young, started a family so soon, he'd only reminded her that she was her own person. If she passed that down to Rhiannon, then she'd honor him. Tears ran down her cheeks and onto the pier.

"This is where Orquídea fished as a little girl," Ana Cruz said.

Rhiannon squeezed her mother's hand. "You can do it. Grandpa says he's ready to swim."

With her family, old and new, gathered around her, Tatinelly twisted open the urn. She tipped it over above the water and returned her father to a place he'd never set foot in before but was connected to because of his mother. He'd been a part of her trying to get back.

They watched the river run.

A silver fish leaped out of the water, and she knew, Félix Montoya had said his last farewell.

20
THE FORTUNE-TELLER WHO IS NOT ALWAYS RIGHT BUT ALSO NEVER WRONG

Agustina Narvaez did not make predictions because she thought others would believe them. She made predictions because she had been burdened with the ability to read the heavens, to decipher the whisper of planets as they related to the affairs of humans. Agustina had never enjoyed it, but she knew, more than anyone, that no matter what people believed to be true, at least she would always be able to make a living without having to be on her back. Not that she looked down on people who did, but she saw the toll it took on the body and spirit after years of watching her mother do the very same at the turn of the century.

Agustina's parents had fled Málaga during the height of the phylloxera plague. Without wine to make, they sought refuge in several South American towns before ending up in Santiago, Chile. Her own journey would take her to Medellín, Colombia, where she waited for the celestial coordinates to be right. For the boy to find a fallen star and begin her new adventure.

She didn't want to be right. Not always. When she'd met Orquídea Montoya, she saw a whisper of a girl who wanted to become a scream. She hated the future she saw for the girl, and most of all, that she was powerless to stop it. But Agustina wanted to try to save her some heartache, if she could.

That was the problem with getting close to people when you were burdened with a magical gift. You wanted to help them. You wanted to save them. You wanted to make everything better because that's what you tried to do when you had good intentions.

When the Londoño Spectacular Spectacular made its way across eastern Europe, Agustina wanted nothing more than to stop Orquídea from making a mistake that would alter the course of her life. The girl had already been born under a cosmic whirlpool of bad luck. She didn't need Bolívar Londoño III adding to it. Then again, she knew better than to try to alter destiny. The way she saw it, they were all fucked either way.

On the eve of opening night for their tour across the Netherlands, Agustina and Maribella were fitting Orquídea for a new costume, a flower that bloomed as soon as the spotlight fell on her. It had been Bolívar's idea, and the plans for the invention had simply spilled out of his pretty little brain after he'd made a wish. Handing it over to the show's stage engineers, they created the glamorous, never-before-seen dress.

Once it was only Agustina and Orquídea in the room, the fortune-teller seized her opportunity. She wasn't going to *change* destiny. More foolish people had tried and failed. But there was nothing wrong with a warning.

"Protect yourself, Orquídea," Agustina said. "Protect your heart from brittle things."

Orquídea laughed her infectious laugh, clutching the delicate fabric of her dress. "You say the strangest things, Agustina."

"But I am never wrong." She tapped the girl's pert round nose and hoped she would listen.

She didn't of course. Orquídea fell in love with Bolívar Londoño the way the sea falls in love with a storm. Nearly seven months after they'd begun their affair, she was convinced that her mother had been wrong. That she'd left her bad luck back in Ecuador.

After their first performance in Amsterdam, Orquídea was supposed to spend a night out with the girls. But something Agustina said had thrummed through her. *Protect your heart from brittle things.* She had left the people who'd hurt her behind. What did she need protection from when Bolívar was the strongest man she knew, aside from the Londoño Spectacular Spectacular's *actual* Strong Man? He doted on her. Spent every free moment he had with her. He bought her dresses and furs. Made her heart feel like the pop of a cold bottle of champagne. He'd given her a new name and chosen her face for the posters. *Her,* Orquídea Divina.

And yet, she couldn't shake the unease in her belly. She abandoned dinner with her friends, vowing to meet them at a pub later that night. Instead, she returned to the hotel in search of Bolívar.

When he answered the door, he must have been expecting room service because there was a note folded in his fingertips. As it dawned on him that it was Orquídea at the threshold, he shoved the note back in his robe pocket. He barred the entrance to the door, pulling his robe closed but not before she could see his naked body beneath, the imprint of red kisses across his torso.

"Mi divina," he said, a strangled high pitch escaping his mouth. The blue of his eyes bright with panic. "You said you were going to the burlesque tonight."

Behind him several feminine voices called his name. She didn't need to see them. Before he could reach for her, to beg her not to hate him — not to leave him — she ran. She took the stairs two at a time, the sharp *click* of her heels echoing in the corridor. When she finally stopped, she found herself in the basement of the hotel.

She heard it then. A resounding boom. Once. Twice. Then the words susurrating on her skin. "Find. Me."

She'd heard that once before.

Hurrying, she turned a corner. A looming figure was at the door — Lucho, whose sole purpose was to guard the cargo. What else was behind that door? He was nearly eight feet tall and his family was from every corner of Colombia. His father had been Bolívar II's guard and Lucho was Bolívar III's. He was blind out of one eye, and still sported a scar from the brawl that had nearly cost him both. When he realized it was her, he stood from the chair where he usually sat for hours.

"Divina? What are you doing here?" He asked, concern in his voice.

Lucho protected Bolívar, and she realized he must have known. They *all* must have known. *Protect your heart from brittle things.* But who could protect her from herself?

She took a deep breath and gathered worry into her voice. "I just couldn't find Bolívar. Have you seen him?"

He scratched at his black beard and averted his eyes to lie. "Not in a few. I'll tell him you're looking for him."

"Not to worry," she said. "Silly me. I checked everywhere but his room . . ."

"Wait!" Lucho's heavy baritone felt like a gut punch. "I'll go find him. You shouldn't wait here, it's cold."

"Thank you." She yanked him close and he peeled her off him, as if he was afraid to touch her because she belonged to someone else.

Orquídea pulled her fur around her tightly and followed Lucho as far as the lobby bar. But as soon as Lucho's back was turned, she returned downstairs to the storage room. A pulse of light spilled from the seams of the door.

Find me, the voice had said once. Now it said it again, and Orquídea wondered if perhaps she'd been wrong. It wasn't Bolívar or the circus whom she was supposed to find that night, all those months ago. It was the Living Star. But why? What did he want from her?

She withdrew the key she'd pickpocketed from Lucho when she'd hugged him and turned the lock. Crates and suitcases were stacked inside. The lioness and horses and dogs were kept on the grounds, but this place was meant for only Bolívar to access.

Within an iron cage stood the figure made of light that she'd seen at every show, every night, from a distance. A trick, she'd thought at first. But now she wondered at him. Beneath the light, she could see his eyes. Incandescent, like the swirls of a galaxy trapped within his irises. It was the only detail of himself that he revealed.

"You found me," he said, and his voice was like the haunting note of an organ.

She stepped closer. "What do you want from me?"

"Your help."

She went closer still. Wrapped one hand around the cool iron bar. Beneath the glow she could see that he was naked. Was he cold? When she blinked, he was in front of her. His fist above hers around the iron bar. She willed herself not to scream, not to jump back.

"What can I do?" Orquídea asked. "I'm no one."

"You do not have to be. I could hear your wish from far away. It is what made me call to you."

She shook her head. "I never made a wish."

"You did not speak it out loud, but it was in your heart. It was in Bolívar's heart, too. I knew his true love would free me from this place."

She thought of Bolívar. *Her* Bolívar upstairs with a room full of women. Every time she blinked they multiplied. She found the courage to laugh. "I am not his true love."

"Oh, but you are." The light around him pulsed. "That is perhaps the cruelest part of it."

"If I am his true love, why would I do that?"

"Because I can give you what he never will," the Living Star said, letting the words hang between them. "My freedom for a taste of my power."

She smelled something burn, then looked down at the hiss of his skin against the iron. She swallowed the scream that swelled within her as the storage door slammed open.

"You're not supposed to be in here!" Lucho shouted, breathless as he barreled in. "Boss wants to see you."

Orquídea might have been born unlucky, born poor, born a bastard, but she was not born to take orders. Not anymore. She raised her head high and imagined her entire body was made of iron, of steel. "There's a poster with my face on it. Tell him to start there."

She heard the haunting chime of the Living Star, followed by a scream as she stormed out. She ran down the damp streets of Amsterdam. Gas lamps lit her way along dark, humid canals until she found the pub where her friends were. She stayed with them until dawn broke but kept her ugly shame to herself. She was surprised to find that there was no amount of absinthe or cigarettes that could cure her of Bolívar Londoño.

When she finally went back to her hotel, he was there, sitting outside the door of her suite. She didn't know how long he'd been there, but he was asleep. He smelled clean, at the very least. She wondered if he'd showered alone. She wondered too many things.

She kicked him awake.

"Orquídea!" Bolívar Londoño III got on his knees and stopped just shy of touching her. She shut her eyes. The steel was leaving her. How could she protect her heart from brittle things? She *was* the brittle thing. She didn't have a "Lucho" to look out for her.

"Don't," she said. "Don't say my name. Don't look at me. *Leave.*"

He pressed his palms together in supplication. "Those girls were a gift from the Baron Amarand. They meant nothing to me. I — I just couldn't refuse him. He's given us so much."

She crossed her arms over her chest and leaned against her door. "Then return to your gift, Señor Londoño."

"They meant nothing," he repeated.

But she should have known. When a man dismisses other women as nothing, he would eventually do the same to her.

"You said that, Bolívar."

He looked pained when she said his name like that. Without the usual love or admiration. He raked his hair away from his eyes. Her belly gave a tight squeeze at the smell of him — lemongrass and sandalwood and smoke.

"The day I met you," he said, "I knew that you'd been sent to me by the stars. You were the one I'd been waiting for because I wished for you, my dearest love. My truest love. And now that I have you, I'll never let you go. I never want to hurt you again."

He grasped her hand, and she was foolish

351

enough to let him take it. She thought he was trying to stand, but he was only shifting. Getting on one knee. He brandished a round pale sapphire set in gold. "Marry me, Divina."

Stunned, she got down on her knees to better look into his eyes, and said, "There's something you should know. Bad luck follows me around. It's attached to me. Stitched to my skin. I believe it now. You might be part of that curse."

"We will make our own luck, Orquídea. Mi divina. Mi vida. Will you marry me?"

She should have said no. Should have known that the world never punished greedy men for their ill-gotten wishes. Instead she said, "I will."

She let him slide the ring on her slender finger, and led him inside. They shared a kiss that made her forget the last several hours. She rewrote the evening so that she saw only him, on his knee, presenting her with a ring. He tasted like licorice and mint, and when he made love to her, he repeated, "you are mine. You are mine."

Later, while he slept, she heard that voice again. The Living Star, calling out to her.

I will be here when you change your mind.

21
A HIGHLY IMPROBABLE BUT WELCOME COINCIDENCE

After scattering Félix Montoya's ashes, they stopped by a farmer's market unlike any Marimar had ever seen. While Jefita did the shopping, Ana Cruz was their guide through the busy rows of vendors. Raw meat hung from metal hooks, chickens, by their feet. Neat blocks of blue crabs were stacked like crustacean citadels. Bushels of corn and fresh herbs. Avocados so large they looked like footballs. Bins of dates and towers of coconuts. Ana Cruz treated them to fresh coconuts. A slender man, who introduced himself as Ewel from Esmeraldas, hacked open the tops with a sharp machete, jammed a straw in, and offered Marimar a straight, white smile she was happy to return. The sensory overload of it all was strangely familiar. Everywhere Marimar turned, she tried to imagine a young Orquídea walking ahead of her.

Back at the Buenasuerte house, Jefita got

to work preparing dishes. She prided herself on making everything with the freshest, purest ingredients, just like her mom and grandmother had taught her. When Marimar tried to help, she ushered her out of her kitchen and into the enclosed courtyard with her cousins.

Ana Cruz busied herself searching for the photographs and keepsakes she'd promised them. While Tatinelly checked on Mike, and Rey and Rhiannon relaxed in twin hammocks, Marimar paced barefoot on hexagonal red tiles. The yard had a palm and mango tree with baby mangos that were just starting to grow. Bright hibiscus flowers dotted a wall of green vines, and fragrant rose bushes bloomed.

"You're making me dizzy," Rey told her.

"I thought you were napping," Marimar shot back.

Rhiannon shut her eyes but giggled. "Uncle Rey said you worry too much."

"I did say that," Rey admitted.

"Isn't it a little strange being in this house?" Marimar asked. "A few days ago you were perfectly happy to stay in Four Rivers."

Rey lowered his sunglasses. "Maybe being in a beautiful house where people are actually nice to me changed my mind."

Marimar rolled her eyes. "Ana Cruz and Jefita are lovely. I mean because of how Orquídea felt about the rest of them."

His eyes were focused, serious in a way he only got when he couldn't think of something sarcastic or petty to say. "We don't know how she felt, though. Not really. Even if the other Buenasuertes were hateful, Ana Cruz isn't. Jefita isn't. If the roles were reversed, I'm sure anyone who has ever hated Enrique would *love* us."

Marimar remembered the Buenasuertes who had shown up at Four Rivers. Had Wilhelm Jr. ever returned to his ailing father the sucre note that Orquídea gave back? She hadn't needed to say that she didn't care for the Buenasuertes. That gesture said it all. In the end, family wasn't about blood. Of course, Pena and Parcha's brothers and sisters were all half-siblings, but it didn't matter who their fathers were. It mattered that they shared a mother, a family. You could be born into a family, but you still had to choose them. Marimar looked at Rey and Tatinelly and Rhi. She would choose them.

"Use your words Marimar," Rey said, then added softly, "I know it's hard, believe me."

She pressed her hand on her stomach. "Being so close to Orquídea's past makes me scared of what we're going to find. I think I'm just looking for someone to blame."

"We only have another day here," he reminded her. "If we don't find anything, we'll go home and figure it out."

She nodded, but she couldn't shake the restlessness that had crept up on her.

"Jefita told me we could go to the park full of iguanas," Rhiannon said. "Are we allowed to keep them and take them home?"

"I'm guessing no, kiddo," Rey said, taking off his sunglasses and biting one of the legs. "But we can try."

Marimar was too tired to reprimand Rey for putting thoughts of reptilian smuggling into their little cousin's mind. She left them giggling in the garden and went back inside.

Jefita had large pots steaming on the stove. Mounds of cubed meat. Seasoning powders and oils turning the pink flesh into a copper brown. She listened to music while she cooked, like Orquídea, and sang along off-key. Every now and then, Jefita touched a small gold Jesus pendant that rested on her chest.

Marimar also reached for the bulb at her throat, pressed the tiny thorn that served as a reminder of the time she tried to cut it off.

"Do you feel better after hearing people talk about Orquídea?" Jefita asked.

"I don't know if *better* is the right word."

"What word would you use?"

Marimar thought for a moment, listening to the high-pitched pluck of guitars. "Curious, maybe. Angry, a bit. I still haven't figured it out. For the last seven years, all I've done is stay in Four Rivers waiting for Orquídea to give me a sign. An answer. Something that would tell me why she did what she did. Who it was that she had run from. And then, nothing happened. I moved on with my life. We all did. Rey and his art. Tati and her family. The twins with their music. Everyone moved on."

Jefita's eyes were filled with more kindness than Marimar had ever experienced from a near stranger. "And then?"

"Then three people died, and I don't know what to do. Sometimes I think it might have been easier for her to leave us behind than to tell us the truth. She became a tree rather than *talk* to us."

Jefita set the rice to cook, washed her hands, and sat next to Marimar.

"I can't guess for you. But when I knew Orquídea, she was just a girl," Jefita said. "They called her Niña Mala Suerte. But that never stopped her from being kind or from helping those who had less than she did. I don't know what happened in those years she was gone, but the Orquídea I knew would have grabbed her destiny by the balls. She would have done what she needed to."

Marimar threw her head back and laughed. "I can believe that."

"Can I ask you, why is your gift different than the others?"

Marimar shook her head. Orquídea had given each member of their family a seed, but Rey, Marimar, and Rhiannon had blooms growing out of their skin. Magic that needed protecting. Enrique had thrown his seed in the fire and he'd returned to Four Rivers worn and bruised. The others had planted theirs and their fortunes had flourished in different ways. Silvia had grown an entire garden. Caleb Jr. had bottled the scents he dreamed of. Juan Luis and Gastón had planted theirs in Four Rivers, and they went back once every few years just to see Orquídea's tree and sing the songs that turned them into international stars.

Marimar? She'd built a house. She'd resuscitated the valley. Was that enough? It would have been so if she didn't feel so unfinished. That had to be it. That had to be why she'd never gotten the flower bud at her throat to open, only grow thorns.

"Just another one of Orquídea's secrets," she said, and gave a smile she didn't quite feel.

"I hope being here will help you find answers," Jefita told her. "It is not natural to be too far from your roots."

Once, she would have agreed. Orquídea had planted herself in Four Rivers. It didn't get more literal than that.

"In my family," Jefita continued, mincing red onions without a tear in sight, meanwhile Marimar blinked against the burn, "those kinds of markings are signs that someone was blessed by God."

"Sorry to disappoint you, Jefita," Marimar said. "But we're nonbelievers."

Jefita shook her head but chuckled as she sprinkled salt. Marimar closed her eyes and imagined her house. The salt in the grain of the wood. Orquídea holding rough salt crystals in her hands like dull diamonds. There was an ache pressing under her belly button. She'd had that feeling before en route back to Four Rivers the day of the fire. Why was it happening so far away?

"I'll believe twice as hard for you. Besides, it doesn't have to be my God. It can be a powerful being. A saint. Something. Otherwise, we would all have such blessings."

"Don't you have plenty of blessings, Jefita?" Marimar was curious.

"Of course, I do. I was blessed by Diosito Santo. A good life is enough. I mean a *physical* representation of that blessing. Like a sixth finger."

"Or a tail?"

Jefita widened her eyes and made the symbol of the cross. "No. No tails."

Rey and Rhiannon came back inside to escape the rising heat. Rey grabbed an orange from the fruit bowl and started peeling it. "What did I miss?"

"Jefita thinks our flowers were blessings from saints."

"I *am* very saint-like," he said.

"Ay, niño," Jefita admonished.

But she wasn't wrong. Since their arrival and visit to the river, word had spread that there were three American-born Ecuadorians with real honest-to-God flowers growing out of their skin and bones. The people wanted to see miracles. For the next few hours, there was a flood of visitors at their door. They wanted to see the girl with the rose on her forehead and the artist with the one on his hand. Marimar was less of an attraction. Most whispered, wondering what was so special about her. They were in luck, because Marimar had spent years wondering the very same thing. There was even a group of teenage girls who brought an offering of chips and chocolate covered cookies with sticky marshmallow centers. They had T-shirts with Juan Luis and Gastón's faces screen-printed on them and had written the initials JLG in glitter on the apples of their cheeks, which made Tatinelly ask for her own.

Jefita put a stop to it in time for dinner, refusing to answer the door for anyone and warning them that the family was tired and not there to be watched like penguins at the zoo. She brewed a special tea made of anise, lemongrass, and herbs she didn't have names for to help comfort "Sick Mister Sullivan" as she called Mike.

Before they sat down to eat, Ana Cruz finally emerged from a storage closet, her hair in disarray, and announced, "I found it!"

Rey helped her carry the box of photographs, letters, clothes, and what looked like a poster.

"My mother kept everything my sister left behind." Ana Cruz picked up a photo album yellow with age. Clear plastic sheets covered grainy photos. Before she opened it, she looked at Marimar and said, "Your coloring is different but you look a lot like our mother."

The first photo was of a woman, her hair pinned up in an elegant bun with a side part. Marimar didn't look like her own mother or Orquídea. For a long time she had wondered if the face in the mirror belonged to the father that had left. But there she was, seeing her likeness in the great-grandmother she'd never met.

"Same eyes and face. It's so weird," Tatinelly said, delighted.

Marimar flipped the page and saw the Montoya-Buenasuerte wedding. She recognized Orquídea in a simple dress, off to the side.

"What was your mother's name?" Rey asked, pointing at the bride.

"Isabela Belén Montoya Buenasuerte," Ana Cruz said. "She was disinherited because she had Orquídea out of wedlock. Took the money her mother gave her and built a house. That's where she met my father."

There was another photo. All of the Buenasuertes stood at the grand steps of a house. Isabela was older, more elegant in her finery. And Orquídea, again, off to the side as if she'd walked into the photo while it was being taken as opposed to being a part of it.

"Our parents were too hard on my sister," Ana Cruz lamented.

But Marimar understood the real issue as she looked at the family portraits. More and more photos, and each one was the same. The Buenasuertes at the park, at the beach, in their Sunday best, and Orquídea always apart. Marimar's words grew thorns. "Surely Wilhelm Buenasuerte had no problem with his wife's little brown daughter, as long as she stayed in her place."

Ana Cruz's cheeks turned pink, but she did not make excuses for her father. Instead, she changed the subject, as if Marimar had said nothing at all. "I see Orquídea never took her husband's last name. She remained Montoya until the end."

"It's kind of hard when all five of your husbands die in a ten- to twelve-year period," Rey said. "Think of the paperwork."

Marimar flicked his ear.

"What? We were all thinking it."

Rhiannon giggled. "I wasn't thinking that, Uncle Reymundo."

Jefita made the sign of the cross again and said, "I hope they've patched up their differences in heaven."

Rey, Marimar, and Tatinelly shared a strangled silence. They knew exactly where their grandmother was, and it wasn't in heaven. Unless the GPS for heaven was Four Rivers, USA.

Ana Cruz put aside every photo of Orquídea so that the Montoyas could keep them. The rest of the box was filled with dresses. A few seashells. A school uniform. A white communion dress, and a handmade veil with dozens of shiny oblong pearls. Rey and Tatinelly took turns trying it on, but Marimar kept searching. Her fingers itched with promise, like they had only just begun to scratch the surface of the mystery that was Orquídea Divina Montoya.

"Is this a hunting knife?" Marimar asked and wielded a small blade with sea-green patina on the rusted copper studs on the handle.

Jefita clapped her hands once. "Orquídea's fishing knife. She could gut a river fish in seconds. Drove her mother furious when she didn't stop."

"Can I keep this?" Marimar asked. She didn't know why she wanted it, or what she could do with a decades-old blade that had all but lost its edge, but Ana Cruz parted with another part of her sister.

There were letters, but they were from Orquídea to Ana Cruz. "My father never showed them to me. I didn't find them until after he passed and I had to clean out his office. She talked about traveling the world, but she was careful not to include too much information. She spoke of the man she was in love with and described life in each city."

Rey let go of a strangled sigh. "I thought she was just afraid to see the world. Turns out she saw, she conquered, and she said 'no thanks.' "

Marimar tried not to laugh. Pieces of Orquídea were coming together. She'd left the abusive Buenasuerte house. She'd met a man. Traveled the world. She went to the valley. What were they missing?

"This still smells like burned sugar," Tatinelly said as she unfurled a poster. It was for an old-fashioned circus with a girl in a glittering dress made of pearls sitting on a crescent moon. *The Londoño Spectacular Spectacular! featuring Wolf Girl, Orquídea Divina, and the Living Star!*

"Holy shit," Tatinelly breathed.

Rhiannon repeated it and ran off deep into the house like an echo of her mother. "Holy shit! Holy shit! Holy shit!"

No one in the room was more delighted than Rey. "Grandmother was a showgirl!"

"You have her legs, Marimar," Tati said.

Marimar looked at the woman on the poster. She tried to remember a time her grandmother had smiled so vividly, so joyously. Like there was life inside of her. But she couldn't quite conjure the image.

On the poster, Orquídea must have been eighteen then. She didn't have Pena until she was at least twenty, she knew that much.

"So, when you said she ran away, you meant she joined the *circus.*"

"My mother told me," Ana Cruz said. "I've been struggling with whether to tell you."

"Why?" Rey asked. "We're millennials. We're desensitized and have no shame."

Marimar wanted to argue, but then decided her cousin was right. She didn't understand why it was a big deal that a girl had run away and joined the circus. But then again, this was not her world or generation. She'd grown up barefoot and free in a valley full of magic. These were all things her grandmother could have told them and known she was safe recounting her past. So why hadn't she?

"She was so beautiful," Tatinelly said, touching the likeness carefully, like she was afraid it would disappear when she did.

An idea came to Marimar. "Is there a museum for things like this?"

"A circus museum?" Rey asked skeptically.

She touched the thorn at her throat. "There's one in Coney Island. The whole place used to be a carnival."

"Let me ask one of my professor friends," Ana Cruz said, tapping her chin. "He loves obscure history about Guayaquil. Don't get your hopes up. These things used to pass through towns, but they wouldn't stay long."

Rey wrapped an arm around Marimar. "It's a good thing we have a cousin who is here to look for ghosts."

Marimar sighed, taking an orange wedge he offered. She bit down, sweet citrus juice running down her fingertips. "They're your ghosts, too."

22

LA SIRENA DEL ECUADOR

The following day, one of Ana Cruz's contacts called with good news about a hole in the wall "historical center" located in the back room of a comic book shop. When they were ready to go, Mike announced he'd stay back and sleep. Mike only seemed to be able to get up to use the bathroom, but insisted he was fine in bed, and Tatinelly had woken up with bruises under her eyes from lack of sleep. Jefita worried and tittered as she made tea and refused to leave the house until they all drank and ate. It felt right having someone care for them. Marimar had almost forgotten what that was like.

She wasn't doing better than her cousins. She'd tossed and turned all night listening to the sounds of the city. The noise of a television left on, cats fucking in some yard, the orchestra of insects. Her insomnia grew so bad she moved to the courtyard, and it wasn't until she was gently swinging in the hammock that she finally fell asleep, the scattered images of half dreams.

As they piled into the minivan, Rhiannon said, "I talked to the moon again last night." She scratched her forehead. Her rose had turned violet overnight.

Rey examined his rose. "How come I don't get to be a human mood ring?"

Marimar grinned and said, "Because your only mood is dramatic."

El Museo del Circo was located in the middle of the cerro Santa Ana, the colorful hill full of clusters of houses and shops, bars, art galleries, and bookstores. It took 444 steps to get to the very top where there was a lighthouse painted in the city's signature pale blue and white, as well as a small chapel and 360-degree views of Guayaquil. The Montoyas and their crew stopped at around step two hundred, winded and out of breath. The "museum" itself was located in the back room of a comic book store, and was approximately the size of a studio apartment, but it only cost fifty cents to enter and the proprietor and curator was eagerly awaiting their arrival.

Ana Cruz knew Professor Kennedy Aguilar from when they studied at La Católica. Back then, they'd been young and fired up to change the world. Kennedy Aguilar, with his empowering speeches about social justice and civil rights; Ana Cruz, by changing the minds of students and fostering kindness from an early age. Of course, she'd done what she had wanted to do for a long time, before she had to dedicate the rest of her life to taking care of an ailing father who, on good days, remembered she wasn't a servant, and a mother who had died with more regrets than aspirations. Kennedy had been off to a good start, publishing in semi-radical papers. But after the murder of his best friend and journalist, Lisandro Vega, his spirit had diminished. His marriage had failed. He'd lost every strand of hair except his mustache. Instead, he dedicated his life to the research of forgotten things, particularly South American circuses. A passion he'd procured from his grandmother's stories about her time with a spectacular to end all spectaculars.

Rey and Rhiannon walked around the room, studying the items on display. There were costumes on mannequins. Posters that still wafted with the scent of kettle corn and the sulfur left behind by pyrotechnics. There was a giant hoop, presumably one an elephant would have jumped through. The very unfortunate taxidermized head of a lion, an iron sledgehammer still coated in rust, or blood. Several flyers that didn't advertise anything extraordinary, just people of different races. The Incredible Indian! The Marvelous Mulatto! The Astonishing Aztec! And those were some of the less racist ones. It made the nostalgia of it all turn bitter.

Rey tried to picture Orquídea smiling with a spotlight on her face in the middle of a European city with people trying to decipher what she was, as if she had been made of something other than bone and sinew and blood. Then again, how much different would it have been than if she had walked through the main street of Four Rivers, also with people trying to decipher what she was, where she had come from? How much different was it from Rey, standing at his gallery shows with people trying to decipher what he was, where he had come from?

"Mamá Orquídea talked to the moon, too," Rhiannon said, and they assumed she was talking about the poster they'd spent most of the evening staring at.

Rey found himself wondering about how Orquídea could have belonged in the circus? Was Seal Boy really from the sea or just a man born with a medical condition? Was Wolf Girl truly a wolf or an impish girl with thick sideburns? How could a star be alive instead of just some clever pyrotechnics?

Rey felt a pang in his chest, and he felt a tug at the root of his rose. He glanced around the room, but they were the only ones around. He took a deep breath. It smelled like air conditioner, polished floors. He'd caught a whiff of cigarettes from one of the employees in the comic book shop's main room, and only then realized he hadn't had a smoke since they left Four Rivers. No wonder he'd wanted to puke his lungs out after ascending two hundred steps.

Kennedy, whom Ana Cruz called "profe," was in the middle of regaling her with the long story of how he wound up procuring the lion head from a Russian circus that had blown up in Buenos Aires.

"Ana Cruz said you wanted to know about a particular circus," Kennedy asked eagerly.

"The Londoño Spectacular?" Marimar handed him the poster.

"You mean *Spectacular* Spectacular! I haven't heard of this one in years," he said, holding the unfurled advertisement open so it wouldn't curl. "Pity the South American run of 1960 was cut short by the fire. Terrible. Terrible day. My father told me about it, but from the footage I saw, it was a sight, a real tragedy."

"Footage?" Marimar asked, something

like hope in the single word.

"Give me just one moment!" He ran off into an adjoining room.

"I haven't seen him this happy in years," Ana Cruz said.

Rey pointed a finger at Ana Cruz. "He's not happy about *us* being here. I mean, maybe. But he's definitely happy to see *you.*"

Rhiannon grinned from ear to ear. Her rose deepened into a mix of pinks and reds. "He definitely likes you."

Ana Cruz turned the same shade of red as Rey's rose. "Ay, sinvergüenza."

"Shameless but honest," Rey said.

"We're a little weird, too," Marimar added, and further explored the exhibits. She leaned in to look into the eyes of a taxidermized mermaid that was surely the skeletal remains of a human and possibly a shark somehow Frankensteined together.

Half an hour later, they'd bought several comic books for Rhiannon in the front room, and Professor Aguilar returned with an old-fashioned movie reel. He set it up on his projector, turned off the lights, and ran the footage.

The scene had been pulled from local TV and had no audio. The news anchor had a serious pornstache and the same drab brown suit everyone seemed to wear in the fifties. Behind him was a black-and-white striped, two-pole circus tent. A mouth made of fire ate its way out. Performers and people ran while a sad-looking firetruck tried to douse the flames. Clowns and stable hands fruitlessly ran for buckets of water. Makeup melted down their faces into grotesque sadness and fear. People picked up children, others ran. Smoke billowed and took shape, like the fire was a living thing. Fury made real. Right before the segment cut out, a woman ran across the camera. Everyone, except for Kennedy Aguilar, took a sharp breath.

"That's my mother. She never said that she was there that day," Ana Cruz said. She brought her hands up to her face, one pressed against each cheek in shock. Rey had always wondered why people did that. As if holding one's own face would make a shocking terrible thing not true. As if you were the only thing stopping yourself from breaking apart.

Still, as he watched his great-grandmother shout, he knew what she was screaming — her daughter's name.

"Why was your mother there?" el profe asked Ana Cruz.

He shook with giddy disbelief as he turned

the light back on. Ana Cruz stared at the frozen scene with disbelief. The Montoyas knew that no one wanted to believe, even when they witnessed the truth.

Marimar picked up the poster they'd brought with them, and pointed at the young woman riding a crescent moon. "She was there to see her daughter. *Our* grandmother. Orquídea Divina."

Now it was el profe's turn to look shocked. "I need to sit down. This is fascinating. Truly my rarest discovery yet. Other descendants of the Spectacular! Of course, all of this information has taken me years to collect. It's a passion of mine, you see."

"Why are you so surprised?" Marimar asked.

"Because so many lives were lost that day. Orquídea was listed as deceased, even though her body was never recovered. Along with her husband, of course."

"Of course," Rey repeated.

"Did her husband work in the circus?" Tatinelly asked.

"Work in the circus? You really don't know . . ." el profe took off his glasses and cleaned them with a pocket square. He smiled so hard, the vein on his forehead sprouted. He walked twenty paces to the other side of the room where he quickly flipped through a black album on a display stand. "Here we are. Bolívar Londoño III and Orquídea Divina Londoño."

He stepped aside to let the small family gather around. It was like looking into the past. Orquídea had her hair pinned in a stylish, elegant chignon with a brooch on the side. The wedding dress was simple, with lace sleeves, a tapered waist, and a floor-length skirt. Even in the old photograph, the beads and pearls on the material looked beautifully done. She held a bouquet of roses and flashed the same smile that contained a hundred secrets.

"Damn," Rey said. "Her first husband was sexy."

Marimar reached out and flicked his ear. "That is so inappropriate!"

"I'm a married woman," Tatinelly said, "But he is foxy."

Ana Cruz shrugged at Marimar, but they couldn't deny it. Bolívar and Orquídea were a stunning couple. From the shine of the fabric, she could tell his suit was velvet, cut and tailored to his Roman sculpture figure. He wore his hair, too long for the age, curled like wisps under his top hat. He was smiling, too. The smile reserved for someone who knew that they'd just been given the world. He gripped the iron lion's head cane with one hand, and Orquídea's waist with the other. A ring on his finger caught the light.

"Where — how did you find this?" Marimar asked, her voice trembling.

Rey looked up to ask what was wrong, but her brow was furrowed with confusion, her eyes glossy with unshed tears.

"My grandmother made the wedding dress. Her name was Mirabella Galante. A seamstress who'd come to Ecuador from Catania, Sicily, and found work at the Spectacular."

Ana Cruz snapped open a lace fan and tried to cool the air around her sweaty face. El profe had to run and get her a chair. They marveled at how intertwined a part of their past had been and they had never truly known.

"What does this mean?" Tatinelly asked. She touched the back of her hand to her damp forehead. Rhiannon, whose flower had returned to the blue of a bruise, offered her water bottle to her mother.

Only Rey seemed to notice Marimar hurry out the door. He followed after her. She took the stairs to the top of the cerro Santa Ana, climbing the remaining 265 steps. By the time they reached the summit, he found her gripping the railing. The humid river air wrapped around them, made the flags wave straight and true.

"What is it?" he asked. "And don't say nothing because you look like you've seen a ghost and we have seen too many fucking ghosts to be scared of them."

She walked to the ledge where the city spread out beneath them. Millions of houses and people and cars ignorant of their revelations. Marimar turned her face to the clouds, but she knew better than to pray.

"Londoño," she said tapping the skin beneath her flower bud. "He was wearing it."

"Wearing what? Marimar, I don't understand."

Marimar opened the purse at her hip. In a hidden zipper pocket was a photo, this one he'd seen once before, seven years prior. It had been folded and unfolded several times since then. He wondered how often Marimar had looked at it and wondered at the identity of the man hidden by a flash of light. The man she believed to be her father. Who'd had a hand in her mother's death. It was the single subject he knew not to broach with her, but here she was, carrying it with her thousands of miles away.

Then he saw it. The thing that had scared her. The hand over Pena Montoya's shoulder. It wore a signet ring with the same eight-pointed star as the ring worn by Orquídea's first husband.

"A coincidence," Rey said, but he didn't manage to sound wholly convinced. "Lots of people have the same jewelry."

She laughed, catching the attention of too many tourists. "Orquídea said the man in this photo was my father. Why do he and Londoño have the same ring?"

Rey shook his head. "Maybe their families knew each other. Like Professor Aguilar's seamstress grandmother who made *our* grandmother's wedding dress. Maybe something went wrong and that's why Orquídea ran, and somehow his kid met your mom. Even as I say it, it sounds fucked."

"It's not enough." Marimar turned, as if someone had called her name. But she didn't see any familiar faces among the tourists at the top of the hill.

When he closed his eyes and took deep breaths, Rey thought he heard someone shout his grandmother's name. *Orquídea!* Perhaps the same way Isabela Buenasuerte had done on that terrible night when the Londoño Spectacular Spectacular had gone up in flames. A woman searching for her daughter. A woman searching for forgiveness.

He wanted to comfort Marimar and tell her that they'd unravel the real truth. But he knew, as the skin around his rose tightened with a sharp pain, as if there was a thorn beneath his tender flesh, he knew something was wrong.

Rey whirled around to find Ana Cruz running to them. "Come quickly! It's Tatinelly."

23
ORQUÍDEA DIVINA'S SECOND HEARTBREAK

"What do you think about when you stand out here on your own?" Bolívar asked her one night, coming up behind her. They were headed toward Dublin for their final European show before returning home. Sometimes it was strange to Orquídea to still call Ecuador her home. The Londoño Spectacular Spectacular had been her home. Bolívar was her home now. Even the sea, cold and tempestuous as it was, was her home.

Bastard Daughter of the Waves, the river monster had called her.

In his fox furs, Bolívar was absolutely breathtaking. He wrapped his arms around her and kissed the sides of her neck. He opened her own mink fur, a wedding gift, and slid his arms across her breasts, down her stomach, reaching between her legs to where she hissed in surprise.

"Your hands are cold."

She turned around on the quarter deck

and leaned back against the rail. The salty Irish Sea breeze beat his cheeks pink. She rested a hand over one.

"This trip makes me think of my father. I met him once. He was a seaman. Sailed in and out of my life. I just haven't had a reason to think about him so much before."

Bolívar bit his lip and gazed at her in that way of his. Like she was the only person on this ship. It was just Orquídea, the moon above, and the sea surrounding them.

"You said yourself you grew up on a river. That wasn't enough to think about him?"

"The Guayas River doesn't empty out into the ocean," she said. When she rested her hands on his solid chest, her sapphire ring winked like one of the infinite stars above. Had he wished for it, like he'd wished for so many things? "And here there is so much of it."

"You know I cannot stand it. How can I take away your sadness, mi divina?"

She didn't know if he could, but she tilted her chin up to accept the kiss he was promising. His mouth tasted like wine, sweet like the dark cherry jam he liked to spread on cake after dinner. Orquídea had tried to be so careful with her heart. It had already been broken once, the day her father shoved a purse full of coins in her hands

382

and told her not to look for him. How could she not look for him when every time she saw her own reflection, fractures of him stared back at her? The parts desperate to be loved but never feeling quite whole enough to be loved.

But Bolívar had whisked her away across the world. He'd chosen her. Yes, he'd had indiscretions, but that was life on the road, on the seas. He'd shown her she was the only one for him when he married her. Now their life would change. Why was she so afraid of telling him?

She deepened their kiss, running her hands along the waistband of his trousers. He pressed his erection against her, and when he lifted her up, she yelped.

"Are you afraid I'll let you fall?" he whispered in her ear.

"I'm afraid of a lot of things. But not of you."

Their corner of the deck was dark. Even the late-dinner passengers would be asleep. He looked around to make sure they were truly alone, then returned to her. His mouth on her throat, he hiked her dress up and over her hips. He pushed her lace under-things aside and eased his erection into her. He gripped the back of her knee and raised it to his hip. The pressure of him swelled and he thought he'd break apart in a single heartbeat, so he slowed. She felt her own pulse drumming in her ears, the hollow between her clavicles. He knew just where to touch her, just where to make her breathless and tight. She shut her eyes and felt the ocean mist around them. Licked the salt from his lips as he told her he loved her, needed her, and shuddered. He rested his face in her cleavage. Then he pulled out and she yanked her dress back down.

He bit kisses at her neck. "Te amo, Divina."

Orquídea took his face in her hands and said, "You can love us both, now."

She guided his hand to her belly.

Bolívar laughed. He laughed the way he did with the other actors and dancers while they played cards and drank rum out of teacups. "Even I am not that good. Besides, it's too soon to tell."

"No, I've known for three months now. Can't you feel it?"

His eyebrows shot up. His pants were still unzipped. He tucked in his wet, flaccid penis and buttoned up. "Are you sure, querida?"

She didn't like his reaction. Didn't like the way he pulled away from her, like she'd become a lit match and he was afraid of getting burned.

"You're upset."

"No!" He kissed her cheekbones. Her nose. He kissed her left eye and then her right one. Her mother had always said that when a man kissed your eyes shut, he is lying to you. The only reason she believed Isabela Montoya Buenasuerte was because her mother had always been too righteous to be superstitious, but that saying she recited like it had been done to her, a personal curse.

"I'm thrilled." His eyes were soft as he squeezed her shoulder, digging his fists in the fur of her mink. "I admit. This was sooner than I expected our family to grow, but we'll make it work."

"All right," she whispered.

He finished buttoning his trousers, shoving his shirt into the tapered waist. "Don't wait up for me, my darling. Fedir has a game in the parlor, and he owes me."

Bolívar walked her back to their cabin, where he kissed her forehead and then scampered down the hall. Orquídea ran a bath. She slipped into one of his soft silk shirts. She wanted to be surrounded by his scent in her sleep.

Was that how men reacted when they discovered their wives were pregnant? A few years later, when she was with her second child, Luis Osvaldo Galarza Pincay would weep and kiss Orquídea's naked belly. He never did kiss her eyes.

She woke to a metallic chime, the kind she imagined stars would make if she could hear them winking. But it was well past midnight, and when she reached out across their rumpled sheets, Bolívar was still not back.

A tugging sensation pressed at her belly button, and out of fear that there was something wrong with the baby, she pulled on her thick robe and her slippers and went in search of Agustina. Her potent teas always soothed her.

Instead, Orquídea took a wrong turn in the labyrinthian guts of the ship's halls. She came upon the parlor, the door ajar. The table empty of players. Cards tossed on the green felt and cigars extinguished in the dregs of highball glasses. She would have kept going, had it not been for the deep, mournful cry of pleasure she knew so well.

She felt weightless, brittle, hollowed out. If she was still standing on the deck of the ship, the Irish Sea winds would have blown her away. Bolívar was standing, his trousers at his ankles. One hand pulled his shirt up, the other held the girl in place. She was on her knees, taking him deep into her throat as only someone called "Mishka the Moscow Sword Eater" could.

She was pretty, pale as cream with wide eyes that gave her the permanent expression of just having had her bottom pinched. She stared up at him then, watching as he threw his head back.

He noticed Orquídea, like she was a phantom in the corner of the room. At least he had the decency to stop, to stutter, to cry.

"Divina, it's not what you think —"

What *did* she think? Her husband, who had fucked her on the open deck of the ship just moments before he learned that he was going to be a father, and what did he do? Reward himself with drink. With another woman.

Mishka wiped her swollen pink lips with one of the cloth napkins. She got up and tried to move past her.

Possessed by her own fury, Orquídea grabbed the girl by the throat and shoved her against the wall. She was so breakable, this girl who ate fire and metal. Orquídea leaned in close and whispered, "If you tell anyone about this, if I see you here again, I will poison everything that touches your lips until there's nothing but holes in your throat."

Mishka muttered something in Russian. A curse, an apology. Whatever it was, fearing Orquídea more than Bolívar's scorn, the girl ran.

"Orquídea, please," he stuttered quickly. "Don't be angry with me."

He went on that way, trailing behind her like a kicked dog all the way back to their cabin, where he washed himself and then crawled into bed beside her. She tuned out the world. Curled in on herself so tightly she wished she could vanish into nothing.

"I was terrified," he whispered in her ear. "This news terrified me."

She knew she shouldn't let him touch her. She knew she should throw all of his belongings in the tub and set them on fire. She knew she deserved better. The world, like he'd promised.

"I was weak. I am so, so weak, Orquídea. When you are not with me, I am nothing. Please, I won't be able to live if you don't forgive me."

She turned around then. They faced each other. He was so solid, so strong. It was then, as her heart splintered, that she realized that he was built of a more fragile substance than she was.

"I don't know what's wrong with me. I didn't want to hurt you."

He didn't want to hurt her the way an alcoholic didn't want another drink.

She said nothing, though. Bolívar held her close, desperate. And for the first time she realized, she liked seeing him scared.

While he slept soundly, she kissed both his eyelids, and crept out of their cabin. Moved swiftly down, down, down into the hold of the ship where they kept the elephants and lions and wild beasts. The Londoño exotics and oddities. For a moment, she wondered if that was what she was to him. If that was what he couldn't help but be drawn to and that was why, when he wasn't at her side, he forgot about her.

Orquídea pushed the door aside, readying her wicked tongue to lie. But Lucho wasn't there, by some miracle. In the years to come, she wondered where he had gone and why he had chosen that specific day to abandon a post he had guarded so faithfully before. Some things were never meant to be answered.

When she opened the ship's cargo compartment, the Living Star slowly turned in her direction.

"Are you ready to make a deal?" he asked, weary but amused.

"I am. But I have a condition."

"What?" he snapped.

"Show me your real face."

24
THE GARDEN OF PLAGUE AND MIRACLES

No one knew exactly what was wrong with Tatinelly and Michael Sullivan. After she'd fainted in the circus museum, they'd rushed to drive her back. Marimar had kept her discovery between herself and Rey and would do so until her cousin was well. While Tatinelly had a high fever and was dehydrated, her husband had worsened. One thing was certain, the Montoyas had to cancel their flight.

Mike's sickness, which had begun with the symptoms of a common cold, had progressed to something even doctors couldn't explain. His skin had become so translucent, you could see the inner workings of him. Like his body was an aquarium for his bloody, swollen organs.

The first doctor who had been brave enough to enter the now-quarantined Buenasuerte house, was Lola Rocafuerte, a surgeon who owed the dead Wilhelm Buenasuerte a favor and decided to pay it by coming to diagnose the foreigners locked in the guest room.

She took their temperature, their blood to run tests, but she was positive she had never seen anything like this. And so, one by one, medical professionals arrived to the house in cohorts to try and determine the cause of the ailment.

One doctor, round and with a face like a mole who had never seen sunlight, protested that it was a plague from God. Normally, they all would have laughed, or disregarded him as being out of his mind, but then pustules began growing in pockets across Mike Sullivan's body. Upon closer inspection, they were pods. After the biopsy of one, they discovered the very early stages of grasshopper eggs.

Tatinelly, on the other hand, displayed all the textbook symptoms of typhoid fever. But when her bloodwork came back, along with her husband's, the only abnormality displayed was high blood pressure on Mike's part.

The doctors all agreed to send the blood and egg samples to the CDC, and a week after that, they received the same results. There was nothing wrong with them, except Mike had become a human incubator for a biblical plague and Tatinelly's body was an oven.

The inhabitants of the Buenasuerte house, who had so far been immune, did everything they could to keep Tati and Mike comfortable. From teas to cold baths. Still, the only thing that would truly help Mike's emotional and physical pain was being sedated with high levels of morphine.

Marimar was in the rear courtyard with Rhiannon and Rey, hoping for some time away from doctors and prying eyes. A few of the medical professionals, unable to cure the Sullivans, had taken to try and analyze the three cousins with the flowers growing out of their skin, particularly Rhiannon, whose rose had turned the color of ash since the day her mother fainted. Although the surrounding neighbors did climb ladders and peek their heads up on the other side of the cement walls to ask how they were doing.

To which Rey would answer, "Just enjoying the biblical plague! How are you?"

No one really tried to talk to them after that.

"We have to do something," Marimar said while Ana Cruz and Jefita were getting takeout. Days of worrying had drained them all. Marimar and Rey were cleared by Doctor Rocafuerte to return home, but neither of them could imagine leaving their family behind. "If it's not a scientific ailment, then it's a magical one."

"We do what we came here to do," Rey said. "Figure out Orquídea's shady fucking past. Let's start with the eight-pointed star."

"Theory one," Marimar said, "Bolívar Londoño is actually immortal and my father. Which, gross."

"In my comic book," Rhiannon said, pulling out dead leaves in the rose bushes. "The superhero married his dad's former girlfriend without knowing it."

Marimar blinked in surprise. "You let her read that?"

Rey gestured at the glass screen separating them from the medical freak show happening in the house. "We've been a little busy, Mari."

"Fine."

"Theory two," Rey said, in a hurry to bypass the conversation. "Bolívar survived the fire, had another son, and somehow that son met your mom?"

"Too Dickensian. It could explain why Orquídea didn't want me to know my father. And why she forbade my mom from chasing after him. Either way, he won't survive this. I will kill him myself."

"Too Oedipal, Marimar."

"Penny is dead. Uncle Félix is dead. Aunt Florecida is *dead.* Tati —" She glanced at Rhiannon, then composed herself. "Whoever this is, they can't get away with it."

"Do you remember how Orquídea conjured those ghosts?" Rey asked.

"I've tried talking to my mom. But if she's a ghost, she's not coming to see me."

"You're both wrong," Rhiannon said.

"Oh yeah, smarty-pants? Why?"

Rhiannon dug her finger in the dirt. She loved all the same things other seven-year-olds loved. Video games and dolls. Glittery dresses and mountains of candy that she would regret in the middle of the night. She loved staying up late, fighting sleep so she wouldn't miss a minute of her cousins' adult conversations. She loved eavesdropping. But she also loved listening to the way creatures whispered at her, the way butterflies said hello and kissed her forehead. The strength she felt when she got dirt under her fingernails. One time, when no one was looking, she ate a mouthful of it, worms and all. Later that day, she could understand what Ana Cruz and Jefita were whispering when they spoke in Spanish. She'd never been able to understand them before that day. In a dream, Mamá Orquídea had done the same: eaten dirt and learned a language. Rhiannon was connected with her in ways she was only beginning to understand.

"You think you want to know but you're scared. He *is* scary."

"Who?" Rey asked.

"The man in my dreams. Usually, Mamá Orquídea is there to protect me. But sometimes, I see him."

"What does he look like?" Marimar asked.

"I can't see his face or anything. But after we went to that place, I think he might be the same. The moon. Or maybe a star."

Rey felt his mouth go dry. He'd painted that light, that prism that appeared in reflective surfaces in New York. "Baby girl, circuses are tricks. It's like magicians. Illusions."

"Is the flower on my forehead a trick?" she asked with a slight grin. "Were Mamá Orquídea's miracles tricks? She shows me in my dreams. She says you both think you want to hear her, but you're not actually listening." Then she raised her eyebrows in a gesture that was uncannily Orquídea. "Especially you, Marimar."

Marimar felt a pressure in her stomach, behind her belly button. She was starting to understand that feeling meant something was on its way. Something was going to happen.

"Can you show us, Rhiri?" she asked.

Rhiannon held out her dirty little hands. Ladybugs crawled up her arms, but she didn't seem to mind them. "Okay, think about Mamá Orquídea."

Rey's lips quirked slightly. They each had a different version of the woman in Four Rivers. For Marimar, she would always be the same. Half real, half legend. She imagined Orquídea Divina Montoya pulling salmon from a lake that was made for trout. She imagined her making salves and ointments for every scrape and burn that Marimar accumulated like battle scars. For Rey, she was all glamour. She was the same grandmother he'd loved and hated in equal measure at different stages of his life. The one who would never be confined and normal. He saw her as the girl she'd been in that photo, hopeful and young, like the world hadn't quite broken her yet. Rhiannon only knew one version of Orquídea — the woman who was a tree. The voice in her dreams that sang pretty songs she was only beginning to understand.

Together, they heard a single voice. A man Rhiannon and Rey had already heard before.

Find me, he said.

And then, Orquídea's clear voice. *Run.*

When Rey opened his eyes, sweat was running down his face and neck. He crab-walked into the wall behind him but something brushed his skin. Again and again, leaves and vines shot out of the ground, growing faster than he could blink.

"Run," Marimar said. She hauled Rhiannon up by her hand, and they stumbled into the house. Rey was trying to close the screen door but there were too many vines. They flooded the house with green, creeping up on the ceiling and twisting around the ceiling fan, the light fixtures.

Marimar slapped her hand on the light switch, but the electricity was dead.

That pressure and ache behind her belly button intensified until she was on her knees. Rhiannon pulled Marimar by her shirt. Rey pulled them both back.

"Marimar, Marimar, get up, please," Rhiannon cried. "He's here!"

She could see a shape emerge in the center of the living room. The dark warbled around him, forcing their eyes to work twice as hard to focus on the outline of his silhouette. The negative of a photo filled in with moving space and time, radiating at the core with the rainbow fractures of a prism. Marimar knew. She knew Rhiannon was right.

The Living Star.

"Why are you doing this?" Marimar asked. She hated the sound of her voice. The fear that squeezed her vocal cords into high notes.

He looked around, and she could make out a snarl outlined in the bright kaleidoscope of his features. "I have to take back what was stolen."

"We didn't take anything!" Rey shouted.

"But Orquídea did." He moved fast, his hands closing around the gifts at Marimar's throat and Rhiannon's brow.

Marimar and Rhiannon screamed. Marimar felt a pulsing sensation within her heart. It was like being split in half, her flesh being turned inside out like skinned game. She tried to move her arms to fight back but the sensation was numbing her down to her bones. She saw the tree back home. Her valley. Clouds rolling in black and gray, punching fists of thunder into the ground. Orquídea's tree bleeding from its heart.

The Living Star screamed and let them go. Behind him, Rey's eyes were manic as he released the kitchen knife he drove through their attacker's shoulder. The Living Star fell to his knees, the light within him was a fading pulse. He reached over and removed the blade from his body.

"I will never stop hunting you," he said, then almost sadly, he added, "It was not supposed to be this way."

Marimar took up Rhiannon in her arms, thin traces of blood running from her forehead and into her eyes. They needed to get out of the house one way or another. But her mind was numb, her body ached from her hair follicles to her marrow.

Then, Tatinelly made her way down the stairs.

Mike Sullivan died in the middle of the night. He felt no pain, only a deep warmth, the gentle caress of his Tatinelly, and then he was gone. The moment of his passing, his every pustule, which had served as gestation pods for the hundreds of grasshopper eggs embedded in his skin, split open. The grasshoppers molted, and shimmering green creatures bounced across every surface.

It was their frenzied song that woke Tatinelly. She kissed her husband, but she did not have time to mourn him. Not yet. Perhaps not ever. She had work to do. The living needed her still. She'd seen glimpses of Rhiannon, her sweet Rhiannon, running from a figure in her dreams. She found that the vines that filled the house felt familiar as they wrapped around her legs and arms like armor and gave her strength. Her fever broke, her eyes cleared. Tatinelly, who had believed she was ordinary her whole life, walked out of her quarantine room.

What no one — except Rhiannon and Mike — knew was that Tatinelly had never truly shed the gift Orquídea had given her seven years ago. After giving birth to Rhiannon, a branch remained, and a single golden laurel leaf sprouted out of her belly button. She took strength from it every day. Tatinelly would never be a painter, a writer, a celebrity, a scientist. She didn't want to be any of those things, and that was okay. Some people were meant for great, lasting legacies. Others were meant for small moments of goodness, tiny but that rippled and grew in big, wide waves. Tatinelly might have been ordinary, but she was not weak. And she'd been saving the gift Orquídea had given her for a moment that mattered.

"Leave my family in peace," Tatinelly told the monster hunting her family.

Using the very last of her power, Tatinelly called the vines to her. More and more, there was infinite life within her. Vines broke the skin of her belly button and wrapped around the Living Star, choking him until he began to fade. She felt the fire of his light, fighting against her. Grasshoppers leaped down the stairs. Hundreds of them descended on him, a cloud of locusts.

"This is *not* over," the Living Star hissed and vanished in a breathless wave of darkness.

After, there was the crunch of glass, the panting of breaths, the crackle of locusts. Tatinelly Sullivan Montoya staggered into the arms of her cousins and her daughter. They brushed her hair back.

"I want to stay here." And with her final breath, she said, "This is a lovely place to rest."

25
ORQUÍDEA DIVINA'S VOW

The Living Star shone brighter within his iron cage. He turned away from Orquídea. "I will show you my face when we have a deal."

Orquídea pulled her robe tighter. It was a flimsy armor, but she would work on finding a better one, a stronger one. "Fine, stay in that cage for another decade. What do I care?"

The air chimed in that celestial way of his. "Wait. Wait. Wait, please!"

She froze. *Please, Orquídea, please.* That's how Bolívar had begged her, too. She shut her eyes against the onslaught of tears. But she didn't turn around. Didn't let him see.

He extinguished his glow, so the only source was a phosphorescent bulb overhead and the strange gleam of his manacles. They had blended into the brightness, except at certain angles where she saw color, the streak of a rainbow. The sheen of water on an oil slick.

Orquídea blinked until her eyes adjusted to the shadows. She was surrounded by sleeping beasts, by the flap of restless caged birds, the stench of animal shit, and the hay and cedarwood shavings that could never quite cover it up.

Then, she faced him.

The most surprising thing was that the Living Star was a man almost like any other. His hair was as dark as the longest night, with thick waves that tumbled down his pale, naked shoulders. His hooked nose was proportionate for his rectangular face, like every imperfection was tailored to make it impossible to look away. Orquídea took another step closer and was able to see the pearlescent beauty marks on his pectorals, his abdomen.

"Do you have a name?"

"Lázaro."

She stepped closer yet. Her fear giving way to curiosity. "What are you?"

"What are *you*?" His mouth tugged with a smile. "Flower. Mermaid. It seems you have to be anything, other than yourself."

"I'm just a girl."

"No wonder you cry out for help."

Heat coiled in the pit of her belly. "If I'm here for your insults, I'd rather just go."

He grew sullen. "I would have thought your darling husband would have told you already."

"He said you're a real, true star."

"I am so much more than that," Lázaro said softly. "There are beings across the heavens, above and below, in the between. Sometimes, we find planets and rule over them. Become gods and saints and prophets. Other times, we become weapons."

"How?" she paced the perimeter of his cage and he turned to keep her in his line of sight.

"I will tell you when we have a deal. When you agree to set me free."

"I can't accept a deal without knowing what I'm walking into."

Lázaro's laugh was the distant roll of thunder. "And yet is that not what your marriage was? A deal with a man you barely knew."

Orquídea hardened her heart and it showed in her smile. "Mock me one more time. Do it. As soon as we arrive in Guayaquil I'm leaving, and I don't have to take you with me."

His light became inverted, a silhouette of shadow and prisms of light in every color. "Think it through, Orquídea. You have done this once before. You ran with nothing to your name, and you found Bolívar. Will you do that once again?"

"I'm not the same girl who left."

"That is not what your deepest wishes tell me." He relinquished his dark light and appeared human again. His skin shimmered as she'd imagined stardust would. The more he moved, the more he looked like a supernova living under his skin.

"You truly are a wishing star that walks the earth."

He leaped to the bars and gripped them tight. He shook. "If the earth is this cell block."

She took several steps back reminding herself that they were alone, and she was pregnant, and he was naked.

"I apologize," he said. "I have been here so long. But yes, I hold the power of wishes. Desires. True, unfathomable want. When I fell here, to this planet, your sun and moon solidified my corporeal form."

"Is that why you are so very shiny?"

"Luminous," he corrected, and laughed, despite how much he did not want to.

"How old are you?"

He resumed pacing again and traced long, elegant fingers across his torso. "This form is perhaps two decades old. But my consciousness is older than that, though I have begun to forget the longer I am locked in this place."

"Are you cold?" she asked.

"I no longer feel it."

"Is your light not warm?"

He looked up. His strange eyes never left her face. "For you, but not for me."

Orquídea finally sat on a crate. Her body ached, down to her bones. She shivered, but she removed her scarf, thin as it was, and offered it through the bars.

Lázaro stared at it for so long she waved it like a flag. He accepted warily, but wrapped it around his shoulders and sat cross-legged on the hay to make her less scared of him.

"Do you get to choose?" she asked.

"Choose?"

"What you become. If you're raw power hurtling through the galaxy, and you don't know what you'll become or who you'll become until the planet gives you form — isn't that disappointing?"

Lázaro toyed with the fringe of her scarf. "There is nothing brighter than a wish. It comes from true hope. Humanity is so full of that. Desperate hope. Joyous hope. Even those in anguish, *especially* those in anguish, I should say, have hope. The anticipation that tomorrow will be better than the next day. I find it terribly amusing."

"Then you're cruel," she stated simply, without a trace of accusation.

"Humans put me in here. Well, one human. Did your darling husband tell you how he came upon me?"

She nodded. "He said his father found you in a crater."

Lázaro turned away, looking at the other beasts in the cages beside him. "When I fell to this planet, I came in a meteor shower. I fell outside his encampment. I was weak and recovering from the crash. I told the man I would give him a wish in exchange for his help. All I had with me was precious alloy from my galaxy, my armor, and my sword. Ah, and my clothes, for I did wear clothes once. While I slept, his son melted it all down and made these manacles for me and a ring. It is the only thing in this world that can restrain me."

"If I break you out of here, then you're free?"

"Not quite," Lázaro said, a sad smile. "Even if I break free, he can call upon me. Control me."

Orquídea let out a frustrated breath. She hadn't thought betraying her husband would be easy. She rubbed her belly then. Could she really do it, when the days passed, and her anger ebbed? When he looked at her as he did the first day they met?

"Your heart need not be metal to be strong," Lázaro told her.

"Stay out of my thoughts," she hissed.

He chuckled lightly. "Ah, but that is the very core of it. I can sense what is in your heart and mind. That is how I know that this is the only deal which will make you whole, if you keep your word. I know you desire more than this. Even the ocean we travel across is not big enough to fill the desire in your heart. Neither is Bolívar."

"You said, if I gave you your freedom, you'd give me a taste of your power." Her mouth had gone dry with a hunger she'd never felt.

He stood slowly, watching her with his night-sky eyes. "And I meant it."

"I don't want a taste. I want a piece of it. I want a sliver of your power to keep for always. And I want you to teach me how to use it." She should have thought about it more. Been more careful about the eagerness in her voice. But it was out there, and she couldn't reel it back.

He thought about this as he silently prowled the cage. Two decades he'd spent imprisoned, bested by a monstrous boy of only ten. Now, he was haggling for his freedom with a girl who had so easily given away her heart. And yet, he knew that it would be Bolívar's true love, the one he'd called forth on a wish, who would set the Living Star free. Agustina had decreed it, and though he doubted the capability and honesty of humankind, he did not doubt her gift.

"You have a deal, Orquídea." He held out his hand and waited. She seized it. His touch was firm, cold, like the first time she held snow.

"Deal."

A sound came from the end of the hall. Voices. The guard, or perhaps Bolívar himself.

"I have to go," she said.

"Bring me the ring, and find the key. It is the same color as my chains." He gripped the bars in front of his face.

"Wait," she stalled, glancing back at the door. "What does his ring do?"

Lazáro held up his palm, and her eye went to his left hand. "It is how he controls me."

Steal a key and a ring that her husband kept on his person at all times. It was impossible. But as she made her way back, she imagined the taste of that power, even the smallest bit. She was Bolívar Londoño III's wife. La Sirena del Ecuador. Orquídea

Divina, Bastard Daughter of the Waves. She'd seen parts of the world she'd never imagined, and when she was done, she'd see it all. And why stop at the world, when she might have a chance to see the galaxy?

■ ■ ■ ■

PART IV
HASTA LA RAÍZ

■ ■ ■ ■

26
Ingredients to
Call on the Dead

The grasshoppers were hard to catch. When they thought they'd gathered them all, they appeared in cups of coffee, in Jefita's purse as she rushed out to make arrangements. They hid in the underside of the car and in the engine. Ana Cruz's approach was to step on them, crush them, but eventually she grew accustomed to the sight of their green faces in the kitchen cupboard and in the tins of cereal and rice.

Ana Cruz was not devout, not the way Jefita was. She'd been baptized, had her first communion. She went to church when her father was alive, but not since. She kept reliquaries of the Virgin Mary in her home, a cross in her bedroom. Sometimes she wondered if it was because she truly had faith or because she feared the alternative. But when she'd come down the stairs to find Tatinelly dead, she prayed harder than she ever had before. She prayed for the

Montoyas, the living and the dead. Ana Cruz had been so stunned she simply stared at Tatinelly's lifeless body. The slight girl looked like a princess out of a fairy tale resting on a bed of vines after her sacrifice.

The vines had been another problem. They'd grown out of the garden and out of her stomach. No one had wanted to take the bodies. Not to the hospital and not to the morgue. There were too many officials, too many gawkers standing outside the house. Reporters and helicopters. Vultures, all of them. Even priests made the pilgrimage, getting past the enclosed neighborhood's guards because no one, not even the guards, would deny a priest.

The official story was this. Intruders attempted to kidnap Mike and Tatinelly Sullivan, tourists from the United States. The perpetrators were chased away by other members of the family and were in the wind. The police had no suspects.

That was the official story.

Others, those who had visited the Montoyas, those who had marveled at the God-given gifts growing out of their skin, knew different. They called it a miracle.

Rey had spent the day after consuming the entire bottle of bourbon Mike had intended to drink in celebration of Félix

Montoya's life. Rhiannon hid in the garden, crying and whispering to the grasshoppers who surrounded her like a rapt audience. Meanwhile Marimar went over every finding, every photo. She obsessed over the Living Star, but there was nothing about him. No real name. No museum obscurities. He was like Orquídea, a mystery they couldn't solve.

No one slept, and they only ate because Jefita forced them to. Mostly, they waited for the bodies to be ready. Marimar called the family at Four Rivers, told them to stay put, stay together, and then she sat there listening to Reina, Tatinelly's mother, wail. It haunted Marimar as she retraced the steps of that night. How had the Living Star found them? Why hadn't he come back? She stood in the courtyard with her face to the night sky. She listened for a whisper, a threat. That strange bell-chime voice that threated at the fringes of her mind. But nothing and no one came.

There were no more miracles.

Miracle or not, there was work to be done. A funeral to prepare. Tatinelly had used her final words to say she wanted to stay here. Despite Reina's plea to come home, they couldn't go against Tatinelly's wishes. Not when she'd saved them. As for the Sullivans, they left a message, but no one had returned their call.

Seeing their desperation, Jefita approached Marimar. She was in the garden with a notebook in her lap, drawing eight-pointed stars. There were pages and pages filled with them, compass roses without a map to give direction to.

"What's wrong?" Marimar asked, upon seeing Jefita's face.

The old woman glanced over her shoulder, twisting the bottom of her apron into a rope. "I know someone you can ask about Orquídea."

Marimar sat up. "Who? Why didn't you say something sooner?"

"Because the person we need to ask has been dead for ten years."

"Tell me."

And Jefita did. All things considered, it was not the strangest thing Marimar had ever heard. She should have considered it herself, but part of her still resisted the possibility of the impossible. Besides, she was desperate.

The following day dozens of people showed up to their house for the funeral. They muttered the words *miracles* and *saints* and *alone.* They knew that the beautiful descen-

418

dants of Orquídea Divina didn't have anyone else. Even Professor Kennedy Aguilar was there, offering to be a pallbearer.

Rey and Marimar did not have to bear the weight of the caskets alone, and together, they flooded the streets like a black river making its way to the sixth gate of the Cementerio Patrimonial de Guayaquil, at the foothill of the cerro del Carmen. People who lived up the hill liked to say it was the best place to live. There were no tourists, they had the best views of the city, and when the time came to return to God, their bodies only had to travel just few paces for a final rest.

During the two-mile walk to the cemetery, the sky turned gray and lightning announced the coming rain. Rhiannon held on to Jefita's hand and wiped at her tears, which had begun to calcify as they were shed from her tear ducts. Those walking behind her rushed to pick up the shimmering pearls. They tucked them in pockets. Others ate them just to see what miracles tasted like. Rey, on the other hand, shed more than a tear. Three petals fell from his wrist. With one of the caskets firmly rested on his shoulder, he turned his face up to his hand and inhaled. The faintest trace of decay filled his nose. It was the scent of

419

roses forgotten in a vase of water that turned to muck. There was nothing he could do, not until after they broke several legal and ethical laws in the cemetery.

Tatinelly and Mike were laid to rest in the Montoya mausoleum crowned by a statue of an angel. Rhiannon said, "the angel looks like it's ready to fly away."

After everyone had left, Ana Cruz, Jefita, and the Montoya cousins remained.

"For the record," Ana Cruz said. "I do not like this. Rhiri is too young to see something like this."

Rey, who had bummed a pack of cigarettes from one of the onlookers, raised one to his lips. "I'm pretty sure *I'm* too young for this, too."

"I'm not a little kid," Rhiannon asserted. "And we're a team. You can't leave me out."

"We won't," Marimar assured her.

Ana Cruz raised her hands in defeat and went outside to keep watch and bribe any guards if she needed to. As she left, so entered a short, stocky man with deep-bronze skin and a canvas hat covered in the same white paint as on the stacked tombs. He had a pickax and a sledgehammer in his backpack and averted his eyes when greeting the Montoyas. Abel Tierra de Montes had been painting the outer faces of the vaults of the cemetery since he was fifteen. He'd apprenticed for an artist as a boy, but after she died, the family had ousted him. He had a practiced hand, and his portraits were favored by the families who paid for the upkeep of their entombed dead. Abel had owed Jefita a favor on account of her introducing him to his future wife, and though he didn't think what this family was about to do was natural, he couldn't turn away from the money. Not when more and more people were forgetting their dead.

It took twenty minutes, but he managed to open the sealed top of Isabela's tomb. Then he made the sign of the cross, bowed his head to Jefita, and said he'd be back at the time they'd agreed to seal it all up.

They stared at the bones. There were still clumps of hair on the skull and thick cobwebs on the simple pale blue dress.

"How does this work?" Marimar asked. The black dress she'd borrowed from Ana Cruz was itchy. Sweat pooled between her breasts, down her spine. When the scent of cement and decay hit her nose, she breathed through her mouth.

"My mother did this once," Jefita said, lighting a stick of wood with Rey's lighter. "On her death bed my grandmother confessed that my mother's father wasn't her *birth* father. But she died before she could say his name."

"Is that to summon the dead?" Rey asked.

Jefita wrinkled her nose, she set the stick on the lip of the tomb. "Palo santo. It purifies. And it smells good."

"The ritual worked for your mother, though, right?" Rey asked, undoing the knot of his tie and the button choking his Adam's apple.

Jefita peered down at the bones. Her mother had needed answers only the dead could give. Jefa, whose real name was María Luz Rumi, chased rumors of necromancy and resurrection until she found the real deal. "Yes. She discovered her real father was her uncle. My mother knew she might not like the truth. The difference is my mother had to dig."

Rey grinned. "Lucky us."

"Where do we start?" Marimar asked.

"You have to focus all of your energy on that connection every family has. It's in our bones, our blood. More than that, it's in the questions we need answered. The secrets, traumas, and legacies that we don't know we've inherited, even if we don't want them."

Jefita's dark eyes fell to Rey's hand. Another petal fell. In seven years, it had never

422

shed a single one. After the other night's attack, he'd shed four.

"A seance would be less smelly," Rey muttered.

Jefita lightly smacked the back of his head. "This is real. Usually, the ingredients to call on the dead involve a blood sacrifice. Your family is still brushed by so much recent death and that is enough. Now, focus. You've never met your great-grandmother, but blood is like a tether, even when the tether is frayed. The connection is there, deep down, hasta la raíz."

Down to the root.

Rey thought of the boy he'd been once, reserved and quiet. He'd wanted to hide in stacks of papers and numbers that added up to neat solutions. He'd never expected to be this person who dug up his ancestor's bones. Though, to be fair, he hadn't had to actually dig, in the literal sense. He tried to clear his mind again. Concentrated on what he wanted. Every other time he'd focused this power, gift, curse — whatever it actually was — his desire had been simple. To make art. So, he had. He envisioned Orquídea's tree. The three of them had been trying to talk to their grandmother before the Living Star attacked. They'd heard Orquídea's warning, too late. He explored the spark of his power, his gift. Rhiannon had said that Marimar and Rey hadn't really been listening before, but where were they supposed to learn how to communicate having been raised in a house of secrets?

Rhiannon closed her eyes and felt the skin around her rose burn as it changed back to the blush pink that reminded her of her mother. Her beautiful, patient mother who had protected her. She didn't want to cry anymore. She wanted to help her cousins listen and see. Somewhere in the shadows of the mausoleum came a breeze, a deep groan.

Marimar thought of the pictures she'd seen of Isabela Belén Montoya Buenasuerte. She'd already had opinions of her great-grandmother and they weren't kind, even if she wore the woman's face. She felt her frantic pulse at the center of her throat and focused on that. How far within her did the bud grow? When they'd taken Tatinelly away, Marimar had noticed the golden laurel leaf on her belly button. Is that what was inside of Marimar, too? Was she made up of roots and vines? Were there flowers in her lungs? Thorns around her heart? Jefita had said to focus deep down, hasta la raíz, *down to the root.* Tía Parcha was buried in New York. Her mother, Tía Florecida,

Penny, and her grandfather Luis were in Four Rivers with Orquídea's tree. Tío Félix was here in the river that surrounded them, and now Tatinelly was in this room with their great-grandmother. Where would she be buried when the time came? And who would care?

A single tear ran down her cheek.

Then, the bones rattled. They aligned, gathering into the semblance of a person.

Isabela Belén Montoya Buenasuerte's skeleton sat up.

27
LOS HUESOS DE ISABELA BELÉN MONTOYA BUENASUERTE

"What have you done to me?" Isabela asked in a clear, haughty voice. There was the faintest imprint of the woman she'd been layered over the bones, like transparent skin. A ghost. A true and honest ghost. "Who are you?"

"It's me, señora Isabela! Jefita Rumi —"

"I know *you,* Jefita, of course. But who are *they*?" The bony finger pointed at Rey, Marimar, and Rhiannon.

"I'm Marimar, and this is Rhiannon and Rey."

"Rey?" Isabela's bones asked. "¿Rey de qué?"

Marimar snorted. His mother had changed the usual Ray to Rey. "Rey," the Spanish word for "king." She would always call out to him and say, "my little king of the earth." Sure, that was cute when he was five. But clearly, his great-grandmother didn't think so.

"It's short for Reymundo," he said and took a long drag of his cigarette.

"I'd say I'm pleased to meet you but, who are you to me that you would wake me? How long have I been dead, Jefita?"

"Almost a decade, señora," she said, and crossed herself.

"We're your great-grandchildren from your Montoya side," Rhiannon explained.

"Montoya? Whose Montoyas? My brother or sisters'?"

"Neither." Marimar said the word like a bite. "We are the progeny of Orquídea Divina. And we have questions."

"Orquídea lived," she said with joyful sorrow. She repeated the name, until the sad spell was gone, and Isabela's bones rattled with the Montoya temper. "She lived, and she didn't tell me. I don't want your questions. I don't have answers. Let me rest in peace."

Marimar and Rey exchanged a knowing look. She said, "Well, at least we know where Orquídea got her stubbornness from."

Isabela's bones made a choking sound, if bones could choke. "How *dare* you talk to me that way? The nerve. It served Orquídea right that she should have such insolent grandchildren. And what is that on your skin?"

"It's Mamá Orquídea's gift," Rhiannon said, clutching the side of the tomb. She leaned in, not away like her older cousins, like Jefita who hovered against the wall out of fear of the dead. "And I'm actually your great-*great*-grandchild. We need your help, otherwise the star is going to get us, too."

"If he does, I might just haunt you for all eternity," Rey muttered.

Isabela crossed her arms over her chest. "And my daughter? Why don't you ask her?"

"She's not among the living and she's not among the dead," Marimar explained. "We'd leave you alone, but we know that you were there when the Londoño circus went up in flames."

"No, I wasn't."

"You're lying," Marimar stated plainly.

"We saw it on film," Rey said.

The skeleton turned to Jefita, dust particles buzzing around her. "Mira cómo me hablan. None of my other grandchildren take that tone with me. Was I so terrible to deserve this unholy disruption?"

"We'll leave you alone," Rey said. "But we have to know. Did you speak to Orquídea the night of the fire?"

"That place." She tipped her nose to the

ceiling and sniffed as if she wasn't a bag of bones marinating in her own decay for a decade. "That wretched place. My daughter dressed like a whore for all the world to see. They told me she was born unlucky and they were right."

"You don't get to talk about my grandmother like that," Marimar said, a second thorn growing from her throat, twin to the first. "Maybe if you had loved her, if you'd done right by her, she wouldn't have run away, and we wouldn't be talking to you right now."

The bones stiffened. A dense cold bit at their skin as Isabela said, "You don't know what I went through. You don't know what it was like. Two years after she left, the Londoño Spectacular returned to Guayaquil. I saw Orquídea on a poster. I took it down, of course, lest anyone in the neighborhood recognized her. I tried to fix things; I did. I tried to tell her to come home. She had a child. She shouldn't have raised him in that place."

"Pedrito," Rey said. "He — he died. We think that night, but we can't be sure. We need to know everything that you saw. Anything Orquídea might have said."

"*Why?*"

"Are all the Montoyas this way?" Mari-

429

mar asked, half laughing, half hysterical. "Just — tell us please."

"Yes," Isabela turned her cheek on them. "If you're going to wake me from my rest, then I at the very least want to know why. And did you bring me any offerings?"

Jefita had instructed them to bring something the dead might have missed from their life. Since the Four Rivers Montoyas didn't know their great-grandmother, they made their best guess. Marimar brought a silver flask of whiskey. Rey contributed a cigarette, and Rhiannon, her plastic *Little Mermaid* doll. Jefita offered her former employer's comfort food, a sweet humita. Isabela made a noise of reluctant satisfaction, and gathered everything into her tomb and placed the cigarette in her mouth, leaning in for Rey to give her a light.

Jefita and Marimar also took cigarettes Rey offered because the occasion felt like it called for such a thing.

"Very well. Tell me your plight," Isabela said.

"We are being hunted." Marimar couldn't help but glance over her shoulder. "Something Orquídea stole from her time at the circus was important enough to murder for. A gift, of sorts. Before she died, Orquídea gave three of us that gift. We need to figure out how to kill the man she took it from before he kills more of us. Did she tell you anything that could help?"

Isabela's bones blew out smoke. She observed the people before her. None of her Buenasuerte children had tried to wake her. But then again, none of them would have believed in such a thing. She wouldn't have either, once. There had been a weight-lessness to being dead. Now that she was, not alive, but awake, Isabela felt every regret she'd once had. They were needles piercing right through her bones, reminding her of her sins.

"When I went to see my daughter," she said slowly, "I wanted to ask her to come home, as I already said. When I got there, part of me hoped that I was wrong, that I imagined her likeness. But there she was. Glowing. Beautiful. She even sang for the crowd. I don't remember her voice ever being that strong. I thought she was indecent at first, because the dresses they wore were so short, but when I saw her up close, she was — radiant. Wilhelm had forbidden me from going to see her. He found out, of course. How could I keep something like that from my husband? He forbade me from telling my other children. But she was my daughter. I missed her more than I can ever say. There were so many things that I should have done differently but I couldn't change it."

Isabela unfolded the yellow corn leaf of the humita. Her movements were dainty, but she ate with her fingers, drank ravenous sips of whiskey. Every morsel that passed through her phantom mouth turned to ash.

"I went to confront Orquídea. She was like a new woman. So sure of herself. Married, too, by the ring on her finger. I met her little boy, Pedrito. He was so sweet, barely a year old. I wanted to hold him, but she didn't let me. She asked me to leave.

"Hadn't I done the same thing to her? Pushed her away because of my own shame? I shouldn't have left, but I did. It's my own fault. We don't talk. None of us. Why don't we ever talk? Silence is a language of its own in this family. A curse of our own making. That's the inheritance my daughter got from me, and I am so very sorry."

Isabela Buenasuerte was an old woman with so much regret that she'd carried it to her grave. It poured out of her in shimmering tears.

"I know my daughter well enough that I knew there was something wrong," Isabela said, sniffing and taking a calming drag of her cigarette. "It was in her eyes. She was scared."

"Did you see the Living Star?" Marimar asked.

Isabela paused, like she was trying hard to recall the night. "Yes, yes I did. I was going to leave after seeing Orquídea perform, but I stayed until the end. They rolled him out in an iron cage. A Living Star, they called him. I thought it was a bunch of horseshit, you know. Trying to fool honest people. But he glowed from the inside out. You couldn't even see a person, only the outline of one. Orquídea watched him, too, from the opening of one of the curtains. That's when I took my chance and went after her. You say this Living Star survived, too?"

Rey nodded and lit another cigarette. "He said he'd never stop hunting us."

Isabela's bones rattled as she shook her head. "I tried to find her, when the circus caught fire. When I couldn't find her, I thought she was dead. She and Pedrito. My poor girl. It's my fault, not the stars'. The only bad luck she ever had was me."

Marimar gripped the lip of the tomb. "We shouldn't have come here."

"Don't say that," Isabela said, like she'd been slapped. "I didn't know my daughter in life, not truly. But through you, perhaps I know her a little more. You know, there is

433

something. . . . When Orquídea was a little girl, she talked to the river more than she talked to me. She told me she made a pact with the river monster. I wouldn't be surprised if she went back there when she escaped the fire."

Marimar brushed the corners of her eyes.

"We'll let you rest," Reymundo said.

"Thank you."

"What will you do?"

"Go to the river," Marimar said.

"Take this." Isabela yanked off the tips of three phalanges and handed them to her descendants. "Keep them with you. Put them somewhere safe. I failed to protect my daughter, but perhaps I can protect you."

Marimar chuckled.

"What's so funny?"

"You just reminded me of her for a moment," Marimar said.

Isabela laid back and rested her hands on her abdomen. She shut her eyes. The impression of her ghost faded. "She is still my daughter, after all."

28
THE FLOWER WHO STOLE FROM THE STARS

A few weeks into her search for the key to free Lázaro, Bolívar had become so attentive, so utterly loving, that Orquídea almost wanted to change her mind. Doubt seeped into her thoughts. Why should she take another man's word over her own husband's? A man who was not a man but a celestial being. A fallen god trapped for the amusement of others by a clever ringmaster.

Bolívar proved his love and desire for her again and again, for the duration of their voyage. When they changed ships in Panama, en route to Santiago, Chile, Orquídea spent most of her time walking on deck, taking in the cold breeze. She talked to her child, even though he was still growing. She wanted to make sure he recognized her voice when he was born.

On one of those walks, another passenger approached her. He leaned against the railing beside her. "What a beautiful sight."

She nodded and offered a polite smile but nothing more.

The man leaned in. He was handsome, tailored. The kind of man who liked to adorn a bowl with exotic fruit but never eat it. A Nordic accent perhaps. "I meant you."

He reached for her cheek, but before his hand made contact, Bolívar grabbed the man by his coat and pinned him against the edge. The threat was clear. Orquídea tried to pull Bolívar back, but she was not strong enough.

"Stop it, Bolívar, please!"

"He was going to touch you," Bolívar shouted, feral.

Thankfully, Lucho was there to stop her husband from being jailed for manslaughter.

Back in their cabin, Bolívar kissed her, pressed his face against her pregnant belly and apologized for scaring her. Everything was fine for a moment. That's what Bolívar was like, moments of love, adoration, heat, betrayal, jealousy. All of them fleeting.

When the moon was full, the tide within him changed. He wandered into the crowded parlors and salons, searching for a pretty girl to fuck in the dark corners of the ship. He was a lycanthrope, waiting for that one night of havoc and rage, of wild reverie that made him forget about his wife and his son growing in her womb.

It was that day, once a month, when he stayed out all night, that she made herself remember her rage. It drove her. It turned her little by little into a new kind of marvel, the woman made of iron. But no matter how many times she emptied his closets, his suitcases, turned out the pockets of his dozens of tailcoats and doublets, his socks and his undergarments, she couldn't find the key. The only thing Orquídea discovered was that Lucho left his post once, every night, just after midnight to carry out his clandestine affair with Wolf Girl. Those were the moments she spent with the Living Star.

Lázaro was getting impatient. They were already making their way across Chile and into parts of Argentina, after which they'd continue north to Guayaquil and end back in Cartagena where everything had begun for the Londoños.

"Perhaps," Lázaro mused, "I will find another girl with a heart of ice who wants her dream just as badly as you, perhaps more so."

She sat where she always did, at the door of his cage on a wool blanket. How many times had he said that to her? Always the same threat. "Too bad, my dear fallen star, you already showed me your hand. I am the one you were looking for."

He allowed himself to laugh with her and accepted her offerings. He'd never cared for human food because he hadn't known that Bolívar had only ever fed him the same scraps they fed the dogs. Orquídea brought him cakes filled with cream, tartes topped with candied berries. She'd made him try wine and tell her the story of sailing across the stars. What it felt like to be pure energy and light and consciousness. She never grew tired of that one, of the promise of infinite wonder.

Every time she left, he'd say, "Do not forget your promise, Orquídea."

"I won't," she'd assure him. But she could never figure out who she was lying to, herself or him.

During the height of her pregnancy, Bolívar treated her like glass. The most fragile thing in his collection. She stopped performing but watched all the same. Watched his eyes linger on a pretty face in the crowd, watched as he auditioned new performers alone, at night, for hours. He wouldn't make love to her while she was in her "condition." After the baby came, a healthy beautiful boy who was a replica of him, Bolívar's habits remained the same.

Orquídea could no longer escape the whispers. Mirabella and Agustina watched her with sympathy. Lucho gave her a kind smile and he never smiled at anyone but his lady love. Sometimes she wondered if this is what her mother had felt when Orquídea was born, waiting for a man to come back while a baby bled her breasts dry. Then she reminded herself that she wouldn't feel the same shame. She was determined to be a better mother to Pedrito than Isabela Buenasuerte had ever been to her.

Soon, Bolívar's cycles became hers. He left, he returned, he loved her, he left again. He assured Orquídea that his promise, the one he'd made to love her forever, was written in blood. She had his name. She had borne his child. Nothing else mattered but that and no tryst could compare.

She decided to put his theory to a test. Though Orquídea wasn't unfaithful, she flirted with the danger of it. While the show was stationed in La Paz, Bolivia, she left Pedrito in the care of Agustina the Fortune-Teller and spent the night with her friends at a tavern. Men bought her drinks, tried to get close enough to count her freckles. They wanted her autograph written on the skin over their hearts. She was mid-signature when she heard the tavern door slam and she knew that it was him without looking up.

Bolívar found her. One of his porters must have followed and snitched. This time, Lucho wasn't there to pry Bolívar off the man who'd touched his wife. He beat the stranger until both his eyes were swollen shut, until Orquídea let out a scream that shook him from his fever, and he was taken to the local jail.

The stranger had lived but went blind out of one eye, and Orquídea paid twice the bail funds in order to bring him home on the condition that the circus leave La Paz that same night.

Bolívar and Orquídea clung to each other out of desperation and fear of solitude. It was only when they fought that they could reignite the passion they had once felt for each other. He wanted her to scream his name. She wanted him to beg. Orquídea knew that it was not enough. Bolívar's words were no longer enough. That life was no longer enough. And so, she made plans. She searched. She learned about the galaxy and magic from Lázaro. In order for her betrayal to work, she needed to be in Guayaquil. She needed his ring, which he never took off, and she needed the key.

When Pedrito was three months old, Bolívar started carrying on with one of the new Egyptian belly dancers they'd taken on for the Peruvian leg of the tour.

Orquídea admired herself in the mirror, taking down the pins from her hair, and he was getting ready to go back out, when she said, "Give Safi my compliments on her performance tonight."

This time, he didn't deny it. He just stormed out. And when he returned a breath later, she foolishly thought he'd come back to apologize. To make it up to her. To fuck her instead.

He'd only forgotten his top hat.

That was the moment Orquídea Divina figured it out. One part of her three-pronged conundrum. There was one item she'd never searched. There was a second item he always wore, and only took off in their private cabin.

With Bolívar gone for the night, she snuck in to see Lázaro. Pedrito slept snug in a sling against her chest.

"I know where the key is," she said breathlessly.

Lázaro diminished his light in front of her and grinned. She'd grown used to his pale, naked figure. The pearlescent beauty marks on his skin. His irises moved like a starry sky. But she'd never seen him smile with

441

such satisfaction. He was rather beautiful when he did.

"Then why are you here instead of getting it?"

"I told you," she said. "We have to be in Guayaquil. I have to be home. There's still the matter of the ring. He sleeps with it on. I've never seen him take it off."

"Then seduce him until he is fast asleep."

Orquídea made a strangled noise. "We haven't — we don't — he doesn't want me that way anymore."

"He does," Lázaro affirmed. "He is simply content knowing that you are his."

"I am no one's."

"Brave Orquídea," he chuckled. "Who will entertain me when I am back among the stars?"

"Don't you have friends? Family?"

Lázaro frowned. "We do not have those words. And my kind have no sense of humor."

She smiled then, truly smiled. "Lázaro. When you share your magic with me, will it — will it hurt?"

"Me more than you," he said softly. "I have to open up myself to you."

"Sounds intimate," she said, worry piqued in her voice.

"Believe me, it is not the fleshy awkward

sex you humans have. I would be letting you into the thing that makes me *me.* I suppose your priests would call it a soul. It would be like opening a vein and letting you feed off me. Consume the very power that makes me what I am. I would have to trust you not to kill me in the process. I am putting all of my trust in you."

"I know," she said. "Thank you."

"Then you are free to go your own way. Make your wishes come true. I truly hope our paths never cross again, my friend." Lázaro reached through the iron bars and touched Pedrito's nose and startled when the baby let out a cry. "What is wrong with it?"

She laughed and sang a nonsensical lullaby that her mother had sung to her. "Haven't you ever held a baby?"

"Of *course* not."

"Can you make them?" she wondered. "I mean, if you remained on earth?"

"Yes, I suppose I could. But I do not belong here," he said, amazed at the way Pedrito quieted at the sound of his mother's voice. "Remember, Orquídea, every time you use your magic, there is a price."

"My dear fallen star, so you've told me again and again."

"If your husband is any example of your

kind, it is worth repeating."

Orquídea looked away. "Bolívar seems fine to me."

"As long as I am tied up here, he will not pay it. That is his loophole. So, for you, well, have a care. Wish for riches, and you might get a million dollars in sucres, but the next day the country's currency becomes the dollar and the exchange rate is not in your favor. Wish for true love, and you might get it, but he might drown in a year because you were not specific."

I wished for you. Bolívar had said. He had gotten her, in his own way.

"So, you're saying *be specific,*" she teased.

"And careful. This is celestial magic, not a birthday candle. And after it is done, I want your word, your vow, that you will not look for me when the magic begins to fade."

"I won't want to," she said, but smiled. "Where will you go?"

He looked up at the ceiling. How long since he'd looked up at the sky? "I am going home."

29
THE GIFT OF THE RIVER MONSTER

After they sealed up the tomb, Ana Cruz drove them back to river shore in La Atarazana. This time, only the Montoyas got out of the car and walked to the edge of the rickety pier.

"What does a river monster look like?" Rhiannon asked.

"Ghosts and miracles, I have seen," Rey said. "This is out of my peculiarities' expertise."

"Orquídea said that it was ancient, part human and part crocodile," Marimar said. The skin around her clavicles itched and she pressed her fingers against both the old and the new thorn that had grown there. "The question isn't what it looks like but how we get its attention."

"I know!" Rhiannon gasped and darted to the murky water's edge, leaning over so far, the slightest breeze might tip her over. She stuck her little hand there and disturbed the surface.

"Rhiannon!" Rey startled and reached for her, but she wasn't in danger.

"Papa Félix!" she said in her small, fairy voice. The water gently lapped at her touch. "I need your help. Can you find the river monster who was friends with Mamá Orquídea? Tell him that she says hello."

They waited. Across the river, the city of Durán was obscured by low-hanging clouds. Before long the sky began to darken. Rain clouds unloaded overhead in torrential showers, and Jefita yelled that they would catch their death before any false god could get the chance. Traffic blared in the distance and pinpricks of lighting tore into the sky. They waited for so long that they nearly turned away.

Marimar felt the weight of her family. The ache at the base of her throat. "We should go."

Rhiannon pointed. "Look!"

A slick creature about one foot long, with a reptilian body and the humanoid head of a crocodile, crept up onto the pier. It clawed up to the top of a post to be closer to eye level.

"Orquídea Divina's progeny," the reptilian creature said in a wheezy voice.

446

"Orquídea's . . . river monster — uh — friend?" Rey said.

Rhiannon picked it up in the cradle of her palms. It was smaller than any of them had expected. This was the creature that had wrestled grown men and made a pact with their grandmother?

"River monster," it spat. "No one has called my name in a long time."

"You're so cute," she giggled in that way of hers. "Mamá Orquídea said you were three feet long."

Indignant, the creature wriggled and climbed up on Rhiannon's shoulder like a questionable Jiminy Cricket.

"My spirit grows smaller and smaller as I am forgotten."

Marimar brushed her damp hair back and wiped drizzle from her eyes. "Orquídea remembered you. She used to tell us stories about you."

"My Bastard Daughter of the Waves."

"I'm sorry, but I have to ask," Rey said cautiously. "You're not secretly our grand-father, are you?"

The river monster snapped at Rey's hand, snatching a rose petal between sharp teeth and ate it. "No."

Rey winced, and rubbed at the spot. "It's been a strange couple of days. I needed to be sure."

Marimar pinched the bridge of her nose as Rhiannon giggled. "Orquídea's mother said that you were her only true friend here. There's a man — a creature — after us. We need to know if Orquídea ever came back to seek your help. We have to stop him before he comes for us again."

The small crocodile spirit smacked its tongue, like it savored the rose petal. With a shake of its whole body, the river monster perked up and scampered off Rhiannon's shoulder, growing six inches in height and width.

"That's better," it sighed. Glossy yellow eyes took in the young Montoyas, and as if seeing them clearly for the first time, the creature spoke clearly. "After our pact, I never saw Orquídea. I do miss her presence on these shores."

"You've seen everything that passes through these waters for centuries," Marimar said. "And yet, you answered Orquídea's plea. We're here now. Make a bargain with us."

The river monster chuckled. "You're as demanding as she was . . . My power has faded, but perhaps I have something that might help you. One thing that is enchanted with a bargain. It will trap a hundred fish or a single man. Once caught, they can only be freed by myself or by Orquídea, as we are the ones whose vow enchanted it."

"What is it?" Marimar asked.

The creature reached into its wide mouth and pulled out a shimmering string.

Not string, Marimar thought. *A net.*

The net her grandmother had used decades ago, when she was no bigger than Rhiannon.

"Take this." The river monster crawled back on all fours, elongating to look more like a crocodile than a beast of legend; as if the more magic it expelled, it became something else.

Marimar took up the net, still perfectly intact. Her vow shimmered gold in the thread, for what was stronger than words?

"Thank you," Marimar said.

"We don't know your name?" Rhiannon said.

"No one asks. Sometimes I forget it." It coughed, like it hurt to speak. "My name is Quilca."

"I'll tell Orquídea you said hi, Quilca," Rhiannon assured him. "That you helped us."

Quilca waded into the river, then stopped. "I am not the only one who remembers Orquídea, you know. Sometimes I hear her

449

name, like a scream."

Rey straightened. So had he, the day Tatinelly's illness took hold. It had happened so fast he hadn't processed it. "From where?"

"Up in the cerro Santa Ana. Once a month, when the full moon is out, I can hear it."

Then, Quilca the river monster was gone.

30
THE SPECTACULAR
SPECTACULAR FIRE

The day the Londoño Spectacular Spectacular returned to Guayaquil was the day Orquídea's life would never be the same. But she had already prepared for that. This time, the tents were bigger, the acts more astonishing. Bolívar's fascination with spectacle and glamour made it an immersive experience for all who entered. Agustina spun the threads of fortunes at her table. Children cracked baby teeth on bright red candied apples. On stage, women walked across tightropes with wings growing out of their shoulders, angels all of them. Orquídea performed in her dress that bloomed like a living flower, and then again as a mermaid swimming across a sea. Dancers and jugglers and sword swallowers. Wolf girls and seal boys and beasts. Finally, Lázaro, the Living Star. At the heart of it all the ringmaster, the visionary, Bolívar Londoño III.

Orquídea had prepared for that day for so long, that when it finally arrived, she couldn't stop trembling. She needed to compose herself or the plan wouldn't work. She took everything into account. Bolívar's activities, the time at which he bathed after the show, then left to play cards. He'd come back one more time to kiss Pedrito in his sleep. Her bag was packed and stowed under the bed. She'd take Pedrito to the storage tent where Lázaro waited. She'd free him, take her sliver of power, and then she'd be free.

She'd prepared for nearly everything, even made the rounds around the circus, saying goodbye without really saying the words. But on the way back to her tent, Orquídea was approached by someone she never thought she'd see again. Her mother.

There had been a moment when she was singing that she thought she'd imagined Isabela Buenasuerte in the audience. Her heartrate had spiked, agonizing over what her mother would think. What she'd say. But Orquídea ran away two years ago. She was a married woman. A mother in her own right. She'd seen more of the world than her mother, who had never even left the province she'd been born in. By the end of her song, Orquídea convinced herself that she was wrong. The faces in the audience blurred together after a while.

But there she was. Isabela Buenasuerte looked the same as always in her expensive dress, her elegant features turned up in distaste at the candy-coated popcorn and wood shavings on the ground.

Orquídea remembered the helplessness and anger she'd endured at the Buenasuerte home. All at once, it felt like trying to surface during an onslaught of waves. But if Orquídea was honest, her anger toward Isabela went further than that. Standing in front of her mother, Orquídea felt like that unlucky runt of a girl again. A stain in her mother's perfect life. The bastard child left behind by a man who'd used her. Seeing her mother was like pressing on a bruise that had never healed. It had festered, rotted. It seeped down to the bone. She'd only learned to live with the pain.

"What do you want?" Orquídea asked, not letting her mother speak. She pulled Pedrito protectively against her chest.

Isabela Buenasuerte ignored the dagger that had become Orquídea's tongue. She tugged off her white gloves and smiled hopefully. "Who is this beautiful child?"

"This is my son," Orquídea said tightly.

"Tell me his name, mijita."

Orquídea didn't want to, but the part of her that still wanted her mother's love relented. "Pedrito."

She should have stopped there. She was a spool of thread coming undone and there would be no one to put her back together. She should have turned and walked away like she had two years ago. Instead, she pointed at the large poster of Bolívar Londoño III with his smile, sharp as diamonds, welcoming one and all to his creation. She held up her glittering sapphire. "And that is my husband. And this is my circus. And I don't want you here."

"Orquídea —"

"Leave."

When Orquídea recalled that memory from time to time, she admired the hands of destiny that orchestrated the longest minute of her life. From somewhere, fireworks sparked. Bells rang announcing the opening of the fairground portion of the night. Fortunes, games, prizes, a perfect storm of cruel fate! And there was Bolívar strutting across the grounds, so beautiful in his signature blue velvet that it was impossible not to notice him. Only instead of his wife and child, it was Safi, the belly dancer, draped on his arm. He'd skipped the card game and had gone straight to her. As he kissed her, he didn't even try to hide his indiscretion. On any other day, Orquídea might have picked a fight. But on that night, of all the nights her mother had chosen to return to her life, she'd been witness to Orquídea's shame.

Bolívar was unaware of his wife's life shattering in front of his mother-in-law. Orquídea couldn't bear it. Something inside her split. It was a tear in her whole being. A fracture that would never be able to be put back together.

"I said *leave,*" Orquídea repeated as Pedrito began to wail in her arms.

"Orquídea, please."

"No. You chose your life and I chose mine. I don't want to see you again."

"At least let me hold my grandson —"

"You have six other children. One day you will have plenty of grandchildren to hold." They were ugly words, but she had an ugly, cruel pain in her heart. "Tell me. Did you always know that someone would come into your life and make it better?"

"What do you mean?"

"I mean, we had a life before Wilhelm Buenasuerte. A life where you could have loved me. What we had could have been enough if we had worked together."

Isabela Buenasuerte shook her head. "You

don't know what it was like being left alone. I was *alone.*"

"You had me." Orquídea tapped the naked skin over her heart, like if she punched through it she'd find it hollowed out. "We didn't need Buenasuerte or my father. He came to the house one day and I never told you. I never told you anything because you made it clear, from the moment I could walk, that I had ruined your life. It's like you were waiting for someone to give you the world you deserved before I came along."

When Isabela had nothing to say, no words to defend herself, Orquídea laughed. "I thought so."

Hurt, Isabela did as she was told. She left but, of course, didn't go far.

Orquídea returned to her schemes but she'd changed. Some people change over time, water wearing stones smooth. Others require the violent clap of lightning that turns sand into glass. Her heart felt like it had split into tiny little hearts, each pounding at the hollows of her body, her throat, her fingers, her toes. Pedrito could feel it, and he fussed and cried all the way back to their tent.

She set Pedrito down in his basinet and ran over to the room she shared with her husband. Bolívar's hat was in the same spot on the bed where he threw it every night before he went out. She didn't think he'd be back, but she seized the boon. She turned it over. She'd never truly held it in her hands. It felt like an extension of him, in a way. She reached inside and ran her hand along the lining. The latch of a false bottom. She opened it.

"Orquídea?" he asked. "Is that you?"

Who else would it be? She wanted to ask but didn't.

Then she felt it. The cold metal of the key made of celestial light. She quickly pocketed it in her brassiere and sat at her vanity. Her dark eyes were glossy, but she hid her distress well. She opened one of her powder boxes and dipped the velvet cushion in, then dabbed it between her breasts. The delicate scent helped her relax.

Bolívar stepped out from behind the bath screen. He was naked. Her heart gave a flutter in reminder of how much she'd loved and wanted him once. He followed her eyes to his lower extremities as he dried his torso. She remembered the times when they bathed together, emptying the tub with their passion. Then she remembered Safi, the prostitutes in Amsterdam, the acrobat twins, the actress in Monaco, the duchess in

London. Most of all she remembered standing in the parlor of that ship and watching a Russian girl swallow his erection whole. She wished the girl had bit it off.

"Are you happy to be home?" Bolívar asked, drying his ear.

He walked up behind her, kissed her while staring at them in the mirror. She accepted his kisses because she had a traitorous heart. They were together now. She, Pedrito, and Bolívar. He raked his hand over her leg, over her breasts. She remembered the key tucked there. Even if she wanted him one last time. Even if . . .

"You're in a good mood," she said, and distracted him by slapping one of his muscular thighs. It was like he suspected something was wrong. Is that why, after months, he'd changed his predictable schedule? "And you're wet."

He cocked a brow and let his stare rake over her. "I thought that's how you preferred me."

She laughed and stood, using their son as a pretense. She rocked him so that the baby was the only one she had room for in her arms.

"I was thinking," he said, tugging on a simple button-down. A flush of heat spread across her skin as she remembered how much she'd loved watching him dress in front of her. "We should take a walk around the park tomorrow. See the city. The river. I know you've longed for it. Let's see how the pearl of the Pacific has changed since you left it."

"You know me so well." She tried to sound sweet but her nerves seized her vocal cords.

He wrapped his arms around her and kissed her cheek, caressed the baby's head. "That's because you're mine. You both are."

Why had he chosen that day, of all days, to remind her of the moments when things were beautiful? She knew that Bolívar Londoño was not going to change. She should have listened to Agustina long ago and protected her heart better. But she'd been naïve. She'd been desperate to cling to something good. The biggest trick, the greatest illusion in the whole circus was Bolívar's love.

"Why? Is Safi busy or did you already fuck her enough today?"

Bolívar looked like she'd slapped him. He bit his bottom lip and pulled on his trousers. "You spurn my advances and then you push me to another woman. Is that how little you love me now?"

"You stopped loving me long ago," she

said softly, and she wasn't sure who she was trying to convince. She tucked Pedrito back in his bassinette and sat in front of her mirror. Tried to summon all the strength she had, steel her heart.

"I have never stopped loving you," he said, turning Orquídea in her seat to face him. He caged her with his arms. "You know who I am, and you chose me, too."

That was the last time Orquídea Divina would see Bolívar Londoño. Sometimes, during the time periods between husbands in Four Rivers, Orquídea wondered how things would be now if she had only relented, slipped the key back into his hat when he fell asleep. Pedrito might still be alive. She'd still be the foolish ringmaster's wife who allowed his trysts and infidelities. How was she supposed to know which life had been the right one? She allowed herself that moment of weakness every few years and then she put Bolívar where she put her other memories, locked away where no one could find them.

Instead, she kissed her husband. She let him trace the familiar lines along her thighs and hated herself for still wanting him just a little. He was on his knees, ripping the seams of her sheer stockings. Orquídea's heartbeat pounded in her ears. She turned her head and watched him through the mirror, the bright lights that showed every detail, even the lines across his back made by someone else.

She reached on her vanity for one of her powders. There were so many reasons she had asked Lázaro to wait until she was back in Ecuador to enact their plan. The most important one was because it was her home. She wanted Pedrito to grow up with eyes on the river. She wanted him to learn to love the land. Guayaquil was an old city, full of old people, rooted to the earth. The world changed around them. Hills covered in grass became paved streets. Houses made of cane and brick and tin became slabs of concrete. There would be new bridges and monuments and art. It would change, but the resilient heart of the people would always remain strong. She needed that strength.

The second reason was because Ecuador was home to thousands of species of flowers. Four thousand types of orchids, four hundred types of roses, and one strange, hallucinogenic lily. An angel's-trumpet, shaped like a bell and used by shamans to divine the stars and expel inner demons. It had medicinal properties, but in the hands of men, it was used for cruelties. She'd acquired the powder and emptied the vial in one of her powdered perfumes.

It wasn't how she'd timed it, but it could work. Would work.

Bolívar wrapped his hand around his cock and looked at her, dazed by her beauty as he'd been that first day. Orquídea grabbed a fist full of powder and blew it in his face.

He choked and sputtered. He cursed and grabbed for the bed, falling on his back. She'd only ever heard stories of the plant, and she didn't know how long it would last. Her plan was three-fold. She had the key. She retrieved the bag from under the bed. Now, she yanked the signet ring from his finger and pocketed it.

With Pedrito safely against her chest in his sling, she ran. While the fireworks went off, she approached the tent. Lucho frowned when he saw her, but she blew a handful of the angel's-trumpet powder in his face. All eight feet and four hundred and sixty pounds of him fell like a great bear in the woods.

Lázaro paced in his iron cage. Orquídea dropped her bag and rested a protective hand over Pedrito's soft curls.

"You are early," Lázaro said, taking in her agitated state. "What happened?"

"We have to do this now. Bolívar came

back early, and I don't know how long the angel's-trumpet will last."

Orquídea thought of her father shoving money in her hands and then asking her not to look for him. How arrogant had he been in thinking she'd wanted to know him in the first place?

"The key," Lázaro said, and held up his manacles.

Orquídea thought of her mother marrying Wilhelm Buenasuerte and telling her to wait upstairs on the balcony, out of sight.

"And the ring?"

She thought of Bolívar's serpent tongue. She thought of the broken pieces within her.

"Here." She cupped it in her palm like a pearl.

She thought of how Lázaro trusted her. But he knew the darkness in the heart of humans, and he should've known better.

As he shut his eyes and became the Living Star, Orquídea did as he'd instructed. She placed her hand against his chest. For a moment, she couldn't breathe. She felt like she'd fallen into the Guayas River. She'd stepped into the hollow space of the galaxy he said he'd come from. The world was all color and light. Then all darkness and stars. Was this what he felt like every time he used his power, like the world couldn't touch him?

Orquídea thought again of her mother and Bolívar. The two people she loved the most once again had split open her wounds. She never wanted to feel that way again. What would she do when Lázaro's power faded? What would she do when she was alone again? Why should she not have the power of the stars forever? The universe had conspired against her, Niña Mala Suerte, Bastard Daughter of the Waves, and she was evening the score.

Overcome with grief and anger, when the moment came to let go, she held on. She took and took as others had taken from her. She heard Lázaro's heartbeat, his pulse within her, slower, racing against her own and losing. She heard him scream her name.

Only then did she snap awake. Pedrito was crying and Lázaro had passed out.

Orquídea kept her end of the bargain, however. She left the key and the ring in his hand.

She felt his starlight coursing through her. It was deep in her marrow, in the composition of her blood, her sinew. Orquídea Divina made her first wish.

I wish Lázaro never finds me, she said. *Never sees me, never hears my voice, never*

464

comes near me.

Then she picked up her bag and left. She made it across the fairgrounds before she smelled the smoke. The others did, too.

"No," she gasped.

Orquídea tried to run back but there were several explosions. Animals and people trying to escape all at once. She dropped her bag and tripped over a net. Later on, she remembered thinking how ironic it was. The very thing that had sustained her as a child would be her undoing.

She heard Bolívar's voice somewhere in the distance calling her name. He was awake. She had done this, played a part in the destruction of everything he had built, and she knew, she knew he'd want to hurt her.

Freeing herself from the tangled net, Orquídea held her baby close. She thought she must have hit herself when she fell, because, as she stood, there was a piercing pain cutting from her heart to her core, deep within her uterus. She began to glow, her insides radiating with light, hot and blinding.

She didn't remember fainting from the pain, but she came around to the wail of ambulance sirens. Heard the screams. Then, a terrible realization claimed her. Pedrito was pressed against her, but he wasn't moving. Wasn't flesh or bone. He was calcified, unbreakable moonstone.

31
The Living Star & The Girl with a Hole in Her Heart

The city of Guayaquil was born on a hill. Nearly five hundred years later, three cousins raced up 444 steps of the same hill to reach the summit of the cerro Santa Ana. They passed vendors whistling for their attention, girls selling candy and cigarettes out of boxes that hung from their necks like parlor girls from the 1920s. Buskers and pickpockets. Young and old couples out for a stroll, families dining in at local favorites. Families so much like the Montoyas and families worlds apart.

As they reached the very top, Marimar felt that familiar pain behind her belly button. She wondered if she'd been wrong when she'd equated that feeling with Four Rivers, with Orquídea. The plaza at the top of the hill was lined with visitors who wanted to watch the sun set over the city. Not one of them was aware that she'd buried her cousin that morning, that she'd spoken to the bones of her great-grandmother moments later. None of them knew how many times her world had shattered and how she'd put it back bit by bit. All because some circus oddity had a vendetta against her grandmother. They'd take the fight to the Living Star. This ended with her, with them.

"Fuck, I need to quit smoking," Rey muttered as they reached the top of the hill, winded, but alert.

The Montoyas formed their own cluster, turning and turning in the direction of the winds in hopes of hearing that voice.

"What about that place?" Rhiannon asked, pointing at the lighthouse.

The lighthouse would be the highest point of the hill. But it was decorative. Visitors spilled in and out to get a sight of its views.

Marimar knew in her gut that the Living Star was not up there. This was the hill that the indigenous peoples had called Loninchao, and the Spanish invaders had called Cerrito Verde, *the Little Green Hill*. Where a treasure hunter, near his death, invoked the name of a saint to save him from death. Santa Ana.

Isn't that what the locals had called her, and her cousins? *Saints*. Marimar knew that she wasn't any of those things. But Orquí-

468

dea might have been. The girl who spoke to the river, the girl who made something out of nothing. The woman who transformed herself time and time again when the world refused her.

"The chapel," Marimar said, and this time she was certain.

They ran across the stone plaza bathed in sunset golds. The stained-glass depicting Santa Ana pulsed with light. The chapel itself was small, with five or six rows on each side. A couple of old women were kneeling in the front pews. Despite the noise of the intrusion, they did not open their eyes, only kept rubbing rosary beads between wrinkled fingers.

Marimar palmed her stomach. Sharp pain tugged at her belly button. She stepped closer to the stained glass windows depicting the stations of the cross.

"There's nothing here," Rey said, his whisper amplified by the acoustics.

"Wait —" Marimar couldn't quite explain the sensation that pulled at her. She heard a faint chime, like the prolonged note of a church organ. It was distant, but there. The Living Star was hiding within these walls and she would rip out the wallpaper, the boards. She'd break everything apart the way Orquídea had destroyed her own house.

Then the pulling sensation grew stronger. She counted each window and found the oddity.

At the other end of the chapel was a fifteenth window that did not belong — a figure standing at the top of a green hill overlooking a river. Above him, stars fell in a torrent, but one was the brightest. An eight-pointed star right over his heart like a compass rose.

"It's him," Marimar said. Her throat ached, and this time it spread, like thorns were growing inside of her chest. She wove between the pews until she stood in front of the glass window. Her abdomen cramped where her power tugged, and for a breath of a moment, she wasn't certain if it wanted her to go forward or turn back. She heard Rey and Rhiannon hurrying to her side.

When she touched the glass, vertigo spun her up and down, left and right, here and there. Marimar closed her eyes and breathed through the nausea that slammed into her. The temperature dropped and, when she opened her eyes, she was no longer in the chapel.

Rey and Rhiannon leaped into the stain glass window a breath after her. Rey had never felt as cold, not even when he did the polar bear plunge on New Year's Day in

Coney Island. Rhiannon thought of the ice that had frozen her hair into icicles when her parents took her sledding, and she didn't mind as much.

The room was empty, dark, with a circular skylight that let in a single shaft of moonglow. She took a step forward. The thick plumes of incense and the sweet, humid air of the city was replaced by a stench that assaulted her — waste and decay. The same rot she'd smelled in Four Rivers, but older still. Something was dead and it was in this room with her.

"What *is* that?" Rhiannon asked beside her, pinching her little nose. "I don't see anything."

"It's another trick," Rey said. He walked into the moonglow spotlight. Up above, he could see the moon, like it had been lassoed closer to the earth. His steps echoed in the cold stillness, as he made his way to the far wall and stopped at his reflection. He spun in every direction but there were no doors, not even to mark their entry point.

Rhiannon touched her reflection. "Why are the walls all liquid mirrors?"

"I don't know," Marimar said. Every instinct within screamed for her to run. But to where? There was no place that was safe for them. Not until she confronted the Liv-

471

ing Star. She pressed her hand against the wall, but this time it was solid. She saw herself multiplied over and over again, an infinite version of herself and her cousins, and then, right behind her, a man appeared where there hadn't been one before.

The Living Star's halo of light flickered, then darkened, until he was the layer beneath, a man with long black hair, milky skin dotted with pearlescent scars. His black eyes flared wide and a deep moan echoed in the room. Thick stitches formed crude exes over his lips, the skin red and raw at the puncture wounds.

Marimar swallowed the scream that wanted to crawl out of her throat. She stepped in front of Rey and Rhiannon and willed her body to become a shield. She pulled out Quilca's net, ready to ensnare him, but the Living Star didn't move to defend himself. He stepped back in the shadows; head bent in sorrow.

It was then that she heard the rattle of chains at his feet, the strange color of the white metal.

"What's wrong with him?" Rhiannon asked.

Marimar had no answers for them. How could this man, this being, have hunted them in this state? She shoved the net into her purse, then rummaged through it and drew out Orquídea's old fishing knife.

She approached the Living Star with one palm held up to show she meant no harm. Not yet. "I'm going to cut your stitches, is that all right?"

He shut his eyes, and something shimmered down his face. Were those tears? He made a strangled sound she took for "yes."

Marimar didn't want to touch his skin, but she gripped his jaw. She wasn't sure what she'd expected but he was just skin and bone, slightly cold to the touch.

"On three," she said, but sliced after she counted, "one."

The Living Star doubled over, trembling as he ripped the thread from his lips and slid against the wall. He kept looking at her with eerie galaxy eyes.

"I wish you had not come," he said darkly. There was something strange about his voice. It wasn't like the man who'd attacked them at the Buenasuerte house — gruff and demanding. This man sounded like torn vocal cords, a soft tortured plea. She realized it was the one she'd heard in Four Rivers. *Open the door, Marimar.*

"A thank you would do, too," Rey muttered.

"Why?" she asked, acid crept up her

tongue. "Who are you?"

His gaze cut to Rey and Marimar. "You must go. He is searching for you now, but he will come back to take more of my power. He will use me to hurt you."

She glanced back, but they were still alone. "Tell me everything. Tell me the truth."

"You are as stubborn as she was."

"Orquídea?" Marimar asked, even though she knew. She knew.

He rubbed at the spot right over his heart, like there was a hollow there, one that matched her own. He shut his eyes and wiped at the blood trickling from the punctures around his lips, and when he smiled his mouth looked like a pomegranate split in half.

"No, you are as stubborn as Pena," he said, glancing at the skylight like he was waiting for someone. He breathed deeply and spoke like he'd lose the words if he stopped. "My name is Lázaro. You are our daughter. This is not how I wanted you to know me. Forgive me. Forgive me. Now you must go."

Rey placed a hand on Marimar's shoulder, but she only stared at the broken creature at her feet. Her father. The shining light, the missing piece, the question she'd thought she needed an answer to. He was before her. She felt the thorns within her, the rage she didn't know she possessed. Mostly, she felt like she was hovering at the edge of a chasm and the only way out of this was to jump.

"You're my father," she said, mostly because if it came from her lips, it would be true.

Lázaro winced and touched the ripped skin around his mouth. Rhiannon crouched on her knees and brought out a bottle of water from her backpack and offered it to him.

"Here," she said.

Lázaro took it and his features twisted into a deep well of gratitude, like someone who had never been shown kindness. The Living Star gulped the water in a single breath, sloshing it down his chin and washing away the blood. "Thank you."

"You killed her," Marimar said. "You killed all of them. You hunted us and now we're here."

Lázaro staggered to his feet. He nodded, slow tears spilled over the mound of his cheekbones where they froze, crystalized, and fell in sharp clinks to the floor.

Marimar choked on her words and only managed a soft, "Why?"

"I did love her."

"I didn't *ask* if you loved her. I asked why you did it."

"Is it not obvious?" Lázaro asked, stepping closer to Marimar. He tried to memorize the shape of her eyes, the color of her hair, her spirit so much like her mother's. "Because *he* wished it. I do not want to hurt you, but I will if he makes me."

The room rumbled. The four of them looked up at the ceiling. A shadow eclipsed the moon for a moment, and then it was gone.

"Marimar?" Rhiannon asked. She pulled out a tiny red ember from her pocket and hissed as it fell on the floor, turning black then white.

"Is that Isabela's bone?" Marimar asked.

Rhiannon kissed the tiny blister on the palm of her hand. "It *was* Isabela's bone."

Rey raised his brows and examined the digit his great-grandmother had gifted him. "She did say it would protect us."

Lázaro gave a cracked, rumbling laugh. "You are keeping him out."

"Who is he? What is this place?" Rey asked.

"I cannot tell you," Lázaro said. "He forbade me."

"Did he forbid you from telling me, or

476

just Marimar?"

Lázaro sucked in a tiny breath of realization. His eyes grew bright for the first
time in so long, like the stars had returned
to the black skies of his irises. "Just her."

"Then, look at me," Rey said. "Direct your
answers at me or Rhiannon."

Lázaro nodded. "There is too much to
say."

"Who locked you in here?"

"Bolívar Londoño," he said.

Rey and Marimar exchanged terrified
glances. Rey shook his head. "He didn't die
in the fire. How?"

Lázaro shook his head. "Everything went
wrong that night. Orquídea and I had a
bargain. I would share my power with her
in exchange for my freedom. But she arrived too early, distraught. When I opened
my soul to her, she did not stop. I felt her
fear, pain, and anger. Overwhelmed me with
them. And then she left. She did leave me
the key to my chains, and my ring. But I
was weak. She took too much. The circus
was engulfed in smoke and flames. A beam
fell on me, pinned me down, and who
should find me but Bolívar."

Lázaro shivered. Rhiannon dug through
her backpack until she found her shawl, the
one her mother always kept because she got

477

cold wherever she went, even in the tropics. He accepted the offering.

"Then you went after her," Marimar said. She rubbed her hands over her eyes, as if the movement would wake her from the terrible lucid nightmare this reality was becoming. "You're the reason she never left that house."

"Mari, let me," Rey reminded her softly. "Did you go after her?"

"Orquídea's first wish severed my connection with her. She never wanted to see me, hear me, speak to me ever again. The next was to ruin Bolívar, and the way to do that was to destroy the circus. I warned her that there would be a cost to her wishes."

"Pedrito," Marimar said.

"He was the first price Orquídea paid," Lázaro lamented. "I wish I had known what troubled her that day. I wish we could have both escaped."

The room shook again. The reflective walls undulated like molten steel. Rey drew Lázaro's attention. "What happened next?"

"Bolívar locked me up once again. He controls me with my signet ring. He drains my power, but it burns through him. I heal, and he returns for more. He has corrupted my power and in turn my power has corrupted him. And still, Orquídea's will was

478

so strong. I could not get near her."

"That's why she couldn't tell us about your bargain," Marimar said and the relief felt like a cruel thing. She wanted to scream but felt the rumble of the room once again, like a battering ram at the door. She met her father's eyes. "And that's why you got close to her daughter instead."

"No. It was not my intention —" Lázaro stopped, frustrated. He glanced at Marimar again, and that seemed to ground him. "I got free, once. I searched for her name. I scoured the world for her, trying to find the link between us. All I found was a name in a newspaper. The list of graduates from the *Four Rivers Gazette.* Pena Montoya. A girl whose name meant sorrow and shared a likeness to my friend. She was only protected from me when she was on Orquídea's lands. When I traveled to her, I fell on the road in front of her car. I loved her from the moment she asked me if I was lost." Lázaro licked the blood pooling on his bottom lip. "I could not tell her everything, but I did tell her my name, that I was a fallen star, and when Orquídea heard it she forbade Pena from seeing me but, because of our deal, she could not explain why." Lázaro shut his eyes tightly, sighed with regret. "She must have thought I wanted to hurt them both for what Orquídea did to me. I never wanted that . . ."

"That's when my mom ran away," Marimar said.

Lázaro nodded. "For six months I lived like a human, with her. I thought if she knew me, my heart, I could tell her the truth and free us all. Then, Bolívar's pull was too strong. Fighting him, even though I had my ring was impossible. He had bound us. It feels like . . . thousands of constant cuts in my soul."

He touched the finger where the eight-pointed star belonged. "It would have been my greatest joy to have known you, Marimar."

She looked at him then, this strange being who was the reason for her mother's death. "Am I — what you are?"

Rhiannon repeated the question and Lázaro shed his crystal tears once again, because he wished he could look at his own daughter's eyes and tell her that she was made of the sigh of the universe. Just as he'd explained his origins to Orquídea all those years ago, he told her descendants.

"I did not know if I could spawn my own progeny," Lázaro said.

Rey raised his brows and murmured, "Romantic."

"Does this mean you're part alien?" Rhiannon whispered to Marimar.

Marimar's laugh turned into a sob.

"Pena tried to call me down, but I could not go to her out of fear Bolívar would uncover what I had done. Still, she broke through and made a door at the bottom of the lake in Four Rivers. My shining, beautiful Pena. She tried to swim to me and I knew if I answered her, Bolívar would hurt you, hurt all of you."

"You still *failed,*" Marimar snapped.

"I have tried to fight against him," Lázaro said. "I have been trapped here for forty-eight years, but he held me captive long before that. I am so very weary."

"What do we do?" Rhiannon asked.

"We leave," Rey said as the room shook harder. The bone in his fist caught fire and he let it fall to the ground.

"Leave," Lázaro agreed.

Marimar pressed her hands against the wall she'd fallen through but it was solid. She closed her eyes and wished for a way out. The ground rumbled beneath her and she had the sensation of falling from great heights. The battering ram sound returned, closer apart than before.

She felt heat in her pocket where Isabela's last bone was.

"There is a way," Lázaro said, his eyes locking with Marimar, then the shaft of light pouring in from the ceiling. "You can make a path using your magic."

"I'm trying, it's not working," she said.

Lázaro extended his forearms. The pearl marks along his skin formed a pattern of constellations so far away, the human eye couldn't see them. She brushed her own skin, tracing the same pattern in brown beauty marks.

"Not the gift Orquídea gave you. Mine. You are still my child. You have your own power, Marimar."

"How?" she asked.

The third and final bone from Isabela Buenasuerte's finger erupted in flames. The room went still. Rhiannon clung to her cousins as the sharp click of boots on stone rang, the rhythmic thump of a cane approached. Bolívar Londoño III was alive and he wanted them to know he was coming.

"Show yourself," Marimar demanded.

An old man dressed in a midnight velvet suit stepped out of the wall in front of Marimar. The skin at his jaw gave the effect of a melted candle, but Bolívar flashed a wicked grin. The blue of his eyes too bright, something about the Devil in them.

"So eager, my dear, for our family reunion," said a deep, disembodied voice. "I thought for so long that this trap would be for my Orquídea, but the three of you will do for now."

He lashed his hand out like a viper. Marimar was aware of the screaming around her, the people she loved trying to come to her aid, her father, failing yet again to save her.

Bolívar's fist closed around the flower bud at her throat and he pulled it out by the root.

32

THE MAN MADE OF BRITTLE THINGS

There was one memory of her mother that Marimar always thought back to. It wasn't particularly special or magical, just another cold October day in the valley filled with tall tales, which was a different type of magic she supposed. Pena Montoya loved the fall because the fruit born from the orchards tasted sweeter. Marimar thought it tasted the same as always, but perhaps her mother knew differently somehow. In that memory, Pena was more beautiful each time, more ethereal as she continued Orquídea's tradition of stories. The dragonflies were their protectors. The trees were their guardians. Even Jameson, neé Gabo, watched over the house and the Montoyas, and that is why he could never die. All of that Marimar had taken at face value, the legend of her family.

But when her mother told her the story of a secret door at the bottom of the lake that led to other lands, Marimar shook her head. Still, her mother stood by it.

"It's there," Pena had said. *"Beneath the mucky ground, the clusters of silver fish, past the cave of eels, there's a door that leads to other lands, even deep into the reaches of space."*

Marimar had tried to write down her mother and grandmother's stories, but the words never made sense when she put them to paper. Was it because she had stopped believing in them? Had she given up on them or her own potential? After all, belief was like glass — once broken it could be pieced back together but the fissures would always be there.

Now, in the hidden room within the chapel of Santa Ana, Marimar was a broken thing in body and soul. She knew she was bleeding. She was aware that her throat was raw from screaming. She couldn't feel anything, not her own limbs, or the floor beneath her, or the connection that had sparked when she dug her fingers into the worm-filled earth. Orquídea's gift was gone. Rey and Rhiannon would be next. Her cousins were the only thing that forced her mind to cut through the pain, and she focused on a bright, white light behind her eyelids.

Marimar opened her eyes. The skin of her chest was sticky, and her insides felt like she'd swallowed a fist-full of nails. A gutting, ripping sensation, followed by a scream that left her hollowed out.

Rey and Rhiannon came into view. The Living Star stood between them and Bolívar Londoño III. The decrepit old man held the long stem covered in dozens of thorns dripping blood. He caught a droplet with his fingertip and brought it to his lips.

"You're stronger than you look," Bolívar told her. "I suppose it's your father's blood, too. You'll do, once he's spent."

"Go back to the circus hell you came from," Marimar spit.

Bolívar chuckled, then held up the green flower bud to his lips and ate it, thorns and all. The green chlorophyl pulsed with the light of the magic within. It made him younger, sagging skin tightening, silver hair peppered with black, giving him back at least twenty years.

"There," he said, turning his eyes to Rey and Rhiannon, who hadn't moved. "Now for the others."

She blinked through the spell of dizziness that slammed into her, and realized they were frozen in place. In Rhiannon's fist was Orquídea's fishing knife, and Rey held the fishing net. They were ready to defend her, but vulnerable. Always too vulnerable.

"I'm going to kill you," Marimar promised. "Why couldn't you just leave my grandmother alone?"

That seemed to catch his attention. He walked through the shaft of light from the skylight, casting his features in hideous shadows.

"Please," Lázaro begged. "You have what you've always wanted. Finish it. Finish it and let this all end."

Marimar looked at her father, the Living Star. She'd seen his name printed on that poster in magnificent letters like he was the ultimate marvel to behold. But it was a lie. There was no marvel, nothing spectacular. He was just a man who had fallen, and in doing so, he'd become as weak as anyone else. Hadn't she wanted to know him? She knew in that moment — it hadn't been a father that she'd wanted, but the truth. Lies carve out holes until they make one big enough to escape through.

"Let this end," Lázaro begged.

Bolívar's eye blazed an unnatural blue. "You're wrong, old friend. It's been decades and I still don't have what I've always wanted. But I will, when I see Orquídea again."

Marimar laughed, and when she saw it drew his ire, she laughed harder. "She's dead, you fucking corpse. You'll never see her. *Never.*"

"Ah, but that's where you're wrong," Bolívar said, waving a wrinkled finger in the air. He walked around the beam of moonglow with ease, like he'd never left that stage. "My Orquídea isn't dead. She's a survivor. She's eternal. She's simply in a different form, and she will be mine again."

Marimar glanced at her cousins. Rey's eyes moved, his form inching at a glacial pace, like they were wading against time.

"Control the girl," Bolívar warned Lázaro. "I have spared her life as she's your child and I owe at least one mercy after all these years."

"Marimar," her father said. His curtain of black hair fell over the side of his face as he turned to her. "Leave this place."

Tears burned down her face. "How? Where?"

"Bolívar was right. My blood runs through your veins. We are celestial beings, made from the spark of the world's dawn. No one can take that from you. Your mother knew that, remember?"

Bolívar stopped pacing.

Lázaro's words came fast and heavy with

488

meaning. "Remember the door."

Bolívar raised his fist and twisted the signet ring on his index finger. "Traitorous until the very end."

"Go, Marimar!" Lázaro yelled as he fell to his knees. She felt the temperature drop, frost creeping against the walls.

The wall of magic that froze Rey and Rhiannon was lifted. They stumbled into Marimar and she seized them. She couldn't wait. She couldn't look back to see her father's fate. She held onto her cousins and stepped into the beam of moonlight. A force tried to pull her back, but she fought hard.

Marimar thought of home. Four Rivers with its great blanket of sky. Her garden. Her orchard. Her house that she'd bled for. She heard her mother's laughter as if she was standing right beside her.

"Did you know that there's a secret door at the bottom of the lake?" she told Marimar.

"No way," Marimar said. *"You can't have doors in lakes."*

"Where do you think all the fish came from, silly?"

Marimar saw it now, the door. A kaleidoscope of celestial light. She stepped right through.

33

THE STARS FELL
OVER FOUR RIVERS

Rey's first thought upon opening his eyes was that he should have taken his mother up on those swimming lessons. The second one was that even if he'd learned to swim, he still couldn't breathe under water. When he looked back, the prism of light that Marimar had created was gone. He made the mistake of being startled by a tiny silver fish and sucked in a mouthful of water. The next thing he knew was that Rhiannon, his seven-year-old cousin, was the one dragging both of them out of the slimy depths of the lake.

After belly crawling themselves onto the shore, they coughed and sputtered, and he was certain he'd swallowed a fish.

"You couldn't have teleported us onto the shoreline with your star magic?" Rey choked. Somehow, they still had Orquídea's fishing net and knife with them.

"I don't know, Rey, I've never *done* that before. I was just hoping none of us combusted along the way. Let's go. We have to warn the others. We have to warn Orquídea."

Rhiannon raised her arm to the lake. "It's them!"

The wind came first, clearing the sky, like someone had taken an eraser to the evening heavens. She thought of Lázaro and their matching constellation of freckles. She felt a pressure in her stomach. The lake's surface bubbled and churned, twisting into a whirlpool, and she knew that Bolívar had followed her.

Marimar, Rey, and Rhiannon ran from the lake to the house, their path lit by incandescent dragonflies and lighting bugs. When she chanced a look back, Bolívar was trudging across the valley and pulling Lázaro along.

"Hurry!" Marimar urged. She opened her mouth to scream when a piercing cry split the valley awake.

"Bless that zombie rooster," Rey said, as they reached the porch.

Marimar saw her laurel leaf was intact. She touched the wound at her throat again and swallowed the urge to wail along with Jameson.

The front door swung open and the Montoya clan spilled out of the house that Marimar had built. There were Juan Luis and Gastón, Ernesta and Caleb Jr., Enrique, Tía Silvia and Reina.

"What's happened?" Enrique asked.

"They're coming!" Rey managed. There was no time to explain. "We have to protect Orquídea."

Marimar tried not to think of that day seven years prior, but she couldn't help it. She knew that Enrique must have been thinking of it, too, because when their eyes met, he was crying. She'd never seen him cry, not ever, not even when he got a compound fracture when he fell down the hill after a fight with Orquídea.

One by one, the Montoyas returned with their weapons. The baseball bat and pocket-knife Chris had left behind, the shovel Enrique had used to dig Penny's grave, butcher's knives, hammers and wrenches, and even a curling iron. The ceiba roots sprouted out of the ground like keloids on skin, the moonstone baby embedded in the trunk glowed as they gathered around Orquídea's tree.

The sky that had been clear moments before changed. Clouds gathered over the valley as two figures moved like vengeance coming to call. Bolívar's aura refracted like light on water. His clothes were singed in places. His long black hair blew in the storm winds. He was younger again, closer to the man in the wedding photographs they'd discovered. A man who believed the world was made for him alone. At his side, Lázaro wavered as if a strong wind might scatter him like dandelion seeds.

"Come out, Orquídea!" Bolívar shouted. "Come face me, Divina!"

The Montoyas stood their ground, but there was nothing they could do to stop the crack of lighting that split the ceiba tree open.

Orquídea Divina wanted to rest, but she had too much unfinished business. She held her head high, her spirit evanescent as she stepped out of the tree with Pedrito in her arms. She'd spent years running from the memory of Bolívar Londoño III. And there he was, in the flesh. He wore his favorite blue velvet, the same damned top hat. His smile, the one she'd loved so much, turned into manic delight, then, distraught.

He punched his chest. "Mi Divina."

"You got old, Bolívar," she said. "It doesn't suit you."

"Mi Orquídea," Bolívar said, his voice as possessive as it was mournful. He breathed hard and fast, trembling in place as he studied her and their son. There were burning white flames within him. Impotent rage at the memories she evoked. He whimpered and extended a fist toward his family. "You took everything, and yet you could never outrun me."

"Not for a lack of trying, querido." When she held her head up high, she was still that show girl, dazzling the world with her smile, her voice, her charms that had been hers and hers alone. "You always knew how to get what you wanted."

"Enough of this, Divina. Come back to me," Bolívar wailed softly, like a wounded beast.

Orquídea took in her family once again. They dusted themselves off from the lightning blast and stood ready to protect her, as she'd tried and failed to protect them. She'd been gone for years, but had she ever truly been present when they'd needed her? Marimar had led an expedition to the center of the earth just to get to know her. Despite it all, her family had blossomed without her, and the realization hurt more than Bolívar ever could. She would never fail them again.

Her gaze then fell to Lázaro, nearly drained of life. His kindness had been a balm and it had turned out to be the worst mistake he'd ever made.

"I told you I was cursed when I met you, Bolívar," Orquídea said. "And yet you want me still?"

"I wished for you, Orquídea. The universe saw fit to bring you to me. I made mistakes, but I gave my heart to you and you alone, and I know you gave yours to me."

She considered this as she brushed a lock of hair away from Pedrito's forehead, the ghost of his infant sounds haunted her still.

"Leave the others," Orquídea said, "and Pedrito, and I will go with you."

"No!" Marimar shouted. "You can't just do that. Not after everything."

"Mom," Enrique whispered. "Mom, please. I'm sorry."

Orquídea held up her hand. She would do this. They would accept it. "I'm so proud of you. All of you."

Then, she made her way back into Bolívar's arms. The winds picked up. The weight of the sky felt like it would crush the valley.

Marimar looked at her father who'd fallen to his knees. This man, who claimed to have sailed through the cosmos, rendered to nothing. She looked at her cousins, her aunts, and uncles. Orquídea's weakness was her family, and they'd led her back to the very person she'd given everything to run from.

Who was she to stop this?

The answer came to her in a flood. She was Marimar Montoya. Her mother chose the name. Mar y mar. *Sea and sea.* In the middle of the Four Rivers valley, away from the oceans, she pulled on that spark that had always been within her. The granddaughter of Orquídea Divina Montoya, Bastard Daughter of the Waves, a girl who couldn't swim, had never even stepped into the sea.

But here, in her family's home, she was river and salt and that same sea found her. She was the mouth of an ancient god who would swallow the world. She was an ocean of stories, memories, thousands of little moments that made up her whole being.

A slick warmth trickled down from her throat as a new flower bud penetrated the wound. When she touched it, she could feel the thick petals of her new bloom.

Rey and Rhiannon closed ranks beside her and held her hands. They formed a chain. Then, Marimar let out a scream that shook the valley.

How do you fight a thing that believes it owns you? How do you fight the past? With gold leaves and salt? With silence? With new earth beneath your feet? With the bodies, the hearts of others?

With hearts that are tender and bloodied but have thorns of their own.

With the family that chooses you.

Bolívar Londoño III's presence in their valley felt wrong, and the land which had protected Orquídea Divina for so long was ready to fight back. It simply needed a little help.

Rey felt the ground tremble. He could feel them, all of them, the earth itself, as they clawed their way out. Roots of faraway trees split the ground. They grabbed hold of Bolívar's ankles. Blood gushed from Rey's nose from the effort. He knew that he was shedding petals, but he didn't feel weak. Instead, he dove headfirst into the sensation of being part of the valley. Rey raised a fist in the air. The clouds split open with rain, feeding the hungry lake until it surged and flooded, like a river racing to wash away their sins.

But as hard as they fought, Bolívar was still stronger. He ripped free from his bindings and lashed out, twisting his signet ring to draw from Lázaro's life force. He shouted Orquídea's name. She remained unmoving, clutching her moonstone child, as her family fought to protect her soul. Her children formed a barrier around her, the rhythm of their hearts so fierce, the whole valley could hear them beat.

Bolívar lunged for Ernesta first, but Juan Luis swung his bat. There was the crunch of bone. Bolívar's jaw snapped out of place, but he popped it back with a low rumble. Enrique swung the shovel. It lodged in Bolívar's side, but he only yanked it out.

"Don't you see?" Bolívar said. "You are fighting the infinite."

He pulsed with blinding light, expelling a force that knocked everyone down.

Marimar coughed up mud as she pushed herself to stand. She thought of her dead. She thought of Quilca in his river, so ancient, so close to being forgotten. Her father was on the ground, a spark of light pulsed faintly in his heart. And she knew, nothing was infinite, not truly. Not even the stars. She reached for her power, the network of veins and sinew and chaos that connected her to these people. She used it to guide the flooding river in a wave. It crashed over Bolívar's head until he stopped moving.

There was a brief moment when Marimar felt a wash of relief, but even mortality couldn't stop Bolívar Londoño III. He rose from the sodden earth and relished the mud, the rain. He twisted the signet ring on his finger, surveying the wild green that surrounded them.

"This is the place that hid you from me," he said to Orquídea. "I would like to see it burn."

A second lightning bolt tore the ceiba tree further apart. Molten fire spilled from its core. Its flowers curled into black husks and withered in the rain. Dead insects and birds pelted the grass.

It was then that Marimar heard a voice in her mind. A whisper hurrying to solidify.

"Marimar." It was Rhiannon. *"Rey."*

They turned to the youngest Montoya and saw the intent in her eyes. The little girl nodded once. By accepting their gifts, wholly and completely, they were connected.

"You can do this," Marimar whispered in their shared thoughts.

"We've got you, little one," Rey repeated.

"I'm not afraid," Rhiannon told them.

She readied the net that Quilca had given them. In their shared dreams, Mamá Orquídea had shown her how to use it, how she'd cast it in the water and pull in her catch.

Then Orquídea whispered in their thoughts. "Now, Rhiannon. *Now.*"

The little fairy child closed her eyes and pictured Orquídea on the river. The sun danced on the water, and Quilca the river monster was waiting for its share. Rhiannon threw the net. There was nothing stronger than a vow.

Orquídea's first pact singed into Bolívar's skin and pinned him to the ground. His face contorted in disbelief. Marimar crouched down at his side and sawed off his finger with her grandmother's fishing knife. Then, she made a wish.

The ground beneath Bolívar's feet ruptured. The earth was hungry, and it would clean its teeth with Bolívar Londoño III's bones.

The valley smelled of smoke and upturned earth. The Montoyas remained gathered around the smoldering split trunk of the ceiba tree for a long time. First in silence. No insects, no night creatures, not even wind made a sound. The valley held its breath, a reminder that they were alive. Then the fireflies returned. Each and every one of them exhaled. Jameson let out a victorious crow as Rey ran inside. Their silence turned into crying, relief, terror, hope, and music. Always music. It poured out of the open windows, and the front door as Rey returned with a bottle of Marimar's favorite whiskey.

Rey yanked the cork with his teeth and

raised a shoulder at Marimar. "You said you were saving it for a special occasion. What better occasion than our grandmother's resurrection?"

"You'll only be able to use that excuse once," Orquídea said, and took the bottle from Rey and drank straight.

The Montoyas laughed together, as they never had before. And then there was another first.

"We deserve the truth," Enrique said, with his head lowered to his mother's ghost.

Orquídea touched his chin, leveling their eyes, and shed shimmering tears that never hit the ground. "It's a very long story."

But she told them everything.

Lázaro hung back at the fringes of a family he did not belong to. But after decades, he languished in a moment of rest. Besides, a part of him did not want to leave yet. He wanted to raise Pena's spirit, see her one last time. He did not want to leave Marimar before he could truly meet her, his daughter, his miracle.

They were pretty thoughts, but he'd been the cause of enough harm on this earth.

"You look stronger," Marimar said, and sat beside him at the base of the hill.

Lázaro inhaled the valley air. Though he

longed for the sky, he couldn't help but touch the living things around him. Dirt and grass and wildflowers. Glowing insects were drawn to him. This valley, after all, was born out of his power.

"I feel stronger," he told her.

She extended her palm and offered his ring back. When she'd separated the ring from the finger, Jameson had been there to rid the valley of any traces of Bolívar Londoño. "This belongs to you."

"I thank you," Lázaro said, slipping the ring back on his pale hand. "I did not let myself believe I would ever be free of him. But I would endure this, just to have known you even for a moment, Marimar."

She licked her cracked lips and found the courage to hold her father's hand. "Where will you go?"

He smiled, and she found they had the same wry grin. He simply looked up.

As the hours passed, and Orquídea began to fade, Lázaro and Marimar rejoined the family. The Living Star and Orquídea Divina faced each other after so many years apart. There were not enough words that could be spoken. They were entangled deeper than roots and always would be, and that was enough. Sometimes silence said enough.

The moment they faded into prisms of light, thousands of shooting stars filled the sky.

Others outside of the valley, who had not witnessed the miracles of that night, would call it an omen, government conspiracy, the end of times, a blessing from the gods.

For Marimar, it was simply a goodbye.

34
NOW

Marimar wrote everything down like she'd always wanted to. First, the trickle of a few lines in a notebook. Then, her words became ocean again.

In the first few months following the meteor shower, the Montoyas moved back home. Marimar didn't mind, even if Rey forgot to replace the wine he consumed from the cellar, and even if Juan Luis and Gastón preferred to write their songs in the middle of the night when not even the valley's animals howled.

Tía Silvia and Enrique were usually in the kitchen. He wanted to learn all of his mother's old recipes. He wanted to learn the things he'd never gotten a chance to. There would never be the curse of silence in the valley again, not if they could help it.

Once a month, every month during the third quarter moon, everyone came to dinner. Even the ghosts, even Orquídea. They announced themselves with Gabo's howl. After Bolívar's demise, the ceiba tree came alive, the wound down its center grafting back together with scarred skin. But the faithful blue rooster that had protected the Montoyas and their valley, had followed Orquídea into the afterlife, and after dying a final time and being resurrected as a spirit, Orquídea changed his name back. Gabo's ghost was always the first to return, announcing the others.

Penny's spirit would hide the twins' guitar picks. Uncle Félix drifted around the ceiling with Pena, while Parcha might smoke the cigars left out on the altar with Martin. But Orquídea was only ever found in an upholstered chair in front of the fire, sipping an offering of whiskey as Rhiannon played with Pedrito at her feet.

Rhiannon's rose never stopped changing and she never stopped talking to the dragonflies that returned, the birds and deer that trailed after her. Mike's parents eventually called to check up on their granddaughter, but it was Marimar who adopted her. Marimar who told her the same stories their mothers grew up hearing. It was Rey who taught her how to paint, how to curse, how to find hidden doors. Enrique who taught her how to apologize. Caleb Jr. who taught her about the science of plants. Ernesta, how to classify the species of fish that should not exist in their valley, but the Montoyas had a habit of ignoring what should be possible.

When the house was full that way, Marimar wondered if it could have been like this always. But that was the way of missing people. You wished for them, you longed for them, you forgot them. Then you wished for them again.

"Do you think they're really here?" Rey asked, as he set the table. There was paint on his cheek. Sometimes Marimar wondered if there was more paint on her cousin than on actual canvas, but he was the expert.

"I don't know. I don't think it matters." She touched the orchid petals at her throat. She didn't know the species, but she was still making her way through the pictures of the four thousand types of orchids that grew in Ecuador. She wasn't sure if she'd ever find it, if the bloom was made especially for her. The petals were pitch black rimmed in red, with a shimmering white heart. Tiny green thorns sprouted along the bones of her clavicles.

"¡A comer!" Tía Silvia shouted from the halls.

The dining table Enrique and Caleb Jr.

506

had built was long enough for all the Montoyas, past, present, and future. A crackling pernil was placed at the center, bowls of rice, lentils, red onion, and tomato salsa. Golden coins of plantains and a bowl of French fries for Rhiannon.

Marimar looked across the table at Orquídea and watched her grandmother hold court. She knew it wouldn't always be like this. She knew they would fight and leave and return again. She knew they would always be a little bit afraid of the dark and silence and loneliness, but the valley adapted with them.

Sometimes Marimar needed to leave, too. She tested the limits of her father's gift. She thought of the things she was made of — flesh and bone, thorns and salt, bruises and promises, the sigh of the universe.

Marimar Montoya flew into the unknown, but she always, always knew how to find her way back.

35
THEN

Orquídea Divina stepped inside. She walked into every room, down every hall. Then, she found her way back to the living room. She took a seat in front of the fireplace. She wished for a spark, an ember, and it flew from her palm and into the dry logs. She'd need more. Music, laughter, safety. But for now, on her first day in Four Rivers, she toed off the shoes from her aching feet. She basked in that feeling, that certainty that this was the perfect place to put down her roots.

ACKNOWLEDGMENTS

This book has lived in my mind since I wrote a short story called "Divine Are the Stars" for the anthology *Toil & Trouble,* which celebrated stories about women and witchcraft. Marimar and her grandmother have remained the same people — wayward, magical, and searching for a place to put down their roots, like so many families all around the world. When I had the opportunity to turn the magical valley of Four Rivers into a novel, it became the greatest challenge of my career thus far. For that, there are several people I want to thank.

Adrienne Rosado, who represented the project at the time. Thank you for being one of Marimar's first champions.

Johanna Castillo, who took a chance on my strange little book about an incredible family that shares roots in our beloved city of Guayaquil, Ecuador.

My Ecuadorian tribe, forever and always.

Parts of this book are set in La Atarazana, where the story of our family began. The same river. The same road that led us there. Here's to my grandmother, Alejandrina Guerrero, who is the pillar of our family. Caco and Tío Robert for always supporting me and giving me a place to write. Liliana and Joe Vescuso. My beautiful cousins Adriana, Ginelle, Adrian, Alan, Denise, Steven, Gastóncito. Jeannet and Danilo Medina, Román Medina, Milton Medina, Jacqueline and Mark Stern.

My brother Danny Córdova, who might be younger than I am, but his music talent and dreams always keep inspiring me.

I thank my father, Francisco Javier Córdova, his wife Jenny Coronel Córdova. My brothers and sisters of the Córdova Legion: Paola, Angelita, Francisco, Anabel, Jamil, Joselyn, Enoch, Leonel.

Melanie Iglesias Pérez, for taking over this project and being incredibly patient as the book morphed into several different iterations. Thank you for understanding these characters and what I was trying to do at the core. You made each version clearer, better. To the rest of the wonderful Atria team at Simon & Schuster, especially Libby McGuire, Gena Lanzi, Maudee Genao, and Hercilia Mendizabal.

Erick Davila for the exquisite cover art that exceeded my wildest dreams.

My agent, Suzie Townsend, and the New Leaf Literary team. I know Orquídea is in the best hands.

My incredible friends have watched my often-chaotic process. Sarah Younger and Natalie Horbachevsky. Dhonielle Clayton, for always giving me the kick in the ass I deserve when I doubt myself, and Victoria Schwab for putting up with my writerly torment. To Natalie C. Parker for being one of the first people to ever read this book and give me a different perspective about my characters. To Miriam Weinberg for seeing who the true villain in the story was. To Alys Arden for witch stories and New Orleans.

Finally, to the pearl of the pacific, and the city that will always be home to myself and Orquídea Divina — Guayaquil de mis ensueños.

ABOUT THE AUTHOR

Zoraida Córdova is the acclaimed author of more than a dozen novels and short stories, including the Brooklyn Brujas series, *Star Wars: Galaxy's Edge: A Crash of Fate,* and *The Inheritance of Orquídea Divina.* In addition to writing novels, she serves on the board of We Need Diverse Books, and is the coeditor of the bestselling anthology *Vampires Never Get Old,* as well as the cohost of the writing podcast *Deadline City.* She writes romance novels as Zoey Castile. Zoraida was born in Guayaquil, Ecuador, and calls New York City home. When she's not working, she's roaming the world in search of magical stories. For more information, visit her at ZoraidaCordova.com.

The employees of Thorndike Press hope you have enjoyed this Large Print book. All our Thorndike, Wheeler, and Kennebec Large Print titles are designed for easy reading, and all our books are made to last. Other Thorndike Press Large Print books are available at your library, through selected bookstores, or directly from us.

For information about titles, please call:
(800) 223-1244

or visit our website at:
gale.com/thorndike

To share your comments, please write:
Publisher
Thorndike Press
10 Water St., Suite 310
Waterville, ME 04901